HAWTHORNE BOOKS & LITERARY ARTS | *Portland, Oregon* | MMV

The
GREENING
OF BEN BROWN

A Novel

MICHAEL STRELOW

Hawthorne Books
& Literary Arts

1410 NW Kearney St.
Suite 909
Portland, OR 97209
hawthornebooks.com

Form:
Pinch, Portland,
Oregon

Editorial Services:
Michelle Piranio

Printed in China
through
Print Vision, Inc.

Set in DTL Albertina.

First Edition

9
8
7
6
5
4
3
2
1

Library of Congress
Cataloging-in-
Publication Data

Strelow, Michael, 1943–
The greening of Ben
Brown : a novel / Michael
Strelow.
p. cm.
Includes bibliographical
references and index.

ISBN 0-9716915-8-4
(alk. paper)

1. City and town life –
Fiction. 2. Male friendship–
Fiction. 3. Chemical
spills – Fiction. 4. Electric
shock – Fiction. 5. Human
ecology – Fiction.
6. Oregon – Fiction.
I. Title.

PS3619.T7456G74 2005

813'.6 – dc22

2004025278

For Lynne.

Many thanks to Kate Sage, my editor, for being able to see what this book could be, for her perspicacity, intelligence, and good humor. Thanks to Willamette University's Atkinson Fund Summer Grants for repeated support in the writing and rewriting of this novel.

THE GREENING OF BEN BROWN

Water is honey for all beings, and all beings are honey for this water. The intelligent, immortal being, the soul of this water, and the intelligent, immortal being, the soul in the individual being – each is honey to the other.

THE UPANISHADS

I. The Greening

IN THE TOWN OF EAST LEVEN, OREGON, THE SOUND OF WATER is everywhere. From east and west, every half mile or so, some creek works through the cane berries and bright fields of broccoli to join the Willamette River on its way to the Columbia.

Each creek came to have its ghost. A blood sacrifice was exacted by the water for the privilege of having the town here, as if along with the location of sewer and water there had been some deal recorded in the original plat.

One hundred and fifty years ago, only a few settlers farmed along the Willamette because it flooded each spring, washing out among cottonwoods and stands of oaks, then receded and produced fields of blue camas flowers where the Calapooia Indians came to dig the bulbs. Farmers staked out the higher ground, and East Leven was little more than a post office and a general store on a raised spot with creeks Y-ing into the river around it. Then in the 1930s, the Army Corps of Engineers regulated the water coming down from the Cascade Mountains in catch dams for hydroelectricity. Citizens uneasily occupied the new dry spots as East Leven sprawled across the creeks with webs of bridges, then settled in to listen to the water.

Anne Doucette was one of the children whose story carried the strongest cautionary tale. She broke her sweet neck at the age of twelve trying to walk the wide bridge railing over Inman Creek. If she had fallen to the left that spring, just after the camas bloom, she might have skinned both knees and torn her dress. But she fell to the right, thirty feet to the creek bed, where she broke her neck and – parents paused here in the story to make sure this registered well on a child's graphic sense of danger – she took two days to die, closing her eyes finally on the bad luck to have stumbled to the wrong side.

The wide bridge rails, those invitations to I-dare-you walks, had come with the WPA crews, all men, who poured into town from the camps by day to winch the wide timbers into place. The men sweating and shirtless, the apricot timbers leaking sap, hand-forged iron chisels and drills, piles of fir curls – America was finding its way out of the misfortune of the Great Depression. The crews originated from everywhere in the West, and some WPA men took note of this place and its waters as a town to come back to when the hard times let up. You could hear the water at night any place in town from bedroom windows. Water with its price.

After the Green Man came, the sacrifices stopped suddenly. Maybe it was the new railings, unwalkable thin steel. But there was still the railroad trestle, the inner tubing through the rapids on the Willamette River, the rock skipping and creek wading and rope swings strung up to cottonwoods so you shot from the trees along the bank and landed in the deep hole just before the highway bridge. Plenty of chances for bad choices, bad luck, but the sacrifices stopped with the arrival of the Green Man, and for a while the whole town held its breath waiting for the next death that didn't come. Instead, the Green Man came to live in a cabin that looked out on the Willamette, bound on one side by old firs stepped down the hillside to the flood plain of the river and on the other by cottonwoods and alders that crowded the bank.

THE ORIGINAL CEMETERY FOR EAST LEVEN HAD BEEN NAMED by nineteenth-century cemetery entrepreneurs as the Bye-N-Bye. The phrase had been taken from the song "In the Sweet By and By." There had, of course, been burials in designated plots around and outside town: under a 400-year-old oak on a hillside overlooking the river, in family plots fenced with decorative iron and let go to weeds, alongside a crossroads in the English manner sanctifying the spate of housewife suicides banned from church grounds or family plots. It was, oddly enough, in the 1930s, when everyone found themselves economically in the February blues, that the housewife suicides (fueled by spousal abuse, alcohol, or rainy winters) dropped off to the same level as the rest of the population. The cross of the crossroads conferred what benediction it could as unofficial burying ground.

When the N fell off, along with the supporting hyphens, the cemetery remained the irreverent Bye Bye. Years later a restaurant chain, the Black Angus, came to East Leven and within two years the g in the sign failed. It was fully another two years before anyone insisted, in writing, that the sign be fixed. The Bye Bye cemetery, at first an embarrassment to some in the community, quickly became assimilated and even a source of local pride. "Headed for the big Bye Bye," the local wags pronounced. "It's Bye Bye for the Johnson kid if he keeps driving like that. Has someone told his parents?" "I hear that old man Everson went Bye Bye three days before anyone found him." Bye Bye came to mean cemetery in general, death, the fear of death, imminent death, and all forms of mortality. Local syntax provided the petri dish of language in which the new forms grew.

The Bye Bye cemetery began as an entrepreneurial enterprise. At one point the Congregational Church took over maintenance during the war years, then handed control back to a consortium developed specifically to continue burials until all the plots were filled and then maintain it as a historical center to the town. Furhers, Willsons, Cobbs, Manheims, a section apart for railroad-worker Chinese, another section apart for Japanese buried between the years of 1941 and 1949. Underground the juices of all the bodies mixed and fed the oaks that canopied the peaceful dead gone bye-bye.

On the surface, the compartments of burial included tall versus short gravestones; stones full of the iconography of Christian dead versus stones of simplified gestures, most often just a name; and then the status of prime real estate from which bones could rise up and meet the rising sun versus marginal and mossy edge plots, which for the ten cents on the dollar purchase price might also include a compost pile or a patch of weeds regularly missed by maintenance crews. Local hoodlums, inspired by moonlight and other lunacy, had tipped a number of the oldest stones so that the Congregationalists had to seek volunteers to re-cement most of the pre-granite, nineteenth-century markers. They bore bravely the scars of amateur reconstruction, white mortar cracks slicing up the identifiers on the stone like surgeries performed by jackknife. The headstones assembled in rows, and just after dusk the ancestors of East Leven assembled too. In the evening's equivalence of dying firelight, the stones lost their words and icons and floated above the summer grass and the gathering smells of honeysuckle and wisteria and jasmine until the cemetery was peopled. Anne Doucette's ghost never appeared, though children who lived nearby would tell their parents they were going to sleep in tents in the backyard, then sneak off to spend hours shivering with delight and trying to sleep in freshly dug graves.

The ghosts that did appear hung in the air and cooed like the doves lined up along the phone wires in the evening. Then they hooted like barn owls or grunted like the great horned owls as the light disappeared. The owl-ghosts begat the dying-light ghosts and these begat the scary-story ghosts. The children ghosted each other as long as they could stand the damp grave, then scampered across the wet grass pursued by ghosts mostly of their own making to backyard tents again. Then flashlight faces, faked voices, hoots of laughter. The Bye Bye cemetery on summer evenings was a kind of amusement park in East Leven.

And the ghosts of the murdered lovers were there, the two graves not far from each other, since both families had long-established plots. The lovers were young enough to qualify for tragic deaths, not the fullness-of-

-time deaths that were community celebrations. Their markers didn't bear the emblem of the full sheaf of wheat, the celestial harvest earned through a life of Christian goodness. She had rose buds, emblematic of her early demise; he had vines of hopeful continuous prayer for his wayward soul. Their ghosts became a concoction for young lust in East Leven.

Every spring as the weather warmed, young couples made their way to the gravesites of the murdered lovers. The ritual became to touch hers first, then his, then somewhere between the two, embrace and kiss. Very quickly the next generation thought that if an embrace and a kiss sealed your spooky love after sundown, then having sex between the two graves would really nail it down. The logic seemed unassailable, a sort of premarriage marriage ceremony could be performed any evening or night the weather allowed with all the guarantees of belief that could blend themselves out of the dead into the living. In the depth of summer, when the earth was dry and the air temperature held the heat of day well into the dark, there was a waiting line. The unofficial order for getting to the prime consecration spot began at the Furher angel then moved into proximity at one of the Willson graves that looked like a bench and served as warmup area, with the final holding spot behind an immense marker, aptly enough of the Holden family, that cast a deep shadow just out of earshot of the ground-worn final destination. Like planes stacked up over an airport, the pairs circled for a final landing in perfect weather. A light spring rain, on the other hand, might give a couple the entire evening to themselves, and some brought prefatory picnics, bottles of wine.

There was rumored to be a thrill that shot through the whole proceedings if you could time climaxes just right; the murdered pair would add their own sexual event to the occasion, and like an amplifier with the volume turned up, everybody would get more thrill than ever before. It was rumored, furthermore, that if this didn't happen, it was okay, because one couple had become so spoiled that they couldn't do it at home any longer. Rain or no rain, they had to try to get the "big one" again, and it always loomed over any lovemaking they tried anywhere else. Mile-high club. Daylight in the park. Nothing matched up to the synchronistic blast they had felt the first time between the murdered lovers' graves.

The owners of the Bye Bye were the last to figure out the reason for the bare patch between the graves. They over-seeded, brought in fresh dirt, and finally resorted to sod transplants. Still, by the end of summer, there was a circle of wear down to the bare dirt. And since the activity was largely among the young, the owners were not privy to the prevailing winds of young rumor. It was years blowing to their ears. They asked the police to enforce the local trespass statutes, posted a prominent sign, but by that time, the police themselves had become complicit, having come through the ceremony themselves – many of them – so that they would only halfheartedly chase couples out of the cemetery and then finally give up and claim to the owners that there were too many other pressing crimes and severe manpower issues. Locked gates didn't work. Once, a summer raid by the middle-aged owner and a rent-a-cop had produced such a melee and destructive running around in the darkened cemetery that the damage caused to headstones and shrubbery was much more expensive to fix than a new application of sod a couple times a summer. And so a peace ensued. And couples continued to try for "the big one." There were attempts when the Green Man first moved into his cabin by the river to capture some of the power of his otherness, but lacking credible reports of a "big one" similar to what the dead lovers supplied, the attempts to couple in the bushes around his house soon stopped. "Rocking" the Green Man remained as a substitute activity, but rocking involved a completely different constituent.

Five years before, when Andrew James was eighteen, his friend John set a case of beer out back of his father's IGA store. Three of them and John – that made six bottles apiece – went to get throw-up drunk and "rock the Green Man." Halfway through the case, they pulled up on the other side of the Green Man's laurel hedge and split the hedge to see if his lights were on, dim lights like he'd hung a row of flashlights around the rooms. A light like a glow from a low fire, it exaggerated stringy shadows against the pine walls of his cabin.

"Let's finish these. Can't you shut that thing off?" The Chevy puffed calmly but audibly as they finished another beer trying to keep from laughing.

"No, the fucking voltage regulator. If I shut it off, it'll either start or not, who knows."

"Whyn't you sell that piece of shit and get a good car?"

"Hey man, it's mine. Where's yours? You can ride on the fucking front fender."

"Shhh."

John gathered rocks, on his hands and knees, serious crawling under the bushes. Someone brought Right Guard and lit a blast of spray, bringing down a moth on its way to the street light.

"The jaws of death!" Another blast.

"Shit. Keep it down. Not yet. When he comes out, then let go with a dragon blast. Back him to the wall. Fry the foliage. Down with green people."

"Hey, shhh. It's not like we've just invented this. Have a little fucking class." General laughter and stumbling. "Just rock the house to get him out. Then the jaws of death. Then get the fuck out of here. He's probably getting pissed about all the hassle."

John straightened up and distributed rocks all around. John, whose one long eyebrow stretched over both his eyes and gave him a look of tractable idiocy. John, as always, in charge of ordinance on any of the forays: blowing up mailboxes, writing on lawns with lighter fluid, executing small rodents, throwing marble mortars into the greenhouse, firing gunpowder rockets off the backs of shovels.

John launched the first rock. It clacked on the roof of the Green Man's cabin and rattled down into the rain gutter. Then they all launched and one short, beer-impeded throw crashed through glass. A voice, deep, rounded, a piece of the shadows broken loose like a heavy bat skimming their heads: "Fourteen dollars and twenty-eight cents – uninstalled."

The Green Man, invisible at night, was above, at the sides, behind, in the bushes, exotic like a dark snake, legion – a myth come alive speaking over their nervous systems. His teeth are green too. Long and green. If he touches you, you turn green. It's a disease. Get close and you get it. Horribly painful. The green rubs off. He's crazy. Grows poisonous plants. Drugs! Talks to trees. Bites! And suddenly Andrew was behind the wheel racing the engine while two poured into the back seat and one clung to the antenna waving through the windshield, mouthing, Go! "Fourteen dollars and twenty-eight cents – uninstalled." Those were the first words Andrew heard from the Green Man.

WHAT DO PLANTS KNOW? BEN BROWN, THE GREEN MAN, REMEMbered reading that if you threatened a plant with a knife or a scissors, even without touching it, the plant began to respond, somehow knew you were out to cause it damage. He watched the plants along his riverfront from the throne of his repaired chair. What did they know? And like people, did some know more than others? Were there smart plants and dumb plants? And like people, did the dumb ones sometimes know things the smart ones couldn't even imagine? Whole categories of things the smart ones couldn't imagine? Trees seemed to know lots of things just by their size, he supposed. Then daffodils and tulips would know what their bulbs knew as well as what their flowers could find out when the time came. Then did seeds pass on what they knew? He rubbed his arm absently as if to test the green again. Did he have special knowledge since he was green? How could you get to the special knowledge? Or was green just the color he was? No, there had to be a payoff for being the green one, the trial balloon. The doctors had given up and just declared him green the same way they had declared him green initially. One doctor, when pushed, began to dissertate on the amazing thing he had first learned in medical school gross anatomy class. That humans came in pretty much just two models – male and female – and skin color was just like hair style when you got to cracking open the cadaver. But there was this other noticeable variation on the theme. Organs inside people could be out of "normal" place and size by quite a large factor. There seemed to be a lot of experimenting going on in humans when it came to the placement, size, and internal arrangement of parts. Most of the variation was small, but every once in a while, just to keep the investigator honest, there was a major variation on the standard themes. Ben Brown had listened from inside his greenness, and though he felt the doctor was trying to go somewhere with this Darwinian observation, he never really got there and finished with a noncommittal, "and so…" The doctor trailed off as if the logic were somehow there in the grammar, in the fracture of the syntax. Lots of consulting doctors had done some version of this trailing off. Most predicted the green would fade. When it didn't, they launched a collective shrug that was nearly audible.

Ben Brown, pondering plants in his yard, laughed. He laughed at himself speculating on what plants knew, but most of all it was his greenness that had come to be funny. He looked forward every day to waking up green, again. He caught himself being tickled at how stalwart the green color had come to be, how trustworthy and loyal to him. He rubbed his arm and wondered if he hadn't become greener over time. There had been descriptions of his greenness, medically speaking, but he couldn't remember anyone taking pictures. Maybe they had. How vegetable he had become. That must have disguised, at first, the fact that along with the greenness he seemed to be growing younger. And both of those facts must have been what drew Mary to him, vegetable Mary teaching the world to read, one grade school class at a time.

The Green Man had become so fond of the denizens of East Leven that at first he didn't realize how he had worked himself into their fabric any more than they did. He had arrived as a strange stranger, stranger than all the strangers who had come before him: the veterans of the WPA projects, the Missouri Willsons' last descendent returned (the vegetarian named Mary teaching fifth grade), the job seekers at Horchow, the itinerant English orchardist, the vaudevillian bakers, the flying enthusiast, and all the rest of the enthusiasts in their many disguises. He had fallen among gypsies and Norwegians and Slavs and Poles and Czechs and Finns. Alysandra Gorham, the local girl who was always strange – who lived in a strange world of her own, doing her strange collecting and vending in town – became much more normal when the Green Man arrived. All these were astounding in their manners that came from living on a river, and the river taught manners that always began with the fundament of what rivers teach in the long run: that you are a guest here; behave as if you are a guest. From the ghost of Anne Doucette to Crazy Leo and his conversations with the cosmos, they are all guests of the river.

BEN BROWN, WHILE BEING THROWN FROM THE HIGH-LINE tower, thought he could see through the wires like telescopes all the way to where the water turned the wheels to make the power. Farther: There was the last western light behind the tamaracks and firs, some birds low against the peach light. The view was startling. All around was green with marks in it like hieroglyphics. He closed his eyes and lazed there in the air, taking all the time while looking forward and backward through these new eyes, bright eyes. In a blue-green crackling hammock like a cellophane bed suspended in the sky, he hung there tirelessly without wings. Beautiful. Thoroughly fire. Suspended over the water and trees.

He was swinging by the threads of his heartbeat – *boomp, bup, boomp, bup, boomp, bup*. Nothing comes and nothing is ever going to come because there is no forward or back, no word but the wholeness of silence. Ben Brown stayed a long time dying on the tower: dying out of pink into green, out of Brown into green, dying out of anger into sweet juices.

The power company wanted to know what it felt like being electrocuted, having the sirloin of their finest voltages. They also wanted to know why he lived when he ought to have died. They looked at him and after a while asked, Were you doing anything special? Try to remember. Try to recall everything you were doing. Where were your hands? Your feet? What was the relative humidity and temperature? Were there birds near you? No, he said, but there was birdsong. How could there be birdsong without birds, they asked while cocking an eye at him, this failure to die, this freak electrical conductor who merely passed the charge on to God. No. No, no, no, he said. It was more like being in love. It was like hitching a ride in the air. It was like being a wave … and a particle. It was photonlike. It was exactly about being lucky.

They cocked their collective heads again, looked at him with first one eye then the other – giant birds with pocket protectors for their spare beaks.

It was like dropping a handful of coins on the sidewalk and having them all balance on edge with all the heads toward you.

The power company wanted a written report. The interview was over.

He gave them what he remembered, something of the detail they wanted, some things they really didn't want. He gave them:

"I slid sideways off the tower, my tools in the leather holster splayed out from my waist: a hammer, the head charged with ringing in the steel; the tip of my screwdriver standing straight up like an erection with strings of lightning chiseling the business end into blue ragged teeth; my pliers clacking open and closed, open and closed, then open again in a shivering yawn, the red plastic grips melting off in droplets that became yellow clouds to hang in the landscape before my eyes. A roll of nickel wire hung suspended in the charged air then unrolled suddenly and shattered to dots and curls like Arabic writing – signs and countersigns. This all in one slow take, one shuddering at the end of myself before I sighed. Then the sigh, the giving in slower yet to the light all around me. And after the giving in, an ease almost reclining in the air. My clothes hissed and were gone. Shoes flew in an odd arc, mincing together in dance. Then the hair of my body, even the finest down, sheared off in blue light.

"One hand of its own will clasped the high line as if reaching through a smoking light into the face of God. The hand reached back through the whirling thrum of the generator and throws and switches and circuits – a thousand years – and for a held breath my body bridged the world, and the heartbeat of time thumped once in me and threw me to the ground clean, naked, wax gray in the blue light. I was zapped. Stark fried in the American air. Sincerely yours, Benjamin Brown."

BEFORE THE GREEN MAN, THE TOWN CAME TO CREATE A SAGA of itself almost accidentally, a greening story that prepared East Leven for the second green coming.

A city council member was idly leafing through a grants list in December 1957. He noticed that a midwestern philanthropist with no particular prejudice as to region was offering $25,000 as an incentive to make a small town or an area in a large city into a kind of arboretum, a model of what diverse tree planting could add to a community. Grant proposals would be reviewed each calendar year, and the grantee had to host officials from other towns who wanted to apply in future years. The trees had to be representative of many different species, demonstrating the range of possible plantings in any given area. From his mission statement it was clear that the philanthropist believed in trees. And he knew that people would themselves become better people if surrounded by more and more kinds of trees. In fact, he saw the species' diversity as a metaphor for human diversity. All community relations would be improved by occurring within a context of greater beauty, greater variety. The councilman found himself reading and re-reading the mission statement to try to hold on to the logic. Finally, he decided that the benefactor attributed some magical power to trees or had grown up in the presence of different trees and thought that everyone else should too. In short, the twenty-five thousand seemed to have very few strings attached – some ceremony, the hosting, photos over the years – and the winning request seemed to only have to plant a bunch of trees of no particular size and then use the excess money for some other beautification project or even other capital improvements.

East Leven had its own western simplicity of trees. Along any water, but especially the river, grew the cottonwoods. Higher ground was filled with a mixture of western red cedar and Douglas fir and the indigenous white oak. Big leaf maples, alders, poplars and the odd valley ponderosa pine were all expendable and usually got sliced off the land before building new structures. The fir and cedar and cottonwoods controlled the skyline. Here and there native hawthorns and dogwoods were the arboreal spice.

East Leven's last big trees formed a kind of ring around the town like a monk's tonsure. And like a tonsure they were the residue of ceremony and the ritual letting in of light that obsessed the town in the late nineteenth century. The rest had been cleared off, leaving the whole assemblage looking from the air like a circle with a highway × slightly off center, an incipient tic-tac-toe game. Closer to the ground it was the water of the north-flowing river that truncated the grid of side streets in every direction as the river S-curved through town. One arm of the × escaped truncation by bridging the river between old and new towns on a four-lane sliver connecting the banks. The park, ringed in the green of bamboo, alders, and tulip trees, marked the old town, whose streets named after pioneer families intersected with tree names and American literati. The shape of the town morphed from the square, the original buildings, and the first streets so that even farther out, away from these original seeds, the town kept a shadow of its initial shape as if it had inherited its form from the simple geometry of the square. Even where the hills rose and the streets fiercely zigzagged up away from the river, the square echoed into a grid up over the hills. The grid, like a safety net, had reminded these western settlements of their civility, that all this hard living was not being done out of vainglory but had its substance in the geometry of the East – circles and squares, boulevards and embankments. And finally, it was the shape of the town that formed its people. Anyone in town could mount one of the hills and look out over what had been wrought: off toward the river to the west, the heart of downtown; to the south, the low bluffs on one side with the cutbank on the other; and to the north, Horchow Chemical Company and its appurtenances of ponds and pits and chain-link fence. While the whole effect was something less than splendid, there was also something binding about the arrangement. The viewer on the hill could feel the plan in effect even if the plan sometimes seemed to be generated day after day, by experience. The viewer could look out and see that work had become manifest here, that work stood over against the river, in the darkness of impenetrable forest, within the uneasy truce of cottonwood and water. Work was the shape of East Leven. The work of constant repair and invention sat side by side in the bridge and the park and Horchow.

The councilman spent two hours writing up the proposal and sent it off without informing his fellows on the city council. Eight months later, he had already forgotten about the application when a call came announcing that East Leven had become one of three towns on the short list. Some final questions, a few clarifications. The councilman decided to announce it at the next meeting and get approval should they succeed. The discussion, re-membered firsthand by some, by others related as a tale of the inherent absurdity of government, established two camps in East Leven government, camps that in many ways remain to this day and cut across party lines and political philosophies. The nativists insisted that the trees God put here, or that evolution worked out over millions of years, were the trees that belonged here. If they could use the money to plant more of the trees that were already here, why then that would be acceptable. But the grant seemed to insist on introducing foreign specimens. One council member used the Latin term *contra naturum*. Words and phrases such as against nature itself, unnatural, perversion of original intentions, alien, all flew in the debate.

Members of the other camp, all for seemingly different reasons, argued that the philanthropist's money represented ancient notions of (and here they countered with the authority of their own Latin), *noblesse oblige*, and furthermore, the library had been built with Carnegie money, the square refurbished with Horchow bucks, and the lion's share of road and bridge construction paid for with federal highway taxes. What the hell was the difference if they beautified the town thanks to a stranger's largesse? As the argument heated, the Latin became vulgar and corrupt, and in some retellings the phrase *quid* the hell *pro quo* was actually shouted out over the objections of the nativists. In one version this produced the absolute silence of puzzlement. Another, maybe revisionist, version held that this only loosed a rain of bastardized Latin phrases that defied logic. Mentioned in particular (revisionist version) were: *quo warranto, quod erat carborundum, in mens sanitas*. It seems that the latinizing escalated quickly and loudly, in this version, into people shouting at each other in a language neither group really knew but that both groups felt carried great gravitas, pith, and moment. No one, it seemed, in any versions of the reports, pointed out the unnaturalness of the language situation.

East Leven came in second on the list that year. The $25,000 was awarded to a small town in Ohio that went on in subsequent years to achieve the rank of All-American City a record number of eleven times. But the green debate in East Leven never really ended, only the Latin phase. Some council members pledged to personally plant "foreign" species of trees everywhere they could. And for a while Persian ironwoods, empress trees, locusts, elms, red oaks, and all manner of tree perversions (according to some) were plunged into the ground even at inopportune times of the year it seems just to piss off the other party. One local nursery grew fat on special orders. And then it really began.

A row of honey locusts, fast growers, drought resistant, but messy twig and branch droppers, was planted at considerable personal expense leading into the crossroad that arrived at the bridge over the river. Behind the one-inch sticks of great promise loomed the deep green of the river's cottonwoods. All the locusts died. Foul play was evident. Each had been ringed quickly and expertly. A razor-sharp, beaked linoleum-cutting knife was found nearby. And as if the slicing through the cambium layer hadn't been enough, someone noticed that each plant had been dosed with a turquoise-colored chemical that proved to be copper sulfate. The poor locust sticks didn't stand a chance. They had clearly been assassinated, and the implication was that any mass planting of foreign species would meet the same fate. But there was civility too.

Several council members of the non-nativist persuasion planted eastern dogwoods in all their pink perversity on their own property. None was touched. All survived, and the next spring an aerial view would have located nearly all adherents of the new-species argument by the flush of pink. They had combined forces and ordered 150 trees from a Tennessee nursery and planted them all at the same time. Nearly twenty years to the day after the planting, all the trees died together as if they had made a monoculture pact to expire on the same date. Some speculated that they had all been the same tree, and that's why they had gone down all at once.

East Leven had a number of opportunities to define itself: in terms of its river, its manufacturing prowess, its coming together of creeks and swales, even its unsolved double murder. But until the coming of the Green Man, it was the great tree controversy that established political and social camps in town. Even more than Methodists versus Catholics, more than GM versus Ford (and eventually domestic versus foreign), Republican versus Democrat, ham versus turkey at Christmas, more than grow versus consolidate and stay small, the great tree controversy informed East Leven's citizens' definitions of themselves. Until the Green Man, when things changed.

The nature of the change was only conversational at first. His advent, his invention, his first coming was an extended event that took months to engage the self-consciousness of the community. His name, his history extrapolated out of newspaper accounts, supposed and guessed into reasonable approximations of a life or what a life being green must be like, gave way eventually to a kind of surface calm. Conversations that had swirled at first, became linear with logic and then, finally, anecdotal.

"I hear he went out of town for a few days. Where do you suppose he goes when he goes?"

"Well, Marjory thinks that he's not well and goes to Salem to the hospital or to Portland to the university hospital, where they deal with the odd medical conditions."

"Oh, she thinks everybody is not well. 'Look at him,' she says. 'He doesn't seem well, don't you think? That can't be a healthy skin color.' But that's just Marjory's way of making herself feel better. She has awful corns."

"He seems to walk fine, when he walks. Not a limp or anything. He's green, of course, so maybe you can't tell, but he seems so healthy just walking around."

"Well, what I know for sure is that everybody who has ever talked to him, like in the stores, you know, they all say he's perfectly nice. I'll go with that until I hear different, I guess. That's just my way."

These two might have been on opposite sides in the tree controversy. Sometimes whole families adopted intransigent positions and passed on those positions for generations; occasionally families split acrimoniously, but the Green Man had created a new civil covenant.

The tireless efforts of town fathers and mothers seemed unfocused until Ben Brown galvanized the town's curiosity if not its civic pride. What to make of a town whose main ways of knowing itself were: ghosts, murders, war over trees, the river and its tributaries, Horchow mysteries? The Green Man insinuated himself onto the scene through the bakery, his long walks, then his island adventures, becoming at once an aesthetic and an event.

The Green Man's island adventuring was his own concoction. Later, though, there was some discussion (but not the polarization surrounding tree planting) about who exactly was responsible for the whole floating-island business, then the ecological disaster that followed, then the shaking down of all the ripe-fruit-and-nut theories about what really happened after that. The floating-island business, it was called, as if Jonathan Swift's islands in the sky had come to earth in East Leven. And the town wits, at least the literati, invoked Swift often in conjunction with local affairs. It was no accident, they pointed out, that Swift, writing at the beginning of the eighteenth century, located *Gulliver's Travels* in some vague northwestern America where the fired imagination of his day could picture anything happening – talking horses, floating sky islands, giant people, tiny people, and the hapless Gulliver flailing through it all.

East Leven had traced its name to origin myths. Most towns in Oregon had the advantage of being able to look themselves up in an extraordinary compendium called *Oregon Geographic Names*. But a few towns like East Leven and Tualatin and others could only rely on competing stories. There was no Leven, no West Leven. There was Leavenworth, Kansas, leaven the loaf, 'leven that comes before twelve. Though East Leven was situated on the east side of the north-running river, it seemed that at one time there might have been a plan for a Leven. Or an inkling. The original (now long drowned) orchards that appeared in the 1849 plat might have been owned partially by a man named Leven or Leeven or van Leewan. Wet records, poor ink. And so East Leven occupied itself with the search for itself.

"HOT FOR A TUESDAY," SAYS THE GREEN MAN, SPEAKING MORE or less in the direction of a wall of blooming forsythia. In the tunnel formed by the hanging branches sits Andrew James, cross-legged, thinking himself invisible. He's a recent college graduate – English major – and has his parents' indulgence to find himself this summer before getting on with his life. Anne Doucette is behind his indulgence and water is behind her. So a ghost has set up this meeting.

The Green Man is hammering out of sight of Andrew and each blow is picked up by the river, rendered as a loud tick fading across the green water. The Green Man is about his tick-ticking in this first real heat that has wilted the yellow flowers falling by ones and twos on Andrew's head.

Andrew had smoked the last of his bad college marijuana as a preface to sneaking under the bushes to watch the Green Man going about his green business by the river.

The Green Man moves away behind the cabin, a small house he lives in, and what gives it the cabin feel are the bushes and vines, as if it had been dropped from above into a patch of tall brush. Only the cedar shingles show clearly from the tangle, and even these are covered with spruce and fir needles, giving the roof a thatch effect – a thatched cottage, some play-house abandoned to creepers, vine roses, and Sweet William. It has an elves-and-trolls look even in the daylight. "Leave him alone. He's got enough trouble and he doesn't bother anybody" was the parental wisdom on the subject of the Green Man; and so no one sorted the piled up rumors and halves of tales and must-have-hads until East Leven arrived at unofficial acceptance of the Green Man named Ben Brown. It was whispered he had had a wife before the accident, had a dog, taught school, had children (or not), a house in another town, a camper pickup parked in front. The Green Man might have become the local oubliette down which the town poured the bad luck from broken mirrors, fear of the unexplainable lights in the summer sky, the residual shiverings of Puritan ancestors, their dislike for one another. Every town had somebody to blame for broken dishes, leaky roofs, poisoned dogs, wells gone rank. East Leven could have blamed Ben Brown, green and living in a cabin by the river, who seemed to draw to himself, like a plant does water, all the town's bad luck with drowning children.

He is dark green. Of course, his greenness depends on the light. Coppery green? No, greener. Like a dark frog, an alligator just under muddy water, reptile green. In shadow, brown like a dark nut. Green enough, though, so you would see he was green passing through the patchy sun around his cabin in the J.C. Penney green work shirt and pants. His sleeves rolled up reveal a continuous green as if the J.C. Penney dyes had not set but ran smooth as lacquer from elbow to finger tip, then crept up his neck, his face, and flowed into a dark brown hairline. His green face – ageless, no notable nose or dimple or line because the only fact of his face is its greenness.

He comes back rolling a spool of wire toward the hiding place. Andrew watches him come and go, watches him absently as if he were a TV program of no particular interest.

After graduation, Andrew had sat in his parents' early American décor, which was lit, throw rug to beam, by the color tube. There was something absolute, final, an entombment to it. Laurel and Hardy, Abbot and Costello, Jane Pauley and Dan Rather. Atomic. Those dots of primary colors, whipped to a froth on a Sony, now Eddie Albert and Ava Gabor, now Yogi Bear, now Bob Vila. Then Yogi Bear and Gilligan, Ava and all the Brady Bunch. Bangladesh, Intruder in the Dust, Fat Albert, The Organic Gardener.

The Green Man lugs a roll of wire through the bushes.

A green man sweating and unrolling spools of wire, green and white wire. This heat would finish the yellow flowers falling like ragged little bells. The Green Man works in the shade and moves toward the sound of the river, leaving the two wires looped from bush to branch to bush. Along the river bank the length of his frontage Andrew sees him, no, hears him, the green of shadows. Andrew loses him again like losing the video portion, and there is the sound of the cold river and green branches crossed in a sloppy grid.

The Green Man comes around again and Andrew is in a blue funk. Green and blue, face to face through the network of branches so they can't see each other. The Green Man knows he's there.

"How about holding these up for a second while I tack them on the tree?" he says. The same measured voice. Andrew thinks, should I leave him talking to the bushes?

The Green Man's hammer ticks away on a big fir to Andrew's left. Time clucks like a chicken in the shade and heat around them, and the sense of distance flattens again – a TV screen – so that the Green Man is left behind, behind and down somewhere, something imagined in the sound of the river. Andrew feels invisible and invulnerable, flattened into the shadows of the leaves.

Andrew falls asleep, and the dark, cool river sounds seem closer in the failing light when he wakes. The afternoon hammering has stopped and the Green Man's cabin has disappeared into shadows except for a glint of light on a window. Andrew watches and the glint fades. The line of sight through the bushes has become a texture of no-light, a dream beach, a rocky coast faintly seen, now a thatch of leaves washed up, rocks without edges, a stiffness of vision needing a stretching.

Then pop! A hundred weak lights clamor in a ragged sudden ring from the cabin to the right, in front of Andrew and off down to the river bank. He wakes to a low-voltage circus in the woods. Birds start up again, having left off twittering for the evening, and Andrew finds himself waiting for tiny elephants, tiny clowns, tiny Mediterranean-looking girls beautiful in blue-and-white satin suits with outrageous hats, and strutting little men in top hats.

But the Green Man comes instead, inspecting the arc of lights, hands on his hips studying the lights like God checking out the effects of his uttered word. Now he's directly in front of Andrew.

"Bring in the dancing girls," Andrew says, his voice new, unused since the morning when he'd mumbled to himself.

"Well, it's the ghost-who-walks-by-noon," the Green Man says. "Drag your ass out here and see what I've wrought." This said in a very ungreen manner. The legends falling away. Andrew unbends from under the bushes and the Green Man continues talking. In the dim light he's startlingly green to Andrew but then so is everything else the lights touch in soft circles. "Twelve volts," he says, indicating with a sweep the lights down to the river. "I found a whole 12-volt system, batteries, charger, regulators – the works. Came out of a farm. FDR, rural electrification, all that."

"Why?" Andrew crawls out to a rain of flowers.

"Yes, why? You want the thirty-second version, the ten-minute version, the two-hour version? Better yet, the never-mind version. The important thing now is it works. Watch."

The Green Man reaches into the bushes and lifts something and the lights in front of them go out. He walks a few steps and lowers the lights and they go on again.

"Portable." Andrew observes, vaguely thinking brevity will pass for all the wit needed in the situation.

"Portable and just the faintest trickle of electricity." He turns and raises one eyebrow to Andrew. "Electricity is why I'm green, you know. It turns people green."

Oh shit, Andrew thinks. He is wacko. The legends come rushing back. Watch out for his bite! Watch out!

"Electricity is one of the main causes of green people," the Green Man says matter-of-factly. He's watching to see if Andrew will spook. But Andrew is ready, has seen the Incredible Hulk, the Bionic Woman, weird things – Julia Child, William F. Buckley. The Green Man continues. "And then, of course, there's black people, red people, yellow people ..."

"All caused by electricity?"

The Green Man laughs. "In a way. Only problem with being green is that there's so few of us, you know. That and you get shy about electricity." He pronounced it e-lec-tri-city this time, like a difficult family name that needs to be repeated by syllables to make it clear. "You get shy about real electricity: 230,000 volts, 880, 440, 220, even the piddling 110. Sometimes I can smell it up in the wires these days. Like the wires are so full that it slops over and runs down the poles. Which brings us to the why. In short: so I can work on the island in the evenings. If the river drops off, I'll never get the island done so I'll have to work evenings now. This way. I'll show you."

He walks ahead along the string of lights stopping to adjust a few. There are broom handles sticking down from each pair of bulbs mounted to a board that clips across the two bare spots in the wires. At the riverbank the lights reveal a three-foot trough between the bank and a small island shored with old tires pegged into the bank like a half-buried freeway accident. There are cables like lacing, plastic bottles, wood, and metal viscera. The Green Man sweeps the trough with his hand, studying the sculpture of short trees, bushes, cables, tires, two-by-twos.

"The island was a little point of land on the bank. I was losing it slowly to the river. I've made an island because ..." He looks up from his handiwork to see what the effect might be. "Because I thought I ought to have an island."

Andrew watches his greenness change as he moves among the bushes and finds himself reminded of his Sony TV with its excellent gain controls. He used to detune it, make everyone green or purple. Crank it all the way over. Give 'em hell, Roger Mudd. Flaming red Roger like an ill dream rising from the pillow case of a Texas right-winger. Green Roger burbling and spurting, aggravated by everything that's happened in the world, disgusted at everyone for taking part. The news green, all guilty as hell for being alive. The TV pulpit, the ghost of Jonathan Edwards singeing asses in the fires of hell. Green Roger Mudd, Japanese technology, and a survey course in "American Lit. from the Beginning," smokable herbs. Andrew was ready for green people!

The Green Man still explains the island and Andrew is mute. Watching. But the Green Man doesn't seem to need a response to keep explaining. He is a fountain of information on hydrodynamics – flow, feet per second. He read a book, he says. The eddies behind the island collect, create deposits. Andrew doesn't know what the hell the Green Man is talking about any more than he knew why Roger Mudd was always angry, always pissed off at America. Still the whole scene seems perfectly natural. Everything in front of his eyes is endless tones of green – the river surface, the leaves, the J.C. Penney work clothes, the little green island growing on the river. The shadows and tires and elaborate webbing of junk that holds the island together all seem to be sketched in with a green felt tip pen. Andrew watches.

The Green Man talks on as if he were showing a foreign delegation through a dam site. As if he had fifteen seconds to commercial, Andrew thinks. As if he hadn't spoken to anyone for weeks.

"… and then plants. Arborvitae. Willows, bush and tree. A ground cover. Saint John's Wort for the sun. Rooty things, as many as will fit on the island." The Green Man talks, holding the bush next to him, feeling its leaves. The island should grow long first, gathering itself downstream. And once it's long enough, maybe twenty-five yards, I'll make wing dams, little ones, to create more eddies and hold the banks steady."

And then suddenly there's the offer, "I pay $3.60 an hour. Minimum wage but no taxes."

Andrew takes the offer under consideration: I'm not hirable, he thinks. I don't sell. I don't buy. I just watch. This island, Nicaragua, Union Carbide, the America Cup races have nothing to do with me. All of this just boils along somewhere over there.

But Andrew hears himself saying, "And the $14.28? Do I pay that off first?" Like a dream of finding himself joining the army, he's standing beside himself. No! Don't say the swearing-in words, asshole. You don't have to do it. Nobody's making you. Don't swear anything!

But Andrew doesn't hear himself. He hears the Green Man talking like Frank Lloyd Wright, Mies van der Rohe, Le Corbusier. An International Style island. Will it blink off and on? How's the reception out there? Will the TV cable company service an island, he wonders.

There's a heaviness in Andrew's feet. He shuffles to keep up with this green leanness popping up there on the other side of a bush, hopping to the island and back. Andrew waits out the heaviness, tugs his T-shirt at the neck. Sleep is what he wants. Not work.

Andrew finds himself trailing Ben Brown, who by this time has gotten encyclopedically to continental drift, plate tectonics. He lifts the portable light nearby and hangs it further on toward the downstream end of his cigar-shaped island. The wires enter the island upstream, run through the center and off again where the stern might be.

He's a green one, Andrew thinks, ruminating on TV nature programs. Very rare. We're not sure if he'd know how to check into a Holiday Inn, whether he'd eat a Big Mac. In fact, we're not sure we've even got a breeding population here or a single example of eccentric nature's …

The Green Man looks at Andrew every now and then to make sure he's paying attention. In shadow his face might be deeply tanned. Then he turns into the light. Bap! Special effects. American green. Andrew asks him, "How'd you get to be green?" He's startled by his own voice again. The Green Man tells him.

They are off the island looking back on the canal between it and shore. The Green Man is telling Andrew the hospital part, a short version, because right from the beginning the whole green story will come out in serial form, possibly even sequels, Andrew believes: The Green Man I, The Green Man II, The Green Man III., etc. The whole thing in his chemically altered state smacks of engineering, fabrication, because of the tour of engineering proportions – bulwarks and cantilevers – and it is the hot dripping oil of "manufactured" that Andrew smells in this story now that he's been robbed of the insulation of his watching seat, the safe side of the TV screen.

What Andrew resents is actually being there. So he turns at the first lull in the Green Man's mechanical voice and goes home.

Andrew is back the next day, much earlier than he is used to getting up. He feels, while eating breakfast, that it would be interesting to hang out over there at the island building. Until it's not interesting anymore. Andrew's light brown hair has taken off on its own today, gone to visit somewhere in space, maybe a zoo. He stuffs it under a baseball cap as a concession to civilization, to not spooking the spook. And he goes to visit the construction site. Andrew's nose stops just short of being significant, his eyebrows threaten to but don't touch. His long face will become longer once his hair recedes, but now with his hair pulled back or tacked under the ball cap he gives the impression of being intelligent, slightly quizzical, as if working out a detailed math problem in his head while loping along. His winter skin tends toward splotchy. In spring he phototropes toward healthy, usually affecting a transition with the daffodils.

Ben Brown is pondering something when Andrew comes through the wisteria. Green Man engineering something, Andrew names the scene. He frames it with thumbs and forefingers. Ready to shoot the movie.

"What's the engineering feat of the day?" Andrew asks as casually as he can. There is some fulsome smell in the air he didn't notice before, something perfumey that probably couldn't have made it through the marijuana.

The Green Man watches him sniff the air, holds up a finger and says, "Daphne."

For some reason Andrew immediately thinks of the Monty Python shtick involving shrubbery. "Daphne," he says back in the affirmative. He thinks, lupine; I think it should be lupine. More Monty Python.

The Green Man moves around the bushes like a dancer. He has let the salal and kinnikinnick grow back after the clearing for the building of the cabin. There are paths worn around the bushes like game trails, and he moves through the paths without looking down. The low-voltage wires are clearly visible now and the mystery of the appearing and disappearing light illusion is more than revealed, it's announced.

"Here it is, the source of the electricity," and the Green Man pops a wooden box open. The top has been paved with shingles the same as the roof of the cabin. In the box are batteries laced together post to post in series. A small Briggs and Stratton one-cylinder motor that looked to have been scavenged off a lawnmower was harnessed through a centrifugal clutch to a light green generator that announced its age with the curves of its design, the recessed bolt heads, the snap-open oiling holes that fed into massive end bearings. The engine was fitted with a new muffler as large as the top of the motor.

The Green Man points to the shiny muffler. "Quiet."

"Very impressive," says Andrew. He traces the cables from the generator to the batteries and deduces his way through the schematics. "Two 6-volt batteries in series, then two more, then two more. Six 6-volts." Immediately he feels like an idiot announcing the obvious with an idiot's pride.

And before he can regain his detached, cool place, while he is teetering on his own vulnerability, the Green Man pronounces, "Very good," like a pat on the head for Andrew, who feels he might just as well have observed that the sky is blue.

Ben Brown lets the silence heal the awkwardness. With his own enthusiasm he indicates how the engine sucks air from outside the box and the muffler is stuffed with a kind of steel wool that makes it virtually silent, as opposed to the original arrangement on the farm, where they might not have had a muffler at all and just run the engine flat out to charge the batteries. "You lose about twenty percent of the power with the silencer," he says.

Andrew feels he has entered into collusion with the Green Man. The show-and-tell phase originally focused on the generator begins to spread. Ben Brown indicates the next feature of his specially prepared world. He had mounted a voltmeter on a tree to monitor the output of the batteries. He had installed a thin piece of red tape at the 12-volt mark. "That's my limit, if you know what I mean."

Andrew nods, but doesn't know what he means.

"I feel pretty comfortable with the whole electricity business again if I stay in the low range." The Green Man laughs. "You can take a hit at 12 volts and hardly get to be any color but what you already are."

Andrew admits he has no particular stake in staying the same color, offers that the tanning season is coming up and he might go for a new shade soon. While he talks he watches the Green Man for signs of sensitivity about his color. After all, not only had he brought it up the first time, he kept bringing it up.

They move to the island.

Andrew begins, "Now why …?"

The Green Man shakes his head. "Start with the hard part, why don't you. Let's leave the why for a while and take a look at the features here."

Andrew feels towed around the set of a weird movie. The Green Man's enthusiasm sometimes just takes the form of excited pointing without much explanation, like a young man showing off his toys to his buddy. Here's this. And here's that.

They are at the downstream point of the island, stabilized on the outside, the river side, but still fragile on the inside, the bank side, where a smaller river slows and shuffles then scoots back out into the main stream.

"See how it goes," says the Green Man, tracing the flow with a finger. "Comes in here." Finger dragging along the flanks of the island. "And it goes out there."

This is new information for Andrew only in that the Green Man seems wholly taken with this obvious water event. Andrew looks carefully at his face to see if he's making some kind of subtle joke, and he's the one not getting it. But, no, the Green Man seems perfectly serious. Comes in here. Goes out there. Comes, then goes. Andrew nods. Yup, it does.

"I was thinking of a bridge but all I have is the plank for now." The Green Man walks to halfway up the island and takes a plank from where it's leaning against a tree. He slides it across to the island and ponders the effect. Then he jumps across the water, not using the bridge, to ponder the effect from the other side. "I don't think I really need it yet, but, well, it's really in the idea stage still."

Andrew notices that where the Green Man is standing on the island, water is creeping up around his shoe. He notices too and jumps back across to the bank and dry land.

"We might have a problem. I'm not sure what's happening, why we're losing ground. The outside is shored up with the bleach bottles and rope."

The enterprise seems to Andrew to be wholly made up out of needing something to do. He begins to watch Ben Brown more carefully for signs that he might be dangerous. But something in this tour appeals to Andrew. He had been concocting his own life from moment to moment until the job offer. He was entering one concoction out of another, or joining a pair of them. There must be a punch line to the whole business. What do you get when you join one concoction to another concoction? Umm. Like Alice in Wonderland's raven and writing desk he didn't know the answer, only the certainty of the question loomed.

The island-building weather held through two o'clock, and then it got hot. They took turns wheeling loads of dirt to thicken the island, and each wheelbarrowful got spread thinly to build up the surface. Andrew remembered seeing a documentary on how the Dutch would buy small hills in northern Belgium and truck them up to the thinnest parts of Holland in the north and spread them ceremoniously across farmland reclaimed from the North Sea. Anywhere you stuck a pole in the earth, water filled the hole. Cows grazed the new land, sucking their substantial hooves out of the fragile mire so that the countryside echoed the thuck, thuck of each hoof extraction. At least that's what the documentary made it sound like.

Andrew's turn at spreading comes in the two o'clock heat. He feels the island grow more substantial with each shovelful, and he finds himself carefully spreading the loam to the edges of the island like spreading jelly perfectly to the edge of the bread. He stops once to ponder why he cared to do this so neatly. What was in it for him besides the paycheck? But the Green Man comes grunting across the plank looking for a place to unload in one motion. Andrew finds himself directing the load to the perfect low spot where he could curry the surface, make the insubstantial substantial. Next, while Ben Brown trundles off toward the dirt pile, Andrew marks four future dump spots in ascending order of need. He thinks briefly of Genesis – firmament and void, substance and anima – and hitches the ropes to the bleach bottles tighter while waiting for the next dirt. Ben Brown huffs on his game-trail paths through the salal, announcing his approach, bridge cross, and dump.

"That's it for me," he says. "No more juice. Too hot. And…what the hell, I'm green. I invoke the green clause in my contract."

Andrew notices for the first time what Ben Brown actually looks like. The word avuncular occurs to him. Ben Brown looks like somebody's uncle. Nice guy. Drove a Jeep. Could make quarters appear from behind your ear. Would finally give you one of the quarters after he saw your frustration rising at not being able to find money behind your own ears. His ears are small and sleek, back against his head as if he spent time riding with his head out the window. His brown hair is full and deep chestnut, with a small widow's peak and the aggressive hairline of a sixth grader. It gives the uncle-look something exotic, as if he were perennial, would always be the same age, always be everyone's uncle. He is about five-ten – short for basketball, tall for soccer. Andrew looks more closely. The green shadows on his face play over cheekbones that could be handsome, would shout handsome, if not inundated in green. He could never play Santa Claus, Andrew thinks. No one would ever buy him playing Santa Claus.

EAST LEVEN IN ITS SIDE STREETS, JUST BEHIND THE BAKERY, the bars, the hardware store, Conroy Burbank's flower shop, and the espresso coffee cart in the street – the original East Leven – sagged noticeably. Like the Green Man's island construction, the town too had cobbled itself together out of what was available. This part of town that wasn't regularly in view could now relax and wrap itself up in a ratty robe and worn-out slippers, could slump into a couch and eat chocolate ice cream. The sidewalks cultivated a spate of crack weeds like untended ear hair. Nothing was so far gone that it couldn't be hauled back from the brink, but with their peeled paint and dry-rotted sills, the storefronts hinted of dissolution.

Once, before the Green Man, the circle of blocks that formed the downtown had all tailed out onto the park – the bandstand for Sunday afternoons, a small duck pond – and had shared in the respectability of being park blocks. Horchow had made a company town but left the company store to the townspeople. What Horchow manufactured was so far removed from retail that they had no interest in vertical integration of economic interests. There had been two centers to the town: Horchow and the unsolved murders. Then lower in importance but basic to everything else came water and the ways of water – its self-indulgent flooding, its rare insufficiency, its exacting of an occasional sacrifice, like Anne Doucette. When visitors came to town they felt its low center of gravity as if its permanence were not up for negotiation; what could be negotiated were minor details on its surface but nothing of substance – all the substance had been decided.

The reason that East Leven had a street named Furher and managed to keep the name through World War II was that the Furher family, though no longer with living representation in town, had left a legacy of kind acts and civic gifts. The space for the park, a solid block of expensive retail space, had been donated by the family as an opening in the center of town. In the cemetery, the family obelisk was topped by an angel either taking off or landing – there was much discussion since one foot was solid in the stone and the other either rising to take off or adjusting for the landing. It had been carved in Italy by a family of stone carvers that traced its ancestry to the workshops of Leonardo da Vinci. The Furher family, unlike the Willsons, who came and dispersed throughout the land (minus Mary Willson, who returned to East Leven as a vegetarian to her meat-rancher heritage), simply petered out into the soil of the river bend. Some wearing out of the urge to send their genetic stuff into the future had left the Furher elders satisfied to have come this far west. With not much farther to go, they figured, this was a pretty good run. And then they were gone. Retail, wholesale, mortgage, and entail; they were gone except for Furher Street, something of a shrine, something of a historical homonymic embarrassment.

Mary Willson came back to town bearing her ancestors on her back, in her suitcases, in her immediate comfort with the angle of sunlight in spring cloud breaks and summer evenings. Something in her already bore the information about East Leven's prevailing wind patterns, the way shadows slid off the eastern hills and rolled up toward noon before bluing into afternoon. Mary brought her ancestors' approval, their original consent before they took their longing to other places. Mary came back and circled the Willson family wagons and stayed.

In between the Furhers and the Willsons were the rest. The valley and its north-flowing river, its fir and pine and oak forests, its mandate of water and clay soil like contending political parties, its stitches of blackberries sewing the whole thing together right on the 45th parallel, which established the middle way and the temperate position. East Leven sat astride the 45th and collected the middle people.

Marge McIntry had been a middle person of middle fortunes and income. As with a number of middle people, her luck came and went with health and insurance vicissitudes. In East Leven she had been reapportioned toward the bottom of the social scale by moving downstream from Horchow. At the same time that Mary Willson moved into her fifth-grade teaching job, Marge began shopping at Goodwill, sold off the last of her middle-people furniture, and emptied her bank account into bankruptcy to pay off an improvident son's medical bills. Marge homesteaded, as had Mary Willson's ancestors. But Marge moved north of Horchow on the river pilings where a grain company had warehoused local wheat in the early twentieth century. The piling tops had the floor joists and some warehouse shack walls still in place. Since it was county land, Marge and a few others squatted outside the town's jurisdiction. The coming of the Green Man, his cabin on the river just south of the Bye Bye cemetery, had brought Marge and her cohorts a measure of normalcy. After all, they may be squatters, but they all sported regular skin colors, and the initial town concern about green people in general seemed to dilute the more generic concern for gypsies and itinerants of all sorts. What could be more temporary and transient than a green person? Unprecedented in all the annals of western towns and probably eastern towns too.

Before the Green Man, before Horchow, the people came. With veterans of the WPA and the CCC came contract workers from California and Mexico, who picked the berry and bean fields, though they found it hard to stay and were encouraged to move on. But some stayed and built themselves into the fabric of the town. Then Finns left over from the lumbering days – neither Scandinavian nor Slavs, they were like mutant cousins the family took in anyway – hammered up shingles and framed and roofed the houses where the Swedes and Norwegians would do the finish carpentry. The post-World War II housing boom demanded houses without eaves (even in this land of rainy winter) to save the board feet of overhang for the next house. What got produced were houses that seemed unfinished, as if a front door were missing or a chimney. The effect of no eaves was like an aesthetic snout creation – all snout and not much pig. Through 1949 the snout house appeared overnight on vacant lot after vacant lot. And then someone must have noticed, there must have been more lumber at better prices, something, and the houses grew elegant, with useful eaves again harkening back to the generous eaves of the early century craftsman style. The postwar houses remained like poor relations living out their days among their well-heeled relatives, an embarrassment, but finally family.

Horchow might have been as responsible for the lengthening of the eaves as the lumber market was. Horchow certainly brought bigger, greener lawns, the country club and golf course, the steak houses, some lobster dinners, and European vacations. The house that Mary Willson came to occupy had lavish eaves to keep the winter rains from dripping on the window glass, craftsman knee braces of clear fir to bind the architecture together, fine mullions across the top of the big front window that echoed in the interior cabinetry. It had been built with the first flush of Horchow money, long before Mary's return.

Three streets named after American transcendentalists – Emerson, Hawthorne, and Alcott – paralleled each other and transected five tree-named streets so that children in East Leven grew up believing that pine, cherry, walnut, aspen, alder, emerson, hawthorne, and alcott were all tree names. The Furher family had its memorial street. Then there were the obligatory Main (South and North), Hill, Salmon, River (Road), and Cross (to get across other streets). It was late in East Leven's development, when the urban growth crawled up the hillsides and headed north and south along the river, that the fancy names were generated out of developers' family names – Marypat Road, Tawny Turnpike (a half block long ending in a cul de sac), Clintnjanet Street, and the unfortunate Tobeyjunejoy

Court, which tried to contain the whole natal history of the developer's family's unbridled joy at the birth of a son. And somewhere beneath the surface chugged Horchow and its genius for nonferrous metals, the engine that made naming of things possible.

BEN BROWN TOOK HIS FIRST CHECK FROM PACIFIC POWER and Light and lit out. He flew to Geneva, Switzerland, without thinking that Europe would be almost all 220 volts. He came to feel the juice in the lines seeping out as if through a leaky hose.

In the hospital he was over a month turning green. Each day his skin tingled as if tiny armies had spent the night marching over it. A war raged along his collar bones; between his shoulder blades mines blew, and he twitched and snaked into the bed table while sweating floods down his chest. Knees and shoulders seemed to glow. And in his right shoulder, then the elbow and wrist and hand, was a pain like a cry far away, unintelligible at first, a word growing louder and finally rushing with multiple eees until the sound became a light, the light blinding, white, still. The codeine, morphine, seconal seemed to wrap around the light then withdraw. He became so used to the light that he could examine it an hour at a time, feel the heft of it, the length and thickness. He would raise it and point at traffic out the window, searing imaginary lines into the world. He drew figures in the air like a Fourth of July sparkler. And steadily he turned green and the fire glowed out.

His early green had a pastel softness to it. There was an agricultural cast to his skin, a far-off alfalfa field in spring. The doctor stroked his forearm and checked his finger. Rubbed harder a second time and held his finger up to the light. He finally scraped with a scalpel and tapped the flakes onto a slide, clucking to himself and sucking his lips in concentration. Days later a different doctor, this one almost beside himself with the announcement, said, "You're turning green!"

"Jealousy," Ben Brown said.

"Green," the doctor said, keeping his dignity. "We don't know why." And he paused as if waiting for a blessing, forgiveness, before he could continue. Red, pink, brown, black, yellow – there are so many colors and combinations of colors to turn. Any one of these and he might have had a life among the other colors of earth's people. But green was the color of things people were not: reptiles, plants, tropical birds, monsters, faces in dreams. Slippery things were green.

"We suspect the endocrine system is involved. The pituitary can darken the skin. Other glands ...We don't understand how it all works. And the epiphysis, the pineal body, a spot really on the brain stem, it often calcifies, forms a sort of sand—brain sand, they used to call it—between the age of about seven and puberty. Our radiologists use it as a reference point to the brain since it shows up clearly in adults."

The doctor paused again as if trying to peer through a wall of logic his training had built, a veil of causes and effects. The world of the body was reasonable. But not green bodies. He searched for the simplest words. "Yours is gone. Your spot, your calcified pineal. It showed on an old X-ray you had taken years ago, and now it's not there. Yours is ... active again probably. Turned back on or something ..." He trailed off, unaccustomed to "or something." The words seemed to catch in his throat. Bad Science.

Ben Brown waited.

"Your heart is fine," the doctor continued. Science itself was at stake here. "That's very important. In fact, crucial after an electric shock. There are SA and AV nodes, rhythm makers, bundles of nerves that easily degenerate under heavy shock. Your EKG looks fine. A good strong thumping along." He smiled, pleased with the picture he had drawn, the comfort of it.

"And the green?" Ben asked, not willing to give up the subject that produced the catch in his throat and feeling as if he needed a little power, wanting to push someone around for his greenness.

"It might fade," the doctor guessed. "Women sometimes get a mask in pregnancy, a little like a raccoon. It almost always fades. Well, not green. No. This is something more complicated. You show unusual hormone levels in your blood. Hormones are always tricky because of the minute traces and how they affect each other. We'll need more tests."

"And this pineal body?" Ben felt himself drawn to the mysterious part. The doctor looked out the window as if the answer might be out there somewhere in the traffic, in the jazz and jangle down on the street. "The pineal body," Ben repeated. It was hard to keep from laughing. Something in the pineal body, the doctor pondering out the window like Hippocrates in a frieze, being green – something essentially silly about it all – a contrivance, a suspension of all the rules.

"Who knows?" said an old doctor he hadn't seen until just before he was scheduled to be released. "Who knows? You're the first green one. Maybe you're the beginning of something new in people. I'm too old to get excited. And I like green. Maybe you'll fade in sunlight like my parlor sofa. It was such a burgundy when we bought it." He had his arm in the crook of Ben's elbow while they walked the hallway. Ben felt he was holding him up. "A year in afternoon sun and it doesn't matter what you paid for it." He threw his hands up, then shoved them in his pockets. "There are worse things. You should be dead."

The power company paid as if he were dead – a lump sum he put into T-bills – and alive, "a little" each month, something like a lottery payment, they said. It turned out to be his full salary for life, cost of living each year, the works. He signed away his rights to any further settlement. Ben Brown had won the lottery by becoming green.

And so, what does a green person do when finances aren't a problem? History is one of the first things a green person looks at. The history of all of us, of course, because green people have no personal history, just new little empires where the laws and rules aren't made up yet. All possibilities possible. There are many things interesting about being green, but the history of the green race wasn't one of them. Now the history of the species – that's different. So at first he studied history, then the idea of the civil contract that towns devise for themselves. Later, botany.

AS THE TOWN GREW ACCUSTOMED TO BEN BROWN, THEY EXPECTED less and less of him in the way of public appearances as the Green Man, and they let him walk in the shadows. Once a year, at first, it was reported in the paper on how he was coming along, this business of being green, and how he thought it was going. First a year-to-year report, like a fiscal statement, then eighteen months, and finally the green man saw only young reporters and only after long periods of time had passed, renewing his status as news.

There were whole segments of the population in which green people never came up at all in polite conversation. But there were other segments in which the Green Man was almost daily fare. "I'm looking for a car about the color of the green guy." "I told her, I said, 'What the hell's the difference? Who does he think he is? The Green Man?'" "Hey, kids, stop that or I'll come in there and turn you all green and set you out with the trash for the Green Man." "I think we ought to get more out of him, you know, in a civic sense. Maybe he could cut the ribbon to open a mall or something. You know, high profile. Or higher anyway."

The Green Man walked in town like a visiting second cousin from someplace else. He belonged by squatters' rights that had been recognized in town for a hundred and fifty years and especially in the last fifty years. Only somehow his green skin, green bloodline, kept him a second cousin on permanent visitor's status.

The Green Man came up not so much as a topic of conversation, but as a reference point.

"I see by the paper there'll be a new moon just right for planting this year." Old man Jenkins, paterfamilias of the "good" Jenkins in town, observed to no one in particular sitting on the bench in front of the hardware store.

"You can tell that without looking in the paper, Ned," from the other end of the bench, a retired fisherman who came here sixty miles from the ocean to roost in safety the way the seagulls did when a big storm blew inland over the coastal range.

"Hell, you could tell that by the way Ben Brown gets out and about. I think he takes longer and longer walks as the moon waxes. I talked to him once and he told me he gets restless and creaky both toward a full moon. I mean that's what he said, anyway. Who knows if he's funnin' you or what. But he says he needs to get out and walk more toward a full moon. To stave off a case of the creakies. That's what he called it. Who knows what he means."

The men chewed this over sitting on the bench line that's continued by power mowers chained together in front of the store window. Three wheelbarrows seemed to whisper together apart from the mowers.

"You can sure see him moving right along. Doesn't seem like the 'creak-ies' slows him down any."

Captain Howard lit his pipe. "I'm not so sure he was talking arthritis"– it came out *arthur-itis* – "when he was talking about it. Not old-fart stuff like you guys grunting to stand up. I took him to mean some other kind of malady there wasn't an exact name for. Maybe a green-guy thing, you know. Something you get with the green skin, don't you know."

The topic was open but there was plenty of time and the sun was warm on thin legs but not stinging in their eyes yet. When the sun started to bother their eyes, they would move across the street in front of the Dairy Lunch to another set of benches near the jewelry store clock that quit eight years ago. They had discussed this before. They'd discuss it again soon.

Ned Jenkins, warmed to the knees now, warmed to his original topic. He was chief of the gardening Jenkins clan, no relation, that anyone would admit to, to that other clan of Welshmen who did as little house and lawn maintenance as possible. Those other Jenkins, the bad Jenkins, owned a lawn mower, it was rumored, but no living soul had ever seen it actually functioning. Once, though, no one could remember exactly when, some-one had seen one of the Jenkins boys working on it, grease and tools and gas stink everywhere in the driveway. The bad Jenkins' grass grew long and then flopped over on itself in croplike patches that greened or browned with the vicissitudes of rare summer rains. Ned Jenkins avoided the bad Jenkins and, in fact, their whole street.

"I wouldn't be surprised," he said, "if this didn't turn out to be a good tomato year."

This was a long shot and he knew it. Cool evenings, cooler nights made Northwest tomato growing a great crapshoot, and Jenkins, who had just stuck out his neck, was looking to get his head lopped off. Every gardener knew more recipes for green tomatoes than for red – chutneys, fried, pickled, relish, layered in lasagna, with eggplant. The green tomato sat atop the Northwest gardener's totem pole.

"A good tomato year." Twice said locked in the prediction. He would be held responsible for it now. It was written down, and Ned would be ragged on without mercy come the middle of September. Calling a tomato year was like Babe Ruth pointing to the outfield stands. You better hit it out or look like a complete goof. But if you did call it, there was a year of privileged pontifications earned as payoff for the gamble. Long shot, then easy money. Ned got bored sometimes and liked to take the assembled fogies for a ride once in a while. He had swung and missed before, then taken his punishment in accommodating silence as the other wits cast about for nicknames, new topics for ridiculous predictions. Ned cleared his throat, looking for takers.

"Okay. We heard you." From the end of the bench. "Tomato year."

Ned took a pitch. "And on top of that it'll be the year of the …" He rolled up his eyes to look at the list of totemic garden critters – slug, spider, ground squirrel, moth, toad, ant, yellow jacket.

He had seen the Green Man last week come up from his river cabin and walk into town. From the top of the ravine you could watch him walk the whole distance, across the parkway, then under the trestle and into town. Ned had watched idly at first, just to see how the Green Man walked, what he slowed for, what kind of purpose there seemed to be in his gait. Ned thought he detected a slight limp, but it could have been only that the guy walked with a kind of lilt, a list to the left that might be mistaken for a limp.

Ned could also see the construction project jutting out from the Green Man's riverfront, a mess poking into the stream that seemed to be generating even more mess from above. Ned was put in mind, at first, of his yard-disaster Welsh countrymen, and he remembered hoping this messiness didn't spread viruslike through the town. And he wondered, too, if whatever Ben Brown was doing might be illegal, needing at least a variance or an easement, city council approval, a riprap permit. Suspicious activity.

"I say, 'suspicious activity.'" Ned said aloud, quoting his own thoughts.

"What's suspicious activity?" Finally the question came from near the end of the bench, but with no particular enthusiasm, as if even asking it had fallen to the member with the least seniority and now he asked out of default position.

Ned arranged himself, turned down the bench, since he knew that good ears and bad ears strategies had been worked out years ago. The ears along the bench made adjustments to hear the answer. "This green man, Ben Brown. He has some kind of construction project going down there along the river. I wonder what he's up to. Maybe suspicious is a little too strong."

"Not that he could do anything in this town without someone knowing about it. Doesn't seem like he's trying to hide anything." A voice from the middle of the bench.

Another opinion. "I saw this suspicious activity a while ago. Looks like he's just fooling around or something. Or maybe adults don't fool around. We putter."

"You've got to be a male to putter. Females never putter."

"They do, in my humble opinion, but they call it something else."

"Tidying up."

"Rearranging the furniture."

"Shopping."

Ned returned to high seriousness. "All I'm saying is that whatever he's doing on the riverbank, it's probably regulated somehow by city code."

"On the other hand, Horchow seems to do whatever they damn well please along the riverbank."

"I think they have some grandfathered rights since part of the plant goes way back to old man Horchow, who could do just about whatever the hell he wanted to. Most of the time."

Ned said he thought that the city had been pretty lenient with Horchow since the state had the real authority over the river. "It's state business since it's considered navigable, you know."

There were grunts of knowing or at least giving Ned the nod. Pockets of authority were conceded among the group members – their previous jobs, areas of accidental expertise like Ned's successful battle against lawn grubs that conferred upon him final say in matters of lawn grubs and by extension any slow-moving lawn pest. The higher mammal lawn-pests authority belonged to Al Jory, who had defeated prolifically breeding ground squirrels with applications of gasoline.

As the Green Man now ascended the path from his cabin, they all leaned forward to get a better view – of him appearing and disappearing on his way up the path, of the Green Man's shore project with its scattering of building materials.

The Green Man had stopped three times on his way as if he kept finding something, about shoulder high in the bushes, something interesting to inspect, maybe the same thing all three times, because the last time he quickly inspected and then went on his way. Saw that before. Another one just like the other one.

After the Green Man had disappeared from sight around the corner at the gas station, Ned decided to amble down and see what was so arresting for the green guy. He had found webs crawling with caterpillars in all three spots. How hard could the call be? "It'll be the year of the moth. Get out your moth traps and oil down those fruit trees. I'm saying 'moth' with some conviction."

There was general grumbling but no particular objection. Or alternative suggestion. And so the year of the designated garden and household pest was locked in. All bets down. Ned figured if the whole thing was a long shot anyway, at least the Green Man seemed to have some kind of insider information when it came to the world of plants and critters. If he didn't, poor guy, he should, if there was a shred of fairness anywhere in the cosmos. The guy was spending his life green in the name of something, certainly.

They shifted across the street to the Dairy Lunch and the stopped freestanding clock, not all at once but in turns as if directed by inner compasses, like geese or caribou. But finally they all ended up across the street out of the hot sun. A tomato grower's sun.

The Green Man had grown elemental, as if attended by the town's stare so long that he began to recede into its gaze. Sometimes he sat on the park bench on the far side of the park the W PA men had built. The J.C. Penney deep green shirt he had found actually minimized the green of his skin. And after a time he even felt as if he had become part of bush, bird, lawn – the fabric of authentic things that occupied East Leven. The town breathed him in, breathed him out, just as easily as it did the ghost of Anne Doucette, Crazy Leo, and the high school marching band in full uniform playing "Under the Double Eagle."

And those murders so long ago now that they seemed to be a story someone once told who passed through and then was gone. The details became vague but the central mysteries – unfaithfulness, betrayal, unseasonal snow, a phantom killer – these grew clear. And though the story yielded to many versions of retelling and gained a kind of universality, almost as if it had happened somewhere else, there was also the sense that what happened, what was lost, was a singular center to what East Leven believed it was. There was a place there, an opening, for the Green Man.

BEFORE THE GREEN MAN, HORCHOW PROVIDED THE GEOMETRY to East Leven, but the residual disorder lurked: in the unsolved murders, in Crazy Leo, in the special pleading of each ethnic group's inherent sense of superiority. Ten thousand Swedes ran through the weeds, chased by one Norwegian. Does your old man work? No, he's Armenian. A Mick, a Polack, and a Kraut were playing golf…

The surface in town appeared nearly seamless – an American dream of singular community. But just below the surface were two distrusts simmering. One was western, a plague beyond the 100th meridian that the towns in the American West all felt to some degree or another. The feeling pervaded business deals and handshakes. The persistent sentiment percolated that all this was temporary – allegiances, alliances, beneficences, and even the daily contract with water supply. Settlers became aware that western weather didn't include the implied God-given mandate of rainwater each growing season, that the mandate that had carried over from Europe to America's East Coast had failed in the West. If the rain could not be counted on, then surely all the rest was temporary too. Let's hold out as long as we can and then move on. The Willson family had been seduced by fraudulent reports of bountiful summer rains, and of rain that followed the plow in some hard-work covenant with God. You plow up the earth, and I'll send the rain as reward for steadfast labor. A few generations later and the new paradigm began to set in: you plow and sometimes you'll lose the whole effort. Are you harboring secret sins that make you unfit for the promise of the promised land?

East Leven had deep wells, aquifers that fed off the side streams that ran into the river. You could drill shallow and get water for irrigation, but the deep wells tapped into the good stuff. Down there was the royal water like purple velvet. Part of the w pa projects in town, along with the bridge building, was tapping into more water than the town could conceivably ever use. Part of what attracted Horchow to the bank of the river was not just that the river was available for cooling water, settling ponds, flushing wastes. The wells drilled on the banks before the first factory foundation blocks were laid produced strong, steady, clear, cold water. And though manufacturing hydraulics didn't need a lot of water, rare earths and metal coatings eventually did. Ezra Horchow congratulated himself on his perspicacity when his engineers announced that the changeover would be accomplished easily, drawing on existing wells already producing on the property. The wells were giant straws stuck into the land; Horchow only needed to suck a little harder, and the water would be there. Some local shallow wells felt the difference; a few went dry in the first months as the new pumps at Horchow sucked harder. But the city water surged clear and strong. The new factory drew more people, more people meant more houses, more flushes, more of everything. The whole question of water, the western question that gathered people into cities along rivers, became for East Leven a problem solved. Out of World War II came pump technology that let everybody suck harder on the straws in the aquifers. Except for the bad Welsh Jenkins family and their fear of becoming enslaved to grass, lawns greened and sprinkler heads pulsed. Winter rains were approximated with daily waterings and the excess ran back into the river.

BEFORE THE COMING OF BEN BROWN, BEFORE THE GREAT AND divisive rage over trees, East Leven developed a fence policy that was at first glance out of a nineteenth century western cattlemen's code. Fence 'em in. Fence 'em out. Whatever you needed to get the job done. But excess reared its ugly head, eventually overcoming reasonable and prudent civic pride and common sense. It was the landscaping-challenged Jenkins who set things off. His unkempt backyard, thicket of weeds, and ground-zero aesthetics begged to be fenced out. His neighbor on the south side took a nine-foot fence to a solid wood fifteen. On the north, not to be outdone, a neighbor attempted a chain-link project with woven slats that came to look like a series of batting cages in a high security zone. Jenkins was twice encircled when his neighbor to the back, to complete the shunning, brought in ferro-cement slabs that had been prepoured elsewhere, buried them in two feet of concrete, and topped them with broken glass set in mortar. He had seen the broken glass set in walls in Mexico. He weed-proofed himself with the concrete, he said, because Jenkins's yard was a plague of every noxious plant found west of the Mississippi River except kudzu. He had identified Russian thistle, English ivy, tansey ragwort, and the standard dandelion / pigweed / poison oak mix. "If Jenkins's yard were bacteria," he pronounced one day, "It would be under lockdown by the Centers for Disease Control." Jenkins didn't bat an eye and kept his own landscape architect counsel.

But the look of the shunning of Jenkins, as it became known, was so stalag, so reeking of incivility, that East Leven decided it needed a fence code. The principle of legislating common sense and good taste has always been tricky. At first the code writers thought they should just borrow wholesale from another town, some place that had worked through this business of good fences and good neighbors. But research revealed that codes were so idiosyncratic that each town had created a mantle to fit its own shape. None would import very well. And so it was decided that East Leven, too, would cut from whole cloth for itself.

The debate and suggestions portion of the council meeting drew the following, each presented with equal passion and intensity. Each was entered into the council minutes.

– no red fences of any height
– no barbed or razor wire on the tops
– turrets would be allowed only where fences made 90-degree angles
– crenellation could only bear a ratio of 10:1, height of the fence to the depth of crenellation
– all fences must be only as tall as an average-size human
– air must circulate freely through every fence

– no black fences

– no electric fences with charges of more than 9 volts or 2 amps

– no searchlights mounted on fences

– no orange fences

– no weapons mounted on fences

– no murals of any kind painted on outsides of fences

– waterfalls, climbing walls, flashing or neon lights must all face in

There were more. And it became apparent that everyone had had some specific experience with a fence, fence trauma of some sort, that he or she wanted legislated for or against. And for a while in East Leven, fences held the town's interest. Fences seemed to bear the civic burden that might transfer into legislation about water, sewage, land-use planning, zoning regulations of all sorts. If the boilerplate arguments for fences could be established, it was felt in the upper echelons of city lawmakers, why then all other standards could be derived from fence legislation. What would be reasonable in a fence would be reasonable in all other forms of civil dogma.

There would be no red fences, not pure red, anyway. And no orange or black fences. The rest of the rainbow would be negotiable. Electrical charges could only be used to contain stock, and since no stock – including chickens and a base number of rabbits – could be kept in the city limits, there would be no voltage whatsoever allowed in town. Air circulation, easements, and the idiosyncrasies of turrets, crenellations, and broken-glass toppings would all be subject to individual case decisions per application or building permit.

THE NEXT DAY THEY WORK ON THE ISLAND TOGETHER, ANDREW wrestling the wheelbarrow across a plank to the island, dumping his load of dirt, plodding back to the pile by the cabin. Andrew sweats his honest sweat. Then suddenly, after dumping what seems like the day's hundredth load of dirt, the island shudders once, then again, and Andrew watches the gang plank he has walked over and over draw back, and the island kicks loose into the current with the Green Man in the bow, Andrew startled astern.

The island had felt solid, more solid by the barrowful, and the shudder seemed to Andrew organic, coming from somewhere deep in the earth, not from the water. The island floats beautifully, as if this event rose out of eventuality instead of accident. The shudder seems to remain in the island in some way – the animation of its birth staying on undiminished.

They take off. Or break off, or whatever happens when an island comes loose popping 12-volt lines with a twang. Andrew looks over to the green person right away to see if he has caught on to what is happening. But the Green Man is busy rigging a steering sweep while the island takes a slow 360 degree turn in the current. The sky, the trees, the water all taking a slow whirl that makes Andrew want to close his eyes and whirl too, like going down the bathtub drain or with Alice down the rabbit hole.

They proceed down the river. But this is no Mississippi. They are headed due north.

Finally the Green Man gets his sweep working, then lifting it high and paddling to steer the island, he shows Andrew how to use it and starts to rig another at the stern of the island.

"It's the bleach bottles that keep it up," he shouts, as if Andrew can't hear him ten feet away. Andrew can't see him behind a bush. The island is completely landscaped with a clump of young birch at the back sporting a sweep. There's a boxwood hedge the Green Man has got scattered around to hold the soil in place, and he perches over it like a great blue heron lifting his feet high and placing them carefully down. Andrew had floated the river on everything from inner tubes to rubber rafts and aluminum boats, so going in wouldn't be a problem. Avoid tangling with the wreck-age when she goes, and live through it. Andrew starts to ask the Green Man if he swims, but doesn't. And the Green Man doesn't seem concerned about going down now or later, so why should he? The first shallow riffle they hit will take the bottom out of the island, or the first fast water they hit will surely induce the sugar-cube effect, and they will melt.

But they keep on going around the first bend without incident. The Green Man shouts how the tires are bound together with a series of cables, and the buried bleach bottles strung together with nylon rope, and he hopes the whole thing doesn't come apart because with the tires and the bleach bottles and the nylon rope and the logging cables, well, the whole thing is an ecological disaster waiting to happen.

The river is calm and green, managing itself with great good competence and clucking to itself. The Green Man is sitting cross-legged among the boxwoods like a chlorophyll Buddha. He's quiet. The river seems careful, more careful, careful and fragile, tip-toeing, balanced.

East Leven disappears with the first bend as the cottonwoods and firs shut out the world behind the island and only the river stays.

Andrew looks at the Green Man, who could be straight out of Saturday morning cartoons, and wonders whether he would eat a bug like Karen Johnson's little brother, Pinky, who lived up the river. As boys, they used to tell Pinky that Anne Doucette's ghost had been seen in the trees near his house, and he would beg them to stop, but they went on saying how she floated above the water wringing her hands and looking for someone to take her place as a ghost so she could get free. Pretty soon Pinky said he'd eat a worm if they stopped, but it was no deal. Almost any little kid could be talked into eating a worm. Okay, a bug then, said Pinky. A potato bug, insisted the boys. One of those armored ones that crunches, so they can hear it. And Pinky ate a bug to keep the ghost of Anne Doucette out of his ears.

Andrew and the Green Man come to the bridge without a word. Above the banks are farmland and new houses, and they smell the animals and the runoff from the fertilizers, the chewed-up soil of new frontyards. The Green Man stands, a hood ornament, nose into the wind. Andrew waits for the word from somewhere.

They pass under the bridge, the Green Man on point like a bird dog. He seems to stiffen, catching a scent, every fiber in him alert. The ghost of Anne Doucette is there under the bridge. They drift on without talking as if this had been planned.

On the bottom side of the bridge, cool and sunless, there is a geometry again, like the geometry of the Horchow Company yard, squared, triangulated, and arched.

EZRA HORCHOW FOUND THIS BEND IN THE RIVER DURING World War II and with some government contracts parlayed shacks and rubble into acres of buildings and offices. And geometry.

East Leven had historically sprawled on the bank of the river. It was a town waiting for something to come along and set it in straight lines. Even the streets wandered until Horchow came, and he lined things up – zoning ordinances and flower boxes bursting with geraniums downtown, a sewer big enough to cruise in a row boat, a Junior Chamber of Commerce, a Lion's Club, Eagles, Elks, the whole American menagerie that signified acting civilized. Optimists. Odd Fellows. The rubble got organized too, and Horchow fell into producing rare earths, nonferrous metal coatings, the hydraulics for garbage trucks. Soon there were two more traffic bridges, and the west side of the river opened up and got itself a mayor too. Real estate became the word: parcels, plots, River Heights Estates.

But years ago, during a rare winter snow that clung to every twig and arched over the streets bringing low the big leaf maples and snapping with the sounds of fir branches unloading, a first mayhem came to East Leven, Oregon. In the drizzle following the snow that had temporarily rounded again all the hard-won geometry, the snow that recalled the rawness of frontier shapes, a Horchow executive was found shot in his car and a banker's wife was found shot in her car not a hundred yards away. The town held its breath. For days people talked in whispers on the streets waiting for Sodom to follow Gomorrah while the snow melted. His wife and her husband had air-tight alibis and grieved in the gray rain that followed the snowfall and buried them both in the Bye Bye cemetery. There was a crack in the fragile geometry of the streets and it seemed as if one more such tremor would break the whole design to pieces. The snow melted away, the fir trees sprung back, the funerals were held three decent days apart. That spring the town had its first golf course carved into the rolling hills upriver, and then the country club, city swimming pool, modest band shell, a full-size Sears store (upgraded from catalog outlet). A brokerage house and a YMCA followed quickly. Some in East Leven claimed that these were the most productive murders ever recorded in the Northwest. As soon as they planted the sinners, all the rest of these civic flowers began springing up as if the lovers had fertilized the town from under the earth. East Leven grabbed every opportunity to assure itself that the murders and the rain would not wash away the hard-won successes.

BEFORE THE GREEN MAN, THERE HAD BEEN THE MAGIC OF
metals that remembered and sought and coated and lubricated themselves like faerie potions made out of dew on the longest day or stump
water under a full moon. Hundreds of people worked at Horchow without knowing exactly what was eventually sold to provide the paychecks
and profits. If you asked, you might be told with raised eyebrows and
voices rising into a question: Maybe medical supplies? I think it's all got
to do with rare earths? Is there some kind of thing for making special
TVs? And there were some working there who knew everything, of course.
Among these there was a kind of bond that occurs naturally in inner circles, priesthoods, in which the urge to explain was suppressed in favor
of mysterious chanting of phrases that became the sufficient in "sufficient
information," sufficient for you who can't come all the way in. And so
around Horchow arose the same mystery of priesthoods everywhere – a
privileged language kept circumspect. Narratives available on various
levels that told different forms of both the mystery and the truth.

Before the Green Man reached through wires into the face of God,
there were sufficient mysteries in place. When the hydraulics division of
Horchow slacked off following the loss of patents on the garbage truck
compactors, there arose the metal memory needs of the Strategic Air
Command, the navy's lust for an antenna the size of Upper Michigan to
talk to its submarines, the army's demand for indestructible engine-part
coatings. Horchow became America's insatiable longing after the next
thing, and Horchow Inc. became a genius at anticipating the next thing.

East Leven in 1956 looked for prosperity where other towns did: in the
economic certainties of the Cold War. The fact that the Soviet Union
yearned to take over the fertile plains of Iowa, the mills of Pittsburgh, and
the market centers of New York provided the economy the healthy flush
of opposition. East Leven knew itself because the Soviets had defined
themselves clearly in the world press; they said they were the future and
they were as inevitable as wind and the planets, the true nature of economic humans. East Leven needed to say its own name, its own destiny,
over and over to itself.

The town fathers included a number of mothers. There was consensus regarding what was good for the town. Employment meant everything. More jobs meant more of everything: school tax, property tax, the dollars floating between stores and services. More safety, security, certainty, and in certain circles, redemption, salvation, emancipation, liberation, exculpation, and finally elucidation about things in general. There were the sacrifices, after all. Anne Doucette's sweet neck. The rope-swing accidents, though largely not fatal, had left a trail of fused spinal vertebrae in later life, and in the case of Carl Endorfer, a fractured fibula that had stuck out the front of his leg so far it was reported you could have hung your hat on it when he crawled up the river bank and his friends carried him to the hospital. He still showed the scar on demand, formally or informally dressed, day or night, public or private, and responded to inquiries about how far the fibula actually stuck out the front of his leg. Carl became a kind of substitute for Anne Doucette, who was not available for interview. Luck was the difference, always the difference.

James Andresson, affectionately known as the Commissioner of Sewers, was in charge of where water went when it was bade. He knew that up to a certain point the town could command the water here and there, but that after an infelicitous February melt in the mountains, after the river rose into a hard winter squall, there was only good luck keeping East Leven's citizens high and dry or bad luck flooding their basements. He looked forward to his retirement when he could pass the water-mantle on to a younger man, who could worry the inches and feet of water and dream ruptured pipes and fountains bursting from sewer grates. He would consult with the Green Man on river matters, site-specific recommendations for the building of Ben Brown's modest cabin by the river. He would ask Ben Brown how lucky he thought he was, because the river respected luck. Ben Brown would reply that he considered himself a rich vein of luck.

The whole business of luck seemed a local obsession until the Green Man arrived and absorbed the issue into his rarity. Old man Horchow had been lucky to make the transition from garbage truck hydraulics to nonferrous metal coatings. The two murder victims had independently of each other found the unluckiest of circumstances in their deaths. The town got lucky with Horchow and the development spurts toward city of substance. There were two camps on the luck of Crazy Leo. One group contended that Leo himself and the people he came from were lucky to have pulled out of a potentially awful situation and found a fine life with the aid of the state. They were good-luck people to have been alive at a time when all this was possible. One main proponent of this theory used his personal history to make his case. "As a young man," he asserted, "my sins of sexual curiosity occurred at the exact moment in all of the history of mankind when those sins could be forgiven with a dose of about four million units of penicillin. Twenty years earlier and I might have ended up with a permanent infection – spirochetes hell-bent on eating away significant portions of my brain in old age. Twenty years later the boys began bringing home from Southeast Asia new strains of venereal diseases that no antibiotic could cure. So I figure there was a forty-year window in all of history when a person could go out and get any damn thing he wanted and get over it like a bad cold. Timing is what it is. Luck is about timing."

The other camp regarded Crazy Leo as ambulatory bad luck – dented head, tight birth canal, Wednesday's child, wrong place at the wrong time. Leo could, with the other kind of luck, have been a physicist, a football star, a Ford dealer. He carried the bad luck around with him in his endless quest for more and better hubcaps. Hubcaps were what remnant of ironic luck clung to his life. If he found a Buick hubcap, apparently he thought his fortunes completely reversed. He seemed to like the Buick shield, to take it as his own shield against more bad luck.

The camps on Leo's luck were never equally divided. East Leven maintained fluid positions on matters of luck. A good economy produced large numbers of good luck adherents. When the money got tight during Horchow's transition from hydraulics to metal coatings, at the height of the (temporary it turned out) layoffs, the fluid tipped the other way. Almost no one tried to talk to Crazy Leo; there was much more ladder sidestepping, black cat avoiding, and salt spill mumblings and tossings.

Horchow's government contracts, it turned out, were not so much a matter of luck as they were greased palms, persistence in the presence of greased palms, and bets hedged by more greasing than the competitors were willing to do. The tricky nature of hydraulics was subsumed in the fact that anyone could do them. Not only was the principle as old as Western civilization, but the whole deal was hoses and fluids and pumps – done. The government, it turned out, had an enormous appetite for hydraulics, any hydraulics. And though there did not appear to be a department of hydraulics or even a bureau or sub-bureau of hydraulics, the government itself could not really function without them.

Horchow, sitting on the green river that flowed north, found itself downstream from a heap of U.S. government demand for things hydraulic. The fluids and the hoses were easy. The pumps turned out to be the heart of the matter. Pumps wore out if you used them lots, and even though there were few moving parts and these were highly lubricated, metal sought metal and wore itself out. The combination of things that wore out and the mysterious government lust for more and more hydraulics actually constituted a case of luck for Horchow and East Leven.

Gear, vane, piston, plunger, the hydraulics of government seemed as endless as the night sky full of stars. Francis, Pelton, Kaplan turbines working away somehow in the great machine of the federal mechanical hunger brought to Horchow the flush of long green in the shape of war contracts, postwar contracts. Then, as if the hydraulics themselves had become obsolete, as if some other newer principle less fundamental but sleeker and more modern had replaced pressure undiminished on a liquid, Horchow found the stack of governmental requests for things hydraulic had dried up. What happened? The American government had gone on a hydraulic fast. France, Italy, and Germany after the war maintained Horchow's flow of hydraulics until they got their own economies and local industries converted to peacetime pursuits. Then there were none.

Horchow had one engineer whose sole duty it was to pursue lubrication, of pistons, of vane to chamber, of everything hydraulic. He had no theory of luck and belonged to no particular party of theories of luck. But he was himself an agent of luck.

Bertrand Ronald Carrollton – two rs, two os, two ls, one t, he was fond of designating – had worked for Horchow long enough to have planted a big leaf maple tree in his front yard for shade, and then when it grew so fast that it shaded his tomato plants and hammered his lawn each fall with plate-sized leaves, he cut it down and planted a *Magnolia grandiflora* for its heavenly smell, part lemon, part vanilla, part ardor, and part longing after. It had grown to manageable proportions by the time the hydraulic contracts began to dwindle. He had avoided war service since he was in a "critical industry." And after the war he could have gone anywhere in the industry because he came out of the war with engineering experience instead of soldiering, a patently unfair but clear advantage over others his own age and education. Bertrand (the experiments with Bert and Berty had all gone awry) found he liked East Leven and its north-flowing river. He liked it well enough to stay with Horchow though the signs for the future portended obsolescence and economic doom. He was party to no theory of luck and therefore free to be Horchow's luck.

It happened the same way branches fall from rotted trees and miss all the strollers beneath on a Sunday afternoon. It happened the way a blind sow finds an acorn, some detractors would say later. Bertrand was looking for a way to reduce friction in the cylinder chamber, which became badly scored when the hydraulic hose sprung a leak and ran the pump out of fluid, which was the only lubrication in the cylinder. He stood with the burned piston in one hand, the cylinder in the other held up to the fluorescent light. Something about the light, its truncated wavelengths washing the inside of the metal, about how as you turned it the wash of light moved around the inside of the cylinder, thicker it seemed here and then thinner there, and he moved the piston into the cylinder. Later, when replaying his discovery for colleagues, Bertrand in his innocence of Freudian principle or even inkling, moved the pretend piston in and out of the imagined cylinder over and over and over while he tried to recall the exact moment of enlightenment. His colleagues kept asking him to provide more and more details, more and more minutiae while Bertrand endlessly plunged the piston into the cylinder and then watched the light when he took it out again. Years later piston and cylinder could be seen being demonstrated across a room at almost any company gathering – piston in, cylinder up to the light, in and out to bursts of laughter. Bertrand himself eventually got the joke too. And though it was too late to save him from his own Bertrandness, his place in the company was so secure, his "Eureka, I've found it!" so storied and sung that he enjoyed a well-paid, largely ceremonial job as vice president of engineering development until his retirement. At the retirement dinner, if you stood in the center of the room you could see in all four cardinal directions someone miming a piston plunging over and over into a cylinder.

THE ISLAND TAKES THE BIG LOOP BEND WITH A KIND OF GRACE and aplomb that surprises Andrew and Ben. They're still trying out the water dynamics of the free-floating lump of earth.

"Well, let's just see how far we get," suggests the Green Man in a tone that smacks of a lottery, a wet lottery. "I didn't ask, but you swim, don't you?"

Andrew says he indeed swims and has been swimming this river for … well, all his life. Since the river was simultaneously the great attractor and great destroyer of children, with Anne Doucette roiling through its green surface, children in East Leven all had to learn to swim in it or stay away from it. These two positions were absolute. "You figure we'll be swimming soon, do you?" Andrew asks.

The Green Man makes a Popeye face, squinches up an eye and Popeyes his mouth, tries out a "I yam what I yam," to no particular purpose in the discussion, bamboozles Andrew, who is looking for some logic to this lark.

Andrew feels stoned without being stoned. There is disjuncture to everything, nonsequiturs inside the nonsequiturs. Funny overlaps and underlays. The foundation of whatever the hell this is seems to shift and then shift again. Andrew feels he has slipped back in time and is replaying what just played. Part of the problem, he knows, is that the river doubles on itself here in less than a mile, going first away from town and then back toward the northern outskirts and then back again toward the Horchow plant that stands above the town, in sight of the town, but nearly two river miles to the north. But the other part of the problem is the Green Man, who seems to come and go as if from some other conversation with some other mortal. Andrew has from the beginning had no problem with the cartoon characters, the voices and the accents. It had taken Ben

Brown a very short time to introduce his panoply of disguises and alter egos. Sanjay, some Indian merchant, he preferred for long stretches as if he were taken over and inhabited by doing the accent. Here on this part of the river seemed to call for one after another – Popeye, then Sanjay, then something Irish. Maybe he did this when he was nervous, thought Andrew. Maybe there's some pattern here. All of it seemed harmless enough except when Ben took off, as with the Popeye, in directions not implicitly part of the initial conversation. Maybe, thought Andrew, the word conversation was too severe a restriction on what was actually happening here.

The river doubled, the Green Man multiplied in his own head, and Andrew began looking for some clear principle – any principle. He loved nonsense with the best of twelve-year-olds. But somehow, if he could just get his mental feet under him … he laughed at mental feet. Just get situated. Get some purchase and leverage. The river doubled.

They would get just so far on the island and then seem to slip back to a beginning to do it over again.

Finally they break clear.

In a stretch of the river that runs nearly directly west, they get clear. At least in Andrew's head the sense of repetition begins to subside, and they come to a bend where the wind picks up and blows directly toward them, slowing the island to nearly a standstill momentarily. The stiff breeze seems to catch the Green Man's attention and he assumes his dog-sniffing pose, searching the wind for molecules of interest. Andrew feels the wind strip the heat of the sun from his head and face. They both face the breeze and fall into sane silence.

ONE DAY THE GREEN MAN ROUNDED THE CORNER IN TOWN. AND there was Crazy Leo poking aside the grass with the handle of his hatchet.

Crazy Leo, maybe thirty, maybe fifty, with straight black hair spiking out from a baseball cap, collected hubcaps by stalking the stretches of highway on both ends of town and stumping the streets and back alleys downtown. Crazy Leo was never Leo, always Crazy Leo, as if this particular kind of angel came in only one form – crazy. If there were kids coming around the corner with a bag of pretzels and cherry sodas, there would be Crazy Leo in the long grass behind the Jenkins' house. Mr. Jenkins was hard Welsh, grumpy and territorial, and he let the grass grow long just to piss off his neighbors. Crazy Leo would see the children and sing out. He sang up and down between two notes struck out at the edges of an octave, and all words were generated at one end or the other. It was impossible to predict if the next word would be high or low, and as many as four or five words in a row could be low and then a startling leap for one word and then back down to finish.

"Turned out to be a fine day after all," said the Green Man. "Nothing at all like yesterday." Only he said it with an Irish accent: "Nothing a-tall," he said, "like yesterday." He had worked at this accent off and on since turning green as a kind of adjunct greenness. He had arrived at something the far side of Brigadoon. Crazy Leo continued to bother the long grass with his hatchet handle and said nothing, made no sign of recognition. Something clanked in his long bag thrown across his shoulder.

The Green Man reloaded: "What are you looking for?" and then, "Can I help you find something?"

Crazy Leo stopped and turned to face the Green Man. This should be the monumental, the mythological part – Green meets Crazy. But Crazy Leo was fiercely devoted to his calling.

"A Buick hubcap might be in here," he sang.

From the long grass he announced, "I'm looking for a hubcap. A Model-T hubcap might be in here." Each syllable was a different end of an octave starting with "HUBcap," high then low; hubcap was always high and then low. There was scansion to it.

"Did you lose a Buick hubcap? This grass is long enough to hide a whole Buick. That would make four hubcaps, not to mention all those little holes on the sides. What are those holes for, anyway?" asked the Green Man.

Crazy Leo said, "He wanted to kill them both. He wanted to be their mother. He said there were hubcaps under the snow. He said there were Buick hubcaps. The dog wanted to go outside over and over and then he came in by the stove. And then out again. And then in again. In and out. Auntie gets mad when I go in and out, in and out. I looked in the snow, and it was too cold for hubcaps."

He had a black burlap bag to carry whatever he found and something always clunked in there. Some thought he started each day with a hubcap or two already in the bag to attract other hubcaps. But there was no discussing with Crazy Leo. All you could do was listen to what he wanted to say, and he said what he would say.

Once Crazy Leo found a small hatchet somewhere. And every day after that he carried the hatchet in his belt and showed it to kids. Crazy Leo was an ambulatory circus; when frogs and gophers and tree houses cloyed on summer afternoons, and the heat percolated out of the green along the river, then Crazy Leo shambled around the corner with his burlap bag clanking. "And it's sharp, too" (sharp is two syllables – shar/arp, high to low in Crazy Leo song). And then he looked frantically around for something to demonstrate on and found: a stick blown down out of the alders along the river; a landscaping timber in the parking lot; the shingled side of Newberry's garage. The chips flew, and he would be satisfied and stand petting the sharpness of the hatchet and then look up suddenly as if he had forgotten something. Then he would growl and hold the hatchet up in mock menace and the children stepped back but held position. There was nothing in their small lives so gratifyingly startling as Crazy Leo.

Crazy Leo roamed the town and could be around the next corner. If there were two or more children they constituted a suitable audience and Crazy Leo would say what was on the fragile edge of his mind, would spill in on whatever cluster of kids was at hand. Sometimes he started simply with fast moves, his arms whirling and stopping in a sort of Tai Chi crossed with Saint Vitus Dance and freeze frame. He began all video and then added the audio in one of the pauses. "I got a new hubcap. A Buick," and he would drag from the dark bag his latest. "Wire wheels." The *Why*, the *Whee*, made high with wide open mouth and pried-open eyes. The *Ire*, the *Eels*, low and almost sleepy, as if somebody kept putting the plug in and taking it out again.

Parents in East Leven claimed Crazy Leo was trained "by the state," that he was certifiably harmless, that he was the one loose loony required by state law to complete a town of this size. But Crazy Leo, in any case, was as "official" as bridges.

East Leven got the Green Man without official sanction, without – and here was the hard part for the town – sufficient narration or history to make a full story of him, without blessing or litany or introduction or certification or tradition. Without even one of the customary skin colors, how would they know how to act? What to build their thinking on? What did they think of a green person who moved in among them? Crazy Leo lived with an ancient aunt who looked like mattress ticking stuffed into a striped house dress. She'd shamble out to get the paper each day from her odd house built in a depression, a small house tossed into the hole left when a big house had blown away. The Green Man's house was a troll cottage plunked on the bank of the river among cottonwoods and old fir trees.

The river slapped the pilings below a grassy slope from the tennis courts. And upstream, through a temple of blackberries and across a holy swale into the woods, lived the Green Man. When he first appeared in town they invited him to a civic barbecue, but he politely declined by mail. He signed, "Yours sincerely, Ben Brown." The Green Man named Brown was a perfect hoot for a matter of days but wore thin and faded into the trees. It was nearly impossible for shopkeepers to look into his green face and say, "Thanks so much Mr. Br… Mr. Br-rown," although Hank Seelye at the Shell filling station took pride in his contact with the green person – every tankful and some discussion about fan-belt wear – and managed to look at Mr. Green and say Mr. Brown without a twitch. It was considered heroic of Hank Seelye.

THE WINTER AFTER THE HORCHOW MURDERS, WHEN THE SNOW was again heavy and viscid on the branches as it was more than a year before, when the streets had begun to run with water under the snow, the citizens of East Leven felt the unease of what had unofficially become known as murderous weather. It could freeze and the streets, crowned to help the water of winter rains run off, would become killers. It would snow and rain and snow and rain until somehow, it was not yet believed but suspected, regular people would resort to violence to ward off the gray sky. Murderous weather. It would be years before the term became official, after it had been brought up tentatively and tried out in the bar-rooms, then a second time, and finally an ease with the phrase would set in, and it became settled. Murderous weather. Within five years the words had spread beyond town to other places, where people casually remarked that it looked like murderous weather might set in if the temperature dropped further. The Ramsey's bakery experienced small economic booms during murderous weather as if the antidote to the malaise lay in the display cases. Pain au chocolat with its name evoking the weather's under-lying metaphor as well as its resolution flew out the door. Most chocolate pastries never got cool in the cases.

So East Leven looked each winter after the murders for additional forms of solace – solace of butter and chocolate, solace of clearings and distances as if the lowering sky begged sideways space to make up for its persistent closeness, and solace of the neon wavelengths of the barroom.

The trains that worked their way slowly through the curves along the river across from town and then creaked across the railroad bridge, through the edge of Horchow with its sidings and wyes, echoed under the low skies of murderous weather. The obligatory hoot as the engine descended off the bridge and across town couldn't break the spell of the glutinous snow and how that snow had come to define midwinter in this part of the valley. Children going to school would pump their arms to beg an extra whistle from the engineers. Between the engineers and the children there was a pact of immunity to the general spiritual failing. In East Leven the murders had come to mean that at any moment things could go tragically wrong again.

And would. Even the most self-enlightened Protestant churches invoked seventeenth-century Calvinism and the burden of The Fall from grace into death, how error was inevitable and shameful and ultimately inex-cusable in the eyes of God and yet ... Somehow, though unfathomable to the puny human mind, there came through the undeserved interven-tion of Christ on our behalf the great redemption of eternal life. Dogma took on the color of melting snow, and raised the suspicion that just under the surface flowed blood and more blood – blood earned by and deserved by human insignificance. As a lead-in to Lent there was no better depth of spiritual need than murderous weather. Easter would release the soul, but East Leven's forms of Calvinism, "the whole damn Reformation" as the Catholic priest put it, needed to feel the depths of its own depravity in order to truly understand He is Risen.

The downtown flower boxes and hanging plants could trace their ancestry in part to murderous weather and the search for surcease. Conroy Burbank put the first baskets of fuchsias outside his store as soon after the wet snow as the temperature climbed into the high thirties. Like butter and chocolate the flowers were an anodyne. The city council saw Conroy's gesture, felt its effect on Main Street, and planned the streetscape of hangers and barrels and tubs of flowers. Even years after the murders, the sudden and unexpected violence was present under the surface of the most civil proceedings. With each fuchsia, train whistle, chocolate confection, and resilient dogma, some crack in the surface of fragile East Leven was filled and smoothed over. Patches, yes. But such a steady supply of patches: rope swing from a cottonwood, three-beer epiphany, steelhead strike while fishing from the railroad trestle, even the mysterious wink Horchow's ponds were reputed to accomplish as a flashing back at the cosmos. The town had developed an unerring sense that the tissue of the world was flimsy and insubstantial. The daring of patch after patch had become second nature. This was, after all, the New World and many of the temporary details remained to be worked out. The Green Man's coming, in some important ways, was an old thing, not a new thing.

THE GEOMETRY OF THE UNDERSIDE OF THE ROAD BRIDGE bristles over the river as the island floats under. Andrew moves nervously up and back in the space he has and is quickly wearing a wet path into his half of the island. The Green Man sits quietly watching downstream. Andrew stops pacing and kneels in spongy dirt. He bounces the island, like trying out a trampoline, and it gives under him and then pushes back as the bleach bottles rebound from the dunking. The Green Man seems content to wait the river with a fine, soft breeze in his face.

The river surface gives and takes: the clouds, a fun-house mirror; the riffles, fracturing light; the inside of the bend slow water, mirroring sky smoke, fast-water standing waves, anathema to bridge geometry. This river seems to feel itself for its one-hundred-mile length – one single piece that gathers and feeds off the creeks and hidden springs. Each mile sings to every other mile. In winter it burgeons and fills its valley even past the trees it abandons stranded in its low summer meander. It experiments with island shapes, leaving short fat ones in the same path as long thin ones. Its deep breaths are slow, seasonal inhales, exhales. In high summer it's green; in high flood of winter, café au lait. Andrew and Ben occupy their little dimple passing north toward the Columbia.

Lewis and Clark missed noticing this river in the pelting rain of an afternoon as they floated the Columbia River past the present-day site of Portland. East Leven came to know itself by its defenses against the river. The Willsons, the Furhers, the Cobbs thought of themselves as river people who must keep one eye on the sound of water in the winter, the other eye on the lack of water in the summer, when the sound of the river hushed to a clear whisper.

Andrew calls to the Green Man's back. "I think we have some seepage problems." No answer. "Leaky basement," he tries louder. "Big plumbing problems."

The Green Man turns and waves as if he'd been asked for a salute. He turns again to face the coming water. Andrew tries out a little dance but feels lonely, without an audience. His part of the island seems to be getting wetter faster than the other half. He thinks the swim to the bank would be quick since they are following the fast water with very little correction from the sweep, and the fast water stays along the bank in this stretch. Andrew begins to muse on the upcoming dunking, then the whole green person episode in his life that was going nowhere. He has taken a job, it seems, playing by the river, a paying job for the same licentious summers of play that his parents had given him as a child, as soon as he was old enough to be left with friends and the river. How long would his world conspire to keep him playing here on the river? Maybe this was to be exactly what he was cut out for, this river-ness, this play. Why not just go with it? Why did he feel he had to keep correcting the island (the Green Man had given up and just sat)? Why did he feel like the CEO of Goofball Incorporated? Who the hell cared about the fate of this enterprise anyway?

The river adjusts under them. Depth and surface squirm against each other. The island bobs in the squirm for no apparent reason at all except that below are boulders the size of boxcars and all the water dances over and around them. Scale is everything: the river also adjusts in tiny correctives around the gravel and baseball-size rocks. The island shows no bob for them.

Andrew takes a corrective pull on his sweep to keep the island from running too close to the bank. He can see beaver slides and then root tangles flowing from the bottom of the bank like colored hair, red and blond and black, waving downstream. A patch of burdocks has crowded out all other plants; electric-blue larkspur and orange columbine share a long stretch of bank that passes and then seems to repeat in front of his eyes. Small creeks come in, one with the final gesture of a modest waterfall tumbling over rounded stones to make a spray. In the spray on both sides grow maidenhair fern with black stems like pen scratchings added to the green.

The Green Man has resumed his role as hood ornament as they pass tight against the bank and then start out again into bigger water. The north-flowing river has always, in Andrew's mind, seemed to run perversely up the map. He has learned that one of the conditions that made a map a map was that north be at the top. Having a scale was another. Otherwise it was just a drawing, not a map. But this river chugged up the map while most of the rest of the rivers of America either went side to side or down to the south. The island's sponginess is exaggerated in the standing waves of the deep water, and the run down a short, fast stretch feels to Andrew like riding a noodle. He watches the bank recede as they coast to the middle again, and Andrew finds himself calculating the distance he'll have to swim when the island inevitably comes apart.

EAST LEVEN WAS SPECKLED WITH SALOONS AS A CORRECTIVE against the ravages of winter rain, when only the light of neon beer signs would restore the proper balance of ultraviolet to citizens deprived of sun. There they liked to bask like iguanas in a patch of jungle sunlight, soaking up wavelengths necessary for basic life functions. Digestion itself depended on these reds and blues. The oranges supplied wit. Philosophy arrived clothed in the coolness around the edges. The green citizen was the topic of conversation at Puddy's Bar.

This bar is fundamental, solid, grounded in the earth of East Leven like an old sycamore. The bar has that same scabby peeling look too, as if patches have been torn off by vandals only to reveal new patches of new colors and sizes. The steady glow of the beer signs assures the community of continuity.

Outside, the bar is not so bitten and patched since the city codes insist on a sort of genteel legitimacy of faux just-about-anything. As long as it's painted and cared for and the windows set too high for passing children to see in and receive the deadly stigmata, then the bar is legit.

The bars are spaced in the downtown district based on some complicated formula of liquor to citizen to square footage to proximity of Protestant church to marginal propensity to fall into the clutches of devil rum. The formula for licensing sin. Sin owned, it seems, by a largely Calvinist licensing agency whose civic charge is to dispense the rights to sell sin to sinners.

"Sure, he's green," said the glazier, the man who prayed for wind storms and juvenile delinquents, "but he's a good customer and pays his bills right on the button. In cash. More than I can say for half the deadbeats in this town who hold out until I threaten to sue the sonsabitches. And then they're pissed off at me." He pushed his beer back to make room for the glow of the neon, absorbed it in the reflection off the pool on the bar. "He has more broken windows than anybody else in town. I guess from living down in those firs along the river where the crap blows out of those trees all the time."

"Well, I hear he's not all there, and getting less there all the time." Bill Bozeman basked in orange, turned his head this way and that to get the full dose of rays. He was the biggest iguana by forty pounds and engulfed his bar stool so that he looked like his considerable ass was growing out of a post suspending him at the bar. He was structurally part of the bar now. He swiveled and a bystander winced as if Bill might screw right down to the ground and the post pop out his head. But instead, the bar stool complained and punctuated his turn of phrase. Squaak. "You never know when somebody like that will go off his head and…well, just be a pack of trouble."

"What about Crazy Leo carrying around that hatchet? Hanging around with kids and scaring them with that loony talk?"

Bill halted this new direction with the raise of hand the size of a picnic ham. "Okay, Okay, but Crazy Leo has been up to Salem to the training school. They wouldn't of let him loose if he wasn't okay. That's what we pay those people to do, take and train 'em so they can live here. Besides, we know Crazy Leo's people and his aunt, what's-her-name, has lived here since what, the thirties?"

"Anson. Margaret Anson." A historian was present, as small as Bill is huge. For the historian, knowing where somebody is from, what stock they come out of, what family name is involved, all this told you what somebody was likely to do. He was a salesman at the Ford dealership and made his living guessing what people were likely to do with their money. "What bothers me is we have never known much about him except that he calls himself Ben Brown. Brown, jeez! What do we really know about this guy?" The historian was notoriously dyspeptic, in need of the red and blue neons, and turned his cheek to the biggest sign to absorb some of those Pabst Blue Ribbon blues.

DOWNTOWN IN EAST LEVEN, WHERE THE MAIN STREETS CAME together just north of Puddy's Bar, the huge yellow Kodak sign in front of the photographer's shop swung and fanned the intersection. Across the street the bakery was engaged in making a twelve-layer Viennese torte that had become a favorite birthday cake among adults in town. The baker was Jewish and noticeably felt less odd, less noticed, after the Green Man arrived, the attention having been diverted from him and his family. The sign outside the bakery said, "Ramsey's Bakery," a name his father took when going into battle against the Nazis in 1944, a name he kept after the war, but he assured his children they could choose Abrahamson as soon as they came of age, could choose it if they left East Leven to go to Portland.

The specialty at the bakery was twelve-layer Viennese torte, light chocolate buttercream in equal layers with thinly sliced yellow cake. The new-world version of this was the much simpler yellow cake with buttercream frosting, no thin layers, no fuss. Everybody can make one. But somehow at Ramsey's Bakery these layered tortes always disappeared the day they were baked, Thursday, even though they were made to last through Saturday. Jews had been exotic in East Leven when Ramsey Sr., fresh from World War II and the name change required to go into battle in Germany, settled on this town, this place, this river to open his bakery. All sweet things, all pleasure, all the time Ramsey had vowed while slogging through the winter mud past the racetrack in Deauville, France. Things that made people smile will take up the rest of my life.

Ramsey senior had been a handsome man. The war, then children, the early morning baker's hours, all had conspired against his handsomeness, but in his sixties he still had the ways of a handsome man. With men he deferred and looked away to keep from confrontation. With women he smiled them to himself, reeling them in with cheekbones and chin and confidence. Old or young. And Ramsey the younger, after a brief stint at Horchow, threw in with his father and the business of sweet joy. He found his way to contribute through the chocolate éclair. His chou pastry floated above the doily. His ganache, darker and less sweet than most, depended for sweetness on his custard filling, richly infused with whole vanilla bean. The éclairs and the Viennese torte gave father and son separate beachheads in the sweet business, and each allowed the other absolute sway so that if a customer, for example, asked son about torte or father about éclair, each deferred to the other with mock bowing and stagey presenting. Ramsey the elder knew his son would need the space to succeed if he were to stay in East Leven.

By the time Ben Brown arrived in town, the Ramseys together owned the building the bakery was in and the photo studio where most of the high school senior pictures were taken. "Two clean industries," Ramsey the elder was fond of pronouncing at family dinners. And the implication was that neither one was Horchow slurping and clanking there on the river bank.

The Ramseys, pére et fils, welcomed the Green Man to East Leven first as an exotic citizen – "an honorary Jew," the father proclaimed.

"What? He's interesting. He's something else when everybody else is everybody else. He's green and they're ... flesh-colored Band-Aids!" Father Ramsey.

"We're flesh-colored Band-Aids next to him," his son offered.

They stood across the dough bench, father leaning against a tall stool, son flour-white to the elbows.

"He's supposed to be some kind of medical miracle. He should have been dead, they say. So instead he's walking around. Your great-grandmother used to say that when anyone asked her how she was, 'Walking around' she'd say. 'I'm still walking around.' And then she'd hold up one finger, like a lightning rod or the way you'd lick a finger to test for wind. And she'd pause after 'walking around' and then add, 'and things are still occurring to me.' We all thought she was very funny. Today she'd be a stand-up comic. We'd all get rich off her. She was funny. A very funny person. Maybe the war took that out of me. I was too young for that business. George Burns. She was funny like George Burns. You don't remember, except the movies he made toward the end. But before that, with Gracie. That funny. Slow funny. Nobody else in the family, none of us grandchildren inherited that. God knows my father wasn't funny. A good man. Just not funny."

Between them they worked the dough on the maple table. Father free-associating. Son returning to the Green Man.

"So he turned green they say, instead of dying. Something like that. Anyway, he's the only one."

"What only one?"

"The only green one."

"So far," and father held up one finger, trying out the old gesture.

"Sure, but he chose East Leven for some reason that's hard to figure. Why here? He's got money from the accident they say. He could live anywhere. Florida or San Diego or Phoenix. Someplace warm, and he settles here to be green. What do you figure?"

"After the war I could have gone anywhere. I came here. And I looked around Phoenix and Flagstaff. Too dry. My skin cracked. My hair broke. Really. My hair broke off, it was so dry in Phoenix. My mother's people were the dry ones. You'd shake a hand, and it was like holding onto a stick, like tree bark. My father's people were the moist ones. Uncle Arthur the moistest of all. He played the Hawaiian guitar across his knees like it was a zither or something. His hands were big and damp. He was something. His hands were big and damp. He was a big, damp guy all around. He'd play the guitar and sweat. I'd forgotten how he'd sweat. You. You're the good recipe. Part dry people, part wet people. I think subconsciously we look for that in a mate. You know, some way to compensate for our genetic errors. Tall men, short women. Moist people, dry people. The long-armed gal flashing her eyes at the short-armed guy."

After turning green, Ben Brown craved sweet things as if some switch had been thrown in his metabolism. Some need to burn hotter fuel. When he looked for towns to hide out in, he always interrogated the local baker. In East Leven, the Green Man figured, he could find the sanctuary he needed in order to learn to live as a green person and make the time here to examine his greenness. He could if the bakery were decent.

He entered Ramsey's Bakery that day as a scout, a skeptic, a scientist of the senses. He could tell from the first whiff what was wafting out of the back room: the quality of the shortening, the pedigree of the chocolate. Ramsey the elder was presiding behind the counter. Ramsey junior was back working the dough bench. Ben Brown was sniffing out the concoctions.

From behind the counter Ramsey *père* looked over the glass case at his first green customer, though he had seen, on TV, people – well, students – who had painted themselves green for football and basketball games at the University of Oregon. Ben Brown's face and hands were nearly that vegetable-dye green favored by the U of O student body. Ramsey quickly checked his mental calendar for football season / basketball season, Halloween, Mardi Gras. It occurred to him there were a number of times during the year that it was legitimate to be temporarily green. But his green, Ramsey thought, this was the best he'd ever seen. And though there was no season-associated greenness he could come up with, good quality was good quality.

"Can I help you? The breakfast breads there are just out of the oven."

Ben Brown hitched up his pants in concentration, unable to take his eyes off the case. "Just a few questions. I have some, um, food allergies, and I'd like to know, for example, what shortening you use."

"The pricey stuff. Pure vegetable. Virgin. No recycle." Ramsey Sr. laughed. "Or maybe it's made by virgins. I don't know. But it's the expensive stuff. We experimented with cheap shortening some years ago and you could taste it. Hell, you could smell it too. It was heavy everywhere. In the air." He pointed up. "In the nose." He indicated his own. "And finally, in the stomach. Heavy, heavy, heavy." Ramsey made a *salaam*: air, nose, stomach.

The Green Man nodded, his eyes still cruising the pastry case. "And the croissants?"

"Butter," pronounced Ramsey with finality. "And then butter and butter and butter. Cold butter. All the As—grade A. We fold in thirds with cold butter in each layer. Eighty-one layers at the end. You don't get that even puff unless you do it with butter. You can buy frozen, already made up, for pennies from some guy in Cottage Grove. Ours cost. We do them here. Eighty-one layers! All butter." He paused to let the proclamation work on his green customer, who was still ogling the goods, tasting them with his eyes.

"Sugars?" Ben Brown asked.

And the senior Ramsey was off on sugar, finger in the air: "$C_{12}H_{22}O_{11}$, cane sugar. Your beet sugar's cheaper but doesn't mix the same. Doesn't caramelize the same. Not the same. Then there's your corn sugars in liquid. Don't get me started …"

"Looks like you're already started, Dad." Ramsey the younger appeared in the doorway to the back, clapping flour off his hands, laughing. "Are you telling him more than he wants to know about our ingredients? Here," he said and reached into the case for a pain au chocolat and handed it across to the Green Man. "See what this says to you."

"He asked," the elder said. "The man asked, I told him. He's interested in ingredients." He waved a finger at his son and looked at Ben. "My son. The genius. He knows everything I know. And, on top of that, he knows everything he knows. That's twice as much as anybody knows."

"At your service," the younger said. "We are," he paused dramatically, "The Ramseys, father and son. Bakery guys. Flour fluffers. Upper crust."

"A lot of crust," his father injected.

"Crème de la filling. Just a little flaky."

"All the horsemen knew her."

"It won't be long now."

"But the tips were big."

Father and son, back and forth, had broken into a battle of punch lines the Green Man figured out, and he stood back eating his pastry while the two men convulsed each other with punch lines both bakery and non-bakery related. It seemed they had gone to circumcision jokes then off into birth control then back.

"So he could come into money."

"Frilly dilly." They wound down.

Ramsey the elder was leaning against the cash register to keep from falling over. Ben Brown was witnessing a father-son vaudeville act without the act itself. The two had obviously done this shtick before many times and now found it just as hilarious as ever in front of a green stranger. It might have gone on longer but two customers entered and broke the spell. The two women tried hard not to look at the green person wiping chocolate off his hands. Father and son wiped their eyes on their white aprons, son disappearing into the back, father fetching from the pastry case. Ben Brown had found his bakery. Found his town.

On High Street, universally called *the* High Street, all the retail held its collective breath against the day of mall onslaught or Wal-Mart invasion, but East Leven hovered just outside some planner's demographics. A few more thousand inhabitants and the retail chain would swoop down. Cinnabon would take on the Ramseys. A chain flower vendor would come after Conroy Burbank's flower shop.

Ben Brown became Ramsey Bakery's best customer. Along with his greenness came the ability to metabolize immense numbers of pastries with no ill effects. Somehow he had become immune to surfeit, and his walks downtown usually started at Ramseys and then variations on his circuits.

ALONG THE RIVER A ROPE SWING SHOOTS OUT FROM BETWEEN cottonwood trees carrying two boys with their feet pointed to the sky, heads down watching the water. They let go simultaneously and split the water like bolts. The rope ratchets back and disappears in the trees, the boys surface together and swim for shore while being carried downstream in the green current, the rope comes out again from the trees this time carrying a single girl who kips up and dives at the last second. She makes a splashless hole in the reflected cottonwoods. The rope disappears again in the trees.

Andrew and the Green Man float past just as she swims back to shore. Andrew knew where the rope was tied up in an old cottonwood. You had to know which tree and where to look. The same rope had been there for ten years, an inch and a half through, a heavy painter someone found washed up on a sandbar. There was no other rope like it anywhere in this stretch of the river. Their shouts fade behind and the raft consents to be pulled north.

The Green Man feels the adventure is just beginning, something in the rise and fall of the island as it floats, his project instantly mutated from one intention to this accidental island. I like the metaphor, he thinks. I only had an idea, but this island has already decided what it's going to be. The ride. It seems to be about the ride.

FROM ABOVE, EAST LEVEN IS A BIG $\times$ WITH ONE OF THE RAYS extending across the river at the traffic bridge and the other western ray splayed out into a housing development with a river view. The eastern rays ran off into hops fields and filbert orchards and truck farms against the slow rise of the hills that take their time getting to the Cascade Mountains. At the center of the $\times$ the traffic light blinked red one way, yellow the other. These could be set to the complexities of red-yellow-green for holiday weekend traffic bearing down from Portland. Now they idled in a steady monotony of blinks. From even higher, a plane coming up from San Francisco, say, the $\times$ marked the spot like a pirate map.

The lining of cottonwoods and firs along the river formed a corridor, a false front when viewed from the river, to make the whole town look like it was scattered in the woods. But after the thin corridor just one lot wide in a green belt, the angles of the streets took over, and the tall trees gave way to the politic hardwoods (both nativist and non-nativist persuasion) and yard dwarf trees (largely non-nativist) that cast polite shadows throughout the town.

DOWNSTREAM FROM THE KODAK SIGN AND THE BAKERY, AND lying back from the bank like a silver snake soaking up sun, the Horchow Chemical Company followed the contour of the river for nearly a half mile beyond the city limits; its settling ponds, sitting just back from the built-up banks, were divided by berms so the ponds looked like huge silvered sunglasses giving back glints of clear sky.

Horchow sat up the hill from town with its drain field stepping to the river like terraced rice paddies. No member of the Horchow family had set foot on factory property since the mid 1960s. Their interests lay in the international metals trade, which floated above the national economies of the world like an extranational ghost. There were always specialized metals being made and stored and marketed, and all this happened in sovereign countries. But the paper that represented the metals, now just electronic signals organized into databases, was always available to anyone with an electronic fund transfer number. So Horchow people bought and sold metals that might not arrive in East Leven for up to four years. Sometimes the steel just moved a hundred miles away in a southern Indian town and that movement precipitated a domino effect that moved quantities across the subcontinent, across Europe, and then bumped the exact quantity across the U.S., where the Horchow yard took the last cascading domino to feed the hammers, presses, and coating vats. The order had passed through the hands of hereditary enemies who would never trade with the devil but would move a load of steel across town to a middleman. And so the metals and chemicals and propane slid into this well-watered town from all over the world. Horchow's ponds in a rainstorm were an eclectic cauldron of drippings from all over the world.

Macbeth's witches couldn't have concocted a more potent brew. The winter rains started easy, riding the onshore coast winds of the great anticyclones. The coastal range took out the heavy water, and then the clouds slid over the low range into the valley as steady rain-walking rain. The winter walkers of East Leven weren't fazed by rain, in fact, preferred it, slow and mild. They compared colors that underlay the gray in the leaden sky. There was almost always a hint of rose or purple, sometimes a metallic green behind the darker rain clouds, and on breaking up, the peach and deeper apricot haze between clouds in the afternoon. Painters talked about the combinations, about the difficulty of capturing the subtle colors and mixes. Painting a sunset in the Midwest or East was easy, with its glare of oranges, reds, and yellow. But the Northwest sky required mixing skill and subtlety.

The Horchow ponds had surfaces like the eyes of dead birds. The rains came pouring in from the coast, ran into the ponds, and the ponds never overflowed. The rain flowed in and the ponds never rose. Somehow the Horchow engineers had engendered a stasis between flow in, settle out, and ground water. The surface remained the same, the same cataract opacity that Ben and Farnsworth would see from the air, an ophthalmologist's nightmare written large along the riverbank. Farnsworth, flying nut of the local airspace, expert on local flora and fauna, spouter of Latin names, and watcher after local terrain, had said that the ponds sometimes in some light seemed to black over for a second as he flew above, and at first he thought of the phenomenon as a great wink. But after the second time, it occurred to Farnsworth there might be an engine somewhere in Horchow shifting gears and the ponds were some part of the transmission relaying what was in the buildings to what was outside. He flew around one whole afternoon to try to see the shift more times, but it only happened once more, just toward evening.

There might have been a crack to accompany the optic flash. The pond surfaces – one pond, and then a second later, another – went flat black as if a metal surface had shot out from the side, covered the pond, and then flashed back under cover. If Farnsworth hadn't been looking down just then, he would have missed it. He wondered how many he had missed through inattention all afternoon.

Some optical phenomenon, it must be. In the air there were all kinds of weird things to see that you wouldn't accept on the ground – flashes in clouds, color shifts, sudden shapes that appeared close then immediately far away, UFOs of so many kinds that a pilot stopped believing what

he saw, flocks of birds catching the sun miles away on the horizon looking like the handwriting of God. Evanescent things. Impossible things. It
was enough to deal with the visual assault of takeoffs and landings, flying
straight and level. The sky was full of marvels with no immediate explanation. When the land started to fire back at the sky, there appeared to be
a suspension of the rules. Farnsworth had begun to watch Horchow each
time he went into the sky and each time he took up a guest, including Ben
Brown. Watch Horchow for further signs of subversion of the land-sky
rules. "The big wink," he came to call it, though he was careful whom he
asked to help him look for it.

Horchow employed 1,100 people. The ponds covered slightly more
than 100 acres, and what was dredged from the ponds was hauled off to a
soil amendment site where thorium, uranium, radium, volatile organic
compounds, PCBs, radionuclides, and heavy metals were composted
into the soil, sometimes producing radon gas emissions from the cooking dirt.

"Stop me when I get to the modern device you want our company to stop
contributing to," the Horchow representative had begun his report to
the East Leven City Council. "Just hold up your hand and I'll stop reading.
Catheters." He paused dramatically and looked around the room as if
searching for a raised hand. "The coating on artificial hip replacements."
Again, the drama of a search for a hand. He was heavy in a genteel way,
the bulk of success, the thinning red hair that might have belonged to
Thomas Jefferson. He had authority and good news on his side. Then in
a list, slowly but without a pause: "Bridge cathode protection, stents for
collapsing veins, drying agents for deodorants, airplane engine exhaust
port coating, optical coatings …" He trailed off and looked around again.
"What Horchow makes contributes significantly to all of these and more.
Much more. We make ingots, plates, strips, sheets, wires, bars, foil, rods,
pipes, forgings, tubing, and powdered versions of our nonferrous metals."
He played the list over the city council's head like a kite in a light wind.
He had been asked by a concerned council to give a friendly accounting
of the mysterious business on the hill. Most of the people who worked

there didn't know the extent of the product line since they were involved only in fragments of the whole. "Imagine, if you will," he began again, "a metal that remembers its original shape and can return to that shape no matter how it's heated, cooled, or twisted out of shape. Shape-memory metals! Imagine a metal that when heated, instead of expanding, it contracts! Imagine. Imagine. That's what we do at Horchow. Imagine new solutions to humanity's problems." He paused and looked around the room to establish the effect of his words. "I would be pleased to try to respond to any questions or concerns of council."

A councilwoman raised her hand. "There has been some concern about your company's settling ponds and the sludge removal. Could you tell us the status of your efforts to comply with state and government regulations?"

He pushed the hair back from his forehead, balancing the gesture between exasperation and studied patience directed at a slow child. "The short answer is that we try to always be in compliance with state and federal guidelines. But, imagine," and he caught himself echoing his early rhetoric and stopped. "Try to think," but this came out even more patronizing. "The ponds may be in compliance in one month then out of compliance the next. Here are two reasons why. First, our own tests of both the ponds and the removed sludge become more sophisticated all the time. In the name of being a good citizen of East Leven, we are constantly upgrading the sophistication of our own self-monitoring. Imagine," damn, there it was again. "Think of the blizzard of state and federal mandates in the past ten years. We have found it best to be proactive about them, and we try to anticipate what the next round of regulation will bring. We're not always successful in fully anticipating the regulators, but by and large we're ahead of the curve. Second, our own product line is never static; we can never stop developing new products with new processes. And so we regularly produce new by-products that mix in with old, highly regulated and filtered and reprocessed by-products. The resultant mixture is not always predictable. We think the ponds will settle out some extra product, and then be rendered harmless in the soil amendment program. But then it doesn't break down as predicted. Then we have to do something else, something much more expensive, with the extra product. To keep costs down, and not incidentally employment full, we are obliged to try the less expensive solution first. This is good business practice. But you must understand the nature of Horchow's business. This is cutting-edge technology with a number of hungry and competent competitors chomping at our heels. We are the industry leader, but many of our discoveries and processes are not patentable and the only protection we have is to dominate the marketplace and service our customers better and faster than the competition. We look for new ways to use what technology we have and then that's the product we have to sell. The 1,100 people who work for us and live in the area are repeated worldwide in a sales and service force that sells and troubleshoots for clients around the world. Our domination in the industry is a year-to-year proposition."

He had broken a sweat making sentences as if the marshaling of his forces had strained his systems. He rounded his vowels with handsprings not of the Northwest – maybe Indiana, maybe Illinois. But the council, which had not in many years heard language strung together like this, such logic, such passion, such belief, sat moving gently with the words like the cobra mesmerized by the snake charmer's sway. Mrs. Albermarle, who had been on the council for eleven years, closed her eyes to better hear the rhythm of the words. She had found a way to shut out the meaning completely over the years, but always listened for the rhythm. She narrowly avoided dancing in her seat. At the other end of the half circle the newest member, a dentist whose son had recently taken over his business leaving him with great pride and time on his hands, leaned forward with his head in both hands and absorbed the rays coming from the Horchow representative, who had shifted gears like a preacher toward the end of his sermon, getting to the "and so" part.

"And so, our commitment to East Leven is long-standing: to the people of the valley, to the children of the high schools and colleges who will be looking for jobs here eventually. Horchow deals not just in chemical processes but in folks. In today's economic climate, when many companies have fled to Third World countries to take advantage of wage and benefit packages that would make a U.S. labor leader cringe, Horchow has kept its commitment to the best workers in the world, the Oregon worker. Our…" ("commitment" occurred to him, but quickly he counted his previous commitments and ran his mind down his thesaurus and came up with …) "dedication, our pledge to our East Leven family is to preserve jobs through good business practices and efficiencies, through forward-seeing and environmentally sound policy. But we need the help of you, this council, as representatives of our workers, our family of workers. When Horchow comes under attack, our livelihood is under attack. All our jobs are being beckoned to seductively by the world's poor, who would try to do them at a fraction of the cost of the worker here in East Leven." (Oops, he thought, maybe too heavy on the seduction; try for a virginal image next).

The dentist then the councilwoman thanked him, thanked Horchow for sending him, thanked Horchow for the time, for the overview, the consideration. The meeting broke up, and Horchow was on record, and not for the first time. The company regularly sent representatives to council meetings, Rotary meetings, Chamber of Commerce, Lions Club, Optimists, Brotherhood of Eagles, Elks, Odd Fellows, and the newly minted Downtown Association in charge of encouraging flower plantings and spruced-up storefronts. The Association lobbied the city council to redo the park and then raised most of the money to do the renovation – fish pond, bamboo grove, geometric walks, duck island (swans were rejected after one member read an account of a swan drowning a three-year-old child), oak trees, angle parking, and playground.

THE ORCHARDIST, EYES AS BLUE AS CORN FLOWERS, PIPS IN HIS HAIR where it stuck out of his baseball cap, straws cut to tooth-picking length poking out of his shirt pocket, the orchardist with something significant left of the southwestern England burr to ward off strangers understanding him too quickly, he pulled each ear to affect a center and then walked up the row of filberts. In much of the rest of the world these low, bushy trees were called hazelnuts, but here they were universally filberts; about 85 percent of the U.S. crop grew somewhere in the valley. Alstot leaned into the trees, his thinness poking around inside his clothes seemed to assail the twig ends with a kind of fatherly authority. Blue jays in love with solving the puzzle of the nuts went off like hacksaws every so often, flowing blue across the tight line of trees that grew together in arches, celebrating the endless row of trees and the manicured ground underneath. Alstot Simpson worked for several owners whose acreages abutted each other. He considered himself the steward of nearly six hundred acres all told: sprayer, straw boss of the pruning crews, groomer of the land under the trees to make a bowling alley smooth surface to pick up the nuts with the mechanized collector. Alstot was mechanic, botanist, and chief theorist and interpreter of filbert tree language: – What did they want for fertilizer? How deeply could you till around their trunks? What was the meaning of a dry winter/wet winter? When Alstot came to town, where he came from was the subject of speculation at the bar. What he had actually said when asked a direct question provided endless local discussion in Puddy's Bar.

"It sounded like 'beet bellywort tuft.' I can never understand him so I quit trying. There may be something wrong with him. He may just be English. I don't know which. John asked him about the time to spray fruit trees, and then he seemed to just make noises. I suppose they were words. I don't know."

"Well I think he thinks he's actually saying something. You look at his face and he's got that same look on it you and I use when we say something we expect people to understand. It's not like he's joking with us. I don't think, anyway. You're right though, he is English, and I watched that *Monty Python* once, and I know they were trying to be funny. Some of it was, but most of it wasn't. It was silly, but not funny. Your Englishman knows how to be silly. Your Canadian knows how to be funny: your Michael J. Fox, your Dan Ackroyd, even your Rick Moranis, your Peter Jennings."

"Jennings is a newscaster, John."

"Whatever. He's funny."

"My experience with the English is that they don't open their mouths enough to get the whole word out. Watch his lips sometime and then look at how we flap ours to get the words out. There's your difference."

"Your Englishman's lost his r. I read where some guy thought that the reason was the court of George the Third. He couldn't really speak English and when he did try to, with his thick German accent, it came out r-deprived like your German will. So the court picks up on it and floats theirs away the best they can to make the guy feel comfortable and, not incidentally, kiss up to him in the process. Kind of like wearing a tie that's like the boss's tie so he'll admire your good taste."

The denizens of the bar considered this for a moment. There was lots to process.

A strict constructionist spoke up. "Alstot's got pretty bad teeth. I'd go with the bad teeth as explanation. Somehow the court thing doesn't seem to fly. How'd everybody outside the court get to dropping the r out? I'd give you the power of court conspiracy on this deal, making it kind of a contest to see who could talk most like the kraut king, but the people picking up the game everywhere in England? Not likely. Has none of your persistent logic, if you know what I mean."

There was beer swirled in glasses. One cigarette lit. The Puddy himself reached for his towel and swabbed down the perfectly dry bar.

Court conspiracy guy rebutted. "There's your natural tendency of any court to set the standards of speech and manners for the country. Remember our peanut farmer from Georgia as president? He had people all over the country saying 'nuke-you-ler.' Journalists, for crissake, would say nuke-you-ler for some goddamn reason even when they knew better."

He seemed to rest his case on this hard evidence. Two guys on the outside edge of the circle looked at each other as if to ask, "What's wrong with nuke-you-ler?"

The jury stayed out and stayed out. Finally someone said, "Alstot Simpson may just be a doofus."

"Yeah well, there's that," someone else said. And it was over. The two nuke-you-ler guys nodded to each other, grateful to be moving on to some other topic.

Among his filberts Alstot was undisputed king. He would walk down a row of trees arching over him like the vaulted ceiling of his cathedral. When he came to a road or property line, he kept his vigil by crossing and continuing his inspection down the next row. It didn't matter who owned what; it all belonged to him in the way that Thoreau said he had bought and sold numerous farms in his lifetime simply by looking them over. But Alstot's walks were deadly serious business. He would pick up a filbert and heft it, tossing it in the air and catching it to feel its weight. Then he'd shake it next to his ear as if to hear its music. Then he'd take out a pocketknife and poke it in to gauge the shell thickness. And finally he'd smell where the knife had pierced and roll up his eyes like a wine taster and then snuff out to clear the palette and sniff again. He was going through this ritual at regular intervals while moseying down through his cathedral when he came to a road to cross and the Green Man on an early summer day.

Ben Brown was sitting on a rock alone, and though his green skin did nothing much for a healthy look, his body was slumped in exhaustion and told an unhappy tale clearly. He had been walking and pondering his island project, walking and building in his mind what he might try out near his cabin at the river.

"Are you all right?" Alstot asked. The Green Man held up one finger out of his slump. Wait a minute, he seemed to say. Wait for an answer. As he collected himself to reply, Alstot closed his knife with a clack and slid it into his pocket.

"I was out walking," the Green Man began. "I was just walking." Then, "Can you smell it? The poison they use on these trees? It's everywhere." He seemed to gain strength from talking. "The wind was coming from the other way; then it switched. Suddenly I found myself … I found myself … gassed. It's thick in the wind now and I can't seem to get away from it anywhere. I tried to walk out but it surrounded me."

Alstot pulled at his chin, confronted with a green person whom he knew only by reputation. He sniffed the air like he sniffed the filberts. Ripeness? A full nut? What was the green person smelling?

Ben Brown started to get to his feet but sat back down. "Smell the chlorinated …" He stopped and tried again. "Could you help me get upwind somewhere?" His voice was airy as if coming through a tube from somewhere else.

Alstot helped him up and together they made a slow way down the road from the edge of the trees and across another country road into a field of sugar beets grown for seed. The waves of waist-high greens provided cool refuge, and the Green Man sat down again on a wall of beet tops. He seemed to grow noticeably stronger sitting holding his knees.

Alstot stood by and waited silently while extracting a straw from his pocket, and then he began working around in his teeth until the straw gave out. He tossed it to the ground and asked again, "Poisons? Tell me about the poison." The accent was as thick as the beet tops Ben sat on. The words seemed to work their way out of his jaw with reluctance, stopping long enough to fill up on diphthongs and southern England rhythms and stops. But Ben Brown seemed to have no trouble decoding. Alstot continued, "So you smell poisons. These are my trees and I'd like to know if they're being poisoned."

"Your trees?"

"Well, in my care. As far as you can see, I'm the orchardist. They're under my care, you see. I know every one of them, what's right with them, what's wrong."

"What sprays do you use?"

"Well, none in this season, of course. But early on we spray for the root rot, the scale, the worm. Can't have an orchard without some spray. I'd like to spray for jays too," and he made a sound that passed for a laugh, "but they get their nuts, we get ours. Used to put out poisoned bait for the birds in the fruit orchards long ago. But not now. The birds get what they get. We get the rest. Oh, and we spray the understory so we can groom it for picking up the nuts with machines."

The Green Man sighed, his strength flowing back tidally. Alstot got around to introducing himself, mentioning that he knew Ben as the Green Man, and seemed to break into unending talk now that his practiced reticence had been breached. He was interested in just what the Green Man smelled, how much, how strong. He used words like ultraviolet breakdown and residual and surfactant as if he'd been invited to lecture. Ben Brown listened to the harmlessness of sprays, how they broke up at the molecular level, how there was no detectable residue in the marketed nut after drying and sorting. The flavor chemistry of roasted filberts seemed unaffected by sprays. Flavor chemistry was heat sensitive, very sensitive at certain temperatures. The nuts could go "off" in a second, a degree or two at too long a duration. Very complicated business this flavor chemistry. Once, Alstot volunteered, he had been giving a talk and had said that while roasting filberts, if you could smell the nuts you'd gone too far, and the audience burst into laughter. He had stood dumfounded and couldn't figure out what he'd said. Much later it occurred to him. He volunteered that he'd felt like a stranger in a strange land though he'd lived in East Leven since the 1950s when it was easy for a British citizen to become American, especially one bringing orchardist skills and knowledge. The only easier transfer from Europe had been the Basque sheepherders and their dogs, who had been officially welcomed into the Northwest since the 1930s.

Ben Brown stood with sugar beet seeds clinging to him. The Horchow ponds he'd seen from the air with Farnsworth now seemed just like a concentrated version of the same goings-on in the filbert business. They had flown over the acres and acres of filbert orchards in Alstot's charge and peered down on what looked from above like even meadows of deep green grass, future golf courses, geometric blocks of verdure.

Ben looked around in the beet field and saw no plants that weren't beets – no weeds.

Alstot Simpson saw his guest to the edge of the field. Between them he had lost more than an hour of orchard time, but he had begun to wonder just what a green person smelled that he didn't. Was there a layer of his business, of his competence, that was invisible? Was there another reality outside his care? And was there some part of the filbert that was keeping itself private ultimately, a part that could pop out and bite him in his ignorance? Alstot walked his rows sniffing the air for a trace of what had made the Green Man so ill, so quickly. But no matter how hard he tested the air, he could smell only the filberts slowing filling, could see only the jays splattering across the rows. Something in his encounter with the Green Man had left Alstot convinced of the invisible. Whatever Ben Brown was talking about that day in the orchard, and though he could never find the smell Ben smelled, the illness that laid Ben low, and though Alstot couldn't attest to some verifiable truth that Ben witnessed to, somehow the Green Man's green sincerity carried the day, and the next day.

And the day after, Alstot had marshaled all the sprays and ground treatments, all the potions of the orchardist's art, and read and reread the labels searching out the devil in the details, lined up the bottles and cans and bags as if reviewing his troops in the battle against leafroller, oblique-banded leafroller, blight – eastern filbert or common bacterial – aphids, leaftier larvae, winter moths, filbert worm. Sprays to discourage aborted nuts and blank nuts, chemical mowing. There was Gramoxone 2-4D amine for sucker control, Casoron, Norosac, Goal, Enquik, Princip, Karmex, Soli-cam, Devrinol, Surflan, and tribasic copper against moss and lichen accu-mulation. Foliar boron to increase nut set. The blight sprays: Kocide DF, Bordeau 6-3-100, Nu-cop. And then the pheromone traps and copper sprays.

Alstot Simpson, orchardist, sat among his army that allowed him to win the battle for the filbert nut. A percentage here, a percentage there, each agent increased his yield. He had never before had all his weapons in the same place at the same time. He had assembled them from storage sheds and warehouses. Usually they came out by season like Christmas decorations, Easter baskets, Fourth of July flags. Alstot watched them as if they might begin to move by themselves and seek out the Green Man and make him sick. Finally he sighed, stood up, and walked among the tools of his trade. He wasn't feeling up to snuff, he thought. He thought he might go lie down for a while.

ANDREW AND THE GREEN MAN FLOAT ON THE ISLAND TO THE bank outside the Horchow Chemical Company. They can just see the Horchow sign over the plant rim. Up until here, there have been blackberry vines all along the cutbank growing from the riprap, hanging almost to the water from undercut banks like the ancient gardens of Babylon. Here at the Horchow bank, the Green Man starts jumping and yelling about rare earths.

He's shaking like a dog ridding itself of water, except the water is some-how clinging to him, and he can't get it off, and so he goes on shaking. Shaking and jumping.

"Rare earths!" and he points up the bank. "I've felt these before. I know they're here." He leaps off the island and scrambles up the bank and over the top, the island making a lazy circle in the still water.

Andrew finds himself thinking comic strip noises: *Zap! Bonk! Kaachiiing! Kapoooow! Bif!*

Andrew hears whooping. The island makes another slow circle in the eddy while he gives a corrective tug on the sweep to hold it there, and the Green Man goes about his business up the bank. Andrew is watching the top of the bank trying to think of some way to tether the island so he can go up and see what's what. With the sweep he bangs the island against the cutbank hoping to run it aground on the loose gravel and boulders. Instead he bounces off, and a chunk of the island dribbles into the green calm of the river. A bleach bottle is sticking out like a polystyrene sore.

"Jay-sus, Mary, and Joseph," comes from the top of the bank. There's the accent of a leprechaun in it. There is clanking and banging, shouts from far away as if they are coming from the blue sky directly above Andrew.

The Green Man comes bounding down the bank suddenly, making two-footed hops in the loose gravel. Behind him and upstream from where Andrew is holding the island against the bank, there's a gushing and the rattle of stones washed together, and over the bank like a brown locomotive comes a river of sludge chugging toward the green river. With a slurp the river receives the sludge. The Green Man dives into the river and comes up on the other side of the island. The smell of the growing brown cascade following the first plunge is like hot tin cans in Andrew's nose, like chewing aluminum foil.

Ben scrambles onto the island, and they shove off just ahead of the brown blob spreading into the river. Just as they hit the main current and pick up speed, the Horchow cops show up along the bank, rent-a-cops in Sigmund Romberg hats and badges that crash and tinkle in the sun. They prance along the ridge after the island until they're stopped by the Horchow chain-link fence.

The floating island leaves the brown stream behind almost immediately. The green river is slow to accept the flood from the banks of Horchow, seems even reluctant to take it at all, and the brown river runs in but doesn't mix with the green. The brown is a stripe soon in the distance and then disappears. There's damage to the island from all that scraping and spinning Andrew accomplished while waiting for the green warrior.

Over and over Ben returns to a solid part of the island and leans to the water to wash his hands again. He scrapes at the skin with his fingernails, scuffing and then dipping his hands in the green river maybe to try to get the green of the water to redye him. Andrew lets him complete his ablutions without bothering him, feeling as if he is interrupting someone at prayer.

"The little defeats – the Great Victory," says the Green Man finally. There's a lilt to his voice as if he had confirmed by his hand washing and hand wringing everything that needed to be resolved – the kitchen clean and the dishes put away. He holds up one finger as if testing the wind, and suddenly it seems as if there are birds everywhere along the river – kingfishers clucking and chit-chitting and dive bombing. The raft is melting like a sugar cube, and the Green Man is posing like a pioneer statue.

"There are low-level radiations in that waste. Rare earths, metal salts …" He shivers a shiver of icky, not of cold. It's hot in the sun. "I got up there and couldn't believe they had these huge sludge ponds right up against the bank of the river. I saw them from the air with Farnsworth once, but not up close. There wasn't a living thing growing between the ponds and the factory. The heat was coming off …" He pauses and looks at Andrew as if trying to decide whether to tell a secret. He swallows visibly. "I feel the heat coming off things sometimes, like waves or maybe like invasions from hot to cool. I'm cool, you see, and the heat seems to be after me in sort of a flow, sort of a wave, more like a gush."

His voice cracks in a peach fuzz adolescent way while he looks around. He continues in conspiratorial tones.

"You see, it's the ten thousand things idea of the Chinese." He squints his eyes just enough to get Chinese, kind of Charlie Chan, as if a character to bear the weight of his thought has occurred to him suddenly.

They are at the vortex of the kingfishers' chit-chittering – all around nature is feeding itself. And the Green Man has finally squared up his shoulders in preparation for assessing his romp on the bank and his attack on the Horchow ponds. The island melts.

"The ten thousand things, the manyness of the world, the opposite of the single force – the force of many."

Andrew sits down, plunks down between two boxwood plants, and then stands quickly while the depression fills with water. The river takes them along in the middle of the current with the island floating lower and lower in the water.

"What I mean," says Ben, "is that Horchow's settling ponds have some of the inevitable ten thousand things, things Horchow developed. Well, they sort of found these things in the bag of ten thousand things and took out these particular ones – the rare earths, zirconium and the like – and then got on with the process of selling them to other people who coat the insides of TV screens …"

As he talks he rubs his hands together, cleaning them in the air as if the rare earths are clinging in a fine hot dust and won't come off. The river is quickly claiming the island's dirt. The trail of brown is thick now, a milk chocolate road behind the raft, and the bleach bottles begin to rattle in their netting and the blue and yellow nylon rope washes out to the side like tentacles. Andrew looks at his feet, raises and lowers them as if marching, and notes the pools growing deeper. The Green Man peers downstream and sinks imperceptibly, seems to settle into the island.

Cool green the river. Hot green the Green Man. Andrew thinks he has got the sound turned off as he sits between the two glowing screens. He wonders what went on with the Green Man up the bank.

Just before, before this: a double rainbow clobbers the sky, and the world happens again for the Green Man. The story is relived, prompted by Andrew's asking. The loosed island drifts toward Horchow again in a fine mist as if nature had conspired for this one, for this event – the high water, the breaking loose, the first corner, and now the melting island on the green water under the adventure of a rainbow. They are alone on the river: no rafts, jet boats, inner tubers, not a canoe anywhere when they pass under the highway. Ben prods the island surface semi-scientifically, wondering if they had worn away to the ring of bleach bottles yet, the ring roped together with collections of yellow and turquoise water-skiing rope.

Besides the brown stripe behind and a little rippling fore to aft as they chug down a riffle, the whole thing feels made for eternity, consumed only by going onward and looking for the Pacific Ocean.

Andrew has grown completely silent now and seems to be enjoying himself, the strings gone from his neck, some other song in progress. And then the Green Man feels the heat.

Before they even come to the cutbank, maybe three hundred yards still upstream, he feels it like a leak from deep in the earth. It is hot on his face as if the sun has dropped into the bank and is shining to get out. Ben starts to sweat and glisten green immediately and squints at the heat coming out of the bank. He signals for the kid to pull over against the bank, and he does, reluctantly, since they had been pulling to stay off the bank. Tires crunch against gravel and drag to a stop.

"Stay here and just hold it against the bank with this sweep. Don't let it get off the bank and it'll stay fine."

Before Andrew can ask why, the Green Man jumps up the bank and scrambles up the rocks, rocks that now feel heated from the inside, each one cooking, incandescent, getting hotter as he climbs over the crest of the bank.

On the other side of a short ridge are open settling ponds separated from the river by a chain-link fence. And just a hoot away on the other side of the ponds is the backside of a low factory broken by some towers of steaming pipes and catwalks and mounds of buff, even-colored dirt piled against the silver buildings. To Ben the heat seems to percolate off the ponds connected by sluice gates. It is hard to tell if the stuff in the ponds is real heat or the heat he felt trickling out of 220-volt outlets and oozing out of high lines. He pauses and feels with his greenness, his glands, legends and texts. It was the leaky heat other people didn't seem to feel, the heat that backed Ben out of the butcher section in the supermarket when they were sealing meat with the plastic-wrap machine, the heat from the side of the road after the county had sprayed against blackberries. It was an audible heat to him, ringing heat, whistling heat, wailing heat.

He climbs the bank where the gravel is loose, finds a length of pipe and begins wrenching open the gates that connect the ponds. The ponds flow together, water turned into hot wine, and the joined ponds conspire somehow to run over and through the chain-link closest to the river. A miracle.

There are shouts. The sludge hums over the bank, hot stew of the ponds mixed, brown elixir of heat. Ben feels as if he were racing back and forth on the floor of hell. It is hard to breathe, the air just out and away from his mouth so he has to suck hard to get it to come near. Ben Brown sticks out his neck and arches his shoulders to get air in, and it won't come closer. The shouts are louder, and coming down from the factory are waving men in blue uniforms. One throws a rock that lands in the sludge and splashes a fiery mist on Ben's arm. Suddenly he sees clearly the uniforms, the Horchow patches, the silver factory straddling the hill with pools of hot excrement below it like stuff at the bottom of Horchow's cage.

The Green Man rubs his arm with dirt, cuffs at the spots that feel like hot grease, but still they burn. The river! There is coolness and air at the river. He runs to the fence and finds his hole while the security is making its way around the biggest pond. Stop in the name of the law, they must have said. Stop in the name of the law.

Ben climbs under the fence and down the bank, the kid holding the island against the bank.

"Push off! Go! Now."

The island moves off while Ben skis down the loose yellow gravel and dives into the cool water, and while still underwater he scrubs at his arm, washes and rubs at himself as if he were covered by biting insects, things mindlessly nipping and nipping.

Andrew has caught a good current, but in the water the Green Man travels faster than the island. He waits in slower water for the island to come by, and then slithers up on the side away from Horchow. As he peers out of the foliage fending off the kid's rapid-fire questions, the Horchow guards appear near where the brown goo lurched over the bank and into the river, several of them with binoculars swinging from the island guys to the trail of brown edging its way out into the current like some granddaddy version of the puny silt tail made with the dissolving island. Ben thinks people should know about the heat he felt even if they didn't feel it the same way, that heat the fish could feel. Ben knows the trout would recognize that heat because they were green too.

Now, as the story finds its stride, it was all the king's horses, all the king's men after them. The kid had been waiting below, out of sight. Ben was the great Humpty in full sunlight prancing around. Horchow's ponds were like the surface of a fry pan ready for eggs. Owch, ooch, ahh, yikes. The ground was cooing.

Sat on a wall: He pauses when he sees that the sign had spawned the uniformed authorities fanning out toward him. Hot enough to fry this big egg! Whew. Hot ponds. Hot ground. Hot pursuit. Hot foot.

He prances, tip-toes across the sizzling causeways between ponds feeling his yoke cooking hard. Three minutes and the king's men would nab him. Cuff him. Bash him around.

He finds a sluice gate that would surely run one pond into another, that one then overflow into yet another, then the whole works overwhelm the bank. But the sluice wheel is locked and chained – chained and locked logically. Where was their sense of fair play? The king's men gallop toward him. He hopes to hell the kid has some swashbuckler in him and has stayed below and didn't skitter off downstream. Still, he has to take a chance and move from trespassing to destruction of private property. Be a good egg, he thinks. Trip their trap. Fire their crops. Or what's an egg for?

In a flash – the heat grows, bubbles around him, seems to cook him to a standstill. He is on the sluice wheel with a piece of pipe snapping, snapping, snapping their chain. In a flash he remembers himself on the ground under the high wire, sizzling on the grass like a naked, poached person. The authorities are still swooping and Ben still snapping when he feels the chain go, give in with a puny click. He cranks the sluice gate open and goo runs into goo like cake batter, cake batter that percolates in waves.

He can see the Horchow louts coming. One with blonde hair is going to be the first to reach the miscreants through the haze of the heat, and Horchow has turned up the voltage on the yellow sign behind him making his blue uniform even bluer. He might have cuffed the Green Man too, but he stops to try to shut the opened sluice gate. Meanwhile, the Green Man has scrammed. And kept scramming until he's pranced down the bank and found the scraggly kid waiting for him on his island, his cool island slowly melting in the eddy. The kid has been a swashbuckler after all.

ONE AFTERNOON AFTER HE HAD BEEN IN TOWN LONG ENOUGH to pass as talk among the town folk, the Green Man climbed the hill toward Horchow on a day before the rains came. The main plant sat above the river, above the town, and the storage yards with shacks and heaps of cast iron, then below the settling ponds with an ironic surface that looked like oily rusted liquid iron.

Ben had discovered the ponds by accident one day when he had accepted an airplane ride from Farnsworth. Farnsworth had a first name, but no one used it and through disuse it had atrophied until no one could recall what it was. Farnsworth would tell anyone who asked, but no one asked anymore. And his one name became even stranger after ten minutes with Farnsworth because he seemed obsessed by the naming of things.

"*Armillaria mellea*," he pointed out to the Green Man as they walked toward the plane. "The shoestring root rot. Bane of the orchard. Gets in under the bark and the mycelium snakes around the cambium layer and kills the fruit tree." The airport sat at the edge of town in the remains of a combination cherry orchard and filbert grove. "Cessna 150 used to be the standard after the Piper Cub and the Aerocommander before that. Not hot like the Waco or Steerman. I'm saving for a used Cessna 182 R RG."

Farnsworth, somewhere in his permanent late fifties, strode ahead as if he had to hurry and the hurrying would speed up his companion. But the truth was that Farnsworth had no particular place to go, no particular place to be, but remained vaguely behind in some internal clock and gave the impression of always trying to catch up. He had the beard and haircut of a man answering to no one. He was known in town to be a man of some means but just exactly what the means were – how much and from where – was never very clear. Like the Green Man, Farnsworth had come to town out of the vastness of somewhere else and plunked himself down in East Leven by the north-running river. Two rumors accompanied his money: early TV patents and Link trainer connections. Neither rumor seemed solid in town, and when Farnsworth's wealth came up at the bar, adherents to either theory of his fortune were about equally balanced. At the bar some swing votes went first one way and then the other. Farnsworth was a fixture in town long before the Green Man, and Farnsworth's oddness – of constantly naming things, of rushing off to no particular end in the pursuit of naming more and more – his oddness shrank before the Green Man's greenness even though Ben Brown's personal life in town was a model of usualness.

Farnsworth and Ben became not so much friends as compatriots, drawn together in a pact of inverse oddness. Ben was regular in his habits, a citizen of the middle way. But he was green. Farnsworth looked the part of a man fading each year into the landscape of daily community. But everyone who talked to him, with the possible exception of Ben Brown, felt dipped in oddness for hours afterwards by Farnsworth's compulsive naming of the world's parts. And so Farnsworth came to invite Ben to fly with him, to share his overview of the valley, the river, and East Leven. The two of them for different reasons enjoyed these outings: Ben, though flying made him queasy, loved the distance and the quick, changing perspective of humming over the river; Farnsworth loved his running commentary, the saying out of the names of the parts of the world as if with enough said it would begin to assemble a sense too.

Farnsworth padded around the plane making his visual inspection and enumerating in no particular order the characteristics and specifications of the plane – top speed, fuel capacity, weight-carrying capacity, design history, total hours on the engine rebuild, oil pressure, wing span, engine displacement. His mind seemed to overflow with whatever came to the surface. He spoke slowly and clearly though with no particular urgency as if, like a hillside spring, a certain amount of flow needed to be maintained for the viability of the spring. Plug it up, and it might never run again.

No crosswind. Clear and dry. Farnsworth pointed out land forms "… that in another landscape, say the Midwest, could be confused for eskers and drumlins. But these, geologically speaking, are much younger than the Wisconsin glaciations and the Cascades, of course, are volcanic and …"

Ben Brown found the flow of information at first bracing. Then, after he stopped trying to keep track of what Farnsworth was saying, soothing, like voices in flowing water that seem just barely incomprehensible with an occasional clear word sparking out of the background.

"… Climax forest of *abies* and *pseudotsuga* with some *Quercus garryana* and a valley-specific *Pinus ponderosa* – technically not the same ponderosa as on the east side of the Cascades. Hemlock, oak, fir – white and Douglas and noble – pine, western red cedar, and some incense cedar." He fell out of Latin names into the vernacular, back into Latin. "*Abies concolor* most commonly associates with *Pseudotsuga menziesie* and *Abies magnifica*. Prairie, planosol, and alluvial soils mostly, some lateritic (the reddish brown). Of course, the new classification system after 1967 changes names – the *haplohumults*, for example. But I find I like the old names. Same with mushrooms. The old taxonomy before the *Boletus* family got broken into *Suillus* and …"

Farnsworth flew in slow esses and filled each sinuous curve with names, like Adam appointed to delineate the world for the first time.

And there were the ponds at Horchow, from two thousand feet the blue of swimming pools gone off for lack of chlorine. Too blue. Metallic blue with a bloom of acid-looking algae, slime molds.

"A perpetration," Farnsworth said, pointing out the pools.

"Pooping in the punch bowl," added the Green Man.

Farnsworth shouted over the engine noise. "A concoction." Looking for its name. "A melange. A cocktail. An infelicity." Farnsworth dropped the left wing and descended steeply like a bombing run at Horchow. The plane shuddered and slid toward the growing buildings with enough noise to make Horchow's yard workers pause and look up as the Cessna flattened out and buzzed the complex.

"A hundred and fifty bucks," Farnsworth shouted. "Every time I do that it costs me a $150 fine. You used to be able to buzz friends' houses just to say hello. No more." And then pointing off to the western coast range, "*Acer macrophyllum, Tsugamertensiana, Shrus rubra*."

The Green Man nodded as if he understood. Farnsworth continued naming the world in and out of Latin like a schizoid monk while Ben Brown flowed with the stream of words and the language of the Cessna engine. On the way back, after flying north along the coastal range for a good look into the high rain forests, Farnsworth suddenly asked, "When women talk about being attractive or finding clothes or makeup that's attractive, what exactly are they trying to attract? I mean, attract whom? Everybody? Men? Other women? I try to figure this out and everyone else seems to understand this except me. 'Oh, that's attractive,' they say. Do they want to attract everybody all the time? Isn't that exhausting? Have you ever been married, Ben? I have to admit I'm at a complete loss in that world. Of attracting and … and being attracted. I can never figure out what I'm supposed to do or say. A friend once told me to be myself. That was a social disaster of some note. The poor woman is still probably telling her friends about that date. Oh, no. Not be yourself."

The Cessna 150 bucked into some updrafts rising off the valley floor up the flank of low mountains.

"Yes. I was married. It didn't work out, so I'm afraid I can't be much help to you in the world of attraction. Now longing-after, I can help you with. In fact something fairly recent – well, someone named Mary – has me doing a little longing. But longing, it seems to me, is the essence of naming, and you've got that down."

The valley tour continued into the afternoon. The plane executing long lazy figures up and down the valley. Farnsworth abandoned male/female attraction for less arcane subjects: plate tectonics, prewhite culture in the Northwest, the Eve gene in Native Americans.

"Okay. Why East Leven?" asked Farnsworth finally. "Just wondering. I had my reasons for settling here. What about yours?"

The Green Man looked over at his pilot as if to gauge whether to use the long answer, the short answer, the ironic answer, the flip answer, maybe the fabricated-but-logical answer, or the complicated-hard-to-believe but true answer.

"I could have lived anywhere I suppose. I thought of warm weather. Third World countries where being green had some real magic power associated with it. That was tempting, let me tell you. A holy man. I thought that through pretty thoroughly." He laughed. "Get up every morning and go off to work as some kind of manifestation of a godhead. Knock off a few cures, a few life-changing encounters before noon. Then maybe comfort the bewildered or fearful until dinner. But no. Finally, no. Finally, after all the pondering was done, I didn't know how long I'd live. Doctors either.

I chose to stay somewhere among my own people. Not that they would understand better than anyone else. I think the whole green thing presents a certain amount of insulation, maybe even alienation."

The plane droned in the afternoon sun. The Green Man paused long enough to regain a foothold after "alienation." And then: "But I was turned green here in Oregon – south of here the actual event took place – so I wanted to stay here. A big city is out because I'd constantly be confronted by a new set of strangers who needed to get used to me. Small town was one possible answer. Then wet side or dry side. I chose wet because ... well, I know the wet side. The coast was a strong contender and still is. Sometimes I think the coast makes even more sense. The principle of 'you can't go any farther.' Then there's all those other people who gather on the coast. Not exactly green people, but people who have come to conceive of themselves as 'other,' if you know what I mean." Ben Brown looked over at his sky host to see how close to the bone this was, whether compulsive naming of things might qualify in Farnsworth's estimation.

Farnsworth nodded vigorously without naming anything, acknowledging the coast as a final catch basin for idiosyncrasy.

"So I finally decided on East Leven not exactly because I had eliminated everywhere else, but because everywhere else failed to qualify."

Farnsworth thought about this and decided it had probably answered his question.

The sky had moved on from blue to an even, cloudless theme of blueness informed from the horizon up by clear peach overlay – strongest at the horizon then thinning and thinning its way up. Both men silently watched the sky begin to thicken with peach color as they flew. There was nothing to name, just sky after sky growing bright in the valley air over East Leven. The final pass over the town, Horchow, the north-running river, the two mountain ranges that carried the valley like cupped hands, and the plane lowered down the afternoon to the airport. Farnsworth touched the runway so gently that the Green Man didn't realize they had come to earth until the speed slowed and they were clearly taxiing on the runway.

THEY PLUNGE INTO THE RIVER ALL OF A SUDDEN, JUST BEFORE the pilings. Below Horchow for two hundred yards the riverbank is sterile, without so much as a blackberry poking out of the riprap. The island begins to disintegrate badly from its whirling escape, flinging bleach bottles and yellow nylon rope out to its sides like a watery supernova. But still the center holds until just above the pilings, when everything lets loose at once and the flotsam goes one way, the jetsam the other. Andrew simply disappears directly through his standing place and comes bobbing out the bottom miraculously unencumbered by any of the cables, ropes, and other devices strung together to assemble the island. The Green Man is sitting on the bank between the pilings by the time Andrew clears his eyes of river water. As Andrew swims two strong strokes to shore, Ben Brown waves to him. "Quick, this way," he says, and scrambles up the bank between the pilings.

They are wet and inside the shack in short order.

"There are a number of problems with greenness of course." The Green Man talks. "Dogs pick up something they don't like in the smell of me. Bright lights still bother me." The Green Man is calm, ticking these off on his fingers like recipe ingredients. His eyes are silver gray surrounded by all that greenness. Andrew thinks puffs of smoke ought to be coming out his ears. "But there are also advantages. No one really sees me, just the green. Sometimes I do pushups when I get chilled. Hotel lobbies, the deck of a ferry. No one cares about the calisthenics, just the greenness. I disappear. Only the greenness is visible at all. I have no face, no height or weight. Only greenness. Children touch me, especially two- or three-year-olds with those tiny fingers, softly as if they're tasting me. Feeling for the tingle of mint." He looks out the window where they have come to rest, where they are dripping on the floor of this shack and waiting for what comes next. He looks at the river recalling some touch. "Of course, their parents tug them away then. But there's darkness too. In the dark briefly, though I know it won't last, I am any color, no color. The lights go down in the movie theater and I disappear. Only the green is there. So I know about darkness better than anyone, except the blind, who must know all its corners."

There is more to be said on being green, Andrew thinks, but the Green Man looks out at the river as if he is finished with the subject. And then he continues quietly, almost a whisper, repeating some of what he had asserted earlier almost as if not what he said but the saying of it counted.

"And the heat of things. I seem to feel the heat of chemicals working, plastics cooking away, the steaming current through light bulbs. Generating plants and power substations are too much. Memory of sucking in all that juice, maybe. They're too hot. I can feel weed killer on a lawn like the heat of a campfire on a cool night. I don't know why. It's interesting. I sometimes feel the heat then look to see what it is. The perfume section of a department store gives off that heat. New paint, floor waxes. Like having an invisible face close to mine, the breath, the heat of the skin. I thought for a while I picked up some wavelengths of light, some radiation. I feel a new plastic raincoat in a dark room, feel it like a touch, almost a touch on my face. I don't know what it is now. It's being green."

The river ticks and pulses in the pilings below the shack, something living under the house, something stirring in its sleep. Below, the pilings smell of creosote and streaks of tar drooled to the high-water mark. The shack is propped over the forest of pilings almost carelessly, with a kind of native carpenter's overconfidence that as long as the water never reaches the top of the poles, then it doesn't really matter how well the shack is fastened on. The architecture is bricolage, found art of mill ends and mixed shingle bargains cobbled together, a wood blur in parody of the forest on the other bank.

Inside, Andrew has a cuckoo-clock feeling: the green bird waiting for some mechanism, some wooden tongue to stick out over the river and announce the hour.

The Green Man speaks again: "I once had a '57 Plymouth like the island. First the frenched headlights flaked and rusted out and snapped against the windshield in pieces as I drove along. Then the quarter panels ..."

"Who the hell's in here?" The voice is female and rattled with disuse.

"A citizen and a green person," the Green Man responds, "drying out from a river accident."

"There's always room in hell no matter what color you are. It's the citizens I'm afraid of. Stand away from the window so's I can see you both."

Marge, tall, maybe old, lumpy under layers of sweaters, shoos them with flicks of the back of her hand, shoos them like cats to where she can see better. She is easy of speech, almost laconic, but her words are sharp wrapped in honey. "What is this? A green one and one that won't look straight at you," she says. "What's the poop here?"

Andrew looks at her. She stands hands on hips, outriggers upholstered in wool, with a gap-toothed Vince Lombardi smile, a coyote smile. Then the cuckoo-clock feeling comes over Andrew again. The cuckoo clock inspector's here. Everybody out for inspection. Cuckoos in front.

Ben Brown: "This will go in my journal as the day my island broke loose, floated north, encountered the chemical plant, then crashed into the pilings of …? … of?"

"Of Quality Seed and Grain Company number three piling patched, cabled, and cobbled together by Marge McIntry."

They both laugh. The Green Man and Marge instantly like each other.

"And who's the citizen?" Marge asks, waving at Andrew, who keeps a chair between him and the question.

"Now, one of the two of you is the keeper, I got a feeling," Marge says, pulling off a layer of sweater. She lights the fire in the oil drum stove while the Green Man and Andrew look at each other to see who is the keeper, who the kept. Andrew asks by raising eyebrows while the Green Man does a yikes face.

"Well," she asks when the fire is going, "Who's got the leash?"

Ben Brown says, "It's more of an employer/employee relationship. Maybe until we hit your pilings, a captain/first mate. And then there's the partners-in-crime point of view." The Green Man seems intrigued by the permutations. "We sort of attacked the Horchow Chemical Company this morning and we …"

"We?" says Andrew. "My green employer here opened a sludge pond into the river and down swoop the chemical authorities, badges flashing …"

"While driving the get-away island," the Green Man points at Andrew, "is the accomplice who …"

Neither perpetrator seems to have any difficulty ratting out the other to Marge. Somehow she is clearly of no particular authority regarding matters of attacking Horchow. Her clothes, the shack, the eclectic Goodwill furniture, the oil-drum heater, the way without apology she scratches where it itches – these combine for the pair into permission. Andrew begins in the cuckoo clock but Marge brings him out.

"Coffee?" she asks, as if this is the beginning of a long story and she'll need hot coffee for comfort. Her shack windows are lined with shelves of bottles of different colors, especially deep blue and one blood-red bottle used as a vase. The light from behind it seems to all come through the red into the room, coloring the exposed beams, the gleam of the heater chimney, the eclectic chairs gathered around a white table with legs so thin it seemed a trick of the light to hold it up. A couch of desperate 1970s orange peeks out from under a sheet trying just as desperately to hide it. The floor is plywood of varying vintages covered in spots by ancient rag rugs. The whole impression might be of impermanence except that the light off the river seems focused through the bottles into a cathedral's authority.

Coffee all around and Marge finds blankets so they can get out of wet clothes. Andrew watches to see if she'll peek to see if Ben's green all over, but she's got her back to them in the kitchen swiping at plates left in the sink. She drags a chair over and sits with the Green Man at the table, and Andrew has the cuckoo-clock feeling redux; he is poised ready to pop out of this loaded mechanism into a room somewhere furnished in Victorian plush, children playing on a floor with fist-size blocks. His imagination is cooking along now with the fresh pot of coffee percolating on the stove.

Marge reaches over and rubs a finger on the Green Man's forearm to test the dye. Spits on her finger and tries again. He lets himself be spit on, in fact holds his arm out to her for further tests. He watches to see how she'll conduct her tests.

Marge is no stranger to accidents, of time and space and circumstances, of economic vicissitudes and whim. She has pulled odder pairs of things out of the river than these two. She checks the colorfastness but, as with each piece of flotsam and jetsam she has recovered, she assesses the salvage worth with a severe eye.

"Industrial accident," says the Green Man. "Apparently it's permanent." He says this with a slight hitch. Waits for interrogation, finds none. Marge lifts her cup as if to toast his greenness. She knows some of this green story, of course. But this is the closest she's come to the actual green critter. His green spit-tests true. But what's under the cover?

The stove crackles madly as it heats, the river ticks against the pilings, and the Green Man blows across the top of his coffee.

"Then again," he says, as if all the conversation is somehow collecting in the rafters, "maybe no one's after us. Maybe they all went home at five."

Marge is looking out the window with such interest that Andrew and the Green Man both turn to see what's going on. The green river has a brown stripe where it's deep as if a watercolor brush had been dragged through the surface in a long squiggle.

"That's what happens after a heavy rain, but I've never seen it run like that on a clear day," Marge says.

"The sluice gate you opened." Andrew turns to the Green Man. "Maybe they couldn't close it."

"Oh, they couldn't close it. I broke off the flange and let the heat out. Look for dead fish."

Each one takes a window, leaving Marge the center, the best view. In the eddies just off the brown stripe are a few white bellies, summer steelhead floating on their sides trying to right themselves. Small trout flap against the current half turned upstream, roiling the water. There would be hundreds of dead fish downstream where the river broadens along the sandy islands in the city. Horchow's waste pools had belched out into the river a metallic brown stream that wailed its way north to Portland with a load of fish bellies. The Green Man's attack was paying off in a slick of dead fish, and if the poison were strong enough, there'd be a second wave of stink when the scavengers came down to feed off fish. Herons, raccoons, beavers, kingfishers, and river rats would make this a slaughter event downstream as the brown stripe eased around the next bend. The Green Man has set loose the Horchow stored-up treasure from its vault of extra things. He pulls the blanket around his shoulders and sighs toward the river. Marge breaks the silence.

"So this is what you two were up to. They're looking for you all right. Horchow pulls mighty big weight around here. They'll be looking for somebody to hang for this one." She looks over the Green Man again. "Good thing you're hard to recognize. Nondescript pair the report probably says. One green, one kind of noodly and scraggly." Marge laughs. What washes up in the river sometimes doesn't tell you what it's good for until much later. Old wine bottles, when you have enough of them, become a window when you cement them in a wall. Those big, flat pieces of Styrofoam make great insulation. The rough-sawn four by fours buried make a fine deadman to anchor cables.

This pair, Marge thinks, what is it they do? Her old life as a woman of sufficient means, so long ago, not so far away, that old life never would have asked the question, much less speculated on the value of this particular driftwood pair.

Ben raises his eyebrows at Andrew, makes them jump like two caterpillars ready to race across his forehead. Groucho.

To hide or not to hide, that becomes the question very quickly. Perhaps to run. Marge seems to have caught on to the felony trespass of it all very quickly and sighs out the window. Just what she needs, an investigation of her squatter's rights one more time, one more reading of the conflicting Riparian Rights Codes, one more trip before a judge. Marge thinks of the awfulness of the ceremony of repeat offender. She had "repeat offender" stenciled on her file at the police station, almost like having a rattlesnake or a satanic dagger icon. She lived now in the day-to-day scavenging of bottle and can returns, seasonal work at the county fair, Saturday market booth for her elephant garlic, Chinese chives, and geranium starts.

Horchow security people appear upstream in white boats, boats like white gloves fingering the banks on both sides, probing inlets and pilings. Andrew jumps back from the window, but the Green Man and Marge continue to peer out at the river.

"I've got a friend," Marge says. "A river person too. Well, first he was a Presbyterian minister somewhere in Nevada. Then he was a lawyer. Or maybe it was the other way around. Doesn't matter. Anyway, now he's outboards – used outboards. Maybe he can suggest someone to defend you two."

"Or maybe salvation would be a better deal," pipes in the Green Man. "Probably cheaper."

"Well, either way, I suppose," Marge drawls as if this is a drawn-out joke making its shaggy way to a punch line. But she thinks she's going to have to bet twenty years of squatting rights on this one, this green one and that other one. She looks them both over again for signs of worth.

Andrew's instinct is to run and hide, skulk and flatten himself along walls, and then pounce into the bushes and be still. Not breathe. Make them find him. He's slumped in a chair out of sight of the authorities and vaguely calculating his rights as an employee who didn't know what kind of vandal he'd hooked up with. Who knew the Green Man would hop off the rafting lark and attack the major employer in the area? Who walks around thinking the person they're with will go berserk? On the other hand, who got onto a raft made of tires and bleach bottles disguised as an island and pushed off for adventure with a green person? Boredom, your honor. It was boredom made me do it. It was the slack economy coupled with a slow news day coupled with slow return mails. It's the pits, your honor. When nothing's happening you take whatever comes along, you know?

He slumps farther down in the chair.

The icy keel of boredom slipping through the waves. Wave after wave, all looking the same, and then there is the Green Man. He's green like a palm-covered shoal in the distance. He breaks up the horizon. He's a new possibility when Andrew had run out of possibilities.

Marge and Ben Brown seem to come to a pact of sorts. Both are impervious to the nervousness, the darted glances of Andrew. Marge pours more coffee. The Green Man lards it with sugar, three teaspoons, and then he looks up to see if it's okay to put in a fourth. Marge smiles and invites him to go crazy, life is short, sugar is sweet. He stirs and stirs until the black and white are one and leaves the spoon sticking out to siphon off the heat. The Green Man slurps his coffee. Marge laughs and pours hers out in a saucer and blows on it, then returns it to the cup.

Andrew watches them play their coffee-cool game while certainly the cops are closing in. Certainly they're all about to be cuffed and boxed and tossed around, these two miscreants and this one large lady harboring fugitives. All very legal it will be.

The rent-a-cops from Horchow are thinking about the same cuffing and boxing as they comb the bank for the perpetrators. There are six of them left from the original group of twelve that chased the Green Man down the bank and into the water, the first six into Horchow's two boats. By the time they got the motors running and out into the stream, the island had sunk low in the water like a comic opera set. It looked to be on the final sinking as it rounded the bend downriver and disappeared. By the time they motored to where the island should have been, it had disappeared and the two had escaped somewhere. The tangle of ropes and tires and bleach bottles in Marge's pilings said, Here! They're around somewhere. They scramble up the detritus caught under the pilings, creep around to Marge's back door by ducking under the window sills, and gather all six of them together to make the nab.

The criminals are nabbed.

There is a wad of bleach bottles in plastic netting caught in Marge's pilings bobbing just below the surface. This too is dragged up by the authorities as evidence.

Marge answers the door moose-style with a "Waddaya want?" But the Green Man pops out from behind her like a magic trick in all his greenness. And without a word he collects Andrew (not exactly hiding, just sort of flattened against the wall, blending in with the wood grain), and they go off in a Horchow tin van without saying a word.

Inside the van the Green Man says to Andrew, "Now don't tell them anything. Make them prove this by bringing out everything. We want them to answer questions about what was in the ponds by the river. Don't volunteer anything. Name, rank, and serial number," and he pats Andrew like a good soldier. We are off to the hoosegow, Andrew thinks. Slammed in the slammer. Ben stretches and his joints pop audibly. "I think I'm beginning to grow again," he says, looking off somewhere along the road toward the river.

II. The Horchow Affair and Affairs of the Heart

MARY WILLSON WAS CERTAIN THAT THE GREEN MAN WAS RIGHT. Not Mr. Right, necessarily, but she found herself wondering if the green went everywhere. Closer to home, she wondered to herself if Ben Brown and the Green Man had reconciled themselves. If they were the same or if Ben Brown had maintained a separate space within the Green Man. She had read about alienation and the permanent state of anxiety attributed to the modern condition. Her own return to East Leven was a conscious attempt to reassemble herself in the historical presence of her ancestors. Ben Brown having turned green somehow fit but at the same time didn't fit perfectly. There was discord and exception to the correspondence, and the longer she was around him the more important the exceptions seemed. How he didn't fit loomed and loomed. His greenness seemed like a wrapping around him that covered more than it revealed. But, in any case, it was through the greenness that she thought to get to the authentic Ben Brown. Mary thought she might like to take a chance here, having not had the inclination before. Somehow hooking up with a green person would be different in kind than hooking up for life with some guy like her stepfather, who had found her mother a convenient meal ticket.

Hooking up, aye, there's the rub. As an experienced teacher she could take her craft wherever she wanted. She had taught for the University of Maryland overseas programs for a while. Then a stint as an English as a Foreign Language instructor in Madrid, Spain. She had thought to try Trieste, where James Joyce had taught English, but she couldn't get a visa. Then back to the U.S., a few more reading courses, a counseling course, and then a masters degree, and then East Leven. The criteria in her search for the right place were: class size, flexible administration, physical beauty of the place (and not too hot), state school funding history, personnel policies, parent support programs, support staff salaries and benefits, recall and referendum. She never figured she'd end up back in the town of her peripatetic ancestors, the ever-unsatisfied Willsons. Her return to East Leven should have corresponded to the pioneer picnic, been heralded by a small parade, but the fact was she moved in by herself, had to spell her name repeatedly – "two ls" – in a town first assembled by her forebears.

Mary stirred the juice she had extracted and looked out the window into her backyard. The bird feeders were filled with thistle seed, suet, sunflower seeds. Juncos at the feeder, towhees on the ground, a downy woodpecker waiting his turn at the suet, one red-shafted flicker going off occasionally like a spike in the air – all's right with the world. And through the bushes drifted a blue cloud of cigar smoke from the neighbor, Mr. Andresson, who had retired a year before and took up cigars within weeks. The backyards were bound in bushes of laurel and forsythia and ivy hanging on the wooded fences. One kiwi plant lopped over the fence and offered quarter-sized fruit to the birds in Mary's yard.

Mr. Andresson had been an inspector for the city – building codes, fire codes, early on before the two had become two different departments, and finally what he had called "inspector of sewers." When the Green

Man had come to town, he had applied to the city, to Andresson's former department, for a building permit for his cabin near the river. That department had forwarded a copy of the request to Andresson as a courtesy because the building site was within one thousand feet of a sewer outlet. Ben Brown appeared in person, as suggested by the building permit people, to inform Andresson of his plans. The conversation had been short and mostly business until the end. Ben Brown had asked about how the storm sewer upstream from his cabin might affect him. Andresson, nearing retirement and frankly looking each day for something interesting to occupy himself, something he hadn't seen yet in thirty-five years of inspecting various things for the town of East Leven, said that East Leven had built storm drains for the future, storm drains for the five-hundred-year flood, drains big enough to row a boat through. "Water," he had pronounced, "was always the guiding principle when the town was established, and water continues to be part of every plan the town made. Did you know," he continued, "that the building site in question is well within the five-hundred-year flood plain and right on the edge of the one-hundred- year flood plain. Mr. Brown, you might just get wet there. And by wet I mean, swept away. Not overnight, you understand. You'll have plenty of warning. But the dams upstream in the mountains can only hold so much and then they let the water go. Have to, or they'd overflow and risk ripping out the whole thing. So we can't stop you from building there since it's zoned for building. But down there along the river, you take your chances with the big one, whenever it comes. Storm drains won't present you any difficulties since when the water comes, it'll get you first from the river."

Ben Brown thought he'd take his chances, if it were Okay with the city. Mr. Andresson started to say something and stopped. The Green Man said, "Go ahead. I know people have a lot of questions about being green. I don't mind."

Andresson stood and hitched up his pants. "Well, since you say you don't mind, I do have one question. Have you got any Norwegian blood in you?"

The Green Man looked across the desk and tried to read whether he was serious or not. "Maybe. I think my people always called it Scandinavian, though. Sort of generic Swedish, Norwegian, Danish. Nobody could remember exactly which. Can I ask you why?"

"Well, there's stories when I was a kid the Norwegian old folk used to tell that had something to do with green people or people who painted themselves green or something. I thought you might know. I'm coming up on retirement and thought I might have time to look up some of that stuff finally. Thought you might give me some leads, maybe where to look."

Ben Brown laughed and said he didn't realize there were Scandinavian versions of green people too. He knew of the English and Welsh versions. He was beginning to suspect that there were a lot more too. Green people seemed to be just below the skin almost everywhere. He figured he was just one of the only ones to have made it to the surface.

Mary caught Mr. Andresson one afternoon raking up under his birch tree. She had planned to discuss his new cigar habit with him ever since she had been sitting in her yard and had been engulfed in his smoke that hung in the windless evening like the aftermath of a forest fire.

She felt for a way to bring up the incursions without offending him. She smiled and thought of peaceful resolution. "I see you have taken up cigars since your retirement."

Mr. Andresson looked up, surprised since she had come up behind him. "Umm," he said and put up his rake at parade rest. He looked at Mary out of the corner of his eye as if he couldn't turn his head very far. "My wife hated 'em. I could only smoke a cigar fishing when she was alive. I'm still not sure if she really hated the cigars or she thought they'd kill me." He turned his head to follow his eyes and looked at her face. "I'm still not sure if I smoke 'em because I like the taste or if I'm working at following her." He wrinkled his face in what Mary took to be a smile.

"Well, I understand her point of view, Mr. Andresson. The smoke always seems to find my backyard, though I am sure sometimes it goes somewhere else. It comes right through the laurel without pausing."

Mr. Andresson leaned his rake against the birch cluster then took off his gloves and tucked them in his vest pocket. "Kind of like your cat, I suppose. She comes right through the bushes like smoke and worries the birds in my yard. I just cleaned up the carnage. I think she got a towhee.

Couldn't find any parts, just the pile of feathers. Did she bring it home for you? They'll do that sometimes, you know. Kind of like a present." He opened and closed his hands to work out the stiffness from being wrapped around the rake handle. "Cats are pretty much like smoke in that way. They go wherever it is they're going without asking much of anybody." He sniffed and wiped at the end of his nose.

Mary said, "Yes, I guess they do. The females are the worst, I'm afraid." She paused over her unaccustomed use of contractions. But she wanted to make Mr. Andresson comfortable. "A neutered male won't bother much with hunting if you get them early enough. Females though will keep hunting for years until they slow down. Mandy's not leaving the birds alone. I've tried a squirt gun, but it doesn't seem to get through to her just what she's doing that I disapprove of."

The stalemate hung in the air like cigar smoke on a windless afternoon. Cat. Smoke. Borders. Mr. Andresson scratched. Mary asked how he was liking retirement. He asked how things were going at school. He said he had seen her talking to Ben Brown downtown. Did she know him pretty well? Did she know him well enough to give him a message for him? She said she did.

"Tell him, about that little discussion we had a while ago, or a bunch of years or so now it would be. Well, just tell him that I found time to look up some more about what we were talking about. Tell him that they painted themselves green, those people. And red and yellow too, it turns out. There weren't any natural green ones that I could find. He'll remember our conversation, I think. Just say they painted themselves green."

He sniffed again and put his gloves back on. The trade-off was established: smoke for cat, even up. She said she'd take his message to Ben Brown.

Mary drank her juice and watched a cloud of particularly blue smoke come through the bushes, hesitate as if looking around, then proceed slowly in one piece across her yard looking around in her irises, her delphiniums, her statuesque euphorbia. Then it was gone.

The Green Man's coming had confused a number of the certainties she had entertained in her life. She liked living alone, and after seeing friends, or weekends at the coast, she relished coming back to her house, her cat, her flowers, and the indulgence of not having to share them with anyone. Toward the end of a three-day weekend, walking along the beach with two other teachers after a mini-retreat, someone remarked on the way the cloud slid across the setting sun and changed the colors in a halo around it. She had been thinking exactly that, but somehow the other person mentioning it diminished her own delight in it, the discovery and secrecy, thinking it privately and savoring the flavor of exclusive secret. Women's magazines mentioned the joy of having someone to share secrets with. Maybe she didn't qualify, then. She only knew that having it all to yourself felt better than saying, "Me too. I was just thinking that." With Ben Brown, "His Greenness," she had called him to herself but not yet to his face, it seemed there were so many odd and idiosyncratic moments that there was plenty to go around. If one private stolen observation didn't stay private, there were plenty coming, just wait. Together they had done the spit test to ascertain colorfastness of the green – slightly intimate; the match-up test where they held up leaves and color chips and magazine décor to look for a match and names for the green Ben Brown had – between deep heather and Scottish verdant – less intimate; the "ask me any question about turning green" and then turn about game – the most intimate of all. How'd you end up in East Leven? Were you married? Why weren't you married? What about your people? Where are they from?

Mary drank her juice and waited for another cloud of smoke to insinuate itself through her backyard. None came. But, like a handful of feathery marbles tossed into the air, twenty or so bushtits arrived as a flurry and settled on the suet like fleas. Then all at once on some incomprehensible signal they exploded into the air like shards and regrouped in a daphne bush. Mary watched them and wondered at their organization: what seemed like sheer natural terror that drove them into the air then also drove them to seek each other in the shelter of the bush. What eats one of us must contend with choosing among all of us, they seemed to say. The community of it. Mary longed for the anonymity of the flock, the wholeness of the endeavor. This was the root of her vegetarianism. By not eating things with faces, things with belly buttons, things that breathed the same air, she joined all these things without having their corpses laid up in her refrigerator. She allowed them their houses and she could be alone in hers. And the Green Man, though he ate all those things, seemed so vegetally connected that Mary, private Mary, independent Mary, found him irresistibly complicated and attractive.

Mary Willson, sweet vegetable Mary, filled her glass carefully and set it on the counter.

The Willsons had lived in the valley since 1838, when the first Willson had come with a group of missionaries. That Willson had left again within a year, but he returned to Missouri with tales of grass as high as the stirrups of a man on horseback. The Indians burned the valley every fall in order to keep open grassland for hunting, and the Willson tales included the smell of burnt grass though he had not stayed through the fall to see the burning and the smell of burnt grass, never lingered into spring since the winter rains scoured the valley clean. Willson told of water everywhere, one creek after another scratching down out of the mountains toward the big river, running bright, fresh, cold all summer. A person would have to do nothing more than plunk himself down on one of those creeks and get into the business of orchards or wheat or cattle. A handful of apple and pear starts and a man would be full time into fruit in no time. Willson told his stories over and over to anyone who would listen in Missouri. More Willsons came after him, but he never made the trip again. When asked why not, the family lore went, he said he had gone and seen what there was to see, and he preferred his farming close to the markets.

And it was markets that were the main problems for the first settlers; they only had each other to trade with, and they all had an excess of the same crops. Eventually wool and flax took over and being nonfragile, these stood the trip back east to the states better than foodstuffs. Mary Willson, fifth generation of Willsons in the valley, was the daughter of a son of a son of a son of a flax trader who would load his wagons with flax fiber he'd bargained for and haul repeated loads the sixty miles to Portland's port. Down the skid road where the logs were skidded to the water, through the mud, his horses with feet like dinner plates, and to the dock where he'd find out what his flax was worth today. And so the Willsons found themselves generation after generation in thrall to market prices. When prices were up, the Willsons cracked into Oregon's middle class, the pride of the Northwest, a solid middle class that loved summer picnics and politics. But during the wild ride of the 1890s, the Willson family found itself strapped to the saddle of an incomprehensible market headed up then down then up again, all the while seeing the dirt floor coming sooner or later. Mary's great-grandfather, living in a time when a man could get away with a front name of Rex, was the one who took a mouthful of dirt in 1897. East Leven by attrition became a scratch mark on the river, a dent in the bank where vegetable gardens from an unusually warm summer bore enough so most families could do without money. But that was the last time until the Great Depression at its wintry depth when currency was the least used option for exchanging the fruits of labor. The valley had never become the pear and apple haven of early promise. Instead plums and filberts and the stinky processing of inedible flax hung in the air over the river like a harbinger of Horchow to come. Many children raised in the 1890s would never eat another plum or prune or very nearly anything purple for the rest of their lives from facing day after interminable day on plum concoctions made from the endless bounty of endless plum trees. The plum tree had become the sustainer of those Willsons too practiced in the ways of East Leven to flee with others back to the Midwest. The Willsons hunkered down. Mary came of stock that had defined themselves as permanent residents of the valley. They had had one great move in them, and that had been the westering, until the 1930s when for all different economic reasons, all the Willsons migrated elsewhere, leaving behind only the soil-enriching Willsons of the Bye Bye cemetery.

Mary Willson found herself for four years at the University of Oregon. Then her wandering teaching, and finally the return to East Leven, which gave her some sense of attachment even if it was the abstraction of visiting the graves of her forebears.

The coming of the Green Man had felt like a disturbance in the fundament, in the bedrock under East Leven, as if something essential were slipping in the very structure of things. Why didn't he go somewhere he wouldn't disturb things so much? Europe. Sweden! In Sweden they accepted everybody. Why come here and disturb everyone? But after a time Mary considered Ben Brown, like the flower boxes Conroy Burbank introduced downtown, perfectly inevitable and even essential to her town. Finally she introduced herself to Ben Brown on the street, and eventually for her, the Green Man, green people, fit into the landscape like the ravines that fed the river and the river itself.

Mary ran into Ben occasionally. Then more often. Then she began to calculate, broadly at first, then more precisely, where he might be at any particular time in town. The Green Man had already established his rounds, his walks to the bakery, past the bar and the benches downtown, along the ravine, past the battlefield monuments to the sump pump wars, then along the park path lined with Oregon grape and salal. It felt good to stretch his muscles toward the end, the odd, painless popping and crackling going on in his joints, picking up speed through the park.

Mary had reading to teach, fifth graders to guide toward oneness with the word, its ease and their uneasiness. Out of the schoolroom window she had seen Ben Brown pass in his green work clothes, his elemental skin, toward downtown. She remembered that the crocuses had just appeared as if he had sprouted them as he walked along past her windows. They weren't up yesterday, that she could remember, anyway. Some of the children pointed him out, but most of the students had grown so used to him by now that they didn't bother. His bite, he'll turn you green, don't let him touch you – all these remained much more plausible in the evening light when shadows crossed his skin and it was hard to make out his face clearly. Walking along like this in daylight past the school, on the other side of the window glass, he seemed as safe as the sheriff.

Mary watched him pass. What he was like, that's something like these reading problems: first you work hard to decode, then you smooth out the code, and then slowly you understand, really understand. Mary used reading – the work of reading – as an infallible metaphor for how the world worked. We learn to pick up the world's hieroglyphs, collect them, look for patterns and repetitions, then string them together until they mean something, if only temporarily. She believed in the working of the word.

AS THE HORCHOW AUTHORITIES DISAPPEARED DURING THE island's short journey, the birds appeared – the kingfishers. It is a stretch of river green and cool like a wallow of willows and cottonwoods, and the birds chitter on perches over the water in a line far downstream. And then something in the island's passing breaks the mold of things in general and the regularness of the world leaks out, leaving the other.

The birds appear all at once – like blue darts hissing into the water all around, impossible and beautiful, so that when Andrew and Ben look up they see blue streaks like Horchow uniforms broken into droplets and raining down. The birds miss the island sometimes by inches as it moves downstream among them, then pop to the surface, each successfully pinching a silver jewel flapping in the sun, and Ben and Andrew, mouths open, pass among them astounded. There are bright blue feathers in the air – thick air, with bird and feather traveling at different speeds, the one lazy and unhurried, the other urgent in a straight line into the water.

At first it is exactly like watching the feather float and the bird zing through the air, as if one were somehow wrong and the other right, but they can't tell which one to watch, which one to fix on, so they look at one then the other in turns like watching wave then trough then wave, one thing completely integrated with the other.

Andrew crouches on the island, watching the birds with his mouth open, the blue colossal rain. The rain of birds is less marvelous itself than just another extension of marvels he'd been experiencing since connecting with a man who had turned green. A story. The extraordinary kingfishers are his summer shower. He expected nothing less. He maybe expected Eve.

They both get instead, Marge, at the end of the raft trip, at the end of slow melting, dissolution, their dunking in the green river with the brown, deadly stripe, the arrest. They are thrown into the slammer, green person and skinny kid, two marvels stripped away from the general marvelousness by the authorities of the State of Oregon. Marge is the instrument of their salvation, legally speaking, but she was not Eve, the green Eve waiting to start the world again.

SEVEN O'CLOCK, JULY 23, 1960S, SOMEWHERE. THE GREEN MAN is still a twinkle in the eye of the cosmos. But East Leven is getting ready for him.

It is hot, it's been hot, it will be hot. Never in the history of record keeping has it rained on this day in this place. The onshore flow crept up the slopes of the coast range and slipped over into the valley, keeping the morning temperatures in the seventies with lyric little clouds concocting themselves on the downward slope of the mountains and then getting zapped by the valley heat. Over and over this ritual weather made a cloud, fried a cloud. One down-slope Christmas tree farmer piled wet slash from a heap that had been sitting on a seep spring all summer and hadn't dried out. When the farmer hooked a cable from his tractor to the pile and pulled it to a dry spot, he discovered an explosion of monkey flower in the shade generated by the pile. He tried to light the pile by starting a small fire with pitchy fir sticks, but produced only elegant blue smoke that stood straight up into the sky toward the tiny clouds that bloomed and died overhead. Then the fire went out with a hiss.

Next came kerosene. He reassembled the pitch sticks, added some slab wood, let the kerosene soak in, and fired it. While the kerosene lasted, while the dry wood lasted, the fire prospered and the farmer walked away to weed his pointy crop with chemical sprays. An hour later he noticed the satisfying smoke had stopped. The fire was out again having just burned a hole in the soggy pile. His ten-year-old son was playing at a friend's house down the road, his wife was at the store. Both had been cautioned against using gasoline to start fires. He looked around to see who else might witness this lapse of good sense and finding no one, doused the entire pile with several gallons of gasoline that was growing old from long-time storage. He soaked a length of old rope in gas to make a long enough fuse so that he might be able to walk away with eyebrows and hand hair intact. And he lit it.

The heat was immediate and cooked the moisture into a small mushroom-shaped cloud so that from the distance of East Leven it looked like someone had set off a small nuclear device to clear stumps in the foothills. As the wet fire burned, the moisture rose hot and high above the fire until it cooled and found one of the forming and disappearing clouds. Just as the cloud was to be beheaded by the valley heat, it received a blast of wetness from the Christmas tree farm, and instead of returning to the blue, bloomed into a twice-made cloud that happened to be in the way of another cloud just cresting the mountains with its load of pacific wet.

The three clouds connived to be in the way of a fourth. And the four of them together stayed the valley heat and moved toward town. Crazy Leo was alone in the field near the highway, lugging his bag of hubcaps and parts of hubcaps. He was intent on hillocks of grass that might have grown over a stray hubcap, maybe a Buick hubcap. It began to rain seemingly out of the blue sky, but over his shoulder was the invented cloud, the lone survivor of any July 23 on record. The rain fell on Crazy Leo. It fell across the field where the low Jenkins sat in his weed-filled side yard drinking beer, down the street stippling the asphalt with drops of rain every two inches, and then through Main Street and across Furher, where the assembled bench pirates were just switching sides of the street to get out of the sun. There were plenty of witnesses who felt the rain, saw it spot cement and asphalt and bald head and T-shirt. The official weather station was on top of the old Masonic temple just off the park, and the rain never got there, running out at the edge of the park with a few splats in the dust around the yellow swings. Not one drop was officially recorded, and so the record of rainfall for that day remained 0.0 inches. But everyone knew that the string had been broken by some miraculous event that, as the cloud exhausted itself and became finally invisible, seemed to generate rain from nowhere, everywhere. In less enlightened times there would have been soothsaying, portend reading, prophesying. In East Leven it would take years more to produce the Green Man, but his way had been prepared.

"I'll be damned. Rain without clouds and only 20% humidity."

"The damnedest thing."

There was speculation that it wasn't actually rain at all.

"The big airplanes will flush their toilet holding tanks, you know."

Several people who had been hit with drops brushed at their heads and shoulders. One man smelled his hand afterward.

"I think they do something to it chemically before they dump it. It's not supposed to reach the ground, I think, like it breaks into such fine drops that it just gets absorbed into the air."

Parties formed. Airplane error. Some other explanation.

"What about, what about some kind of emission from Horchow? There's always something coming out the stack. Maybe they had a burst of something wet and it scattered out." A third party formed.

"I think it was rain." An essentialist chimed in. "I think we just had our first rain ever on July 23. It felt like rain, fell like rain," and with a nod to the hand smeller, "and it smelled like rain. I'm going with rain on this one."

Eventually, rain won out over more complicated theories. But, finally, it was not just rain but "the July 23 rain," said with a knowing rise to the eyebrow that indicated the special contrivance of the event. Two flat tires at once on a car might be dismissed as a July 23 event. Zucchinis grown together to form a V as big as a riding toy – July 23 at work again.

THE HORCHOW AFFAIR BECAME A BIG DEAL IN REAL LIFE. ALL around the Green Man there's hot news: Horchow is just one of the great chemical offenders on the river. It seems there are stored wastes all along the banks, some seeping, some waiting to seep. The politicos have picked this up and see that it's time to run some of these guys in before the next election, and the green person has become a handy symbol, though a confusing one, for the forces of truth and rightness this year.

The newspaper explained him at length. Why did he have to let the chemical plague loose, killing fish and wildlife? Why didn't he just denounce Horchow for storing wastes too close to the river if he knew about the ponds and their contents? How did he know about the ponds if he hadn't worked for Horchow? – the disgruntled employee theory. Or was he in the pay of Horchow's enemies? And by the way, how many jobs would this cost if Horchow had to shut down or move? Was he just some vagrant, some nether hippie? Destroying private property, committing felonious assault on the polis and the rights of all citizens to pursue a profit?

The Green Man seemed to have some vision that had very little to do with the world as Andrew was experiencing it – the political world, the world of budgets and getting and spending. He talked about the ten thousand things of the Chinese. A blue-haired lady in a perfume shop might be one of those ten thousand, some way to get at the vision of the whole, the one that swallowed up the ten thousand.

Andrew had had the strong urge to get stoned before the trial, just to get a little distance on what was happening, and given the crew in the jail cell overnight, getting stoned for the trial wouldn't be a supply and demand problem. One fellow prisoner plunked down on Andrew's right, with the Green Man on his left – this guy from a nineteenth-century Russian novel and called the "titular clerk," the mousy guy with the glance that always comes out of the top of his glasses, always trying to please and clearly for some ulterior motive, his fingers stained with ink, his nose always itching, him always scratching it backhanded.

The guy offers Andrew one kind of chemical after another as fast as his no-lipped mouth can move, and Andrew figures he's the in-house connection. But something feels wrong about all this to Andrew. The guy's five o'clock shadow is out of a Bogart movie, a production number cultivated hair by hair in makeup just for this scene. He's got to be a character actor hired for this by some agency, some form of authority.

Andrew listens to this peddler of chemicals, this acolyte of Saint Tim Leary, who would have him be in touch with his brain stem and the successive layers of consciousness waiting there. Andrew says nothing to all this lipless speaking, this lizard talk, which goes on and on and only requires the occasional nod, the wordless eyebrow raised in amazement, in agreement, in assent. Andrew has confidence that this confidence man will become what he is eventually, will tire of all this gesture and selling and step out of his costume, peel it off like a jumpsuit fitted with glasses and vest and buttons.

Suddenly the Green Man is talking across Andrew's face to the titular clerk. "Got anything from the human endocrine system? That's where the real stuff is. Though renal cortex is always nice too. Maybe some pituitary? How about a nice pineal body? You can rub those suckers right in the corner of your eye, shove 'em up under your eyelids to get 'em in your bloodstream. I hear the pineals – maybe you got 'em under the name of epiphysis? – are good from babies. Real active." And on and on he goes, shutting down the Russian novel character completely, who fiddles with his glasses anxiously, waiting at first for a way to get back into the word stream, then stops from trying to get in and waits out the barrage while the Green Man runs through *Gray's Anatomy* on the endocrine system. He's getting off now into certain arcane versions of reptilian systems, talking a green Hunter S. Thompson character streak and some contentions about the layered brain and all the history of the world being available through the chemistry of the layers, and then Andrew's mind begins to wander as he watches the Green Man's eyes glow in the shadow.

And then as suddenly as he started, the Green Man stops talking, holds his hands up to the titular clerk, palms out as if the clerk were a fire to warm hands on, and moves his green hands up and down the fire to find the hottest spot.

"You're from Horchow, aren't you? You've been in the Horchow plant not long ago." And then the Green Man adds his green humor to all this, humor that rings in as that of a twelve-year-old to Andrew.

"You're from Horchow, aren't you? You've been in the Horchow plant not long ago." Then a pause. "And if you work for Horchow, then you must be a Horchow whore." Pause again. "And if you sit down to eat, you'd be eating your Horchow whore chow. And if you drink white lightning with your dinner, you'd be drinking Horchow whore chow hooch. And if…"

The titular clerk from the Russian novel moves away to the opposite side of the holding cell. Andrew asks how the Green Man is sure about their new acquaintance being from Horchow, and he reports that he can feel the heat on him as if the clerk had been dipped in one of the holding ponds. Andrew feels the rising, serious plot against them both, and it's authored by Horchow. Andrew squirms on the bench and brings his hands together across his chest as if to shield his vital organs. The Green Man studies the Horchow whore like a curiosity in a junk show, his greenness nearly popping from the surface of his skin and threatening to surround the man like ether.

PIRATES: BEN BROWN, AFTER TURNING GREEN, FOUND HIMSELF longing for the days when they wore eye patches, said "Arrrgh, matey," had bright macaws dug in on a shoulder. The story of being green includes pirates.

Apparently, the fact of being green, this chlorophyll approximation, is a valuable commodity. The first offer came from a carny. He wanted a series of tests first to see if the green was really green, if the green was really everywhere, and then he proposed a few tattoos just to set things off, to guarantee that folks were startled.

The pirates kept coming in all different forms and the Green Man, not recognizing them, was thinking: So I could make a fine living being green; this variation on a theme, this greenness, seems to stand for money in one line of thinking. My green ass is worth greenbacks! They'd buy and sell me, rent me out and cut me in.

But this is real green, he told them. This is the real thing, not some production number in Las Vegas. I'm the first of the series, the original, the only living, the singular.

The most interesting offer came from a small circus on the edge of bankruptcy with nothing to lose but a hundred pounds of sequins and the elephant that walked with a limp. The owner – the chief shareholder – opened his books and offered Ben a 51% share of the whole works. He could use his greenness to buy tents and hay bales and clowns and a modest debt. And he was assured that with the Green Man as the main attraction, the whole thing would turn around financially within weeks, and he could mine his own gold from there. He had the necessary cigar stub sticking out of his face like a beak; the suspenders; the baggy, sweaty shirt that used to be white a number of years ago but now possessed an internal yellow glow; the one-eye-bigger-than-the-other squint. Perfect. He was the rounded-off stereotype, so Ben had to believe everything he said. His dog's name, his dog about the size of his double fists and with a lock of hair in its eyes, his dog's name was Rags!

So the friendly Charles Burley says to Ben across his squint, across his stub of a cigar, he says: "You see, son, your accident can become your fortune. And, of course, you'll be right at home here with people, if you'll pardon the metaphor, greener than even yourself. Ladies with beards, folks whose gender has never been clear even to themselves, little people littler than people are, big people bigger than it's easy to be. You'll find everyone completely at ease with you from the start." Here he lowered his voice. "You've probably noticed how the public is startled by your greenness, I dare say. They'll never be less startled than they are now. That's how a circus stays in business – being startling.

"And if we had a little cash flow we could have the elephant's front foot fixed. It's got a crack in it growing sorer every day. She has to be anæsthetized to take care of it properly. Very expensive in elephants." All the while Mr. Burley waved a blue work bandanna around to emphasize his points, and Rags sat with his ears up, watching the bandanna as if a bird would fly out.

The Green Man got an offer from CBS, too, for straight money, a number of appearances. No elephant, he thought. What is this? No Rags? Ben called their toll-free number and said no thanks.

He was tempted by Mr. Burley's circus, but his visit to see what he'd be getting was like a visit to a leaky snake pit.

The electric lines drooped everywhere with unfrosted bulbs like white hot spikes ready to fall from the circus tent and pierce his brain from above. Electricity ran down the tent poles and pooled in the sawdust. The generator that electrified the popcorn machines growled in a corner, full of electricity like hot grease ready to explode out of a pan. Ben walked beneath a grid of singing hot wires, craning his neck to keep track of where they would fall with their hot spikes, and there, buried in the sawdust were 220 volt cables, anacondas fat with amperes.

His shirt was soaked with sweat. He lifted his foot high over a 220 line and turned his face away from the temporary service box where they'd sloppily tapped into the city electricity. He felt like he was walking out onto a schematic, a nightmare plan of his own nervous system.

The elephant, the elephant, he said to Mr. Burley. The elephant to cool off.

Rags barked twice as if a signal to someone, maybe to inflate the elephant, to bring in the clowns. Ben had come to the circus on a lark, to not be alone with his greenness, and now he felt a circus trap closing. He sweated. Tucked under a tent flap around the corner, with her face in a stack of hay, was the great cool elephant. Ben was so compromised, so zapped by the careless use of electricity, the unshielded, bare-wire use of the yellow-white stuff running out that he could swear he heard the elephant's name was Sophie, and he saw SOPHIE written up somewhere in gold on burgundy velvet. Her name can't be Sophie; her name has to be Sophie. She had her right front foot lifted slightly and blue-green antiseptic glistened in a fissure between her toes. But Sophie felt cool.

The Green Man leaned against Sophie's side, great gray Indian side in the half dark of her lean-to. She was quiet, chewing, so large she didn't need to push back as he collapsed against her and slid down to rest against a cool rear leg.

Burley was fanning him with a program for the night's show. Sophie stirred and turned to look at Ben. He was much taken by how far her heavy neck would allow her head to come around toward the rear. He would have signed the papers to buy the circus if Sophie had asked.

In came a clown dressed as a pirate – eye patch, wooden leg, stuffed parrot in orange day-glow, a blue beard. Ben felt himself falling again, but he couldn't have been falling since he was still sitting in the hay leaning against the resistant Sophie.

He was saved by the pirate and by Sophie. The pirate had a lisp and a high squeaky voice, a cartoon voice, a high-speed voice in a low-speed world. Something like this: "Mithter Burley, they thed I had to wear thith leg for the whole sthick tonight. I thed it hurths too much to wear it that long …" There was a whine of machinery to the voice too, something needing lubrication. But the costume with this voice coming out of it was so real in all the unrealness around Ben – the leaky electricity, Mr. B, the temptation to sell his greenness – it was what he'd always suspected pirates had to sound like. And then Sophie farted.

A great organic breaking of wind as if she'd stored up the evening breezes along the Ganges and mixed them with alfalfa hay from the new world for a perfect perfuming of life itself. Ben was still leaning against her leg and heard the rumble begin at his back, rise up through his neck taking with it his shivery tingles of electric overdose for the day, and then rise tube by tube in Sophie's great moist insides where the wind adjusted itself with a rumble and broke out to silence the cartoon pirate and the evening breeze. Sophie turned one wet eye on them with a sway of her head as if to see what she had wrought. Next she swung her head back into the shadows and commenced chewing again.

Saved. All his resolve not to really buy a circus had returned. His loneliness was broken with Sophie's wind. He left Mr. Burley and the pirate discussing a wooden leg.

NBC called the hospital when they found out about his being green and apparently asked a number of questions about the shade of green, tonal qualities, brightness, zonal scale. The hospital staff handled the call. NBC never called back. Burley either.

Ben decided that the green part of him was what attracted the pirates. After the circus, NBC, ABC, he thought he had dealt with the obvious range of offers. But there were other offers, other pirates he had no notion about.

First there were the offers of women who simply wanted to sleep with someone who was really green. These ranged from the "If-you-can-prove-that-you're-really-green-I'll-fuck-your-ears-off" offers to the "I-want-to-have-a-mint-green-child-with-you" to the more gently curious about what "it" looks like when it's green. None of this was too astounding since Ben had read the tabloids that document the versions and perversions not necessarily of human behavior but of what writers could conceive of people doing.

It took Ben longer than you would think to realize he was growing younger. He wasn't the incredible shrinking man of the movies, no daily effects, no growing smaller at all in fact. What was it, this notion that he was growing younger on the inside but staying a fresh green on the outside like a salad in the refrigerator?

At first it was singing. The sound was wafting in and out somewhere over there, something remembered and then quickly forgotten and only the feeling that something was there and then it wasn't. Or maybe it was like light. A lighting up from the inside of all the affairs of the brain. Somehow no one thing itself seemed as important as it was before. He cared more about things in general and less about any given thing. He felt as if he wanted to play.

The island was his playing; he needed no reasons to give himself to work and think about ways to make the island bigger. When he was awake, he was thinking about it completely: what he needed to buy, what he could salvage in the way of bleach bottles, tires, cables, forms, and small plants. The light system, the helper.

And when Ben became sure he was growing younger it was because he felt like delicious meat. He was walking near the river and the heat of the sun was gone, the wind coming up off the water and ruffling his hair, caressing his greenness, touching him on purpose as if from some finger of Now. He realized that the pleasantness was missing some adult notion about "This is nice but can't last. Why can't it last?" The wind only was and he felt as if he were being tasted by the wind, savored and rolled over and over without end. This sensation was more remembered than discovered.

And the other clue, again at first like some sound far away that he slowly discovered was music, was that he found himself becoming more and more shy, and each time he had to talk to someone, it was as if he had to wait a second, two seconds, then later even more, until he could arrive from far away where he'd gone to be with himself, and then as soon as he had said his say, he'd go back immediately.

And everything smelled knife-edge clear and whole.

Brain sand was gone.

There were a number of things disconcerting about growing younger, the most important of which came to be: What is the end of growing younger? We know the end of growing older, a well-documented cooling off toward death. But how about a warming up, a taking off of sweaters?

WHILE WALKING THE STREETS OF EAST LEVEN WITH THE CREW from the shacks down along the river with the hatching of the whole green-and-skinny-guy plot to unleash on the court, Andrew and the others looked around and the green guy was nowhere.

They were about a dozen river denizens, including Jake, Marge and her sweaters, and assorted other shack people who are generally pissed off at Horchow for storing up ponds of ugliness next to their river.

They split up to go look for the star of the trial. Andrew backtracked toward the jail but they had been walking for almost twenty minutes, and he could be anywhere. Andrew found him first and answered for himself Marge's question about the keeper and the kept. I'm the keeper, he thought, and he is the kept.

He was with a bunch of young kids who were either colorblind or hadn't noticed that he was green. They were on an embankment along the river, down on hands and knees around a sewer grate fishing for something with a string and didn't notice Andrew when he came up. Andrew paused at this scene because it seemed to be out of yet another movie, or Saturday morning TV.

Andrew arrived on the sewer grate scene, and stayed back and out of sight to see what had drawn the Green Man here. The kids were about ten or twelve years old, the perfect age for adventure of this sort but not yet scared off by all the green lore. The Green Man had begun to carry various kinds of tackle with him: string, hooks, pocketknife, wire, found nuts and bolts. Andrew found just walking with him difficult because he was always looking at the ground in search of what? What he found: golf balls! – an incredible number of golf balls in city and country as if the world were filling up with golf balls in some subversive way, and it was the Green Man's job to find them: He found golf balls and squirreled them away in his J.C. Penney pockets. Who's hitting these golf balls into the world and from what tee, wondered Andrew?

The Green Man had his tackle involved in this sewer-fishing project. Hand over hand he was gingerly bringing up something from the sad sewer while the kids waited, entranced. Pretty soon, there was a general sigh, and the Green Man looked apologetically at his crew and lowered the line again. The group concentration began again as if whatever was being raised depended on the collective power of concentration and squint-eyed effort. Andrew leaned over, trying to see the stakes in this project. The prize was white and coming up to the grate slowly. The Green Man paused and waited for it to swing around to fit through the slots, then jerked up and a Frisbee leaped out of the sewer. There were cheers and some clapping, much nodding, and the chattery beginning of replays of the hard parts, how many times it was dropped, how it fit through the grates.

The green guy was congratulated with pattings and cheers, and the Frisbee owner lifted his prize with a piece of newspaper and looked for water to wash it off. The Green Man spoke Andrew's name without turning to look.

"We've just rescued the twentieth century from the nineteenth," he said.

A kid came up and asked: "Hey, do you know you're green?" and the Green Man answered that he certainly did know, but it's Okay. The kid made one swipe with a dirty finger along the Green Man's forearm and left satisfied.

Andrew saw his green friend straightening out and brushing off, stretching too as if he'd been fishing for quite a while. The kids were off on the grass celebrating the liberation of the Frisbee. It's found, he's found.

This is beginning to feel like a job, Andrew thought, and I still haven't seen a paycheck. They walked back to find the rest of the search party, and Andrew mentioned the fact of money to his employer. He looked at Andrew, used Andrew up with the look, and when he was ready answered that Andrew would have an installment as soon as they got near a bank. And how much would he need then? Andrew mentioned a figure in keeping with a keeper's keep, and the Green Man nodded.

Andrew planned to continue the conversational gambit of money, but the Green Man seemed overcome with the notion of a Frisbee: What did it look like when it's flying? What flies like that? Anything? Does Andrew remember seeing his first Frisbee? Was he stunned? Amazed? Or had this thing always existed in our minds and did we just recognize it when we saw it for the first time? Why does it seem like a game even though there's no game in the Frisbee itself?

Someone hauled them back up the river that night to where the two-day whirl began, and they got what the Green Man called the proletarian warning. There was a knife in the door of his cabin, a kitchen knife with a wooden handle, stuck through a cartoon message: TOO MANY JOBS TIED UP IN THAT COMPANY. LEAVE IT ALONE NOW. There was a drawing of a dead guy in some grass, or maybe it was only a pile of clothes or dead flowers. Andrew took it as a serious warning. The Green Man puzzled long over the drawing, trying to see what was there.

"Now these guys," he announced, pointing to some low rhododendrons, "If they get too much light or too little, they won't produce the kinds of toxins they need to keep off the strawberry weevils. And at night the weevils come out of the ground and up the trunk in rows like marching armies and munch the leaves into lace. You can actually hear them chewing if you lie here near the trunk at night, and I did once and watched them march up the trunk with the moonlight on them. *Hump, flat, hump, flat. Hump flat.* They traveled blind and white, sniffing the wind for the weak leaves above, I suppose. I guess, anyway." Andrew watched the Green Man's hands fly around making the lying down, the marching, the chewing.

The Green Man stood straight and felt the rhody leaf while going on about the toxins. Stroked the leaf, pulled it between his fingers, and then reached over to pet an azalea as if it were a cocker spaniel horning in on the affection he's showing for his Great Dane.

"A healthy rhody will poison its own invaders." The leaf was wet. The world was deliciously wet, washed off without a real rain having fallen. They stood outside his cabin washed off too: the impending trial was washed away and the Horchow whore melted for the time being as if the rain had cleaned away layers that built up around them recently. They stood in the wet and green, listening to the river. "When you spray a rhody," he continued, "with say malathion, you kill the weevil for a while but the plant doesn't get stronger and the weevil just waits somewhere for the malathion to age and weaken and then the weevil comes back and makes lace of the leaves again because the leaf-toxins still haven't built up. Now if you fertilize, mulch with compost, cut back the weak wood to the strong wood, move it to more sun if that what's required, more shade if that's the problem, soon the weevils disappear because the plant has become strong and the leaves toxic and bitter again."

It was early May, and the leaves began to drip, forming a kind of bass note under the fir trees, a bass note for the river bird chatter, the click and *tank-atunk-tunk* the river made as it sucked on its teeth. The Green Man was silent for a long stretch and then without transition, he was talking about shields, escutcheons. Andrew's mind is on the knife.

"There is a twelfth-century town in Spain, Pedraza, and nearly every house has its escutcheon cemented in over the door to remind everyone, including the owners, that there is a responsibility not to be forgotten: that fathers had owed fathers, and favors offered and accepted passed on generations of debts, and mothers were the blood underpinning it all, and cousins bound lions to eagles to serpents to castles to towers to portals paraded across the escutcheons." He paused as if he'd been speaking a long time, wiped at a wet leaf. "The terrible responsibility of it all, I remember. Who will carry the Virgin Mary in next year's procession? The world did not begin yesterday, and you came to life with many strings running off in many directions. If the well fails, whose family knows about finding the source again, clearing the waters?"

Andrew couldn't wait any longer to find out what the Green Man had been doing in Spain. So he asked. The Green Man said that he'd been trying out his greenness on the world and launched again into his twelfth-century village.

"Even the houses are one continuous line, wall depending on wall. And each day in front of each, someone comes out and mops the dust from the cobbled walk and splashes bleach around to scare away germs but mops only far enough to encourage her neighbor to do the same, to carry out the same ritual beneath the escutcheons that look down and wag all those symbols at the people of the village: 'Hurry up,' the crests urge. 'Clean up. Another generation is coming soon. Just over there. Here they come. Are you ready? They'll be hungry; feed them! They'll want your rooms – grow old and die. Clean off the walk. Here they come. Have you the names ready? The sheets clean? The baptismal font full to overflowing?'" His hands flew up and formed walls and shields.

"I stayed there for two weeks, watching the people and the escutcheons, the sidewalks wet each morning. I ate in a local restaurant whatever they had each day. They called me 'the stranger.' Not 'the green stranger.' Just 'the stranger,' the same as they called everyone who came from somewhere else. It seemed no worse to be green than to be from Madrid or

Barcelona. And no better. The circle was closed between the escutcheons, the walks fresh with bleach, the local nose that found its way onto a large number of local faces and was reported to have come from the hidalgo centuries ago who had the appetites of Pan. We were all strangers who were outside the circle."

The rain went on, the Green Man went on, and Andrew waited for the two tales – the rhododendrons and the twelfth-century village – waited for them to come together. All this must be connected somehow, Andrew thought. Everything will eventually make sense. Just wait.

And so Andrew waited for the Green Man in the rain that wasn't really a rain yet. He noticed for the first time the rhododendron he still fondled as he talked; it was full of buds with cracks of scarlet like neon lights against the green leaves; there was clearly something living in there wanting to get out. Andrew pulled his hand back as if it might bite him, as if there might be knives in there too.

The green adventure. Andrew stood waiting for the rest of the information.

There is the threat of a kitchen knife in the door of the Green Man's cabin. He seems to think the note and knife are not worth worrying about but that rhododendrons, azaleas, two varieties of laurel are. Andrew is less taken with the plants, although he begins to see the green point. He sees the point of being good to plants, being good to yourself – something like that.

Andrew had the feeling early on that someone was making a movie out of all this, and somehow he was being paid out of the edge of the gross to keep the green star punctual, to keep things chugging along. But there was also the feeling that another camera was turned on and aimed at the whole comings and goings here, and the main chemical event, the trial, even the celebration dinner were all being recorded by cameras without film packs; the only real film was in the camera he couldn't see, the one catching all this far and near. Andrew wanted to write down what he remembered the Green Man had said with a hooky Irish accent or the Chinese thing he always seemed to be affecting or the comic book sounds. As if the silly-dream troll had visited him and said, Okay kid, what you get from all this is only what you don't expect; expect anything at all and that's what you're not getting.

Andrew went back to his own house.

THE TRIAL IS PART CIRCUS, PART PRANK, PART LATE 1960S guerrilla theater.

It occurs to Andrew again that he has found himself smack in the center of the Green Man's movie without having auditioned, without a screen test, without consent, if you don't count stepping off onto the island that became a raft. An excellent adventure. There could be many tales to tell, tales superior to rocking the Green Man because there he was, talking right to you, hopping around the island and the Horchow bank. Then Marge, harder to corroborate, then Jake, the lawyer/priest/outboard repairman, splendidly everything. But Andrew feels uneasy about refusing his parents' offer of a "real" lawyer, a family friend with a strong record of defense, a man known in East Leven legal circles, who lunched with judges and police chiefs and civic luminaries.

John and Margaret James found their only son an accessory to felony trespass and mischief. He was driving the getaway island. John felt his job as public relations man for the state was obliquely under attack by association. Horchow had had some problems with the State Department of Environmental Quality because waste solvents routinely dumped in a pit in the yard had reputedly leached into the river. Nothing proved, just that there had appeared downstream some of the chemicals from the solvents and Horchow was a "likely source," the report said. They had relined the pits to let the solvents evaporate but admitted no guilt. Still, sometimes in heavy winter rains the pits filled, though they never ran over according to Horchow records; once they spilled into the dirt. And now there was his son mixed up in this clumsy public-relations monster that could turn on Horchow and then come tumbling toward everyone, where he would have to field the inquiries, maybe even with time, the accusations and demands for public responsibility. He had seen it happen before. The public remembering, like wet snow, clung to the business of East Leven, and now this Green Man caper with his son sent the hairs on John James's neck erect.

Margaret James was a young girl when Anne Doucette sacrificed her sweet neck for the young people of East Leven. With Margaret's dark-haired beauty she never needed rail-walking to gain attention, and she floated through grade school and junior high and high school then into the arms of John under the protection of the redeeming ghost of Anne Doucette. Her marriage was blessed and white; her son, Andrew, was a pearl of singular price. This trial and two parking tickets (paid within twenty-four hours) were the whole of her encounters with the forces of law and order. In what Jake had called the "friends pew," she waited in the courtroom while John conferred with a lawyer friend, who had as a favor agreed to give John a running judgment about how Jake handled the proceedings on Andrew's behalf. The lawyer had advised that smart council would have separated the two defendants into two trials and then distanced young Andrew as far as possible from the unpredictable Green Man.

EAST LEVEN HAS ALWAYS HAD SOME VERSION OF JAKE AND Marge living downstream. The old pilings always gripped the river bank tight and offered footing for the two-by-fours and roofs; the salvaged windows with blue, green, and white peeling sashes; the aching sheets of peeling plywood; the driftwood decks and stoves hacked out of oil barrels.

Marge claimed she was "socially readjusted downward" by her husband's short then her son's long illnesses into which she poured her house, car, pension fund, and family jewels. Insurance covered eighty percent, but it was the twenty percent that ruined her. She waved her hands vaguely toward East Leven as if it were the seat of all insurance and maybe even bad luck itself: "MRIs, CAT scans, two 'er three tankersfull of blood, gas passers, pill pushers, seventy-five-dollars-a-bottle pills – it was crash and burn from the beginning. I used to live on Tenth and Furman." She pushed her beer away to let Andrew and the Green Man appreciate the prime real estate she had occupied. "How the mighty are brought low!"

As a twelve-year-old, Andrew's summer river adventures always included the shacks just outside town with their sheets of plastic and blue tarps under the cottonwoods, icons of the forbidden itself. With the ghost of Anne Doucette and her broken neck brooding, the shacks were deliciously dangerous. At the dump were rats to shoot with a pellet gun, twenty-pound feral cats come to the dump in search of rats, and old Miracle Whip jars. There were always the different versions of Marge and Jake: some snarly, with an arthritic limp, they gave a wide berth; and some, such as Marge, waving to them from an old lawn chair with circus-colored webbing like festive fringe, they hailed as creatures visiting from another galaxy. When things were good at Horchow Chemical, there were jobs that drew out the shack dwellers with the poultice of steady wages, and then most shacks fell into disuse, rattled in the wind off the river, and began to return to the earth. But when the company rosters were full of citizens, a second village collected on the pilings and hummed into the evening with kerosene lanterns and husbanded campfires if the night was chill. There was always talk in East Leven of annexing the land from the county and clearing up the menace to health and building codes, but then Horchow would lay off again and the tax roles would plummet and there was no money to buy the acreage from the Seattle landlord, who always seemed to be using the land as some kind of tax loss and didn't care about temporary squatters on his pilings.

Marge and Jake came to be permanent in one form or another. Jake fixed the unfixable, the throwaway outboards thirty years old. Marge held out rent free on social security. During the winter rains it was the hardest. The group in the bar downtown absorbed their long and short wavelengths from the beer signs, and the rain poured down. At the shacks there was mud and modest fires, beans and hard bread, wool Goodwill sweaters.

And Marge was the mother of wool. Even in summer she seemed a warehouse of wool layers as if she were personally storing garments against a world wide shortage. She laughed too loud. She shoved up the sleeves – various sleeves – as she prepared to talk.

She had also become the unofficial mother of the piling dwellers. She knew the time to apply to deliver telephone books, to sell stew to carnival workers setting up in an open field, to work at the food stands for the historical pageant and the county fair. Marge McIntry watched the economic tides of East Leven ebb and flow and always kept an eye out for what might wash up on her beachhead. Andrew and the Green Man were a surprise but no more surprising than a v-8 block to sell for scrap or a parka blown off the deck of a passing boat. She had closed her eyes at their arrival and sighed at their worthlessness as flotsam. At the deadly brown stripe in the river with its metallic smell, she had sensed the change in the flow of everything that depended on the river. Horchow was a hard neighbor – fenced, private, about some secretive business fueled by government contracts that rarely monetarily leaked over onto the pilings. Horchow was like a secretive, tight-lipped neighbor who nodded each morning and went to his work in sullen silence. She thought Horchow might be full of sons-a-bitches, might not.

Marge had told Jake Miller the same day Andrew and the Green Man were collected by the Horchow cops.

"Might be business for you," she said, while Jake hauled a small outboard out of the seething running barrel. "You're still licensed here, aren't you?"

Jake said he had kept up the license to defend himself on a couple of occasions, though he had lost interest in the direction the law took when he had set himself up in the old outboard business, the 5 horsepowers, the 7½s, long shaft, short shaft.

Marge looked over his inventory of Johnson, Mercury, Evinrude, and the antique Scott-Atwater lining one wall of his work room.

"So you'll do it, if it comes to that?"

"If it comes to that. But tell me the story of what you know."

She did: from the pair's appearance, from what the Green Man had said.

Jake listened and took notes by staring into space where he made his notations.

"The kid was not much help in putting this together," she continued. "Wasn't either one of them too nervous about what might happen, though the kid seemed about to run for it. But didn't."

Marge had a second son who worked in Houston in the sheet-metal trade and spared her some money when he could. But he had a wife and child now, so she sent back the last check and said to open an account for the grandson, and that was the final check. She had plugged herself in firmly on the pilings. She had planted zinnias on the land side of the pilings, had sowed garlic and chives on the sun side of her shack. Zinnias and garlic and chives, her gifts.

Jake put the latest outboard in the line hanging from saw horses and considered his work. "Another iron soul sees salvation," and made a sign of the cross over the assembly. "Pax whoa-bisque them all."

Marge knew that one of Jake's careers had taken him through the ministry, then "out the other side," as he related it. She thought of Jake as all the competencies that got you a good job rolled into one without any one of them taking over. He was industry, the law, salvation. He just wouldn't actually take the job.

THE RIVER PEOPLE WOULD DWINDLE AND GROW WITH THE economy. Each one might purposely reject a Horchow job during good times, and during bad times the river people numbers would descend to just Marge and a few plastic tarp folk in the woods along the bank. When the Green Man had established himself in his cabin by the river, they considered that he was a river person too, though it was code not to presume upon mere closeness. Al Miller, Marge, and others held sacred the right to be alone. The river made a good neighbor for the being alone types since it would cover one's flank, always. If they were going to sneak up on you, if there was an assault, if the authorities ever got organized and determined, the river would always be there covering one part of your ass.

Al Miller fixed outboards using the name of Jake. He had considered Jackson, Jean, Georg (pronounced Gay-org), and finally Max. For a while he had tried each name for a number of days to see how it might wear. He had to resort to posting the name du jour on the door outside, over the fifty-five-gallon drums where he ran the motors in static tests. Max, the sign pronounced, and his customers, who had come to tolerate his constant remaking of himself – his transcendental phase, he declared it – bore the name changes stoically.

Al operated out of a shack on a pie-shaped piece of land, one point of which touched the river, and the base of the triangle touched the road with a gravel parking lot. He worked on outboard motors he called "the lost souls," ancient wrecks dented and dreary with faded colors, usually very small horsepower and questionable parts availability. People found them in their parents' garages, in attics, and not infrequently snagged them up from the river bottom.

A man stood in the doorway with a lost soul in hand. "I got this for forty bucks in a junk store over on the dry side. Doesn't run. But I heard you do miracles with these things. I don't have much to spend on it though."

Jake turned on another light to see what the cat dragged in since the outside light behind the man framed guy and motor with bright light and left them both mysterious and dark in the light bath.

Jake assessed. Two-and-a-half horse Elgin from the middle fifties. "Jeeze, I haven't seen one of those for a long time. Used to be you could buy these from Sears, I think." History done, Jake plunged on. "You can't tell on this one, it's so faded, but they were a nice, soft green." He took the motor from the man and hung it from the bench. He tried to turn the flywheel where a rope was to be wound to pull-start it, but it wouldn't budge. "That's not a good sign. When we're talking about resurrecting one of these, it's good to have the flywheel turn, if only a little." Jake began to sniff the motor, first in general and then in the gas tank, then in the cowling that covered the carburetor. "Varnish," he pronounced. He unscrewed the plug to the lower unit and pronounced it "dry." He patted the pale green shell as if to reassure it during the examination. Finally, he tightened the motor to the bench transom and pulled down from the wall a device with a long bar on it that locked into the top where the pull-start rope would go. With one arm he cleared himself a space and worked his way out to the end of the bar. "The secret here is hard enough to tell and not so hard to break." From the end of the bar he worked back halfway and tried to turn the flywheel. When it didn't budge he held a finger up to the man and pronounced again: "Ceremony. This may take ceremony." He muttered something else and tugged again with a steady pull that increased until the veins stood out on his forehead. Still muttering some litany from another life, he worked out to the far end of the bar and braced himself. Slowly he applied all the pressure the bar would afford and then the flywheel turned a quarter turn and stopped. He shortened up on the bar and finished the full revolution. "Born again, I do believe. New main bearing, bore out, oversized rings, and it will run again. Soak out the carb, juice up the lower unit. But you won't have a two and a half any more. Maybe two horse or less. Eighty dollars."

The man scratched his chin. "Eighty and forty? That's something like a hundred and twenty? Can you cut some corners, do it on the cheap? Maybe fifty bucks somewhere?"

"The difference you're talking about is what I have to give for the main bearing. If that flywheel turned around easily, why we'd just let that bearing go and scrape out the crap and fire it up. But when you can't turn it over … well, that's seriously bound up, you know. There's a chance that bearing would loosen up with some penetrating oil. But I couldn't say how long it would last. When they're frozen, usually the metal's damaged and they're ruinous as sin."

The man pondered some more. "Let's say you could get into the engine and let's say you got that bearing free and it didn't look so bad, okay? And you get it turning and turning …" The man's face was lighting up with hope. A kind of prayer rhythm seemed to creep into his words. "… then slap her together, put her in the barrel for fifteen minutes or so. Why, I'd take that as new life. No guarantee, of course. I couldn't really expect that. But she might just go after that, don't you think?"

Jake saw the hope of saving thirty dollars glowing on the man's face. The narrative in which the semi-miraculous intercedes on behalf of the unlikely, he'd seen this before. Eternal springing hope and its good buddy self-delusion. Jake could just picture the bearing in question. It would have a white crust along the edge. This motor had to have been dumped in a lake at least once, maybe even finally. Then it was a while before someone got around to pulling the sparkplug and dumping the water out of the piston. God knows they didn't think to squirt some mineral oil in there. Then the crank bearing surely had a bath too. So the whole thing sat in the back of a garage somewhere until the old man died and his kids sold the motor and a bunch of other stuff in the garage as a lot, and it ended up in the junk store. One damn tragedy of human neglect after another. What could be done? Who could be made responsible? The man was tapping him on the shoulder.

"Well? Well, what you think? Jake? You in there?"

"Okay. Fifty bucks and no new bearing. But if I get in there and the bearing is hopeless, I collect for labor for the disassembly. And if I get the bearing loose, get it back together, clean the carb, grease the lower unit, and it blows the bearing in a few minutes running in the barrel, you owe me the full fifty bucks, and you've got yourself a ninety-dollar anchor."

It was always this negotiating that made the outboard-fixing business interesting for Al Miller, doing business as Jake. His story was an old story. He was easily bored and needed to change what he was doing and pursuing with a frequency that would baffle most people. Just as one major in college began to become apparent in its complexity, the direction of its discipline, he would swap it out for another. In the first two years of higher education he had majored in philosophy, biology, geology, literature, and a brief encounter with psychology. He found a way to assemble a humanities major by the end and graduated to, in chronological order: divinity school, law school, two years at a composting commune, and eighteen months in a cave on the Greek island of Mykonos. Reversing somewhat the Buddha's search for the middle way. Al Miller, guy from Wooster, Ohio, arrived in the Northwest by way of a Rainbow Family Gathering in several clearings in a national forest, then, like Zarathustra, came down out of the mountains carrying his blanket roll and apprenticed himself to small-engine repair. Finally, he found his specialty in outboards in order to avoid blade sharpening for lawnmowers and hose repair on irrigation pumps. And negotiation. Always negotiation and his fascination with the social construct of the bargain. What the eighteenth century called "cheapening" goods by talking the price down. Wholesale, retail, and the great interstices. The coming of the Green Man to East Leven was, for Al Miller, the miraculous made commonplace. Like the transcendentalist insistence that the miracle of seeing the stars in a night sky should not be lessened by the fact that they were available almost every night. Rightly viewed, the fact of their miraculous beauty should be unaffected by their commonness. And so the Green Man became for Al the manifestation of everything he had always been looking for – something else, otherwise, and a set of new propositions. Ben Brown was the ultimate outboard fetched up from the bottom of the bottoms and reconstituted and ambulatory.

Other people in town had become closer to Ben Brown, had talked to him easily through the haze of greenness, but Al, until called into the legal fray by Marge, had kept a lover's distance from the Green Man. To go closer might have taken the glow off, revealed feet of clay. But over there, appearing on the river bank, his head sticking above the bushes, his green skin revelation and testament, Lazarus-like witness to a breach in the logic of the world, the Green Man for Al seemed to show the way to the other side, philosophically speaking. Like hard evidence proving the existence of ghosts would show the way to a whole unseen world on the other side, so the Green Man was a crack in the inscrutable mind of God, a peep hole into cosmic mystery. Al Miller, who changed his major so often, found Ben Brown the ultimate mutating study.

The Miller defense team – Marge, the Green Man, vegetable Mary, the kid, borrowed tort books, and Al – gathered to plot strategy for the first time, and Al found himself tongue-tied in the presence of his avatar. Al kept watching how the Green Man moved, how he stood, gestured, laughed, spoke. Each act was a kind of revelation, a peeling back of the surface of the world to reveal what was underneath, the undoing of the onion's lower and lower layers, and Al caught himself recording the action as if for a documentary to be cut and edited later. It was Al's turn to talk and lay out the strategy for the trial.

The Green Man took a chair and listened. Marge and the kid hovered. Mary, a guest here, hovered behind and lower.

"Well," said Al, affecting a mid-winter depth to his voice. "There are all kinds of ways this could go, according to the torts."

"Torts?" piped the kid.

"The legal precedents, the stories that get told in the name of establishing ground rules for the particular situation." Al paused and searched the ceiling for more specifics. "The narratives that are like our story here."

"Green Guy and young man go berserk and defile a Northwest river." The kid tried it on for size.

"Yeah, well except for the green, the age, and the region of the country. Those are all species specific to our little potential felony. The torts don't cross-reference green people." Al looked quickly at Ben Brown to see if he had offended him. Ben held up one finger as if to indicate, no problem. Al continued, "I wish I could say we had a unique situation here, but we don't. Adjusting for green, for young, and for where, there is some potential in the alphabet of felonious crimes."

"Felonious Monk," Andrew interrupted, showing off his jazz knowledge. "I'll change my name to the felonious monk." Everyone looked at him and then back to Al.

"So we're talking doing some time. The possibility of doing time rests with the judge in this state under these conditions. Lots of latitude. He could swing the mean gavel." He paused to let his constituency ponder the consequences. "On the other hand, I was calling around about Judge Meyerhaus. Seems he's the salt of the earth – fair, broadminded, almost evangelical in his calling. Looking for good faith, so to speak." He chuckled at his own joke, but no one else seemed to get it. "So, what we'll do is court his mercy: first offenses, contrition, full disclosure of motive …" He put both hands on top of his head. "Shit. That's losers' strategy. We need a crack in the logic of the narrative. Some perfect idiosyncrasy that frees us from compelling similarities in tort law. It's not vandalism, it's … it's not aggravated trespass and fleeing from the scene of a crime, it's …"

The assembled group looked at Al hopefully. The kid offered an Elizabethan rendition of the prevailing sentiment: "Methinks we're screwed."

The defense team relaxed. Finally Al continued. "If we get the shit end of the stick, I can't see more than sixty days. Best case, suspended sentence, community service. The difference between these two doesn't really depend on your attorney. That's why I'm not charging for my services. I'm just here to think through contingencies and procedures. We'll plead not guilty and let the prosecution make the case. Okay?" He looked to the assemblage, eyebrows raised. "How say ye one and all?"

The kid. "I vote what the hell."

The Green Man. "Sure."

Mary and Marge raised hands to be recognized at the same time.

"Marge, then Mary."

"Al, I'm not sure we should have quite so much slop in the rigging, don't you know. Horchow pays lots of salaries around here, and if they want to make examples of these two they can put big pressure on the DA's office. There's really just a bunch of kids in there right out of law school, except for old what's-his-name-Peabody or something like that. Pea something, anyway. What a pirate robbing the public booty that sumbitch is." She had sounded her warning. She thought for a second. "That's all."

Mary began in one direction then adjusted course then collected her wits. Finally she said, "… and as soon as the sentence is pronounced we will rise all together to protest anything but exoneration. Horchow is the criminal. Horchow should be the defendant."

"Alas, Mary. That's true about half the time in law cases," Al said. "Used to drive me nuts. Drove me out of the law in the first place. You could look around any courtroom and with a little imagination see who the real guilty people were. The precipitators, I used to call them. The people who caused the whole mess that other people were trying to untangle by putting the hit on one unfortunate SOB who was in the wrong place at the wrong time. Luck, I kept thinking. It's just luck who gets stuck in the hot seat. It's important not to be much of a strict constructionist after all is said and done."

But Mary, even as a new guest at this party, constructed strictly: out of habit, out of inclination, out of constitution. There were right and wrong constructions, figures in the landscape, that kept coming and coming at a person. And the job, she felt, was to pick the right ones, even make up some right ones, and then make sure the wrong ones didn't get a foothold anywhere.

JUDGE MEYERHAUS SAT AT HIS BENCH RIDING HIS CHAIR LIKE a horse into the sunset of East Leven circuit court. His left knee had picked up what he called "the ache" from being immobile too long. His powers of concentration had waned long ago and now were sustained by sheer will. Listening had always been the hardest part of the job, listening to people, lawyers included, who were mainly casting about among all the possible words for the words to make sense. Some took longer than others to find the words that would suffice. And so his job consisted largely in listening to people speak in order to find the words that might do.

Brown suit under black robe to ward off the air-conditioning. Shoes off, wing-tips; East Leven shoe stores sold more wing-tips per capita than anywhere else on earth. Whatever truths Meyerhaus's courtroom pursued, wing-tips were the standard bearers.

But ever since the Green Man and his faithful companion and the sideshow dress-up circus, somehow Meyerhaus found himself letting the little stuff go.

He had seen so many cases float past his bench that he had developed a kind of screen on his consciousness so he would catch the big pieces and let the details go right on through. Then he could divert his energy from screening the moment in front of him to dipping into the past where infinitely juicier chunks of his courtroom smorgasbord heaped up. Crazy Leo's day in court. The Green Man's theater of the absurd. Now those were worth staying awake for.

Anna and Otto Meyerhaus, palindromic pair, had escaped from the big city to raise children in East Leven. The sound of water maybe. The sound of the valley wind through cottonwoods by the river, certainly. His trip from lawyer to circuit judge was nearly inevitable because he saw himself as hard, fair German stock – it was all he was absolutely sure about in the world – and East Leven voters quickly came to see this truth too. He ran unopposed, election after election. And when the Green Man's trial came up, it was also clear that the adjudication would run directly through Otto Meyerhaus.

Ben Brown and accomplice *vs.* Horchow: malicious trespass and reckless endangering. Their lawyer fixed outboard motors and was reputed to be a defrocked clergy of some indistinct ill repute. But he checked out okay with the bar association. Licensed with the state. As far as Otto knew, the defendant was a model citizen, the kid no priors. It looked like they had been caught in the act, well, pursued from the scene, anyway, then hauled in by the Horchow security police some distance downriver. Downriver, upriver, these were cardinal directions in town; everyone knew what they meant.

Upriver: farm land that used to flood regularly with sloughs, tangles of blackberries anywhere it was untended, good sandy soil that used to be all orchards and dairy because the dairy men could turn their cows out onto the flood plain in the summer and the occasional spring flooding didn't seem to bother the apples and cherries. Downriver: below Horchow, below town, where all the East Leven creeks ran into the river and sump pumps wrung out the soggy land, lay deep pools and churning water headed north toward Portland and the Columbia River. Each mile away from East Leven anything wild gave itself up to everything tame. There were developments crawling uphill away from the river and intermittent small industrial parks with pipes and hoses poking into the water.

In court all chases and fleeings tended to be along the river in either direction, and bridges like the paddles in a pinball machine could cause sudden changes in the direction of either. The Green Man and the kid had been going downstream in a northerly direction. Horchow's effluent, not directly relevant to the case, had followed the fleeing miscreants. The torts on this business were crystal clear on all points but one, another irrelevancy but sure to arise in court – greenness: of a person, of an action, of an ideology, of a set of local sympathies. This case had the potential to dredge up all kinds of irrelevancies that would give it flavor and texture. And Otto looked to see if his American flag, his state flag, were in the prescribed position, if there were accommodations for all participants, if his gavel made of rosewood like a guitar fingerboard was lying where he wanted it, next to the striking block. Like a director on opening night sneaking in early to a theater to feel the vibes of the empty house, Otto paced his courtroom to take stock. He secretly hoped there would be shenanigans.

And there were. Otto raised his gavel above the striking block as the first of the faux green man tall skinny kid pairs made its way into the gallery. But before he could bring it down, the second pair appeared. And then the pairs kept coming and coming until the back rows were packed solid and pairs began to make room for themselves among the reporters and other court curious.

"What the …?" Judge Meyerhaus raised his gavel but couldn't bring it down. "Is this a mockery of my …?" But he stopped because the legal principle had occurred to him. The defrocked outboard repairman had rigged a line-up for the court in which, short of a confession – and there didn't seem to be any in the DA's papers to the court – the identity of the perpetrators of the alleged crime was what had come to trial today. The DA's case ended up depending on the aquatic fact that the kid and the Green Man were wet when they were picked up by the police.

The wet-dry principle, thought Judge Meyerhaus. What the hell is the precedent in that? The Horchow guards saw the green person open the sluice gate then dive into the river ahead of the brown goo from the set-tling ponds. That which was dry, he intoned in his head, hath become wet. The ID the police make eventually hangs on the wetness.

Green people kept filing into the courtroom paired with what began as lanky male companions but now included females in gender-neutral jeans and shirts. And still they came.

The gallery filled with Mrs. Little looking for adventure and Conroy Burbank, the florist, she green, he with a shaggy wig and worn jeans. The antagonists in the sump pump wars had both come green, one with a wife as the kid, the other with a cousin. Jeffrey's wife was out of town tending a sick mother. Ramsey, the baker, Marge the barge, and vegetable-breathed Mary entered green in J.C. Penney work clothes. Three kids behind them were eleven, nine, and thirteen and the juridical likelihood that they could have been mistaken for the six-foot kid rested entirely on sartorial evidence. Fragmentary at best, but in concert with actual doppelgangers, a dozen right-on duplicates at least, the circumstantial evidence, the pos-sibility that the police could have nabbed the wrong guys, was becoming overwhelming. Thoreau said that certain circumstantial evidence could become compelling, such as a trout in the milk. Judge Meyerhaus looked out over the assembly and sighed. He made his index finger into a pistol and shot the DA, who rolled his eyes. And still they came, one and one, though slower now, lined up looking for empty seats like late couples at a movie having to break up and sit in different rows.

Judge Meyerhaus returned his attention to the assembled lawyers. Ben

Brown sat at the defendant's table with his hands in his lap. The kid had spun his chair around to face the gallery, turning his back on the assembled legal minds, and had begun waving to friends.

The florist turned to Mrs. Little and quoted Emerson in a loud whisper: "'Poetry was all written before time was, and whenever we are so finely organized that we can penetrate into that region where the air is music, we hear those primal warblings …'" He stopped and gestured grandly to the assembled dissemblers. "And Mrs. L, here we certainly have 'primal warblings.'"

Mrs. Little laughed and made gestures of blessing over the crowd, gestures she had seen a priest making on the seashore in Ceylon when the people had put candles in paper boats and set them on the outgoing tide at night. Her greenness made her feel like she had woken to find herself in a Balinese shadow puppet show.

The gallery was full, and a line of green men, gangly kids, stopped pushing forward. There were excesses of green people stacked up in the doorway as if the courtroom held enough putative green perpetrators already to bamboozle the case. These reserves stopped pushing in through the door by some silent signal given from chlorophyll to chlorophyll.

Judge Meyerhaus muttered to himself: "Class action. New meaning to the term class action. There's only one green one and you got him" (this to the DA). "Then there's a room full of them and it looks like you've got them all. Or they've got you. Anyway you slice this it's going to be baloney, I'm guessing. What say you? Counselor? DA? Can we agree on ground rules? Who's responsible for the Halloween show? Let me guess." He looked back and forth at the two men, but neither claimed the weird assembly. Al Miller spoke for the first time, "Scout's honor, your honor. I did not assemble this gallery as part of my defense."

Meyerhaus raised both eyebrows and sighed. "But," continued Miller, "if the prosecution had planned to prove more than the allegation that the green — I mean the defendants — were present, I think he would have informed me of it as is required by law. If his prosecutorial plan is essentially that there is one green guy and a green guy was seen committing the crime, why then, I'll move for dismissal."

Judge Otto Meyerhaus fingered the controls on his chair. *Hiss*, it said. And *hiss*.

Alysandra Gorham sat in the gallery, neither green nor gaunt, wishing she had been in on it, whatever it was. But no one had called her. No one ever called her. She had come to the trial not out of civic duty but because her father used to take her to trials like other parents took their children to zoos. They would sit in a back row, and her father would whisper to her the names of the principals – judge, court recorder, bailiff, prosecuting and defense attorneys, sometimes teams of lawyers and paralegals. He named them to her tenderly, as if recounting the names of long-gone relatives. Her father considered himself a buff, a hobbyist, of the first water. The East Leven courthouse had been his model train layout, his hunting and fishing, his stamp collection. And since his death Alysandra had taken up coming to trials in order to evoke his memory, his barely audible whisper as he recited the naming of parts in the courtroom. Ms. Gorham – like the silver not the bridge, her father said – kept up her father's court hobby. He would laugh at the end when he had taken to his bed for the end game. He laughed in the last week of his life and proclaimed that of all the things he thought he had learned in eighty-four years, only one true thing held up in the final inspection. All those competing truths clamoring for attention and it seems just one made it to whole truth as far as he could tell: "Buy good shoes!" he pronounced in a voice suddenly full and clear. And then again so there was no mistaking the sermon: "Buy good shoes!" this time a little less hearty, but certain nonetheless and ringing. Then he sat back in bed exhausted and closed his eyes and breathed shallowly as if his revelation had exhausted all his powers of life. Alysandra had been the sole witness to the revealing of this singular truth. She didn't know what exactly to make of it but resolved that if a man's whole life could conspire to come up with a single truth, the world, especially his only child, could attempt to honor it. Alysandra, the day before her father's funeral, spent $140 on a pair of comfortable, butter-soft shoes for his funeral. She had just turned fifty years old and thought that even though the proclamation might have been partly raging "against the dying of the light," as Dylan Thomas advocated in his villanelle, just maybe also lives percolated into singular forms at the end and the hidden became revealed. What truth was available was available only finally and then through the exhaustion of all falsity.

Alysandra sat in court surrounded by green pretenders sitting silently while Judge Meyerhaus held the conference at his bench. She had been present when Crazy Leo's day as a witness had come undone for the prosecutor. She felt that as moments of jurisprudence went, this one might outdo that one.

The coming of the Green Man to East Leven had, Alysandra remembered, afforded great relief to her. Her father's perfect oddness, her own idiosyncratic ways at her gift shop, her motherless family, just the two of them hauling off to Portland in winter squalls to go to the opera while clacking noisy bowling alleys were East Leven's passion – this condition of being a stranger in a town where she was born and raised was suddenly relieved by the advent of this man.

At the gift shop, the English teapots with matching cups in the shape of hives and bees, the doilies from another century, the carnival glass great monuments of the world, antimacassars, African violet self-watering pots, cloth butterfly finger puppets, gold pen nibs, photos of severe old people in tintypes and daguerreotypes, pot metal picture frames cast as elaborate bouquets, the doll shoe collection of thirty-six pairs of elegant footwear for an absent doll (to be sold only as a collection), Alysandra's eclectic wares amused and amazed East Leven. Customers would drop in just to see the oddities, and Alysandra would continue to supply the shop with what she thought were perfectly ordinary goods, goods that had caught her eye at trade shows and second-hand shops, at estate sales.

Her sense of kinship with the Green Man increased. As East Leven grew easy with him, it grew easier with her and her father. She had two weeks ago taken a small piece of emerald-colored ribbon from a doll's hair and pinned it on the lapel of her blazer. When asked about what she was supporting or protesting, Alysandra blushed and stammered. She collected herself finally and declared that she was supporting the Green Man.

"Supporting him how?" asked one of two ladies who had always found

Alysandra's shop to be a kind of island in East Leven's woodsy status quo. "Is there a club or group sponsoring him now?" she continued, and set a small black panther on the counter for Alysandra to ring up.

Without hesitating Alysandra removed the price sticker and rang up the panther with the white circle stuck to her finger.

"There are only a few of us," she said, raising her eyebrows as if to dismiss the entire business. She transferred the price sticker to a sheet of light blue paper that constituted the entirety of her inventory control, income tax record, and bookkeeping apparatus.

But the ladies were not to be put off so easily. "We might like to join too," said number one, continuing her club or group inquiry. "If it's not expensive."

"Or too much time," said number two. "I have so many church-related meetings now. I was just voted onto the board and that's every week. Then there's the women's circle and the men try to do the pancake feed but never seem to pull it off by themselves and always call for help. And I can't tell yet how much time will go to …"

Her friend interrupted. "We're all very busy these days. It seems like there's never enough time for everything." But she needed to know if this Green Man club had the right people in it. "On the other hand, Ben Brown has grown to be a part of our community, though I thought he was really very well off from the, you know…the turning green part of the business."

Alysandra sighed. "There's really no money involved. Just a few of us. Some friends and acquaintances." She heard in her head the echo of the Winnie the Pooh category: friends of the hundred-acre wood. "It's just moral support and … a kind of solidarity with him mostly." She lowered her voice. "We don't have meetings or anything."

Number two perked up. "Now that's a good idea, no meetings. I would join up. He seems like such a nice man, but no one knows him very well. I wonder which church he goes to? Does he go to yours, Claire?"

"No," said Claire.

"He must be a Catholic, then," and that settled it.

"Alysandra, do you have more of that ribbon for us?"

She asked the women to wait and went to the back room. She moved boxes. She climbed on the step stool. She closed her eyes to remember where on the shelving she had left the box of old ribbon since she knew there was none exactly like what she wore. She could always claim that color for charter members or something. And it was there. A box of grosgrain with a satiny stripe. Just the thing. Just the green to proclaim but not shout …what? Kinship? Support? As she descended from the stool she cast about for the word. Loyalty? Booster? Friendship? She made her way back to the ladies, and it came to her: allegiance. Like the pledge of allegiance. An allegiance to the greenness of Ben Brown. And that seemed satisfying to Alysandra.

Back at the cash register the ladies had discovered the sterling spoon set Alysandra got from an estate sale in Portland. She made them both twists of ribbons and fastened them with tiny brass safety pins from the front so that the brass pin stood out on the field of green like a small sculpture. Alysandra looked at her work as she pinned the ribbons on the ladies. A safety pin, she thought, is really a very beautiful thing, and these tiny brass ones (of which she had cards containing one hundred from an auction at a defunct dry goods emporium) were especially elegant installed against Ben Brown's special green ribbon. Both ladies left satisfied with their new membership, and Alysandra put the card of pins with the ribbon behind the counter in case more of her customers wanted to declare their allegiance.

It was the next day near noon that the next ribbons were requested. It had got around church apparently, and the new petitioners came asking how much for their pins and ribbons. Alysandra quickly saw the ribbons bringing in browsers and gladly made up the new twists with the properly installed pin holding the loop together. Handsome, she thought. Each one is handsome though slightly different from every other one. Briefly she considered whether there should be words said with each installation, some kind of pledge maybe. Then pledge and allegiance occurred to her, and she laughed and dismissed any further ceremony.

By Tuesday afternoon Alysandra had sold one hundred and thirty-six green ribbons. As sales dropped off slightly, then precipitously, she began to suspect her patent had run out. She hung out her "back in ten minutes" sign and made for the drug store with a creed of purpose in her walk. There she asked for a card of small brass safety pins. All out. At the fabric store. Just reordered. Green ribbon? Grosgrain about this wide, something close to this color? Had some but it was all gone. Some kids came in and got the last of a whole roll sold all this week. Had that roll since we opened eight, no nine, years ago …

Alysandra sighed. Indeed her patent had run out. But she had been rewarded handsomely for the idea, thank you very much. A person could sell anything. Anything.

Judge Meyerhaus's wife had come home sporting a ribbon two weeks before the trial, after the "arrest," the release on bail. When he asked her what it was for, she was vague, waving her hand as if brushing away annoying gnats.

"I got it at the beauty parlor. They gave them away. No donation," she said, as if that posted enough explanation.

"But what do they represent? What should we remember?" The judge himself was of the paper poppies for Veterans Day generation. The poppy fields of France were to be remembered, the blood interred there. The triumph of good over evil that cost blood and bone, which fertilized the poppies and sent them into the bloom of remembrance each spring.

"I think," she began, cornered now by his insistence, "that it's sort of in support of the Green Man, Ben Brown." And then as if it had never occurred to her before this, she stopped. "Ben Brown. The green man. Listen to that, dear. The green Mr. Brown. Mr. Brown is green." She pondered these revelations, breaking into a grand smile of satisfaction.

"And blackberries are green when they're red," the judge added. "I didn't realize the Green Man had a fan club."

"Not a fan club, exactly. I think it's more a kind of sympathy. Maybe solidarity."

He thought of Lech Walesa and the Polish ship yards. Welders on strike. Banners.

"Anyway," she continued, "you'd be surprised who's wearing these. People who don't join anything. Even some very crabby old people who don't really like anything anymore are wearing green ribbons." She paused.

"And," she continued, "I can get you one to wear to work if you'd like."

Jesus, thought the judge. That's all I need. Sit at the bench wearing the badge of the litigant. "Blackberries are red when they're green. Works that way too."

The Meyerhaus court murmured. Many of the green people sported twists of green ribbon with a tiny brass safety pin in the center. But most important to the judge was that a circus, a medieval fair, had invaded his courtroom for which ten years ago, hell, three years ago, he would have started to hand out contempt citations. Now, while the litigants gawked, the DA and defense lawyer stood patiently for him to continue, Judge Meyerhaus took his time and surveyed his territory from on high. The circus, the zoo, the fair was his. All his. And he saw it wasn't bad, anyway.

What ur-law! The people speak. What cunning the people have. How they redeem themselves again and again just when the daily parade of bad-acting, infelicitous scofflaws had grown toward intolerable. See what they've done here today: they have measured the legal system and found it wanting. The citizens have risen up and stripped tort law naked. Pounced on tortius duty altogether. Look at them swiveling in their seats and smirking at one another, celebrating collective consciousness. They're constituting themselves into all the camerae of law. Fast fish, loose fish, he recalled from a history of law course thirty years ago, when the professor had read from Moby Dick to illustrate some historical source of law.

The whispering among the green gallery rose to a significant susurrus that filled the room and threatened to overflow. No distinct words, just indelible sound of folk.

Judge Meyerhaus smiled and raised both hands – *pax vobiscum* – over the heads of the lawyers, over the assembled representatives of Horchow, over the green and gangly pairs, faux and true.

"May I talk to both sides?" Judge Meyerhaus gestured come hither with the handle of his gavel.

Al Miller took his time and gathered up papers to bring with him in his briefcase.

"That won't be necessary, counselor. I just want a word with you both before we begin. I see where you're headed, I think, with the defense. What's the prosecution's case?"

The DA mumbled, "… apprehended … crime scene … scrutiny." And still green people worked their way into the courtroom. "… apparent identity … eyewitnesses with unobstructed views … affidavits … charged with felonious …"

The outboard repairman said not a word but stood with his hands clasped behind him looking up at Judge Meyerhaus as if he expected monumental truth to flow down from the bench and cover him.

The DA went on and on: "Crime against property, decency … of malicious … entity … apparent … maligned party … public outcry …"

The peace that passeth understanding, thought Judge Meyerhaus.

"Statute … simulacrum … torts … essentialist …"

Roman centurion. Pavlov's dog. Bellicose entreaties. Judge Meyerhaus adjusted his new chair by its side levers that allowed him to raise or lower with a flick of his finger tip. Recline, tilt, soften. A small hissing noise accompanied each adjustment. *Hiss*. Party of the first part. Party of the second part. *Hiss. Hiss*. Sanity clause. Sanity clause? Everybody knows there's no sanity clause.

The DA was not going to wind down by himself, so the judge judged a spot to stop him by raising his hammer. The DA stopped mid spurt.

"And you, counsel for defense. How are all these people, these green people, connected to your defense?"

"Your honor," Al's voice was surprisingly deep and sonorous for a small man. The pulpit was everywhere in his voice. "Your honor, I can assure you that who comes, what public comes to the court today, in no way is implicit in my defense. And I use implicit in the precise Thomistic sense that precludes …"

"Jesus, people," Judge Meyerhaus interrupted. "One of you is as bad as the other. What I want to know is whether we have a valuable trial today, one in which community standards and a valuable legal tradition will prevail and individual rights will be upheld. Due process. *De juridica*, gentlemen. If the prosecution's entire case is based on 'somebody saw a green guy,' then let's get home early. My wife has a pork roast in the oven.

Roasted garlic mashed potatoes. Brussels sprouts, gentlemen. On the other hand," and here Judge Meyerhaus lowered himself with a *hiss* so his face was closer to both men, his gavel lurking just above both heads, "we can guess the luck of the defense that all these green people showed up today in court. The extraordinary luck! And we can hope that the defense counsel is not making my courtroom into a circus featuring green clowns. We seem caught, gentlemen, at an impasse of puny proportions. What say you both? Defense first."

"It seems …"

"In the simplest form," the judge insisted.

"Okay. If there's no more to the prosecution than placing the defendants at the scene of the alleged crime, we feel the defense will be … will be obvious," and he pointed over his shoulder at the gallery.

Judge Meyerhaus turned to the DA and raised both caterpillar-like eyebrows at once.

The DA turned to look around the gallery rife with green folk and faux lanky kids. "That's basically all we've got, your honor. And they were wet when …"

Judge Meyerhaus snorted and hissed back up to full height. "Wet. Dry. Wet Dry." He cleared his throat. "Bring me something more substantial than this. Case dismissed."

Andrew thinks the cuckoo-clock revelation is about to descend on him again, the whole affair explode into prolonged, slo-mo cuckoos ending with the judge's bench opening up and a large black-robed bird flying in his face. Andrew wonders how his green friend sees this judging, but Ben Brown stares off at a corner of the courtroom as if there is some text there he is trying to make out.

Marge and a small contingent of river squatters sit at the other end of the friends' pew looking to Andrew like got-up pretenders to citizenship – hair brushed into unaccustomed dos that mimic the surrounding coifs but still reek of parody, sweaters and slacks pressed in affirmation of serious proceedings but finally seeming to be rescued from a Salvation Army box, backhanded whispers among them while waiting for the judge.

The Green Man blows out a breath as if blasting a mosquito off the tip of his nose.

Andrew checks his shoes, the same work-scarred sneakers he wore the day of the river escapade, just as Jake insisted. He and the Green Man are dressed exactly as they were that day on the advice of their lawyer, who waved away Andrew's objections with a "You'll see. It's important to our argument." Andrew tries to hide one shoe under the other since both can be seen from the bench.

The next morning is crackling with newspaper people who didn't get enough copy outside the courthouse. They form a semi-circle in the drive that leads down to the cabin, and Andrew figures out what is going on, hears the clack of cameras and sees that His Greenness is holding court. He wonders, oh shit, what version of all this is coming out of his mouth?

There is some little acclamation when Andrew arrives but quickly the photographers return to the Green Man. One of them wonders out loud how the greenness will photograph and begins to ask around among the gathered camera people about backgrounds and lighting. The wire services will pick up a photo if the green is good. Andrew notices how someone in the crowd is edging nearer to the Green Person. Mary Willson dresses late-sixties revival with that herb-tea and granola look.

Andrew had seen enough newsreels of Jack Ruby, Sirhan Sirhan, John Hinckley, Squeaky Fromme to have a feel for the fiend-in-the-crowd who lurks on the edge of things and then commences to shoot. He has seen so many versions of this – the slow-motion hand coming up with the pistol, the blur and grimace, the jerking of the freeze frame so we can see it all better – that the reporter scene seems to freeze too. Mary moves in from the right but instead of shooting, waves and smiles. Her hair is an event in itself, brown and as if too much had been stuck in each follicle; it sticks out trying to find horizontal – electric. Andrew wonders if the Green Man feels the static charge coming at him, the ambulatory cat fur charged on an amber rod? She seems to Andrew to be a variation on Crazy Leo, though he knows her from the background of the planning sessions, Marge's friend; she has some status there. But Mary places herself so carefully in the landscape that she draws attention to herself as if she were superimposed over the top of the scene instead of in it.

The Green Man has infinite patience with inane questions, insinuating questions, questions-that-aren't questions but rambling statements. Are he and Andrew a conspiracy? That seems to be the main thrust. Are they aligned with Greenpeace, the Green Party, the Communist Party, Friends of the Earth, Earth First, Spaceship Earth, Soldiers for the Living Earth, the IRA, the UJA, the CIA? How are they connected, and how does this connection make a plot, how does the plot make a story, the story a sensation? Does either of them know Annie Dillard? Buckminster Fuller? Barry Lopez? Linus Pauling? Paul Newman? Christopher Newman? Cardinal Newman? The questions fly and jabber.

And all the while Mary Willson smiles and waves and finally just smiles. She wears a long, gray voluminous skirt, an earth-colored vest dusty pink with flowers embroidered here and there as if she'd wandered through an arbor and a few pink blossoms accidentally stuck. This theme of the accidental is important for Mary, a movement apparently without design.

Andrew finds himself watching, remembering how in high school it was almost required to take a first date to park near the Green Man's house, use him to scare her into your arms. That was the theory. And since he lived closest to the object of fear, it was logical that he would know the most about this thing, its habits and its natural history: What did he eat? Was there a Mrs. Green Man? Was she green too? Green kids? Was it a disease that made him green?

Mary Willson stands and smiles, and soon the reporters thin out, tiring of his reasonable greenness, his patient repeating greenness. They inform him – Andrew is hunkered down on the edge of the reporters, lying low – that the Horchow spill, as it has come to be called, eventually reached Portland, where the water slows down and spreads out, and the whole food chain became a victim as the brown stripe that had sizzled along without mixing much with the side flows of the river hit the turbulence and mixed just before the city. The fish dead from the metal salts lay like broken kites along both banks, then herons, raccoons, ravens, ospreys, turtles, crayfish, and various other river critters, not to mention myriad feral cats and several neighborhood fish-eating dogs that got sick and died. There was general critter devastation and stench. And as the Green Man had predicted, dead fish was one thing; dead mammals and birds quite another.

People wanted to know, thus the rush to find the Green Man and his accomplice. People needed to know what was ready to fall into their river, and what about the consequences. They have looked up the newspaper files on the Green Man's turning green and ask questions leading from old clipping information, but the Green Man doesn't seem much help, even stumbles and hems about until they give up, thinking he's not partial to personal information. And then the reporters go and Mary Willson is still standing there smiling.

"MARY WILLSON," SHE SAYS HER NAME TO ANDREW. JUST LIKE that, like snapping your fingers without being asked. "Mary Willson. I was with Marge and Al at the planning meeting."

"Well, how do you think we did?" Ben asks.

Her vegetarian breath. She tells him she was feeling much better now that she understood the plan of letting out the Horchow poisons, and that somehow the cost was to be amortized over the whole world from now on.

Well, this was a little larger scale than he was willing to concede just yet, but the idea was intriguing. What was Ben Brown thinking when he ran up the Horchow bank, and what was the intent? Looking back, he thought he only attacked the heat, the wearying, broken-wing heat of it all – the smell of dead angels.

She seems perfectly comfortable to just stand and continue to smile. Andrew gangles nearby, idles like a lawnmower alone on the lawn. Ben thought of the guy in the jail, the guy from Horchow who approached them with the chemical rattle and jangle of the poison plant. He thought of holding out his hands to feel if Mary too might be sent by Horchow, but without holding up his hands he could smell the sweet barley of her, feel her coolness; all his special antennæ told him again that she was okay. Andrew, on the other hand, had turned from idling by to suspicious parent somehow looking out for his innocent green charge.

Ben was glad the kid had begun to feel protective because he had begun to care less and less about practical matters, such as cashing paychecks, buying groceries. He knew what was happening and had been happening for quite a while, the growing younger stuff. He just didn't know exactly what all this would entail. So far he found it pleasant, like watching some exotic desert plant bloom, its once-in-a-hundred-years show.

Mary Willson standing there smiling still: her hair chestnut and outrageous with the deep shine of a Morgan horse, her skin tones milky clear as if polished and buffed daily so that shadows lay across her face in stark geometric forms, the smile so easy that Ben didn't feel anxious or even expectant for it to mean anything or be the preface to something.

They stand, an odd triptych, waiting for what the Spanish call "the angel to pass," the silence that falls perfectly in a conversation, the silence that informs the noise and asks us to listen to it, that hushes us and stills all the other rhythms and fills us with waiting. Mary speaks and sets time in motion again.

"Suppose you tell me more about yourselves, both of you, about yourselves," and she turns to smile and include Andrew too.

"Are you going to report on this business? To the papers?" Andrew asks and slowly raises a wild grass stalk to pick his teeth discreetly. He's pulled the grass stalk out of some movie in his mind. Ben finds himself doing accents sometimes just to sort of play along with what he thinks is a movie game Andrew's playing.

No, she's not a reporter, she tells them, not a reporter at all. She is resplendent in cotton and doesn't use contractions. "I am not acting as a reporter," she reported. Ben could smell the natural fibers about her: no cheese, no perfume, no plastic. There's cumin. There's oregano and lavender and the sweet powerful celery smell of lovage. She's a garden – an ambulatory, curious garden. Ben feels pleased that she has stayed and tells her.

They sit down, and she asks Ben again to tell about himself, as if they were opening up some sort of analysis, cracking into some kind of hard green nut.

When the reporters had asked him to fill in what he did before he had been turned green, he put them off, demurring. But when Mary asks him, he thinks it would be fun to tell her something interesting, to interest her. Maybe something about … Something about …

But he can't find anything. Ben searches, as he had for the reporters and finds the same thing. A gray cloud of sorts like a math problem too hard to figure out, a story problem that purposely confuses you and you have to read it over and over and the sense of it doesn't become any clearer: If two dogs that hate each other live three and a half miles apart and one dog is on a chain two meters long and the other is on a chain forty-eight inches long, and suddenly … Which dog runs farther to fight?

He tries again to tell Mary something about … About what was it? Did he have wives and children and cars? Did he watch the newspaper for sales? What did he like to buy? Who did he like to buy it for? What organizations did he belong to? Did he keep good tires on his car? Was there a church, a board of trustees, a managing group, a syndicate in his life? Which sound principles did he defend? Could he be bought? Had he found new uses for 3-in-1 oil?

Mary seems very patient and sweet-smelling about all this reticence prefaced by a huffing and chuffing as the Green Man tries to remember some one thing to hand her in good faith. In frustration he gets up to get lemonade for all three. When he comes back, she is talking with Andrew, who is charming her to keep her smiling. He was telling about the island breaking away, lurching and going off into the river. Ben joins in and finds no problem recalling even details the kid missed: He names all the plants on the island, tells of the structure from bleach bottles to tires and airplane cable, recites the address of the farm where he'd found the Roosevelt-era 12-volt generator, fills in how badgers dug under the rocks piled at fence corners in that part of eastern Oregon. Almost breathlessly Ben rambles on, chocking full his visitor and gangly friend with details of his world after he'd turned green, the stark clarity of his altered world, the trolls that lived in service boxes and what they liked to eat. How kingfishers might conspire to all at once make predatory love to the fingerlings in the green river – the blue with the green and the silver.

Mary and Andrew are both looking at Ben, the one slightly aston-ished – Mary, but still smiling – and the other flabbergasted and not smiling at all but with that worried-man look Andrew has come to affect so recently, so quickly in the few days they'd traveled together. Apparently, Ben Brown is babbling.

Andrew thinks of retiring from the Green Man-and-Mary lemonade fest, thinks of moving off upriver toward his house to ponder these last two days and make what he can of the raw materials. All of this needs time in front of the tube, to settle out better in phosphorescing light, to see the pattern or lack of pattern, to contemplate the chaos of the dots on the screen, the Brownian motion of all this newness. Moving off upstream from the Green Man and his lemonade friend, Andrew feels a relief as if the singing far away that he couldn't really hear has finally disappeared altogether and ceased to make him strain to try to hear it.

Andrew suffers. He stands and suffers, and then he sits and suffers just to try out the difference. Damn his green imperious highness! Andrew raves to himself. The presumption of the whole damn thing. Andrew wants to slink back into his comfortable slough, twinkling with its little dots of colored light, the warm mud with just his eyes peeking out.

They are outside sitting in lawn chairs near where the island broke off, which now looks like a loading dock for miniature steamboats. They sit among the rubble of construction as if it is a park and they are having tea. The conversation has turned to her. He's turned on his 12-volt system and hung a pair of lights away from where they sit so a soft light works its way through the leaves toward them on all sides, but where they sit is cool with a perpetual twilight, the river dark and making talking, faraway noises. He's not green in this light; they're both the same no-color. Andrew crackles through the last bushes.

Mary Willson and the Green Man sit in aluminum lawn chairs facing the river. Mary wears mismatched denim and the Green Man his J.C. Penney dark greens. He sits looking downstream with his hands folded in his lap like a child. Mary has turned the whole top of her body toward him.

"The reporters seemed to think the trial was a great success," she says. She smoothes her skirt with both hands.

"A great success, yes." The Green Man's voice is so soft that Mary has to lean closer to hear, and even then his voice trails off into an inscrutable murmur.

Mary Willson wears denim like a club tie. Through it she certifies her background: vegetarian, utilitarian, gardener, liberal of politics, conservator of the earth. She teaches reading skills at the East Leven grade school named after a mid-level bureaucrat in the school district who had distinguished himself by nothing but length of service – forty-five years of ministrations to the people's children – Charles Judd.

"Sometimes I hate the river," she says. "It's too cold to swim safely. It runs too fast. It collects all the evil chemicals in the valley and concentrates them." She is smiling and ticking off the river's bad points on her fingers. "It flows north unlike the most respectable rivers. It's green ... oops." She laughs and opens her brown eyes wide to see what the Green Man's reaction might be. She wonders whether he is sensitive to the point of humorlessness? Was he bitter about the green trick the cosmos had played on him? She touches him on the right shoulder at the same time as if to see if he will recoil or fall over dead. "Okay. The green part is fine. But I like your green better. A softer green, a ..."

The Green Man raises an index finger to command an interruption. "A natural green. A broccoli state in a desert world." He laughs and turns his chair toward Mary. "A Green Knight to fight Sir Gawain. A vegetable love. A race of one."

"I can see you've thought this over."

"Oh, I've had lots of time to think this over. Really look into the cracks and crevasses of this greenness, so to speak. And, yes, I am everywhere the same green."

Mary Willson begins to protest that she had not meant to be so familiar, but the Green Man continues.

"You're a vegetarian. I can smell that you're a vegetarian. I smelled it at the planning meeting. And you're not a reporter."

"I have heard vegetarians smell different," she says. "But I did not know reporters had a distinct smell."

The Green Man studies her for a second as if to decode some text he finds in her face, her hair that is puffed out to the sides of her head like escaping cocker spaniels. Finally he decides it is all right to go ahead with his considered line of conversation.

"The truth is I can smell everything. Well, everything in a sort of extension of what humans can smell. And then a few things humans can't smell."

He waits to see if she might bolt, or maybe excuse herself. He gives her time to do both, but she stays and the river light reveals swallows skimming and diving.

Mary notices how the failing light seems to draw the green off him. She thinks, what is the offense here? What is it that has made him a target of some kind. What's at stake? She had had a student of mixed race, Tony, whose features and skin color corresponded to no particular race, who floated somewhere between identification – lips, eye color (that extraordinary bright gray) and shape, skin color – nothing too much and nothing enough to certify him in any particular group. Tony was the shape of things to come, a fifth-grade enigma wrapped in what was already an enigmatic condition, fifth grade. A colleague-wit had suggested that fifth graders might be harnessed in some way to produce electricity for the benefit of society, large hamster wheels, maybe to light old people's homes. That the condition of fifth graderness might be declared a separate race among humans, with separate conditions and responsibilities. How like this green man who could smell, what? The way the world was? A kind of super-realism? What else could he smell on her besides her vegetarianism? Could he smell her interest in this shy, funny Ben Brown who was green, the way he slyly fiddled the conversation toward her like a soft pass she couldn't see coming until the last minute?

She had never married, though there had been close calls once, maybe twice. It was pleasant sitting with this green person next to the river, siting and smelling the evening come off the cool water. Mary's hobbies ran to wild mushrooms, birds, wild flowers. She attended land-use planning sessions in the city council's chambers. She was a returned Willson out of the ancient, founding Willsons. Listened to bluegrass music, wove natural fibers with the Card and Loom Society, learned the constellations by heart.

Mary captures a handful of dark brown hair on each side of her head and tosses one then the other over her shoulders and then shakes her head to convince the hair to stay back. The Green Man fixes his eyes on the last light downstream, but his yard stays steady in the glow of his 12-volt system.

He speaks slowly, as if struggling out from under some ponderings to flesh them out with words. Mary leans close to hear him. "They'll be back in some way or another because what I am threatens them somehow. I'm not sure exactly how. Or maybe it's the whole green thing that's unacceptable."

She can tell that like a child he hadn't located the fear and so was speculating in and out and around from it. And then, as if he had got a hold on it and let the threat float away, he turns to her. "How long have you lived here?"

"Ten years. And you?"

"And what do you do for a living?"

"I teach reading at the fifth-grade level, Judd."

"I have lived here for what seems like a long time. But it's not clear anymore just how long. I could look up the newspaper accounts and get the exact date, but I'm not very interested anymore how long I've been here. That sounds like I'm just evading your question. Not at all. Maybe the green change has something to do with it. I don't remember everything very well, just some things. And not even important things. Just odd moments are clear and focused. The rest is not so much gone as run together, like a movie out of sequence when things only happen but aren't tied together and so don't make sense. Then some parts are interesting all by themselves – for their… their what? Texture. Their texture: color or light or pattern. Something like that."

Mary wonders whether it was Ben Brown's skin color that fascinated her from the beginning. Or the sad, low-talking man who watches the river so carefully as if something might rise up out of it at any minute, something like a sign he waits for, a beautiful woman holding a sword. She chuckles to herself at her own imaginings, and he turns to her.

"Yes?"

"I was just … I was just thinking about your being green."

"It's not that hard to get into, is it? Sometimes I wonder if everybody couldn't be in this skin just thinking about it. But it takes having someone actually green for the idea to occur. Some of the local merchants, after the initial bumbling shock, the ones I go to regularly, seem to be trying the green on for size sometimes. There's a kid at the Safeway store who goes into a kind of trance when he bags my groceries. And then he comes out of it when I take the bag and head for the door. It's like he's been abducted by aliens, then set free again. All in a matter of seconds."

The subject of his greenness seems to animate him. He laughs. "As Kermit the Frog sings, 'It's not easy being green.' But it is kind of fun to imagine, I think." He looks at Mary and she wonders if "fun" is what she is thinking – the river, the knife … Maybe it is, she thinks. It was a color that could be fun.

Mary finds this water watching, this green guy, lovely. She had used the word too much, and on the advice of a friend, worked at getting it out of her vocabulary. Lovely this. Lovely that. Such a gloss on what she really meant. It hid her joy instead of revealing it, so she worked the alternatives, and they all came up the same: grand, wonderful, perfect … even nice, for a short while. She thought of herself as mostly pleased with the world even though it was clear how the world failed and failed and failed. A colleague had asked her if she had been diagnosed as manic oppressive at any time in her life. She took it as a badge of honor. She was free to do as she liked, self-supporting, engaged in interesting work that never cloyed.

The light from the Green Man's improvised yard lights holds dimly steady against the evening.

She begins a story this evening that recalls light, swallows, water. She realizes that she is supplying the part of her life that corresponds to part the Green Man said he couldn't recall.

"We would go on picnics to a relative's farm. Some kind of second cousin or something. And there would be a tub of soft drinks in cold water and one horse trough completely filled with iced-over watermelons and then an old refrigerator that chugged rather than hummed. A yellow extension cord ran off away from it like a beautiful snake into the barn. We played in the barn, and it was …" she searched around "lovely" to find something worthwhile for the barn. "It was so fragrant, and at first I could not see when I ran in out of the sunlight. Then spots of sun coming through the boards looked like stars. Then I could see. But I smelled it first. I think I became a vegetarian because of playing in that barn, the smells of the different hays my cousin made. Alfalfa and timothy, and the kind of hay with wildflowers sticking out in dried bunches, which he cut from the meadows where we rolled down the hillside and made silver paths in standing flowers. There were blue coneflowers and manzanilla, forget-me-nots, wild flax, buckwheat, black-eyed susans, and monkey flowers around the spring. I always thought he cut that particular hay to keep the barn full of dried flowers. Somehow none of this seemed connected with the animals they kept. The alfalfa bales were hard and green. The timothy hay was pitched in loose and good for jumping in. We came out covered with tiny pieces of hay and laughed at each other and pulled hay from our hair. Then we ate the iced watermelons."

She pauses to taste the watermelons again. "We played softball in grass so long it caught at our legs and made running seem like dream running. That's how I still remember it. Dream running, where you cannot get going fast enough. But in meadow softball, there was someone slowly looking for the ball in the long grass too, and so the whole thing was slowed down, everything but the ball exploding off the bat. Then these slow motion children. And one tipsy uncle looking hot and red in the sun, holding out his cigar at arm's length to examine something."

Mary waits and waits and then says, "Watermelon so cold. That was lovely."

Mary began talking about her childhood easily after Ben had given her selected renditions of the island and his greenness. He was still trying to poke back through a kind of veil that seemed to have formed, sealing off his life before turning green from his life after turning green. The before became so murky it seemed to physically hurt when he tried to concentrate on thinking about it, to look for details that would lead him to something general – to try to see the house by getting the number of windows first.

And when Mary slid back easily to her family reunions and aunts and uncles and family friends, Ben recorded them – the names, what they did – to fill in his own life. He repeated to himself the names as she told them, repeated the place names, the colors of things, the smells and the flowers she named. In a kind of liturgy he reinstated a past for himself. He kept her talking any way he could, and when she tired or tried out of politeness to turn the conversation to him or the kid, he prodded it back to her own past, the one he was robbing from to make up his own.

At first it was easy. She was a talker and like good talkers she figured that what she was saying was valuable and fun for the listener. She was relaxed, worked the air with her hands like a lover of talking. Once Ben gave up the idea of trying to get at his own past and decided to use hers, the plan was to keep her talking. When the kid came she talked a while yet but tried to turn the conversation over to him. Then Ben wanted more of her lilting past, as if he were hungry and it were food. He had great spaces ready, empty shelves, warehouses, silos to store a past in, and she couldn't talk fast enough, her talk like a trickle when he needed a cascading of stuff to make himself.

Flax, blue cornflowers, forget-me-nots, monkey flowers near where the spring soaked the meadow.

A BOAT STARTS UP ON THE RIVER BUT NOT FAR AWAY, A JET boat, a plague on the river, the Green Man has pontificated to Andrew. They hear the motor first and the rush of water out in the black. Then, like a firefly or the glowing paper hanging in the air after fireworks, something comes arcing in toward them slowly, painfully slow as if they have all evening to sit and watch the arc define itself in the black air that seems to open in front of the missile and close behind it. The Green Man and Mary and Andrew are waiting maybe for the sparks to write out something in the air.

Andrew's yell gets swallowed up by the sudden sound of the jet boat cracking open the night as exhaust pipes are suddenly straight out of the manifold with no water to baffle the noise. The sound is like being struck alongside the head. Andrew dives and knocks down the Green Man and Mary, and the sparking missile zings overhead and into the side of the cabin with an explosion of flame.

Molotov cocktail: Beirut, Dakar, Saigon, Cape Town, Seoul, Watts,

Managua, Panama City. The smell of gasoline, the frying, and orange light.

All three are in a pile in the weeds and the jet boat is a pinpoint of sound downstream. The house is on fire. The Green Man is oddly calm on the bottom of the pile, telling Andrew to get the hose from the other side of the house, that it will reach easily, to turn it on and use a fine spray at first to get close to the fire and wash the gasoline down. All this in measured tones like an instruction manual: "How to put out a gasoline fire."

Andrew goes for the hose thinking the Green Man and Mary will be doing something else in the name of putting out the fire, but as he comes clambering around the corner of the house dragging the hose, there they are standing back as if to wait for the flames to get small enough to roast marshmallows. They're back far enough so that the light just touches them, and Andrew pauses a second to see them flickering like the final scene in *Blithe Spirit*. He passes between them and the flames, dragging the hose, still expecting they'll jump into the rescue operation at any moment now, and they will all be involved in saving the house. Andrew shouts just to keep up with the rhythm of the flames, which have now grown to illuminate the pine eaves on the cabin. He is searching for the proper spray on the nozzle and half pissed off that he seems to be involved in this fireman imitation all by himself.

The fire is engaging to Andrew, even consuming, and he thinks that maybe the Green Man and Mary figure there's only interest enough for one person, and they're letting him have all the fun. Andrew reports that the fire is not really difficult to control and put out, that the spray indeed seems to shut down the size of the flames, and then the direct water washes away the rest of the gasoline into the soft ground.

The house is scorched, the paint bubbled and the foliage fried. But it's lucky the Molotov cocktail didn't go through a window and spread flames through the living room; there are two it could have gone through. It hit between them.

Mary and the Green Man have set the chairs up again in the same spot by the time Andrew finishes washing down the house and the surroundings, having seen forest fire crews on TV mopping up, making sure the hot spots are out. The Green Man has gone for more lemonade as if to say, "Now then, where were we?" Lemonade has become his drink recently: he drinks it insatiably, keeps quantities in his house, and has made pitchers constantly since the trial.

Andrew has returned, puffing slightly. He is perched and looking over his shoulder regularly at the dark river. Sitting ducks, very foolish, if you ask him. He listens for another jet boat and has rewind anxiety. He is afraid the tape of this will be rewound and run again. The conversation has turned to who was behind first the kitchen knife and now the gasoline bomb.

Horchow they all agree is the obvious choice but …

"Yes, but …" Andrew says, holding up a finger of reason, not a pose he is entirely familiar with but one that seems to have been growing on him these past few days. "On the contrary, Horchow is clearly not the one behind this." He looks at his finger to see if it means something too. It means, on the contrary, and he finds himself redundant once again.

Andrew continues. "Horchow is so much the obvious culprit that they couldn't be so dumb as to mess with us this soon after being publicly ridiculed. It has to be someone else who hasn't been uncovered yet and doesn't particularly want to be. Or wants Horchow blamed." Andrew hears himself as the voice of reason, the passion of science, of rectitude and sense.

Mary and the Green Man are looking at him as a unit, like some four-eyed creature that looks things over carefully, much more carefully than any two-eyed creature could. Then Mary says she's more concerned, "worried" she says first, then changes to "concerned," more concerned about the next scheduled spraying for the gypsy moth. That there's so much at stake for the chemical companies, they're liable to do anything. None of this with actual contractions. She speaks carefully as if picking up each word and turning it in the light first to see how it shines, and then slowly and without contractions so that at first she seems to have a foreign accent. It wasn't from any place and so it seemed her talk was suspended in the air.

She sits, her back to the river sounds, with hands in her lap and the Roosevelt light just outlining her mane. The Green Man seems now to have found something more interesting in the broken fabric of the lawn chair and has begun to pull apart the strapping separating the silvery mylar central thread from the other weave. He's pulling it farther and farther until he's begun to unravel the good part of the webbing in order to get a whole length of shiny string. He seems completely engrossed in the project while Mary continues talking about the moth spray.

"If they spray – if we let them – the bees die too, and the flickers feed on the poisoned insects and then …"

Mary continues to outline the danger to flickers – red-shafted – also goldfinches, and the osprey feeding on fishes full of residual and runoff poison. Andrew thinks back to more present dangers – bombs in the night, knives in the door, agents in the jail.

They sit there next to the steaming cabin, the green-black river, the swallow and bat infested air, sit in light insufficient to see one another clearly, and so each one can be doing something completely different: Mary is dissertating on bird and beast, while Andrew begins planning a campaign both circumspect and cunning regarding the dangers facing the Green Man. And the Green Man is very busy unraveling the fabric of the strapping on his lawn chair. Having casually arrived at his own crotch with a length of shiny silver, he's now bent nearly double, about to follow the trail where it inevitably leads – up his own … but no. He carefully stands and without letting go of the thread pursues his unraveling now kneeling in front of his chair with his back to Andrew and, lack of light or not, clearly ignoring Mary's essay on the birds and the bees.

Andrew is losing his own thread of planning a cunning counterattack. The Green Man's fingers tug the strapping fabric loose so he can carefully extract the central shiny thread and pull it clear, like watching someone peel an apple without breaking the peel: slowly, carefully, exquisitely, he peels and the curl hangs down in an impossible spring.

Mary has stopped talking and is watching him without apparent embarrassment as if she, too, wants to know where this shiny string leads, or how long it will be, or whether it will break before it's all out, or if it leads to the land of the wee people, or whatever it is the Green Man has in mind. They are all silent. For Andrew the cuckoo-clock feeling is back.

The Green Man follows the silver line past the horizontal seat of the chair and starts up the back. Hand over hand he pulls the silver plastic carefully through each tangle of fabric. Mary and Andrew now by mutual consent are engaged in watching something they have no idea about. It's like having begun a long sentence, and now they just have to wait to see what gets meant.

No one talks. Andrew has a notion to glance at Mary and raise his eyebrows Groucho-style to see if she is appreciating the drama properly. She seems calmly interested in whether he'll get the whole thing out. She pushes her hair back with both hands and holds it on each side of her head like a pair of captured rabbits. She leans into the obscurity to see how close Ben Brown has come to success.

"Got it!" exclaims the Green Man, and holds up his prize. "I got the whole thing out." He hands one end to Andrew and the other to Mary and pushes them apart so they can hold up the silver ribbon to catch the light. "Look at how long it turned out, much longer than the webbing itself."

Mary goes along with the idea that this is some kind of world record for pulling silver ribbons out of chair webbings, that she is in the presence of greatness, a witness to history, eminence, and prodigious achievement. Andrew is dumbfounded.

The Green Man isn't smiling like an idiot; he's convinced he's done a good service, having unraveled what was raveled and revealed the nature of something that was hidden.

"I just wanted to see how long it would be." The Green Man looking much like the Green Boy now, not sheepish or contrite but young and as if he really didn't have any responsibility beyond what he'd already made clear: "I just wanted …" And then Mary helps him roll his silver thread neatly and tie it up. He tucks it in his pocket, and they all sit down to another round of lemonade.

Andrew goes home shortly after the next lemonade, leaving Mary and the Green Man sitting in what Andrew still considered a dangerous spot on the river bank. It's not lightning he expected to strike twice, but the bad guys.

Andrew is still asleep when he hears the sirens. He looks out to see the Green Man's house in the hollow is all orange flame and the fire trucks are circling in trying to find the nearly hidden drive through the bushes to his house. Andrew runs out in pajamas thinking that he is still on the clock, that he's punched in and responsible for all this, that he should have made them get out of there because he knew the fiends would be back.

Andrew crashes through the woods cutting his feet on sticks and sees that the whole inside of the house is an orange ball of flame while the outside is dark. In front of him pops then pings a wire from the Roosevelt-era electrification system. He is shouting frantically for Ben, but the noise of the fire is impossibly loud now and pyrelike it breaks through the roof and snaps at the fir trees that over hang. The firs are slow to catch fire, seem to hold off the heat, then finally with a sigh ignite and fry the sky with the updraft. The fire truck, having found its way into the bushes and trees, narrowly misses Andrew as he dances around from window to window in his pajamas, convinced that the second fire-bomb attack certainly caught Ben asleep, and this time certainly the molotov cocktails found one of the windows and hit the floor with a smear of fire and the Green Man is no more.

Andrew is not familiar with death. His grandparents are all four alive, parents too, and aunts and uncles. He understands that someday it must start and he will go to funerals, become used to funerals, will even be comfortable at funerals. One of his classmates in ninth grade died sledding in a rare valley snowfall by shooting down a long hill and into the exhaust pipe of a parked car. That's the death he is remembering while stumbling over fire hoses. He remembers the murders, too, then. Another rare snowfall, as if snow were the signal for death. Then he remembers David Brinkley on NBC news explaining that what you were about to see might affect some viewers strongly. Children should perhaps be taken into another room. And the Vietnamese police chief put a pistol to the head of his Vietcong prisoner, shot him while the reporters recorded it for the evening news. It was run in slow motion to show the grimace and the jolt and the death and then the face of the colonel insolent and self-righteous in good color with the sun in the proper quadrant for the mini-cam. The student sat two seats behind him in math – but he had to imagine the death by exhaust pipe, the sharp circle cutting open a head like a cookie cutter. The double car murder was an East Leven mystery. And the Vietcong he knew electronically, could study the face, how unhappy the victim had looked being pushed around by the short colonel, how his hands were bound behind him, how the police chief spoke to the cameraman, raised the pistol (an expensive pistol), how the dead man's face jerked to the side with the shot. It was just another TV death except that this death was certified by the evening news and had the prestige of NBC behind it. A short snuff movie.

The burning of the Green Man, Andrew thinks as he wanders from window to window on bleeding feet, this is death. The firemen find him and take him to the fire truck to bandage his feet. They think he is an escaped resident wandering dazed, and they question him about the fire: Who else is inside? How did it start? Is there any natural gas or other flammable stored inside? They can't locate a hydrant close enough and begin to draw directly from the green river. Andrew tells them there is one, maybe two people inside. One green and the other, maybe, with hair, lots of hair out to here. And in the pocket of the green one is a silver thread.

The firemen leave someone to watch Andrew until the ambulance comes. He is not to be left alone, they tell the watcher. He is in shock and might try to get back into the house looking for the other people.

"No, no," Andrew tells his watcher. "I live upstream in a different house, and the Green Man lives here, lived here. There was an attempt to kill him earlier tonight with a gasoline bomb and I put out the fire using the hose … There was a jet boat … and then the silver thread we, all three of us, followed to its end."

Andrew finds his hand being patted, and thinks that patting hands is not so much reassuring as it is sort of a warning, a distraction that says: "Stop that now! You'll be all right if you just stop that now." Pat, pat, pat, pat, pat.

He is hauled off to the hospital to have his feet looked at properly, but first they believe him enough to go upstream and inform his parents that he is fine, but he needed the cuts looked after.

He is returned home at daybreak, and the firemen have left a message that there were no bodies in the house; they tore the wreckage apart and found no bodies at all. They must have escaped and gone elsewhere. Did Andrew know where they might have gone? Call the fire department.

Andrew shifts on the couch. His feet are tender, a tender foot, and he feels someone has absconded with his life.

He picks up the remote control and holds it. It feels heavy, full of channels laden like a Christmas stollen with candied fruits: red, yellow, and green. He points it at the TV and holds it there. Maybe it will make up its own mind.

Andrew leans back with a little bit of a codeine buzz from the painkiller the hospital gave him.

He falls asleep clutching the remote control, dreaming of where to aim it.

At noon the Green Man calls and tells Andrew that he's been at Mary's, he's heard about his house. Come right away. Andrew starts to tell him about being wounded, having a stitch in the bottom of one foot, taking a fistful of Tylenol IIIs, not getting any sleep last night. He starts, but stops. Gets the address and says I'll come over.

Andrew suspects this "growing younger" motif of the Green Man's has its sexual component, if the whole thing is not a metaphor. He stands in the parking lot with his bicycle.

Mary, her hair like a brace of patient cocker spaniels sitting one on each shoulder, hails him from the porch. "Right here," in case he had forgotten what the Green Man told him on the phone. Andrew can hardly wait to see the nest, whether the Green Man is wearing a bathrobe.

There are brightly colored pillows spread seraglio-style around the living room, some piled in a corner that looks to be the reading place with a spring-loaded lamp like a giraffe poking its neck from the brick-and-board bookcase. The bookcase is full, and other books are stacked around the walls.

The Green Man comes out of the back in full dress as a green person: J.C. Penney work clothes – greens to go with green.

"Good thing you moved the party," Andrew says to get things going.

"Well, yes. The police said my house is burned to the ground." This a flat, green statement.

"They said they had to push the walls in to make sure the fire was all out and didn't want to take a chance with the standing wall falling into the woods."

Mary has an interest in the crime aspect. "Did the firemen think it was the same people who threw the gasoline bomb at night? We told them about the jet boat and …"

Oh, it's WE, is it? Andrew wonders if she's getting minimum wage too.

"… and they said on the phone …"

Said on the phone! Said on the phone! Andrew's mind buzzes. How did they know to call the Green Man here? How did you know any of this burning was going on? Who are you anyway? What's going on here? He wants to hold his hands up to her like the Green Man did with the guy in the jail cell and read out who she is and where she comes from and where she's been in the past eight or ten days.

Andrew feels like a paranoid-for-hire rented by the Green Man, who apparently no longer has the proper paranoid facilities functioning.

Mary is pondering the crime still. Andrew is pondering Mary, not for the first time. And the Green Man seems only vaguely interested in the fact that his house burned down, clearly more interested in Andrew's descriptions of the fire equipment and what he remembers of how they put out the fire.

"How did they get in touch with you?" Andrew asks.

"What's the matter with your foot?"

Andrew tenderfoots around the biggest pillow and then sits down.

"Did they have any suspicions about who did it?"

All questions and no answers, the three of them like three people who have begun to talk at the same instant and now fall silent and wait for the other. The room passes into a quietness that becomes theatrical, thick and palpable, a topic of discussion all by itself. There is, at least for Mary and Andrew, a knot being tied and tightened in the air; they see the cords pulling and cinching on each other. The Green Man is not partial to seeing knots tighten in the air. He cultivates a kind of goofy grin.

Finally, it is Ben who insists on seeing Andrew's stitches, and Andrew takes his shoe off for him. He and Mary admire the stitches and the clever padding that allows him to walk. They make him show the other foot too, though it's just scratched. Andrew is pleased by the feeling of having things evened out – admire one foot, admire the other. It is the balance he likes.

Mary and the Green Man. Hard to tell as they coo over Andrew's soles just where the one leaves off and the other begins.

Mary says, "Oh, Marge called us when the fire people called her. They knew from the newspaper, it seems, about the trial. They called Marge because her name was in the paper, then Marge called me because she thought I might know how to find both of you." Here she grabs two handfuls of hair, her capture and release gesture Andrew has come to think of it, and moves them off her shoulders. She has known Marge a long time from Mycological Society meetings and gatherings in the woods to collect wild mushrooms. And the Audubon Society.

Andrew listens for clues about what went on last night but gets instead a running account of forays in the woods with Marge and other members of the Mycological Society. The Green Man is silent on the subject, but Andrew has the feeling that if he were to ask him directly about sex and the liberated Green Person, he would get an answer right in his face. First, Andrew thinks, my keeper status doesn't extend to proctoring nights in the hay. And second, what he needs is a similar break in the tension of the past days, and this is what makes him so nosy in the first place. Recreational sex, he's thinking.

To Mary and the Green Man, Andrew makes the suggestion that maybe they all ought to lay low and wait for the police or the firemen or someone to see what the poop is here, and just how likely the fiends are to strike again. It's them against the fiends. The scenario is clear to Andrew. They hide out for a while until these people make themselves known by asking around. They are part of the public record here. Andrew's house is out of the question for early American reasons as well as the risk of burning out his parents too. Marge's cedar palace is also known to whatever fiends are out there. What they need is a fiend factor to figure in, some kind of Planck's constant by which they can multiply any of their movements to see how they'll come out, how likely they are to become victims of fiendery.

But they don't have a fiend factor, no probabilities, no bell curve for this one. So they decide to do the American thing – the only certifiable, New World, sound American move: they hit the road.

III. Going West, Looking for Water

IN THE LOWLANDS OF EAST LEVEN, HOUSES HAD LONG AGO reclaimed land that once belonged, in season, to the river. The sloughs would back up, then the ravines and little canyons, and in fifty-year flood plains the river would flood the land with deft fingers of brown water. Wing dams, flood control, and hydroelectric dams in the mountains helped East Leven civilize the water. But in the low lands, the sump pump was the warrior that stood between river and basement.

The Green Man knew about the Barken-Jeffrey sump-pump jousts. He had the habit of walking out in the evening when the light was beginning to fail. Even the first loss of light was enough to slur the green skin into shadow. He thought he couldn't startle his neighbors as he passed: wished them a good evening, kept on walking, blended with the deep shadows, kept from confronting them, grew inconspicuous, disappeared. He had walked by each drainage project at its heyday, had been witness to the silver grating, the gold grating, the sumptuous sumps. In the light rain the Green Man walked his regular walk past Barken and Jeffrey and listened for their pumps.

Warren Barken primed his new pump with a hose. He filled the reservoir on the silver pump as big as a cocker spaniel then went to throw the new 40-amp circuit breaker he'd installed. A warm hum came from the hole where Warren had set aside the cap, also silver, and where fresh pipes snaked away into the soil to send the water to the street. Warren put his ear to the pump as if listening for a heartbeat and kept his ear there out of pride. The pump went silent, having done its job and shut off.

Warren stood up and surveyed his work. He was fifty-nine years old and now ran the finest sump pump on the street. After all the others failed, after the brown, still water crept into every crack and interstices in the neighborhood, his pump would keep him dry. The water could run at his house from all directions and 1400 cfs protected him like the Virgin Mary. PUC four-inch drain, the city wouldn't let him put in the eight-inch ones. Within code he owned the finest sump system in the lowlands, industrial or residential.

Warren looked at his sump pump and saw it was good.

The sump pump had come to East Leven with electricity. In one form or another the water pump came to stand for survival: the way to irrigate the fields during rainless summers and the way to drive back the river plump with itself in the winter, when water crept up the ravines and backed up the creeks and threatened to reclaim the land where East Leven stood. What the sword was to medieval knights, what penicillin was to the second half of the twentieth century, the sump pump was to East Leven. A dry basement was a sign that your house stood in delicate truce with the river and rain.

Just down the street from Warren, the UPS truck pulled up to William Jeffrey's house and off-loaded a collection of boxes great and small. William carted the boxes back to his garage, where he had pipes lining the walls, where a blueprint was nailed to one wall and spotlights clamped to the rafters to throw dramatic light on his plans. The sump pump wars had begun.

The Green Man lived in the five-hundred-year flood plain, below Warren and William. His house would go first, way before either sump pump even kicked in.

Warren showed up in William's frontyard with his hands on his hips.

"I saw the UPS truck stop by, Jeffries. What's up with that. Lots of boxes, I thought. I said to myself, that Jeffries is getting lots of boxes this far away from Christmas." He laughed, more of a serial grunt, to show that he liked a joke. Warren had retired six years before from his job as city architect. He never really had to design anything more complicated than a greenhouse in thirty-five years with the city. His job was approving the designs of others: sidewalks downtown, the municipal parking garage no one used, the gazebo in the park. Under Warren's stern gaze, East Leven was allowed to sprawl carefully with full regulatory cooperation – state and federal guidelines. But Jeffrey always to him was Jeffries.

"Some things I needed for a project," William said coyly. He clicked his remote and down came the garage door on boxes, blueprints, spotlights, pipes. Warren stepped to look around the side of the house, but too late. William thought of himself as a scientist, though he never did science. As Warren was an architect in his day, so William Jeffrey was an engineer each day for a warehouse company. He oversaw the same plans built repeatedly in different locations. On weekends he dedicated himself to matters of drainage and moving the fickle waters of East Leven.

Warren considered the impasse, proffered a fragile offering to get things going. "I just tried out my new sump pump, half-horse, submersible, 250 gallons per minute. Has its own 15-amp service. Backup's smaller, one-third horse, own circuit again, 150 gallons per minute."

William thought about this collection of facts, took his time to let them settle in his engineer's brain, each in its own pigeonhole. He took a breath and let it out as if drawing a line under the new sump-facts. "That should be …" he paused slightly, just enough to get Warren right between the eyes, "… adequate." The word hung in the air between the two men, the young man who had served it up, the older man a groundwater warrior of some renown. "I mean that should keep you pretty dry. Under most conditions."

"Why," asked Warren. "Have you got something …" better, was what he wanted to say. "Have you got something … else?" Warren unzipped his jacket. He was warm suddenly.

William took his time, knowing it was up to him just how much escalation would be enough for today. "Well, you remember when I trenched along both sides of the house? Then I pea-pebbled the trench, then the perforated pipe with the gravity feed into the big sump in the backyard? You remember, don't you, Warren? I had all that reseeding to do. And then I had to top dress …"

"Yeah, yeah. I remember. Your yard was a mess. So what you got planned?"

"Well, that sump drained pretty well with just gravity feed away from my property, but I got to thinking. What if I pull the water out of that sump with a little more force than just gravity? You know, Warren, when the ground is saturated, even supersaturated like it got a few years ago, and then you get that snow melt in the mountains that's raising the groundwater, why the whole hydraulic system just needs some help." He thought that might be enough information for now, but Warren wasn't having any treaty talks.

"So what'd you get? A Sears 4480? What's the capacity? What's your gpm?" William looked into his heart and decided he would string Warren out as far as he could. "Well, I thought maybe something in the way of a … professional pump. Of course, the Sears 4480 is a good homeowner pump. But your heavy-duty pumps are all rated … Excuse me, is that my phone?" Both men listened intently. "Maybe not. So anyway, a municipal-rated runs you a little more. No. A lot more. But in the long run … Wait, I think that is my phone. Excuse me, Warren, I'll catch you later."

William almost skipped into the house leaving Warren flabbergasted and in the state of information *interruptus*, half-fucked as it were. Warren walked home slowly knowing his new pump was shriveling in its housing with every step he took.

In the next weeks William would leave cardboard boxes flattened for recycling with crucial parts removed so that you couldn't tell what they had contained. One box was of especially thick and sturdy cardboard.

William had to saw it to make it bend into the bundle. And Warren crept down the block to survey the boxes for weekly pick-up. The heavy cardboard really got him. Nothing shabby or weak would come in a box like that. The husk said heavy-duty all the way. It shouted of significant gpms and a deep satisfying hum that would tell a tale of oil-light brass bushings and bearings oozing stability. Damn, thought Warren, and went shopping.

When his new industrial pump came, Warren left the box outside his garage. He was vaguely dissatisfied by the quality of the cardboard, but the pump itself was magnificent. He would have to replace all the fittings and connections he'd installed for the 4480, and the housing and grate were too small. The new ones came in an even more impressive box. A new pile of dirt alongside his house revealed where the new pump housing and grate would be installed. This pump would suck the water from his property and fire it into the storm drain.

And just down the street William began to leave ten-inch to two-foot lengths of huge diameter PVC pipe as if lengths had been lopped off giant drains. One day, a six-by-six foot grating arrived by truck from a local metal fabricating plant. It announced: "Heavy-Duty Round Drainage Grate." It was big enough to cap a bomb shelter. It was unpainted, and William leaned it conspicuously against his garage door, fully visible from the street and painted it blaring silver. It weighed 390 pounds.

Warren, seeing the size and color of the thing, slunk home and plopped into his recliner in front of the TV to regroup. Six by six, he thought. How big could that sump be? Jeffries must be doing something else with that, that silver monstrosity. Finally, after the news, he decided to call in a few favors down at the city water-processing plant. They'd have the big cement sumps with the locking grates. Warren hoped the boys down there remembered him, how he took care of them in the old days.

The East Leven pumping station had one section of cement pipe you could row a boat in. Warren had it shipped to his frontyard not knowing exactly what he could do with it, but he knew Jeffries would crap his pants when he saw it. An old circular grate was dropped off the next week by a city crew. Warren handpainted, slowly, taking two days with a small brush. He painted it gold and let it dry for a month next to the cement pipe. William Jeffrey folded his tents, cleaned up his mess, and slunk away from the battlefield.

It had begun to rain, and the ground was so saturated from a rain ten days before that with this new rain sump pumps above the Green Man's house began to pump. The outlets were arrayed along the edge of the ravine above his house—white pipe poking out at the river like so many small cannons. Warren Barken's pump started first, then William Jeffrey's pump—these being the newest and most sensitive to groundwater levels. The Green Man closed a window on the rain side of the cabin and opened one on the lee. The pumps spit out groundwater. Anne Doucette stirred abroad.

Ben Brown could feel Barken's pump drawing heavy juice through the line when he walked past. The pump hummed with a deep resonant whir like a dynamo. Barken's industrial-grade pump gobbled 220 and established hegemony over all the spongy earth around the Barken house. The Green Man thought he could feel the land drying out.

Down the street, Jeffrey's new pump ran nearly silent with a low tone like whale song, as if metal bearings had been replaced by crystal and friction had become so minimal the pump could run without electricity, with just the will to pump and redeem the land again and again. The Jeffrey pump was religion to the Barken pump's engineering. The two realms worked side by side to save humans from human nature, and the pumps extracted water to save the houses temporarily from the East Leven legacy of water. Down the ravine went the water, back to the river, back to the sky, and back through the pumps, the sound of water going somewhere. The Barken pump fired the water into the ravine in a parabolic arc. The Jeffrey pump launched the water straight across the ravine and onto the other side like a gold-mining water-blaster and then shut off and waited for more water to accumulate. The Green Man passed the Jeffrey pump and appeared to cross himself, quickly with fingertips, a small, quick cross in the center of his jacket. Or maybe Jeffrey didn't see clearly from his window, across the yard in the rain.

Mary Willson sits in the new chair and listens to the Green Man's rendition of the sump pump wars. She could hear her father's voice-over, running commentary. Row to hoe. A hell of a row to hoe, being green. Her father liked to editorialize the evening news for the whole family while everyone strained to hear David Brinkley. Once he had been silenced as David calmly read the contents of a package of nondairy creamer he had received on an airplane. Then David continued with the news as if nothing had happened. Mary's father could not believe his ears. Mary's family could not believe the patriarch's stunned silence and endured editorial-free news, indeed got a newfound taste for it. Mary hears the voice-over run parallel to Ben Brown's tale of sump pumps. *And I don't think the row gets any easier to hoe down a ways either. Jee-zuz, this is the stuff of nightmares, Mary. A green person, this is a flagrantly green person. What's with all this concern for where water goes? Who makes it go faster? These are crazy people! Who would be this crazy? These people have nothing to do. Absolutely nothing to do, and so they invent this stuff to worry about. What a bunch of crap.*

Mary listens to the early skirmishes in the sump pump war, fascinated by the teller and the telling. But still her father's voice chirps along with Ben Brown's narrative. *So who's the biggest boob at the end of the day? Jeffrey or Barken? They're both well over the qualifying height for nincompoops. What? Hundreds of dollars later – thousands?! – these guys are some kind of warriors? What's that about? They're telling this Green Guy their secret proto lives for what? Like he'll absolve them or something? A wave of the hand? Et cum spiri and all that jazz. What is it, Mary? And what's the deal with you and Mr. Green/Brown? What are his intentions, anyway? Who needs green-gene? Wasn't that Captain Kangaroo's sidekick? Mr. Green Jeans? And he was Clarabell the Clown on Howdy Doody so the whole thing hangs together eventually, doesn't it, Mary? Mary? Are you listening? Mary?*

She shifts in the chair. The old lawn chair had been undone on an evening not unlike this one, thread by thread.

"So Jeffrey stopped me on my walk to fill me in on what happened. He had run a four-inch pipe out from the pump so there'd be no back pressure from the sump pump. But it seems that Barken had not only seen his pipe-diameter raise, but upped the ante. Barken had built a sump you could climb down into. Not just a hole for the sump pump but a what? A kind of actual sewer where the pump lived and could be serviced by someone small enough. Well this was a trump card, you'll forgive the conceit. The machinery of war had become the war."

Mary nods. Her father, long dead now, prattles on in her head with his parallel text.

"So Jeffrey is looking for a way to counter this walk-in sump business. And he tells me, 'Ah ha. I've got it.'"

THE MURDERS HAVE BEEN COLD HERE FOR YEARS. EVERY NOW and then the newspaper retells the story, asks the questions, and speculates on who is still walking around with blood on his hands. A number of authorities have tried to talk to Crazy Leo about the murders, but he can't find them again among the Buick hubcaps, the Model Ts. And so he keeps his secret and his own counsel.

Crazy Leo belongs completely to this place the way the land curves against the green river and the cottonwoods grow thick along the banks and reach under the earth for the cool water on a hot summer day. He operates in the fields and along the roads with a certainty and elegance that fills each place. Head down, taking direction from the grass and twigs and white butterflies on the blue chicory flowers, Leo arranges a world for himself just far enough off the end of his nose so that his next step propels him into it.

Crazy Leo foraged in Forbes's field along the highway curve, where any escaped hubcap would roll through the ditch into the long grass. He seemed to sniff the field for hubcaps, and then his homing genius picked out an Impala hubcap with its flecks of red, and he shuffled to where it lay. He brushed it off, polished it with a sleeve, and then with great care entrusted it to his bag. He paused as if some kind of prayer of thanks were due, then shambled forward with his head down again.

In East Leven, Leo is so well known that "Crazy" has become only a front name like Billy. It seems it is always the river that comforts both Leo and the Green Man, the voices there and the seep springs where the monkey flowers sport surprising yellow in the mud, the camas and twin flowers and trilliums and wild ginger of spring. These are the land's full occupiers. Ben Brown is the green dream among green things here. His greenness seemed more and more the greenness of plants and the felicity of one root system lapping another like holding hands under the earth. But there was at the same time the feeling that the greenness had been manufactured, forged in orange-hot furnaces, then quenched and hardened in oil that sizzled as he was plunged in and tempered. He was dug up somewhere, green ore, purified and shaken with the hair fried off him until he was worthy of greenness, the newness of being green. He felt rolled and extruded and forged and arc-welded finally on the tower until one end of him reached the other in a perfect ring of green without a detectable seam. He was ready to roll, to ring with his making, with having been made. This was another kind of green dream.

The dream of fire. Ben had the fear of fire that green things have, though he was from the fire. That's the dream. He was one thing made into two, and the two are at war and the dream is the stretching of the one thing in two ways until the breaking point and then beyond and beyond the breaking point until the two-ness itself is perfect and impossible. The dream is that the one green is not the other and that at the same time it most certainly is the same because the manufactured green is so much cleverer than the plant green that includes it. There is one green fleeing from another. There is one green lapping over the other like two strokes of two paintbrushes. This is the same kind of dream as the hot-oil version but a variation, one of a large number of variations.

And another kind of dream with just as many variations as the other two but a dream less frequent, as if it carefully chose its spots to appear, to fill in between the other dreams: He was a hat – a green hat? it's not clear – hanging on a hat rack in a restaurant, maybe a coat, too, that went with the hat that someone carelessly left hanging there, and other garments came and went. This was a puzzling dream and a simple one. Each time he had it, he was the same hat, but sometimes there was no coat, no other visiting garments, but always the same restaurant.

Almost always in sleep he dreams now, and more and more he begins to dream if he as much as lets his mind wander standing or sitting wide awake in the middle of the day, sun in his eyes, left shoe pinching. In or out of dreaming Andrew circulates as a character in the tales concocted out of his greenness, cobbled together to entertain him, his Sancho Panza.

Since the fire – fire of dreams, of reality: a refining crucible and a house on the riverbank, this pair of emblems, two selves fired fast and slow – like Leo, Ben Brown can't seem to concentrate on basic kinds of things, such as where he left his shoes and socks. The weather has become warmer. He takes off his shoes and socks when he can and, it seems, when he shouldn't too. He knows what this shoelessness is all about: it's the growing younger. It's Merlin the Magician's odd condition of knowing and growing younger in the knowing that only comes by having grown old. More than other paradoxes, this one is worthy of Merlin and magic, of the privileged seeing into the world where the dream is absolutely real and what is most pleasing of all is the difficulty, the complexity, the knot tied into itself worth untying.

THE FLOWER BOXES ALONG THE MAIN STREET HELD PINK trailing petunias, lobelia in electric blue, white alyssum to soften the edges of the box, verbena in another pink, dusty miller like small towers of gray hope in the center, then blue scabiosa like small tufts of toilet paper dyed for a prank. And variations on these lined the street high and low. Occasionally some exotic flower stuck out, such as the gaudy trailing double fuchsia hanging in front of the florist as a sign that here was knowledge of flowers, not just flowers. The fuchsia he hung out front had an unnatural look to it as if it had been manufactured somewhere in an Asian country between desks of young women tying flies and other desks assembling silk flowers. Like a decapitated tiny dancer, each flower with its opaque purple skirt in full ruffle with an overskirt of sharply pointed red sepals announced design errors at the DNA level, fundamental misuse of genetic material dipped in a chemical to make it diploid then dangled in front of the shop like a dare to the public, a personal challenge from the shop's owner. Conroy Burbank was asking customers to come in and debate nature itself. Inside the shop Conroy continued the assault with the sayings of Ralph Waldo Emerson: (personally) Who so would be a man would be a nonconformist; (cosmically) Hitch your wagon to a star; (celestially) The sun shines also today; (autumnally) A foolish consistency is the hobgoblin of little minds; (floristically) He that watereth shall be watered himself; (and cryptically) Let a man know his worth and keep things under his feet. This last one always baffled Conroy's customers.

"But what does it mean? What things under his feet? Is it like keeping your 'feet on the ground' or what?" Conroy's best customer, Mrs. Little, would interrogate. Her hair avoided the old-lady blue. It was tightly curled to her head but brilliant white surrounding her blue eyes like clouds drifting just behind her head. The effect was arresting and since she was short, alas little, it was the effect that helped her hold space in a room. She looked at Conroy quizzically.

But deflection was his strategy. "What does it mean to you, Mrs. L? Mr. Emerson loved the indirection, dontcha know? He loved to sneak up on you like nature herself. Take my shop plants. Please! No, no, buy my shop plants, Mrs. L. But seriously. Emerson is my spiritual father, you know. The reason I came to be a florist. I don't know if I told you or not, but my father was a farrier and had serious relations with the horse. He was kicked many, many times, in fact." Here Conroy paused and reviewed his father's kicks, looking ceilingward as if to count the kicks there. His brown spiky hair gave him the look of constant cartoon surprise and with occupation-related additions looked like winter grass in field with the seed heads sheered off by winter winds. A florist's inevitable vest, in winter and summer weights, was the badge of his occupation, and in his estimation a florist without a vest was a bouquet without decorative greens. Mrs. Little had heard variations on these themes before, but East Leven was the smallest town she'd ever lived in, and she sought out the town characters to give her a big-city boost once in a while. It was the occasion of her regular visits to Conroy Burbank. She liked to send flowers to friends in other towns, especially to cities like New York and Chicago. She felt that somehow she was exporting East Leven's bucolic countryside, gathering up the colors and foliage and exporting it directly to less-fortunate friends. She had found East Leven just after the Green Man. The town, she felt, had come fully equipped with exotics: Crazy Leo, unsolved murders, the ghost of Anne Doucette and, of course, the Green Man, Mr. Brown. She had lived all over the world with her husband working for Exxon. In

Algeria for two months living on a dry, stone-strewn peninsula, she had the servants arrange in every sight line to the gray hills pots of the most brightly colored flowers she could find. They called her *Madame Fleur* in the village nearby, and her shipments of flowers became a significant part of the gross domestic product of the village. The plants, watered or not, would live only a week or two in the heat that rose in strings into the baked blue sky. Donkeys, motor scooters, an ancient Plymouth Valiant, and camels were involved in the steady supply of petunias, carnations, and geraniums – whatever could be procured – to supply Madame Fleur. The company easily absorbed the cost into the huge exploration expense. And Sam Little would return each evening to find his wife plunked happily on the rocky plain surrounded by her unnatural garden. When Sam died, in Indonesia, on a monsoon evening full of the chirping of tree frogs, Mrs. Little found herself a widow in a spectacular tropical garden occasionally raided by orangutans and seasonally by fruit bats. She picked East Leven for its climate, rhododendrons, and zone seven gardens, where rosemary hedges proved hardy and the occasional winter wet snow left three days of fantastic garden sculptures and then was gone.

Mrs. Little had bought, during her first days in town, an "Entertainment Pak" of discount and two-for-one coupons that promised savings up and down the Willamette Valley from Portland to Eugene. As she spent the coupons, she found herself more and more in Portland, where the density of restaurants and art galleries beckoned her cosmopolitan self. Finally, though, it was the Green Man that awakened her attachment to East Leven. She, who had lived in the exotic much of her life as she followed Sam around the world, felt the presence of the Green Man as her way into the center of town. His being green seemed to her a sacrifice of sorts on her behalf. She wasn't sure exactly how. Her first months of lusting after the bright promises of her Entertainment Pak began fading away in the presence of Ben Brown walking the modest streets day after day in East Leven. She felt gently rounded up by a green cowboy and comforted by the fences of the corral. She had decided she would stay in East Leven long enough to die there.

Conroy Burbank's shop, the Green Man, the care and feeding of nearly one hundred rhodys and azaleas on her property, these sustained Mrs. Little. And in between times she kept several tropical plants in pots to remind her of the Indonesian garden and Sam: bougainvillea, banyan, mandevillea, carefully hauled in and out of doors to fool them into blooming, simulating their natural winter without a freeze. Mrs. Little was a gardener who extended her garden from Burbank's shop electronically to her friends across the country. Just an occasional glimpse of the Green Man in the parking lot of the grocery store or walking the sidewalks of East Leven and her need for the exotic was satisfied.

"And dianthus, then polypodia. A simple boquet delivered, let's see, Thursday," she said. "Here. I'll write the card message, Conroy. Address it three ways. These people don't know each other, and they'll never find out I got a triple-header out of the same message." She stopped and looked at Conroy as he fiddled his pen from a vest pocket. "What would your Mr. Emerson have to say about this little deception?"

Conroy studied several of the Emerson signs as if he were looking for an answer in his shop texts. He already knew what to say, but the ruse of study pleased him. He hooked his thumbs in both vest pockets and finally pronounced, "I believe Mr. Emerson would wholeheartedly approve of the surprise of unexpected flowers. I know he would. He always welcomed the unexpected in any form, Mrs. Little. You can be sure of that. He walked out from his house almost every day looking for surprise from nature's great store of the unexpected." He rolled his eyes up in a gesture of looking for a quote from the texts in his head. "Let's see, his 'Lords of Life': surprise, temperament something, something, succession … But above all surprise."

Mrs. Little seemed to find this satisfactory. Her whole morning had been satisfactory, and now she needed to get back to her garden that she tended herself on the advice of Voltaire in *Candide*. Travel the world looking, but come home finally to tend your own garden. Ultimately that garden will be the only thing to make sense.

Out on the street, Conroy Burbank's gaudy fuschias gave way as she walked to the pedestrian flowers in flower boxes. The Kodak sign in schoolbus yellow swung and bloomed in sympathy. And just in sight, past the bakery and the hardware store, there he was high stepping around the power mowers chained together on the sidewalk with wheelbarrows and bags of mulch. The Green Man crossed the street in the middle of the block, waited on the center line for a car full of kids to slow and pass, and then skipped up the curb on the far side and was gone.

An east wind in East Leven usually brought rain. Storms came in as counterclockwise rotations off the Pacific packed with water. The coast range milked off the heavy rain, and what trickled over pelted the valley. For the Green Man, the best rain was the light rain, so light the wind carried it up sometimes, that came from the north along the river following the certainty of the valley.

Downtown East Leven seemed to have every light on, every kilowatt sucked up from the river employed to crack open the gloom of late afternoon in winter. The florist shop leaked a bluish light onto the street, the bar flooded orange neon from beer signs into the gray afternoon, and the pharmacy and the bakery conspired to cast a snowlike presence on sidewalks. East Leven downtown held out against Wal-Mart and wholesale clubs by being demographically too thin to merit invasion. East Leven couldn't pay yet and so remained in a retail past tense. Like the Green Man, East Leven was an anomaly, idiosyncratic, insouciantly unaware that the world hadn't arrived quite yet.

The Green Man hid out in East Leven without really realizing he was doing it. The world's interest in its unique green member seemed to fade after an initial frenzy of interest. Somehow, follow-up stories petered out in a quick decrescendo. He never did anything after the initial adventure of turning green. That was the problem with the Green Man as news.

On this wet, spring Tuesday, Mrs. Little shook out her umbrella before entering Conroy Burbank's flower shop. Emerson chattered from the hanging signs. It had been rainy all morning and it looked like it might rain all afternoon.

Conroy was excited. "We need to do something, Mrs. L. We really do. This town's at a crossroad."

Mrs. Little arm-wrestled her umbrella into submission and sealed its geometry away with a swirl of the velcro strap. She looked up finally. "Now, Conroy. What is it?" she said, trying to portray the soul of patience. She had found that in growing old there were fewer and fewer listeners among her acquaintances, and she set her mind to the project of listening as well as possible everyday. She found that this practice, this cultivated habit, made her welcome in many different circles young, old, everywhere in between. She had applied for the job of professional listener and found absolutely no competition for the position.

Conroy hitched up his apron over his florist's vest. He had been cutting flowers for an arrangement and the ends drooled sap and left stains at the slightest touch to any fabric. Dianthus was the worst. Narcissi next slobbered like Saint Bernard's. "A crossroad. And here's why. Main Street is becoming more and more fragile, don't you see. Right now there's almost full occupancy but every dip in the economy produces victims. Empty shops up and down. It's like Paraguay or Uruguay or something."

Mrs. Little raised both eyebrows and cocked her head. She called this to herself only, her "smart puppy" face, and it never failed to bring out the listenee, the one being listened to. Sometimes she tucked up her bottom lip to complete the effect of rapt attention. The speaker might have been holding up a Milkbone.

Conroy continued. "I mean, sometimes it seems as if people get disappeared right out of their shops. Some economics gestapo just comes to get them in the night. Then there's a real-estate sign in the window. That sad, empty look, through the window, of a chair by itself, some tired shelves. You know, of defeat. And it happens every time there's even a little dip in the Dow, if you know what I mean."

Mrs. Little nodded that, indeed, she did.

"There was that import shop with cute stuff from around the world, remember? The little flags in the window of all nations. What? A year? Eighteen months, anyway. And they were gone. Where do these people go, anyway? I suppose they could disappear into the great bowels of Horchow and never be seen again."

Conroy felt flush with his rhetoric and knew, at the same time, that he could get away with only so large a gesture before customers began backing out the door looking at their watches, holding up a finger for a kind of time-out. But Mrs. Little was always safe for trying out a new program. She seemed never to be inclined to flight.

"Horchow feeds the downtown, of course. Everybody knows that. As they go, we all go. But they seem to supply us only so much foot traffic here on the street. Then, any little thing and the bubble breaks." He gestured into the air to pop bubbles that might be there. He made popping sounds with his lips. The apron came off. Mrs. Little settled in against the counter. Conroy dusted off his vest. He had begun to frequent city council meetings though he hadn't presumed to public office. Yet.

"We're a one-trick pony, Mrs. L. And Horchow is our one trick." He picked up a dianthus stem to conduct with. "And you know as well as I do … well, we could use another trick or two. So I'm thinking the other day, inspired by Ralph Waldo's essay 'Experience,' that we've got a pretty rich soup cooking here in East Leven. We just need to appreciate all the stuff in our broth. So to speak. Anyway, you know what I mean." He cocked one eye at Mrs. Little. She knew he was rehearsing this for a city council meeting. She debated whether to mention that the pony/soup metaphor seemed a bit crowded, and he might reconsider one or the other for the final version. He was breathing heavily now, the stem in his left hand with the flower end in danger of being decapitated at any moment against the counter top. "So it comes down, on one level, to the Green Man. There he is, a what? Cultural resource. An attraction, whether he wants to be or not. I think we might approach him with a reasonable proposal. In exchange for featuring him as a tourist draw for East Leven. We could have a day for him in the summer, and he'd be a kind of king for a day with a court, a parade-kind of like Mardi Gras. And then, I don't know, we give him a tax break or something. Make him our number one citizen."

Mrs. Little held up her hand as if she were in second grade.

"Yes?"

"Would you like that, Conroy? Really? If you were the green one? Can you see how difficult it might be?"

"No, no, Mrs. L. I don't mean anything negative at all. I mean as a celebration of our most famous, our best citizen. Now after the trial he's stunningly famous again, almost like when he first showed up here. He could be our nature guy, you know – can't you see him as Emerson's doctrine of compensation? The antidote to Horchow? He'd be kind of a mascot of our clean living and keep Horchow honest. Why they'd have to look lively, wouldn't they?" He decapitated the flower against the counter on the word "lively." But he kept going with the stem conducting his thoughts into the air. "I guess I don't see that it would do any harm if we asked, is all I'm saying. And I mean asked in the nicest way, of course."

Mrs. Little couldn't see a nice way to ask or even what the question might be. Will you be our town mascot? No. Will you let us use a picture of you to bring tourists? No. Would you permit us to dress you up as a ... as a shrub? A tree? A plant? And then have a parade and a picnic in order to ... her mind raced. Would you like? Would you like "a cup of tea?" she said out loud.

"What?" Conroy held the limp, headless stem so it drooped to the countertop.

"A cup of tea, Conroy," she said. "I think I'll run and get a cup of tea at Johansson's. They have such good teas, and I need to get off my feet for a while. So if you'll just send a number six to my friend in Pittsburgh – you have all the information – and put it on my bill," she said brightly and went out the door, accompanied by the tinkle of Burbank's spring bell on the jamb.

Outside she opened her jacket to the sunshine, which broke through the rain clouds in rays that made her think of the Hudson River School painters. The Green Man was crossing the street again a half block down, coming over to her side, to Conroy Burbank's side. Mrs. Little found herself hoping the Green Man didn't have business in the flower shop today. She had never spoken to him before. Never had reason to. He was walking along slowly, hands in his jacket pockets. Mrs. Little marched along the sidewalk toward him.

"Excuse me, Mr. Brown." Her voice sounded loud to her. Had she spoken too loud? Did people talk to him too loud because he seemed like a foreigner and maybe he would understand better if you spoke louder? Oh dear, she thought. Oh dear. But the Green Man stopped and took his green hands out of the green pockets of his J.C. Penney jacket.

"Mrs. Little, isn't it? How are you today? Looks like we're having something of everything in the weather department."

Just say what I want to say, not what I'm thinking, she thought. "Well, I wanted to warn you about something, Mr. Brown."

"That's hard, isn't it, calling someone Brown when he's clearly green?"

"Oh, dear, yes, it is."

"I actually thought about changing my name to, well, you know. But I couldn't go through with it finally. A warning, you say?"

"Oh, nothing dangerous. I don't think. It's just that the florist, Conroy Burbank, has a kind of harebrained scheme afoot. One that involves you. Or could involve you, anyway. So I thought you should know about it and be as prepared as you can be for this kind of thing." She looked at him closely for the first time. He had nice eyes, she thought, and fought not to say it aloud. "He's thinking, and that's Conroy's problem, sometimes. He overthinks things. He's a big fan of Emerson, you know." Ben somehow made it easy for her to talk to him. "Conroy's thinking that you would make a kind of civic symbol, an attraction really, for East Leven. I don't think all this will go very far, but you could be prepared for him."

"A civic symbol? I guess I'm already a kind of attraction. You wouldn't believe how many times … But that's a long, endless story. I'm green, Mrs. Little, and that's the beginning point of every day I'm alive." He leaned over into a conspiratorial whisper. "And the green doesn't show any signs of fading, unfortunately. It looks like I'll be green the whole rest of the way in this life. I've made adjustments. It's okay. I'm even going right now to look at green cars. I think it should be green, anyway."

"But Conroy will probably catch you some day on the street and propose that you allow yourself to become some kind of East Leven mascot." She tried to catch herself, but worry infused her tone. Was she whining? "I have to tell you, when I heard him say it, I thought of those awful baseball mascots they have dressed up in chicken suits or as pirates with big plastic heads. I'm sorry. That sounds dreadful, I know. But I couldn't help it. I thought of a big plastic green man in a parade or something."

But Ben Brown laughed. "Certainly there'll be some franchising opportunities. Spin-offs and action figures. Why didn't I think of this? Oh, yeah.

I guess I did. But it seems like a long time ago now." He patted her arm and she didn't flinch. It was his test as to whether people were still seeing green or he was having an actual conversation. If you could get away with touching them, the green had nearly gone. "So don't worry. Thank you for the warning though. I had all kinds of offers actually when I first turned green. When I was news, you could say. Haven't had much in a while. But I can handle it, Mrs. Little. I think I've had most forms of commercial exploitation offered to me. You'd be surprised."

Mrs. Little felt better immediately. "How did you know my name?" she blurted.

Ben Brown cocked his head to one side like a bird. He smiled, considering whether to give her the long answer or the short answer. Not the whole phenomenological answer that included Indonesian jungle, flocks of butterflies, the pharmacology of ponderously perfumed blue-haired ladies – all that. But a substantial answer with a certain amount of decoration, something of a world view.

Ben Brown gauged Mrs. Little's patience and capacity. "It might sound odd, but I consider it my job to know names in town. I know the names of most of the people because … well, because most of the people know my name. Or at least that I'm the Green Man. Come to think of it, it's a little like a minor movie star learning the names of his fans. But that's how it is. I think I started out just trying to make people comfortable by calling them by name. But after while it was like a game." He paused to give her a chance to look at her watch or check the sky or say she had to go. Instead, she registered full interest on her face. He began again. "And the game was to know all the names not only of everyone I met, you know, grocery or gas station, but people I might run into. And then finally, people I would never ever talk to. It was like collecting pretty stones at the beach. Then when my pockets were full, collecting plain stones, then heart-shaped, then …" He paused.

"I think I see, Mr. Brown."

"Ben."

"Ben. It was something like I do with sending flowers. I do spend a lot of what my dear husband left for me on flowers for friends."

"It's connection. Adam in the garden of Eden. Dominion and authority."

Mrs. Little laughed. "Mr. Brown, you are a poet."

"Or maybe I just exercise the poet's license, Mrs. Little."

She thought of inviting him into her first name, Vernie. But she liked the distance her last name provided, though she was comfortable calling him Ben. The greenness maybe in both cases.

"Anyway," he continued, "There are odd things to discover about yourself once you're green. For example, I thought of myself as by disposition something of a hermit. I remember going to the grocery store as a social chore. Now I can't wait and sometimes purposely leave something off my list so I can go back. And I think it's more than just being green. There was a bigger change." He knew he had reached a crossroad in his answer. One way lay impossibly complicated, speculative details tangled around each other in heaps. The other way lay the quick and merciful version of the answer. He concocted a quick end. "But that's another volume of 'How I know your name.'"

"Well, good luck shopping for your car. Green is a good color for cars," she said, "but like black very hard to keep clean." She found herself cocking her head at him in what she recognized as a kind of a flirt, or would have been a flirt some years ago. Oh, I'm so out of practice, she thought.

They went on their ways after pleasantries and the Green Man thought that the meeting was like a meeting anywhere in time, any place. As he walked slowly in the sun, he felt like he was sliding through time, a European medieval village fair, and he had stopped to trade a local woman for her eggs, an exchange in the surly heat of a tropical afternoon at the beginning of time, East Leven saluting its best green citizen as casually as mowing a lawn.

Ben Brown hitched himself up to go car shopping. It had become time to go mobile.

BEN AND ANDREW ARE DRIVING UP IN SPRING INTO THE coastal range, the green Pontiac station wagon wanting to go on to where the earth drops off into the Pacific Ocean, Andrew driving and holding her back, the Green Man in his green-mobile at ease, pondering out the out the window with his seat belt on as if hunkered down to go where the Pontiac insisted. They are pointed west with not much left of the country before they hit the ocean. Still, it's west. A good start. An American start. In an hour or so they will hit the Pacific and then figure out what to do from there. The Green Man makes the case for completely running out of westering before they make their next move. He talks out the window, and Andrew hears him reflected off the glass. The air conditioner is on, the car is quiet in the wind chasing the sundown, and Andrew is wired through the toes to the road. Andrew looks straight ahead out the windshield, listening to the Green Man as if he's coming over a phone line, reporting from somewhere on up the road. Andrew finds himself gripping the Pontiac wheel tighter for the plain foolishness of it all. The heavy-handedness of it all.

Andrew thinks, and so we'll find the end of this new world first, carve an X somewhere and then start. It seems to me we've "started" a number of times before.

The Pontiac chirps along as they enter the big firs. The Green Man turns to the job of naming the Pontiac. They still climb into a corridor of trees with isolated houses and shacks stitched together by satellite dishes all pointed at the same heavenly spot in a cozy communion.

"Jesse. Shem. Jepheth. Ham," the Green Man burbles. "Old Testament, judges and sons of Noah. Then there's the obscure: Yorick, Don Diego de Miranda – the gentleman in the green coat, Trim, Sophisbonsiba. Then cow names: Daisy, Bertha, Bess, Gertrude. Then common: Tom, Johnnie, Max, Pete, Dick, Old Dick, Nick, Old Nick, Bob, and Bob's your uncle." Pleased with himself, Ben searches the roadside for more names. "Prescott, Kraken, Æthelred, Manx ..."

To Andrew he's just making sounds to try them out on his tongue, an alliterative honking and whistling in search of a language.

The idiocy of all this hit Andrew a day ago when Ben bought the great green beast of a Pontiac. They loaded sleeping bags, tent, frying pan, Coleman stove, and lantern – the wherewithal of survival on the run. The attacks had been fresh in mind, and there was an urgency to the loading, but it mixed with the clatter and banging of the great back door of the station wagon that regularly announced their flight. Andrew kept thinking that stealth should be the watchword. He lobbied against Mary going with them, because of the danger, and eventually he prevailed against Ben's wanting to invite her along in the fleeing. Ben kept clanging pan on lantern on propane tank with symphonic enthusiasm. If they were being pursued, the pursuers had an easy job keeping track of their departure.

But the idiocy has worn off, rounded down like a stone washed on a long, hard stream journey now rolling onward without edges. The Green Man sits next to the window cooing out at nothing in particular. They plunge on.

The Green Man had wanted to buy a 1958 Buick Limited: "A by-God symbol of America, an icon, the CAR that will always stand for car," he said to the guy on the used-car lot in town. "Forty-eight hundred iron-and-chrome pounds with the gas tank empty!" He was waving his hands around with two and a half tons of enthusiasm. At the previous lot the salesman became more and more anxious as the Green Man grilled him about compression readings on the cylinders. Then finally excused himself to answer a phantom phone and never came back.

"Solenoids," pronounced the Green Man, as if offering a gift. Getting no surprise, no bite, nothing but a blank face. He went on to sing the praise of solenoids.

"Solenoids and mercury switches that '58 Buick had, so if you just leaned on it, walked up to it and held a conversation and leaned on it, sort of just hitched a cheek up on the fin to rest your feet, why it would hike itself back up to its original level as if it knew to put the world back right again. Jack you right off your feet. A cast-iron goose for you!"

Arms flying but the rest of him amazingly still.

Carl, the salesman, seemed to be holding up all right though he doesn't have a '58 Buick Limited for sale, doesn't even know where they might run into one if it's not at a classic car place, where they get the big bucks, or in one of those car fan mags for restored older cars. But Carl let on he had the moral equivalent of the Buick they were looking for – something in the two-ton range anyway – but it won't be on the lot for a day or two as it's a trade on a car they've got out for detailing just now. It turned out to be the green Pontiac and, after calling around '58 Buick-questing to no avail, the Green Man settled for the Pontiac. Andrew looked at it and thought, What the hell. It sure is green.

The naming of the car continues as they assault the coastal range. Finally, Holly is what Ben calls her. And Holly it is, as they skirt an enormous Christmas tree farm with sidelights in rows of holly, variegated and plain. They wester in Holly for as long as the West will last. They're after good water, the Green Man proclaims.

"Here!" says Ben on the crest of a slope surrounded by fir trees. Like Brigham Young. Here it will be.

They stop, and off the Green Man goes into the woods, and Andrew finds him squatting at a small stream bringing the water up to his face as if he's listening to it. The creek is coming off the hillside through cedar and salal and fir. It's lined with big rocks to make its way around, and then small pools of pebbles limited to three or four colors until you pull up a handful and find no two are the same color. They burst into color in the air. Cedar roots flow and hold the banks firm.

"I'm feeling it with my face," Ben says quickly, "to see what else is here besides water itself. Pure water makes the soul pure. There's a clear-cut somewhere back there for sure. And then there's spray to keep the side of the road from being invaded by blackberries; there's a hunting cabin or rusting trailer back there with a drain field for the septic tank, maybe a little giardia bacteria, a liver fluke or ten, some tree faller taking a piss during his break. What's the parts per million?"

"What have we found here?" Andrew asks him.

"Water," he says. "What we want is water worth our souls." He holds the water in his hands again and listens with his face, the holy green man stooping by the creek.

Holly the Pontiac is back humming through the coastal forests again. They have failed to find water worth a soul in four separate places on the crest of the coastal range. Holly hums sadder, though the Green Man is perfectly at peace riding off into what remains of the West.

Andrew had told his parents that he was going on the lam with the green person, good son that he was: son of them and Mr. and Mrs. Brady, of Lucy and Ricky, Fred and Wilma, Barney and Betty, June and Ward. Andrew's mother packed a lunch with all the food groups represented and tiny salt and pepper shakers.

Andrew had been a picnic lover, a picnic practitioner, all his life.

On toward his fourteenth year, Andrew would creep with a friend in the direction of the Green Man and the growing stories, drawn by the tales, drawn by his parents' prohibition. Armed with a picnic lunch, they crept along the property line to try to catch a glimpse of this Captain Marvel, this singular invitation into the mysteries and awe of life. The Green Man, if he were true even faintly to the stories, made all the comic books, all the TV programs, all the lore and myth, family fabrications and tall tales potentially true – all of it became possible. Really possible: werewolves, Rapunzel's hair, Rumpelstiltskin's foot stomping, Jack's beanstalk, Alice's Wonderland, Coming of Age in Samoa. They hunched in the belly of the bushes waiting for all of imagination itself to be verified by a green movement through the foliage, a green promise.

The Pontiac looks thirsty with all this westering. Andrew mentions to the Green Man the days when he would haunt his bushes, but he wouldn't show.

"Those were hard times," he said, as if talking about the Great Depression. "But clear in my mind, as clear as …"

He trails off, and they pull into a two-pump-and-a-shack filling station with sunbursts of rust breaking out from under the paint on sheet-metal bread advertisements. They're near enough to the Pacific that the salt air gets here. They sell Shell, or did. It's generic gasoline now, but Holly doesn't mind much unless you put a foot down too far on the accelerator, and then she knocks and pings with pre-ignition longing for the days of 101 octane. She holds nearly a barrel of gasoline. The gas kid with his faded baseball cap and T-shirt full of surf slogans can't hide his pleasure at standing next to a tanker of Holly's length. So pleased is he, he cleans the windows front, back, and side without seeing that one of the passengers is nearly the same color as Holly herself. Finally he sees His

Green Eminence through the tinted front windshield and does an honest country double take.

Andrew watches Ben closely to see how this will work. The kid moves around to where Andrew's window is down to get a good look without the tinted glass. He chews gum fervently, his day already made by Holly's presence; now he seems to want this green-person part to last like the end of an ice cream cone. He stares across Andrew's chest at the Green Man without speaking.

The Green Man sighs. "I suppose you'll be wanting my autograph too." He's been through this before. "I tell you what." He holds up one finger as if he's going to enumerate the conditions – for looking, for autographs, for breaking up the kid's day, for slowing down the ravages of rust on the walls of the station. "I'll give you an autograph if you tell me where up that hill behind the station there's a spring coming out of the rocks clear and clean, one you can drink out of when you're out for walk."

The kid backs away from the car momentarily, maybe to ponder whether he wants to break up his day this much.

"Are you really green," he asks. His voice is strong and confident, as if he'd dealt with green people before, or people who said they were green anyway. He's seventeen or eighteen, charged full of gas-pumping purpose, and he sniffs adventure in all this.

"Yup." The Green Man is direct, the mountain rhetoric having taken hold. He rolls up a green shirt sleeve, holds out a green forearm. "This green."

The kid seems to consider whether this car, this green shirt, these tinted windows have conspired to deceive him. Finally, he steps back from Holly to see in the window better and talks across Andrew directly to the Green Man. "Next left there's a dirt road that goes into the woods about two hundred yards and stops. Get out and walk then, follow a trail through the woods uphill. There's a spring maybe a quarter mile in and a cup on a chain hanging from a tree. My pa put the cup there. Don't take the cup."

For Andrew paranoia kicks in: for people who were supposed to be on the lam, skedaddling and scramming, they sure were leaving a bright trail through these woods. An autograph signed "The Green Man" seemed about par for their camouflaging skills.

"Watch," and the Green Man spits on his fingers and rubs his forearm. Then he invites the gas kid to try it too. The kid spits on his fingers, he chooses a new spot on the forearm and rubs the greenness, testing deep and surely like biting a gold coin in a pirate movie.

They park in the dead end where the kid had directed. The Green Man is out front, up the old road that's now just a sinuous patch of ferns running through the forest with fir seedlings sprouting in the path. They find the cup on a nail in a tree. The water's a trickle coming out from under a substantial rock. The Green Man is down cupping it up to his face in his water-master ritual, his eyes closed, his nose swinging back and forth almost obscenely across the water. "This is it, the good stuff," he says to Andrew. "Drink this. Here."

His hands are full of water, and he seems to be handing the water to Andrew, who takes up the enameled cup instead and catches the water as it drips off the rock. Andrew looks at his water as if there's something he'll be able to see. Why am I drinking this, he thinks, on the say-so of this person who pays me out of boredom to keep him out of boredom while I accept the payment to stave off boredom? But he drinks.

There are the moving shadows of easy fir trees in almost no wind, ferns bristling with fugitive sunlight so that each frond seems stamped clear of the surrounding chaos of green. Even the sun is green here under the canopy and the slow chlorophyll cooking all around like soup.

Soon Holly rolls on toward the end of the West.

Andrew drives and begins to put together some of the water events as if they coalesce around this water from the rock; the water events tinkle down out of some storage place, some warehouse of water he hadn't understood before.

Andrew remembers floating the river on inner tubes, and the Green Man would appear along the bank near his house like a green raccoon. He'd be squatting on the bank cuffing water up onto his arms, his face, even onto the back of his neck, wetting his shirt in a huge dark circle. He'd look up and see them bobbing down the rapids toward him, hear them crack open the hot afternoon with shouts and challenges to each other, legs and arms tanned whipping up froth. There was always, in Andrew's memories, the Green Man just downstream, turning summer idylls around on themselves with that little bright string of fear when they spotted him, and he, having finished cuffing water, would retire into the willows and disappear. They would drift by his section of the bank a little quieter, only the boldest shouting out the same as upstream like a dare for him to appear and do whatever a green man could do to children. Anne Doucette's sweet broken neck was in all the shouts. Somehow the Green Man's danger and Anne's interminable fall had worked their way together in their minds. Trolls, their parents might have said. Beware of trolls. Look under every bridge in this land of bridges. There they will be. They come with having bridges.

And there was the island ritual before it broke loose. The Green Man would wash his hands often in the river. Not just his hands: he'd wash as high on each arm as possible, scooping the water and letting it run down over and over. "Cooling off," he called it. Time for cooling off every hour or so of work, but he lavished the water on his arms as if there were more than cooling at stake, some requirement like watering a plant or drawing water from a well. He seemed to Andrew to be maintaining his color by drawing out the greenness from the water, something liturgical about it in this new religion of being green.

There was the floating island, just after the attack on Horchow, when the Green Man scrubbed the chemicals of the settling ponds from his hands.

Holly has found the alder woods along the creeks that smell the ocean now. The road winds down as anxious as the water to get to the Pacific. Andrew thinks someone's been following them the last four miles, but then the follower turns off just as they pick up a creek alongside the road. Everyone in these last miles before the ocean has a rifle strung across the back window of the pickup, even though they are months out of hunting season, sometimes a rifle and a fishing pole. Andrew feels around in the silence of the last miles waiting for the Green Man to come up with more instructions. Do we go north? South? There's a Y ahead and we're going to have to choose soon. Where the hell are the bad guys, Andrew wonders, and are they really letting us get away? Where's "away" anyway?

THEY ARE FOUND. THEY CAMP ALONG A RIVER, HAVING TURNED north as they hit the ocean. And back up the river at a campground they wake the next morning covered in dew and there's a multipage message limp on Holly's windshield. They have been to the source of waters and drunk from it on their way to meet the Pacific – a spring that to Ben's green tastes is honeyed through and through with its own sweet clarity. Andrew was afraid of germs, but drank anyway. The paper of the message from Horchow is puffed up with the dew as if each page could be carefully separated into two, like a cocktail napkin.

"We know who you are and what you are doing!" This all in bold 16-point type like a headline. Ben begins to have the feeling that he is reading about himself in a newspaper again. He remembered looking over the newspaper stories about his having turned green.

The note says he left teaching because he couldn't get along with his colleagues, having called one a nincompoop and another a bean brain. Harsh words. It says he left in disgrace.

It says he went on a "rampage" trying to get Ted Turner to colorize all film footage of World War II and stop colorizing old movies: He enlisted his students, anyone who would listen on street corners; he got the students to carry petitions house to house for signatures; he organized bake sales and car washes and garage sales to get money for mailings. Ted Turner never returned his calls or letters.

His coworkers thought he was suffering from burnout. Others thought, the report went on, he was just an asshole. Still others thought of him as mentally ill. Many people were "relieved" when he quit teaching and became a trainee lineman for the power company. The PTA, the Local School Advisory Committee, the Teachers Union all "breathed sighs of relief…"

All of this could be true, Ben thinks to himself as he reads the soggy pages. World War II would be a good thing to colorize to make it as real as, say, the Vietnam War. All of this could also be a complete crock, he thinks. His life seems to stretch behind him just back to the tower and no further and then end. Or begin.

ALL THE WHILE, IN THE BARS OF EAST LEVEN, THE LIZARDS ARE basking through a spring rain. Gordon Lightfoot is on the jukebox and there are visible wavelengths and ultraviolets cooking everywhere. There is no end of hating ignorance in here, of filling in, fleshing out.

"Horchow had to back down. They've been in bed with the commissioners since the beginning. If all that back-scratching and zoning for those ponds got hauled out …Well, just let me say, there were plenty of asses kissed in those deals. And the others just watched to see which way the wind blew to see what they could get away with too." Blue wavelengths seem to favor this particular avenue of investigation.

"Didn't that commissioner, Bauer, what's-his-name? Didn't he get the big subdivision deal right after the settling ponds were put in? That whole business smelled bad."

"But that Green Man is just nuts. How the hell does he figure? He cranks open the ponds to kill the river? How does that figure?"

"Well, he seems to have everybody's attention, doesn't he?"

"So much attention somebody tried to burn his green ass out. The police don't know where he took off to. I'd hide out too, I guess, if somebody painted a target on my butt."

"Horchow'd be nuts too to screw the guy after the trial went that way. Did you see the CEO when he saw the argument of the Green Man and the kid turn on him?"

This from the Ford salesman.

"So that old Judge, Meyerhaus …"

"German. Old stock."

"Yeah. He hammered the whole thing into the ground."

Beer, once more around against the rain.

(On the corner of Furher street someone is trying to start a fire in a pile of tree trimmings and only gets smoke.)

"SAYS HERE I WAS — AM — AN ASSHOLE. MAYBE A CRAZY ASSHOLE." The Green Man assesses the text before him.

"I can't say yes, I can't say no." Andrew says this in the spirit of science, of objectivity, of getting His Greenness's attention. "But it seems to me you haven't been an asshole since I formally met you this summer. And," Andrew gestures to show how he appreciates fiscal responsibility, "and I have been paid regularly and fairly to accompany you on this what? This quest. This adventure. I think you have behaved soundly through fire and automobile purchasing – a record not everyone can claim."

"Thanks," replies the Green Man.

They have obviously been followed by some low criminal types, Andrew thinks, who skulk about at night and leave typed volumes on princess Holly. Andrew speculates: They have a portable fax machine, and they get their text from some central text-churn, where the head monkish fiend is attended by thrones and powers of researchers wearing cut-out Spencer Tracy masks so they don't recognize each other on the job. They are secretive. And slick, and shuffle their feet in order not to disturb the main fiend, who sits at a word processor connected to a fax connected to the authorities, the author authorities, who send the copy where it must go to create this version of the Green Man. How do they know he doesn't remember before the highline fry? Maybe they're only telling him they know. Whether he knows or not.

But what bothers Andrew is that whoever put the paper on the windshield was close enough to their tent to kill them both, or write slogans on their heads in permanent Day-Glo magic markers so they'd wake up branded and rounded up.

Ben finds himself fascinated and willing to believe this document, but it is also like old photos in a dusty box. One by one he might pull out the photos and try to erect a life out of similarities between noses, brows, hairlines, and the cast to the eyes of these strangers; he finds himself hoping for some good stuff as he runs through the bad stuff the papers proclaimed, like looking at the photos and slowly realizing your whole family is the Jukes and the Kallikaks. And still he keeps hoping that he would turn the page and out would pop "on the other hand ..." And here there would be the kindness and generosity and all the civilized gestures to make up a life he could be proud of. But the evil text of his obsessive life goes on: Ben Brown the teacher who alienated his colleagues and who ran away to work for the power company like a child hiding because he could not have his own way.

After reading a few more pages of detail, he thinks he can recall a PTA meeting or something, maybe standing up and embarrassing everyone. More a feeling than really remembering. He thinks he could have done that, might still do that, is capable of that. But the circus is so much clearer, almost as if what he lived since turning green is overlaid on top of the previous life until he can't make out the depths way down there under all those layers. The circus is clear: Sophie's great rumbling gray side and how warm she was but also how like a house.

The Green Man sits in the sun on the edge of the massive picnic table that's bolted into the poured concrete slab as if someone expected earthquakes and picnic table marauders. The table is a monument to paranoia. As the Green Man reads a page he passes it to Andrew, and they contemplate this tale of his life wordlessly.

The "crazy asshole" remark hangs in the air. This is the ultimate twentieth-century insult impugning connections a body might make with the rest of the world: the company of Benito Mussolini, Son of Sam, Charles Keating, Ivan Boesky, Michael Milken, George Patton. All the fuckheads, Andrew thinks. Is my Green Man really a "crazy asshole"?

Andrew and the Green Man cross the dune and see the storm surf is crashing heavily and rolling huge peeled logs against one another with each surge. Every now and again a log shoots from the pile when the surf blasts in from the bottom. The logs shift like a giant game of pick-up sticks being probed from the bottom. The sky is clear and the wind gentle off the water, but the surf is informed from somewhere else: a thick gray water attacking the orange-red driftwood pile, dishwater foam, spindrift violent in the air. The two of them watch the logs heave and shift, the waves unfurl and explode in the huge sticks.

Andrew turns to Ben Brown to see if he has seen the same thing, the same apparition here at the end of the West. The Green Man confirms the appearance of the end of the West.

Andrew is certain the noise is part of some kind of conspiracy, feels compelled to say so and finds that the Green Man, pointing wordlessly at the bouncing logs, the chugging ocean, is then quickly more interested in retelling what happened when his house was firebombed, a reiteration of the story they both knew perfectly well. But Ben persists and wants to say it again in the presence of the log dance, delights in the details about the Molotov cocktail arching through the air in the evening gloom. How like fireworks it was, how neat the trail across the sky before it slammed into the cabin. He made the noise of exploding, was unsatisfied with it. Made another one and another one until he had it right.

The Green Man now slips from sentence to sentence with all the green organs of his green body conspiring to punctuate, concatenate in deadly seriousness all the stuff of the tale; his body sways with the fire, and his face puckers for retelling smells of perfumes, plastics, the Horchow mess. An onshore wind picks up, but they are protected in the lee of the dunes, and the tops of the trees catch it and play the rising air so Andrew has to lean in toward the Green Man (whose voice has never been loud) in order to hear clearly. Finally it occurs to Andrew that, with all the body swaying and the saying without being clear about meaning, what he's hearing is the Green Man speaking as a child would, and he looks under the picnic table and the Green Man has one foot anxiously on top of the other, working the top one, bouncing the bottom one while he tells his green story.

The wind on shore has picked up even more, and the surf and wind mix and soothe louder and louder as if to make talking itself useless. Andrew feels he alone continues to be worried by the biography-terrorism of the early morning.

It is the light on the coast that gets to the Green Man, really distracts him, he thinks, so that he finds himself looking at the light when he should be paying attention to what Andrew says or what else was going on. It is early summer light: there is lilac beneath everything, then a stronger purple as if layered in below that if you look hard enough. Ben finds himself staring through the light and there it is. To get those colors, you would have to wash the world in lilac first, then add whatever you need in the way of buildings, gray sea, bright green growing-tips of the coastal pines and deciduous azaleas that seem sharp in thick air. There is a persistence of vision that makes the groves of pines shudder in the romantic lilac air. There are fox glove, phlox, fireweed, penstemon, Queen Anne's lace, wild parsnip, vetch giving up their colors to the air. The thickness in the air is a heaviness like compression as they move against the sand of the coast, north again, the air stacked up over the Pacific Ocean. At the ocean edge is relief from the land smells that sometimes blast Ben Brown's senses.

He feels the closing at the ocean, as if he'd run out of everything by coming to the edge, as if the fight is not there but at his back as he stands facing the gray water, as if he had truly found an edge between a sticky place and a slippery place. The ocean full of critters seems to say, "Turn around. Go back. There's nothing to be done here. Everything to be done there."

The next morning there is another biography. Another biography claiming further basis for the Green Man's insanity, this time historical.

Henry Adams, the bio claimed, thought that Teddy Roosevelt was not just the boor and jerk that many in Washington claimed he was. Adams insisted that Roosevelt was certifiably insane. This was the premise for the biographer claiming that many versions of insanity are walking around the streets, insidious and dangerous and unrecognized. And so Ben Brown was certified crazy as a long line of crazies who have had their way with the public. The biography was actually funny, a kind of parody of biography or those high school social studies books that display genetic criminality at great length.

There was, for example, written out in that indelible laser printer way, the history of Bowie Knife Peters, on his mother's side, who on the floor of the U.S. Senate in the nineteenth century was insulting a fellow senator and when challenged to a duel, his choice of weapon was bowie knives in a dark room. This was followed by a litany of loonies from his father's side: 1959, a suicide; 1939 in Seattle, a crazy great-uncle named Otto, who leaped from a balcony into a socialist rally with a butcher knife between his teeth like a comic-opera pirate, broke a leg in the jump and, the bio reports, after having his leg treated was thrown in the city jail for twenty-four hours, where the jailers pampered him like a hero, but his family had him examined by a psychiatrist who found he was schizoid; 1955, an aging aunt who went to live among the Indians of the Amazon Delta and was recalled by the Methodist Church board after she returned to civilization covered with burns, self-inflicted burns it was learned, as she had tried to impress the Indians by her closeness to God and ability to resist pain; more eccentrics, more aberrance, more anomaly—all in the name of making the case that the Browns were crazy in an unbroken line throughout the twentieth century.

The shore pine grows tight-needled with its back humped away from the onshore wind, duff making a sweet floor to lie on and listen.

And the smell of the place, like the stitches in lace, ties fern to sand to gull carcass to spring water percolating up through the shale and around the basalt fingers that point out to sea. The wind, hard onshore, a vacancy filled by heavy pine pollen, the snap of kelp whips cooking on the sand, and in the eddies behind buildings there is tar and creosote and sour old lumber and sweet cedar shingles. A wet dog somewhere. Gasoline and oil. Waft: the tangy reality of God's dream. Ben laughed at the biography but wondered what Otto looked like.

They talk late, the Green Man saying out loud again East Leven's characters and history—East Leven, the place that contained all that had happened and percolated up from the sound of water.

Even with a resident ghost, an unsolved dual murder, a few gypsies, an official crazy person, a green man, everything seemed to fit the place as if this collection had fit the contours of the land. The river cutbank and the ravines accommodated Anne Doucette and all East Leven's dead children in the cool bottoms and cracked banks. The murder had become part of the spot it happened in, and now there were park benches very near where each of the victims' cars had been found. Everyone knew for a while that the benches had been installed near where each car had been that snowy night. But the knowing slowly changed and then everyone agreed the benches marked the exact spots of the murders and then, even further, the benches became memorials to the murderees—her bench, his bench; there became the women's bench and the men's bench. And it was settled, all of history adjusted into place. The Green Man's revelations about Crazy Leo being witness to the murders fleshed out the historical formula but also seemed flapping around, looking for a place to get into the meaning of East Leven. Crazy Leo somehow knew everything. Big deal, thinks Andrew. The man in the moon knew everything too.

The Green Man goes about making tea, still talking.

Andrew is what his second grade teacher called "wool-gathering," looking attentive but tuned to another channel. Crazy Leo, Anne Doucette, the bar baskers are all the business of East Leven. East Leven (East Lemon, East Twelve, East Levitate, East of Livin', East …). But here on the far coast, perched on the edge of the world and about to fall off, they pour more tea.

Later that night, they catch the mad biographer.

They are drinking tea and talking until the moon is up and the sound of the ocean down. The Green Man and Andrew split up the sleeping places. Andrew sleeps in Holly, the Green Man in the tent. Andrew thinks he has a chance of waking up if someone tries the dastardly biographical version of toilet papering, maybe even a chance to apprehend the flimflammer.

He lies low in Holly's back like a kid at the drive-in, seeking shadow. He'll keep one eye open, and when the nefarious faux-biog comes skulking … zzz, zzz.

Or that's what happened, because by the time he is fully awake, the chase is not only on, but has been on for some time.

The Green Man, with the kidneys of an active twelve-year-old, has risen to pee in the moonlight – the tea is indeed involved. And as he's peeing in the moon shadow of a shore pine, the bio-basher appears furtively scurrying from tree to tree with the scroll of the latest biography in one hand: assassin with words, presumer of history.

The Green Man is watching, and peeing from the shadows, his green making him shadowier and more a part of the moon-mottle in the landscape. And the biog tiptoes up to the car and lifts the windshield wiper to make his literary deposit, slurp/click.

The Green Man swoops, but in the moonlight, he's only a piece of shadow broken off from the general shadow and his "Hey, you, freeze" seems to appear in a comic balloon over Holly's grill. A talking Pontiac, it seems at first to the startled biography deliverer.

"Hey, you, freeze," Holly. The scoundrel flies away through the shadows as if he knows the paths and trails by heart, with the Green Man sort of traipsing along behind and losing ground with every second. Andrew awakes with the "freeze" part, which has some direct correspondence to his dreams, and for a second, he is half in and half out of the dream, and the dream world is more certain and clear than the moonlight on the pines at the coast.

"Stop. Wait!" the Green Man calls. It's the real words that bring Andrew out of his dream, out of the back of Holly with only his socks between him and the prickly floor of the forest and off in pursuit of this real-life dream sequence. It seems just for a moment that he has his choice of chasing in his dream or choosing this moon-lit weirdness. For the long thread of a second Andrew wavers between the safety of the dream and its sepia tones and the Green Man bounding after the bounder.

Andrew is tiptoeing across the asphalt road and then into the woods, where he instantly regrets the fact that he hasn't stopped to find shoes. He's still sore-footed from the night of the fire. The duff of a coastal pine forest contains something like naturally occurring "jacks" – the most dangerous floor toy. Small spurs of twigs like ninja-throwing stars begin collecting in his socks as he pursues the Green Man and the bashing biographer in and out of the patches of moonlight. Andrew drops behind and gets off the woods path, pulling angry stars out of his socks, and finds the nearest dune to get some altitude and perspective on the situation. He sits to relieve his feet altogether and feels the cool sand reach up to receive him.

He can see the Green Man flashing through clearings here and there as he pauses on top of the dune; in the soothing, antiseptic sand he pulls off his fiery socks and rests on the ridge of sand, sand like cool liquid running slowly away on all sides.

The tops of the dunes between here and the sea are lit by the moon and the valleys between are sin-dark and absolute. Andrew can't see Ben any more or the bio-raider, but he knows they're off in the labyrinth of beach trails that branch between the campground and the dunes. He has some thoughts about heading 'em off at the pass, cutting 'em off by taking a shortcut. He squirms his feet deeper into the sensuous sand. For Andrew the black-and-white dune world goes flat and turns into shapes on a canvas – odd white patches wrapped around black cutouts. In the disorienting moonlight he loses track of the chase scene and time.

The Green Man is galloping through the woods, sort of randomly, because he has lost contact with the pursued, and anyway he begins to think what he'd do if he did run across him at the juncture of two paths or just simply caught up to and brought down the quarry. Indeed, he says, what would I do? Would I pommel him? Would he pommel me? Would I bleed? He bleed? Who would catch whom?

The Green Man hears a crunching in the trail ahead. The miscreant is doubled over a stump holding his crotch and moaning low. The Green Man lets out a *Ya-hoo* and a *Whoopie* and pounces on his prey.

Andrew hears the sounds from his perch on the crest of a dune.

By the time Andrew gets his socks back on and works his way down the dune, the Green Man is just finishing a rodeo hog-tie astride the captured raider. The capture scene is glistening in a patch of moonlight. Andrew arrives late to hear the confession:

"Hey man. I don't know nothin' about it. Some guy pays me fifty bucks to bring those papers in and put 'em on your windshield. That's all I know about anything. No wrecking anything. Just the papers."

He has a local address in his wallet and, yes, five tens, and a local carpenter's union card, though he says he's laid off and not collecting "a damn thing" from the union. Says a guy came up to him on the street, city guy, and offered him fifty a night for three nights to put the papers on Holly. Says the guy told him it was a complicated joke. That's all, just a complicated joke between friends. And then he proceeds to describe an average guy with average hair color and average height with average …

The two captors ponder this hog-tied story.

The Green Man prevails against Andrew's call-the-police suggestion, with the argument that letting him go contains the possibility of him reporting back to them any information about "the guy" worth a counter fifty bucks. Keeping him/turning him in to some local police for "paper piracy" would get everybody a good laugh. They secure him in the moonlight and have a new installment of the Green Man's bio to read over more tea. To wit:

The Brown family was really Braun and hailed from the Danzig corridor. Prussians, they were, not the "falsely claimed English heritage"—something like the English royal family. The first two installments claimed: teacher, burnout, colorize World War II, asshole, long line of insane relatives. Having made claims to establish his life and his genetic stuff, the biographer turned to history.

The papers claimed the Brauns were farmers living on the outskirts of what is now Gdansk, Poland. "I won't Gdansk, don't g-ask me," pipes in the Green Man over Andrew's shoulder as he reads.

The family was noted for its collection of six strapping male children, "louts," who were for sale or rent as a kind of early twentieth-century hit squad directed by their father, a wiry local farmer who floated in on one of the waves of mercenaries that collected in the Danzig in the previous century. The hereditary locals viewed the Brauns as upstarts and unsuccessful farmers, though it seems the family always had plenty of money to throw around. The mother, Rose, was vaguely connected to the area through a peasant family of strong potato field origins and so gave the whole family a provisional legitimacy of place.

The Green Man is riveted by the fullness of the description as if someone had brought him some news he'd been expecting and at the same time fearing.

The boys were the scourge of the region and were feared either singularly or together by all the other males of the area. Their boy-mischief always had a violent and destructive edge to it so that the folk could not just shake their collective heads and relegate the boys' misdeeds to the boys-will-be-boys heap of bad behavior. Someone always got hurt. One townsperson contracted his limp from a Braun boy's prank, a young man fell silent and morose after a harvest dance and never could be pumped for the details of what happened, a city cousin visiting a local family suddenly packed his bags and returned home. And, one by one, the six boys picked off handsome wives and four of them left for America in staggered fashion as if trying to sneak into the New World one at a time. And as they left, the level of local petty larceny tapered off: tools no longer missing, shoats safe in the night, no more barn fires...

Andrew and Ben begin to discuss how these sheets of fabrication seem like their conversation of earlier in the evening, the strange saga of East Leven. All the while, the carpenter is politely asking if he can go now, as if he'd dropped in on a family argument, an argument he'd rather not get involved in. And Ben finally prevails on Andrew to release the prisoner with the promise of a counter fifty bucks if he should find out anything about his biographer/benefactor: a car license number, a real name, or who might be paying him to ghostwrite what may or may not bear some or no resemblance to fact.

Ben has become interested in the possibilities of the three installments of the biographies delivered by the carpenter to the windshield of Holly. The Prussian-lunatic-asshole assertion of the text. Without reading any part of it over a second time, it all sounds familiar. Either he had become gullible and was ready to be told anything and believe it, or the whole concoction was true. If it's all true, then the biographer is fairly sure that this version of a life is news to the Green Man: or disturbing, or confusing, or simply dislocating in some way. Ben thinks, what an odd thing, to try it out on me as if this biography were both definitive and in the process of definition, as if I would disappear or become harmless myself, or fly up my own asshole.

There is a coastal rain today as they finish packing and head back east. The rain is delicious, clean, and cool: an end-of-the-world rain with a kind of sigh of finality. They had come to the edge of the continent and without much ceremony had decided to return inland, where the light seems to be. Andrew tells Ben not to believe a word of the biography though he admits some of it jibes with what rumors and bits and snatches he knows of the Green Man legend. But he steadfastly holds out for another reality to be ascertained later.

THEY COME AWAY FROM THE OCEAN IN A RAIN, THE GREEN MAN riding shotgun on Holly's Naugahyde, virgin vinyl. Andrew is pondering their mission now, though the Green Man seems uncommunicative on the subject.

The fates seem to gather in the rain and wash off the salt air, fates foreknowing that they need to be clean and scrubbed for what will be. They climb the coastal range gently for the going back.

The valleys are deep and Swiss-looking and the river a steel gray road with patches of log rafts pegged to the banks. The gray water, the brown logs, and they see the hundred greens working their way up the valley walls in washes of color.

Andrew thinks of himself in the laconic, stoned tennis court days and sees Sergeant Schultz of *Hogan's Heroes*. Colonel Klink has just asked him what he knows of some untoward event in the stalag, and Shultz rolls his eyes to heaven and declares, "I know nuh-sing, nuh-sing." Now, at least I know greens, Andrew thinks.

The Green Man has begun to talk about what he calls the germ theory of why things are the way they are. Holly hums. And as long as Andrew doesn't shove his foot down and ask her high-compression engine to run hard on low octane gasoline, she hums. If he tries to pass, she knocks and staggers and belches.

The germ theory in short is: once things get going, it's hard to stop them.

Holly climbs without complaining, yet, into the mountains. The big rivers are behind on the valley floor and a small stream animated by the light rain rushes past them toward the coast. In the middle of ramblings on the germ theory and its possible connections to the One Great Enemy – Gravity – something else rushes past them going the other direction.

"Mary," shouts the Green Man mid-ponder. And there she is, she was. They enter a Laurel and Hardy movie in Andrew's mind. She must have seen them too, having become acquainted with Holly before they left.

She stops somewhere down the road and comes back. They, having to drive farther to find a place to turn around, take longer to turn around. Of course, they run into Mary coming back to look for them, but they can't turn off anywhere safely so they wave, make generous circling gestures and pass again. On one side is the creek swollen with rain and they need the widening after a bridge to get a turn-around place since the shoulders are so narrow. On the other side is the canyon wall having narrowed now to boulders and rock walls. They pass again, but now they've worked themselves father apart because of missing exits and the difficulty of getting Holly turned around. There's some mathematical formula to all this, Andrew thinks. It's a story problem, seen from some great aerial camera.

This time they pass again going opposite directions but slowly and they wave and point up the road meaning for Mary to turn around, and they'll meet her up the road going the right direction, east: Plan A. They pull over in a county park with lots of tire tracks already in the entrance and wait. Obviously, after a decent interval, she has done exactly the same thing.

They wait and wait in their parking lot in the county park while Mary waits and waits in her logging road turnoff. They decide to go look for her but change their collective mind in favor of her coming to look for them. They wait. She waits a vegetarian's wait. It occurs to Andrew that they are playing scissors/paper/stone and each throws out the same stalemate time after time, figuring the other will change.

A half hour later Mary comes east in full vegetable time, just as they prepare to saddle up and go back west after her.

General hilarity in the county park lot. Mary fills them in on what's been going on in East Leven, on the pilings, along the river, in the newspapers.

Great numbers of people are interested in where the Green Man went after his house burned: Who burned it? Why? Was the river-raider rumor true? And where is he now? Does the Green Man really have mental problems, as one of the newspaper accounts contends? Can't he remember anything? Does he black out while you're talking to him? Is he from another planet?

Brouhaha in the city it is. Leaving the town was the most newsworthy thing the Green Man could have done, it seems. His face, a photo from the trial in desperate newspaper color, has been blown up to fifty times life size and plastered in rows along the streets while headlines declare him the VICTIM of plots and counterplots and criminal excesses of various sorts. The newspaper has found its story: it's not his greenness, although that makes for newsworthy photos, but his status as victim of… of… And here's the real news – mystery! Who or what is behind this persecution of green people, green person, anyway, and how underdog can you get? Green underdog.

Mary explains.

Horchow is the obvious suspect but either is covering its collective ass carefully, has hired the job out, or really has nothing to do with this particular session of green baiting. In any case, Horchow appears clean, and the Green Man turns out to be the smoldering center of a smoking mystery. The police commissioner is urged by the community-minded to get something or someone to stop this victimization. The city commissioners find taking the green side reaps calls, cards, and letters of support. While they were gone, it seems, the town has fermented and churned out a fresh green brew.

All this Mary tells them breathlessly while the Green Man stands close to her side with his arm around her shoulder appearing to listen to her but really sniffing out her vegetable air while wearing his indelible, goofy smile.

The way back home begins by the Green Man jumping in Mary's car with her, leaving Holly and Andrew to sort things out.

Andrew has rain and Holly all to himself. He's thinking he doesn't know what the next thing in the sequence is, where this series is going. And he is thinking, too, of when he moved in next to the Green Man years ago.

Rumor had already created a kind of past for the Green Man, complete with contradictions and inconsistencies and paradoxes – just like a real life. He lived downstream through the bushes in the spring rain when Andrew's family moved into their house. His parents had been assured by first the real estate salesman, then the local public health officer that their green neighbor was, in fact, a model citizen and perfect neighbor; nobody saw much of him, he didn't complain about anything, he kept to himself. Rumor, like the paper on the car windshield, had fabricated a version of his life, and there was something liberating, an invitation to civic invention, in not having the life written but just hung out there like sheets on a windy day. He was divorced before he'd become green. Becoming green had made him a recluse. He had left Oregon, maybe the country, for a long time and then returned to the house by the river.

Andrew drives Holly. He admits to himself that he's grown fond of the Green Man without knowing exactly what it is he has grown fond of. He has accommodated one change in his nonlife after another, all in the name of seeing-something-is-better-than-being-completely-in-the-dark. And the Green Man always enthusiastically tells Andrew the truth as he sees it. Something refreshing about this. Other soothsayers in his life – parents, teachers, college professors – always told him what they thought it was he should know, that canned stuff on safe sex, the role of slavery in the American Civil War, the Manichean proclivity among early Puritan settlers.

Andrew drives Holly; the Green Man and Mary chat in his rearview mirror. Andrew turns the radio on for comfort, seeking a tincture of reality as the weirdness of this procession overwhelms him.

He finds himself pondering like a citizen. As if this green person has usurped his postadolescent rights: to loll around while pretending to come up with a plan for the future; to test the capacity for excess in various internal organs, most prominent among these liver and gonads; to cultivate confusion as a viable state of mind; to feel pissed off as a general wash on the world; to snack into the heart of existence; to feel something so clearly, only the heart's singing is sufficient delight. It is as if His Greenness has worked on Andrew like wind and water to carve him into wind drift and water sculpture, and as if the Green Man were sent by other authorities to be the force of his becoming. Andrew is more and more "finding himself" doing this and becoming that as if he had given over control entirely to this green entity. I am helpless, he thinks. But I'm going some direction, clearly, only I don't know what direction it is. This driving – thinking all while avoiding small mammals scurrying across the road.

Andrew leads the way into East Leven, and when they get downtown past the swinging Kodak sign, they turn off Furher and go down Salmon Street, and there is a procession of billboards using the Green Man's face as advertising for a newspaper, the story of the week, during the time they were gone. Andrew knows to expect this from what Mary said, but the fact of these green-faced redundancies and the slowness of their caravan as they gawk and hold up the considerable weekend traffic reminds him of a movie version of *1984*. But Big Brother has turned green through some inexplicable and complicated joke, and green is being proclaimed as The-Thing-To-Be: Be green! Don't you wish you were green too? GREEN it is. GREEN.

This is the dream-within-the-dream version of *1984*. Holly percolates along the street as if she's looking from side to side with Andrew. The essential fact is greenness, no nose or eyes or chin to remark about. And plied in posters here in the late-edition form, greenness is the ONLY fact of his face. The running footer of the poster, the part closest to the street, asks rhetorical questions about the conspiracy to do away with his Green Highness – Who's responsible? Why is this green citizen being persecuted? Where is he now?

Then suddenly Andrew hears horns honking, and thinks it's because he is holding up traffic here. He begins to look for a way off this street, but soon it's clear that other cars are honking at the Green Man behind him in Mary's car. And the Green Man starts to wave out the window at the waving drivers and pedestrians. A parade. The bars empty. People pour out of stores. The bench in front of the hardware store empties.

Andrew is in the lead and ostensibly headed toward Mary's house, but now so hung up in traffic that he can't even get out of the way to let traffic through. He sees in his mirror the Green Man is broadly waving his green arm out the window. Somebody on the sidewalk has an American flag all done in shades of green. The whole parade is coming to a halt with shouts and wavings and hellos.

Andrew sees in his rearview mirror an earnest young couple has approached Mary's car and are giving the Green Man what has become the "GM rub," the licking of two fingers (index and the next finger) and then a quick rub and a fast check to see if the color comes off. After he passes this test, they barrage him with congratulations about surviving? His triumphant return? Being green? None of this is entirely clear to Andrew in the rearview mirror; it's all backwards. This "GM rub" has been occasioned by an editorial in this very same newspaper asking why the judge didn't simply make everyone in the courtroom during the trial, the green ones at least, submit to some kind of "lick test" to see if the court could discover quickly who was colorfast and who was not. Of course the editorial writer's colleagues all pounced on him in print with imagined scenarios graphically detailing the orgy of licking going on in court, the small but persistent percentage of lickers who couldn't (or wouldn't) stop, the green tongues (the political cartoonists joined in here), the jokes (how does Judge Meyerhaus hold his licker…?). In any case, the couple right there on Salmon Street go through the established ritual that has been and will be repeated over and over. It will spread.

Traffic, such as East Leven can produce on short notice, completely stalls and they all sit. The green version of the American flag gets passed up and down one side of the street as if the town is trying it out as a new banner. Is Conroy Burbank responsible? It seems to have his touch. The newspaper just created a new star. Are there talk-show royalties in this somewhere? Andrew wonders.

The Green Man gets out of the car and is walking among his people like Charlton Heston's Moses, making gestures of an odd kind of benediction.

Andrew feels uneasy. There's something dangerous out there he can't identify. But the Green Man moves into the crowd as if he's drawn by some vacuum occurring just ahead of him, like a politician, he's smiling, he's confident and like a saint, he's not afraid of death, of craziness, of the human bite. Andrew's uneasiness increases, and he squirms on Holly's Naugahyde and begins to sweat as the Green Man disappears momentarily, then resurfaces in a sea of well-wishers and is overwhelmed again by wave and trough of folk on the sidewalk. Horns from the end of the plugged street add acclaim to the festive press of flesh. The next version of the cuckoo-clock feeling has arrived: it's the beehive feeling this time, with buzzing all around in celebration of the green queen bee who is different from the rest and yet buried in the mass of the hive.

Andrew is taken by this beehive notion, pleased with himself as if the naming of the phenomenon will steady the whole rocking motion of the show. He longs briefly for electronics again: gain controls, a remote with pause, a plug to pull on this whole surging thing. But, strangely, the longing is only a flicker, almost a memory of wanting to have this event dancing out there on the delicate end of a beam coming from his remote.

Salmon Street seems full under the poster-gaze of the Green Man while the Real Thing moves like the Pope in mufti. Andrew can see heads plying a wide circle now to the other side of the street, and he assumes the Green Man is just there in front. Here they come around again to the chorus of horns, huzzahs, murmurs, and song. Someone is singing a high, thin anthem as if no one were listening. And now there appears to be an honor guard, and the Green Man comes full circle back to Mary's car. She has watched the whole tour with a grin. There's been no time for newspaper reporters and TV crews to assemble. All this free publicity and nobody really interested in it.

The Green Man is out of the car greeting people in the name of the spontaneous celebration. He's green and the face on the poster is green – though not the same green at all. No one seems particularly interested in what his name is. The most important thing is that he's simultaneously larger than life, and then this smaller ambulatory version, as if the connection automatically bestows on him a secular sainthood. People are looking up at the posters and then pointing out the Green Man moving among the crowd.

The traffic is tied up magnificently, and three police officers arrive on the edges of the crowd. Andrew thinks responsibly that maybe the Green Man should get back in one of the cars and be ready to move or they'll all end up in the clink, clapped into irons, hanging from the damp prison walls. Surely all this is illegal, he thinks. But he waits in Holly while the crowds still swirl. The Green Man is now working both sides of the street like a politician running for office.

Andrew sees a cop working his way through a knot of people toward the Green Man, but the cop is smiling and when he gets inside the honor guard, he's shaking hands with the cause of this green traffic jam. Andrew shuts Holly off because it looks like he is hunkered down here for a while. He checks out Mary in the rearview mirror and she's peacefully watching the proceedings; she catches him looking in the mirror, waves and smiles.

In something just under a half hour, the Green Man makes his way back to the cars escorted by the ad hoc honor guard. Traffic has somehow found its way around them, and the parade has had this block of Salmon Street to itself the whole time.

Mary leaves her car and comes to join Andrew in Holly. She brushes in across the seat and closes the door gently, almost as if something will break if she shuts it too firmly.

"Well," she says, her lips drawn into a line, her eyebrows raised. She gestures, palm up, out the window wordlessly, shaking her head. And, "Well," again.

"Yes, what to make of all this?" Andrew says. He looks over at her to see what kind of sympathy he will get. He looks out the window. "Frankly, I'm just amazed by how my life has turned into one event after another as soon as I signed on with him. That's my personal view. On the other hand, the cosmic view: this is the only green guy going, so far. There must be some historical merit in that. But, not to be forgotten, there are some kind or kinds of fiends chasing us, blowing things up, who knows what."

"No, really," she says. "What do you honestly think of what's happened here today?"

What's she after? Andrew thinks. Is she like his English teacher in high school, who knew what she wanted for an answer to what-does-the-poem-mean and kept asking around the room until somehow, someone divined what she had in mind? Mary Willson looks at him happily but with a permanent worry crease across her forehead. She raises her eyebrows again soliciting gently.

What does he really think about the Green Man and this public celebration of him? So far they have been suspected of urban terrorist activities in the press, attacked by gonzo boat guerrillas, biographically insulted and unnaturally accused. Now he is being street-acclaimed as a hero. Hero of what exactly? How did this come about in their absence as they raced Holly west looking for good water? What alignment of planets? What winds of fortune? Maybe this is what the Green Man means when he asks for a good theory of luck. Where have they come to in this … this partnership: Cisco and Pancho, Don Quixote and Sancho, Roy and Dale, Chip and Dale, Frick and Frack …?

Andrew answers, "I think we are seeing the worm turn, a new direction in the green business. From persecuted weirdo to social hero. Soon everyone will want to be green!" He looks over to see how Mary's taking this rendition of the surrounding events.

She seems to be agreeing with something and pondering an addendum. "This feels like an Indian gathering I once attended. It was a powwow in northeastern Oregon, a gathering for no particular purpose I could figure except just to gather."

Her upper lip is sweaty, and she's flushed a little by the spin she's just taken with the Green Man. East Leven's small population seems to have been available on short notice to mill around behind him while the Green Man takes more vague congratulations.

Andrew pokes Mary and nods as confirmation out the window at this rendition of what's going on. "Powwow seems to fit, somehow. Goodwill. Happy faces."

"Maybe," she says cryptically, apparently unwilling to trust all this goodwill. Vegetarian worry, mellow but persistent. She suspects a pillory. Andrew's paranoia is reinfected by Mary's.

"These people seem just as happy as if they were in their right minds," Andrew contributes, quoting his father's all-purpose observation, useful when any crowd gathered for any reason. Quoting his father? How did this come about? He shakes it off as an accident.

Mary says, "What we lack here is palm fronds," and laughs.

"And a donkey. Blue birds on his shoulder," Andrew tries, and he gets an odd, searching look. "You know, Uncle Remus? *Zip-a-dee-doo-dah*? 'Mister Bluebird's on my shoulder. It's the truth, it's actual, everything is satisfactual.'" He receives a bemused and tolerant school-teacher look.

"That movie is way before my time. And yours."

"The benefits of a liberal arts education." Andrew thumps his chest.

Andrew is thinking that whoever was responsible for the fire bombing of the Green Man's house might be in the crowd. Whoever was behind the biographies. Or, worse yet, whoever will be responsible for the NEXT attack on the Green Man is in the crowd. He mentions this to Mary since she's more likely to be sympathetic as a kind of professional worrier herself. She nods, ever alert, watching the Green Man shake hands and smile and nod. Jesus, worries Andrew.

But when the Green Man comes over to the car after the crowd has thinned, he brooks no talk of evil lurking in the crowd. He refuses to worry or even string together the occurrences of the last weeks in a net-work of influences and conspiracies. "That's what you two are good at," he says patting Mary and Andrew. "I don't need to worry about these things with you two here."

Andrew casually mentions the idea of powwow. Trails off. The Green Man is green flushed with his parade. Animated, can't stand still, like a twelve-year-old prancing in place.

"Sorry," he says. "I don't know," and he holds his hands out empty-hand-ed toward the crowd. "I don't know. Just green, I guess. Green. I think it's just the green." Indelible and bright as grass stains on the knees of new pants.

The Green Man gets through with the crowd, which disperses like a cloud over the desert; suddenly there is no crowd and the three of them are back in their respective vehicles off to Mary's place. But something has certainly changed. From being fugitives, running for their green and scrawny lives – one each – Andrew finds himself cohort to the celebrated Green Man, the autograph-signing Green Man, the eco-hero, the symbol, the prophet, the one come again. Andrew finds this difficult to take, having been with him from the larking down the river on the disaster island.

They get to Mary's house. Andrew is the odd man out clearly since he has brought with him none of the moony-eyed invitation Mary has clearly extended to the Green Man. Andrew says he will walk home while they rest and relax. "No," says the Green Man. "Take Holly. Come back to-morrow afternoon." He's called a twenty-four- hour hiatus in their activ-ities now that he has graduated from fugitive to hero. Andrew goes home.

MARY EXPLORED THE GREEN MAN IN THE AFTERNOON AND declared him thoroughly green in crevice and bump. She was oatmeal and Linzer torte, this vegetarian Mary. Filbert and butter and gathered seeds. Raspberries. And she cared so deeply about everything.

Ben suggested that they keep their good fictions and throw out the bad ones. Keep the ones about getting to the top of mountains; throw out the ones about The Fall. Keep the fictions that tell us we are like gods; throw out the ones that insist we are worms in the sight of God. Mary said she will try, but she remembers the stories of her childhood that asserted The Fall and Ruin. Ben said, that's it. You have to forget everything. Forget all the claptrap and follow the god in you. And she said, "I'll try." She laughed and said, "I will then."

"WE'VE GOT TO DO A MEETING AT MY PLACE," MARGE SAYS on the phone to Andrew. "There's a bunch of shit just sitting by the fan and we've got to be ready according to Jake."

"What sort of shit?" Andrew wants to know.

Jake gets on the line. "What sort of shit?" he asks redundantly. "I'll tell you exactly what kind of shit."

But the good reverend never tells Andrew exactly what kind of shit. Instead he tells him there's a good chance a lot of people are unhappy about the Green Man's new fame. For example, he says, there's the lawn and garden chemical people, sure. And the artificial flavor enhancer industry, the perfume cartel – not people to be taken lightly since they've had these great scams going for so long now that they're not about to let anyone call attention to them. And the combined utility companies who have lobbied against burying cables since time immemorial. Then there's the plastic people.

The lawn people, the perfume people, the plastic people – a science fiction all-star line up. Why should these people worry about the Green Man, anyway?

Speaking *ex cathedra*, Jake announces: "Because of the bell curve. All those industries are tolerated by the great majority of people – everyone beneath the center of the bell. But out at the edge, where the bell tapers and tapers and finally drops to zero, out there are people who can't stand Alar on their apples or drying agents in paint or pesticide residues on their roses. And every day there are more and more of these folks. No BHA, BHT. No resins, no gassing plastics, no aromatics, no high gluten."

Andrew listens to Jake, knowing he's got onto the minority case here. The Green Man makes the minority case loom like a majority. Horchow looms like Chernobyl. Horchow Company is all raging geometrics at the molecular level.

"So these industries have a lot of moola at stake. Simoleons by the mega-gross!" Jake insists. "And they're going to come after him. No, check that. Have already come after him. We're pretty sure that the house burning and the knife in the door were not Horchow but other people under the smoke screen of Horchow's screwup. It was costing Horchow more and more each year to keep the ponds there by the river, anyway, and the cost-effectiveness of pay-offs was disappearing every day. I think they were relieved a little that our green friend blew the whistle, though their public affairs officer has a lifetime of work to do – or undo."

Andrew finds all this easy to follow but hard to believe, too sudden. Maybe Jake found his day in court to be heady stuff and figures to come out of retirement. The money's better than in outboard repair. What exactly is the story here?

Jake is taller on the phone than in person. His nine-year-old hairline, for one thing, isn't visible. Then his tendency toward "moola and simoleans" loses its silly edge when the phone company takes the hi-fi out of his voice, almost makes these sound like real words to Andrew.

Marge is back on the line. "No foolin' around. Jake doesn't know all this. He suspects it though, and he suspects it strong enough to get my son-of-a-bitch warning system operating. Our green friend is on some hit lists, Jake figures. And that's enough for me. Tomorrow at eleven?"

"Um, that's fine if we can get to the green guy and Mary," Andrew says. Oh boy! A meeting with the whole cast of characters, Andrew anticipates.

EAST LEVEN HAS GONE ON A KIND OF ALERT SINCE THE RETURN of the Green Man. Only Crazy Leo is about his business as usual. In a bar, big Bill Bozeman and the Ford salesman are full of news and opinion.

Bill whirls around, his bar stool complains, and he jabs the air with one porky finger. "Turns out we've got the only green one there is right here in East Leven."

Ramsey the elder, the Jewish baker comes in, though this is not his usual haunt, and takes a seat at the bar just down from Bill. "Maybe we need to be thinking of a statue. They turn green all by themselves in a few years."

Big Bill looks to the Ford salesman who nods and certifies Ramsey, a Ford buyer for years.

Big Bill continues, now including Ramsey. "Turns out he's a green by-damn hero even after polluting our river. Horchow's ponds were leaking, the paper says, and the Green Man just sort of blew the whistle on the whole shootin' match."

"It'll all cost jobs," from the Ford guy. "Jobs, and the whole service network suffers – cars, vans, light trucks …" He trails off in contemplation of cars, vans, light trucks, which circle in the neon like sugarplums.

The Green Man as topic of conversation has become nearly inexhaustible. Suddenly he is the sole repository of the extraordinary in East Leven. He's subsumed Anne Doucette, Crazy Leo. The shack people have become only some kind of link engineered by Jake and Marge to be part of the green hero system and are enjoying a wonderful new legitimacy, although a fragile one, as always.

Ramsey orders a beer. "You would think the green Mr. Brown had discovered a new element. Found another planet. Brought Pavarotti to town." He loses his audience temporarily with the Pavarotti reference, sees his loss, jumps right back in to take advantage of his newfound social success. "I may be way off on this, but Mr. Brown may mean big things for this city. More than put us on the map. New development." Eyes brighten around him. "Talk of a riverfront development with condos and shops. Land prices shooting up. Hope you boys are holding a little land somewhere." Bill and the Ford salesman look at each other conspiratorially and then back to Ramsey.

"Maybe," they say, almost together like a comedy sketch. "Maybe," and both the big head and the small head pivot in slow take.

All of East Leven is poised to hatch with the ascendancy of the Green Man, though the mechanism of this is not entirely clear. It is as if there was general husbanding of energy until the Green Man set it loose. The island raft. The Boston Tea Party thing at the sluice gates of Horchow dumping the hot tea into the cool green river. Marge and Jake and vegetable Mary Willson. What a hatching! It stays as festive as the green parade. Even more festive.

ANDREW GETS THERE EARLY FOR THE MEETING AND THE GREEN
Man has become the green tailor. He's surrounded at a sewing machine
by mounds of forest green cloth, maybe Sherwood-forest green. Green
to the core, anyway, in heaps and cascades of indisputable green with a
green guy in the center of it like he's being born out of a green cocoon
that's falling away on all sides. He's making a uniform with a large, white
G on it, thinks Andrew. Mary's in the kitchen, and Andrew is struck dumb
by what this has all come to. He supposes he'll need at least a mask and
a cape himself, maybe some kind of off-green with accents. The Green
Man's flair for comic opera ought to hold them in good stead in this cru-
sade. Rather than just slinking around in an enormous green Pontiac they
can wear capes, masks, and boots and show up at movie openings and
government-sponsored events as a kind of media pique.

Uniforms, of course! Andrew watches quietly as the Green Man plows
ahead seemingly in control of the heaps of green. There's something ceremonial in the uniforms. Mary, though, seems an odd collaborator on this
project. Surely she can't have agreed to this stuff. After all, how like targets
they'll stand out in Sherwood Forest green and then driving around in
the green-mobile on top of it. How like nincompoops, indeed. Andrew
doesn't see how sensible Mary can ...

She hasn't. This green heap is not uniforms, she announces when
Andrew bypasses the green tailor and heads straight for the kitchen to
examine her on this foolish project. The Green Man is sewing a green
banner long enough to go clear across a city street to announce The Second
Green Day. The First Green Day was declared after the fact by Jake and
Marge and Mary concurring. The green celeb had so much fun on Salmon
Street that he enthusiastically endorsed his own second public coming.

But now Andrew's talking to him seems odd. Saturday morning TV
is all he can liken it to: the way advertisements run into programs and
programs run right on through station breaks as if some seamless, demon-
ic, impetuous mind insists that all is one and one is all no matter what
you see and hear. It's as if he would skip – maybe edit out would be better – whole chunks of what you'd expect from a conversation, even a conversation with a green man. There was this odd feeling Andrew had that

maybe someone else was doing the editing in a booth off over there somewhere. No. Slippage, it was like, something slipping that normally held: brakes, transmission, stretch in the rope. There was the feeling that if any of this conversation were examined too closely for real sense, well, the bottom would fall out, the handle would come off, it would all spill out in the dirt.

Andrew is also interested in the physical logistics of the banner – wind resistance, the process of stringing it high enough to avoid traffic and low enough to be seen, what ropes to use, how to fasten banner to rope. He is immediately taken with any physical problem, answering the call of an internal alarm; his ears actually prick up in response to this set of banner problems.

Andrew says, "You've got pretty heavy cloth there. Have you thought about what it might weigh?"

The Green Man looks up from his sewing machine. "Andrew, Andrew, bim-bam Bandrew," he says. The Green Man has become an uncanny mimic recently, and he's perfectly picked up the exquisite line Andrew is trying to walk, the serious tone of his voice, the serious inquiry about fabric weight. The Green Man continues, "Oh yes, the banner will be weighty. And pithy, too. Not to mention of moment. Not to be confused with momentous. The occasion will be momentous. The banner weighty."

Andrew politely waits out this Marx brothers movie dialogue. Patiently he waits for the green humorist to wind down. And Ben does and begins to sew again, like Penelope absorbed. He's humming some green reprise over his green folds and tucks. He's found four of the huge white letters stacked next to the cloth. *Goof.* He spells *Goof* to no particular end, in no particular direction.

Andrew hefts the material piling up on the floor, the wheels whirling, the calculations calculating. "I'll get some rope to string this," and he makes to leave, but the Green Man stops him.

"Mint," he says, dreamily. "What we need is something minty, with a mint wind blowing off it like a glacier. Peppermint. Chocolate chip mint." Andrew's ears prick up. He's had no breakfast. "Feenamint." Triumphantly, "The Philadelphia mint!"

Ben pauses and holds up one finger for Philadelphia.

"Didn't they close that?" asks Mary from the kitchen.

Andrew finds his own mouth is saying, "That's not what he mint."

The Green Man, like Groucho, is in charge here though. He's not going to let this get by him.

"Now another country heard from," he says, more Jack Benny than Groucho. "Let's do this on Saint Patrick's Day."

"Too late." Andrew apologizes for the calendar, keeping his finger on cosmic order.

The Green Man looks off into space, suddenly dreamy as if a sleep has come over him, an irresistible, sleepy thought. Then finding the folds of green cloth suddenly under his hands, he begins again to sew, then stops again.

The Green Man fumbles around in the letters, dropping a few, but finally comes up with the next word: hypotenuse.

Mary applauds, joins in. Then Andrew, for the cleverness of it.

And the Marx Brothers movie ends when Marge and Jake come in. Here we are, the whole wacky crew stuffed in Mary's apartment like too many pimentos in a small olive, Andrew thinks. He peels off to go look for rope and ice cream for when the inevitable planning meeting needs a sugar boost. The green person sews and sews and sews.

Andrew eventually strings the banner – green with white letters sewn on in more or less straight lines. It called for a green day to celebrate: the first green human? A victory of the forces of greenness? The general hatching? Maybe only to celebrate the day on Salmon Street? Marge figures Salmon Street was just a beginning, and Mary adds, that they need a possible way out of the harassment the Green Man is surely in for.

THEY COME TO THE PARK AS IF PULLED BY THE PEOPLE WHO are already there. And as the crowd grows, the power of attraction becomes larger and larger still. As a critical mass converges on the park, the attraction becomes irresistible. People in cars and trucks passing by three miles from the park in East Leven, later reported feeling an impulse to turn off and come into town for no particular reason: no gas, no food, no potty stop. Around the park churn more and more people. One man had brought his baby camel to the park and was an instant attraction in one corner. A woman with a bright red bandana had chickens for sale in wicker cages. She touted that they laid eggs of pastel colors-green, blue, teal.

But the commerce was minimal.

It's Saturday morning; Green Day dawns blue and unusually hot. The banner is still in place, stretched across the corner of the park where Andrew had fastened it to trees after the planning meeting and ice cream eating contest. The agenda is full of open spots "to be announced," since Mary figured these spots would fill in themselves. There are bluegrass bands, jug bands, a chamber orchestra from a college, a fifties rock group, and the rest are TBA. The food booths are set up and lean toward the Mediterranean and Middle Eastern if you count kosher hot dogs. There is granola in the wind – whole grains, plastic sandals, earth balls, boffing, and crystals. But there is also, though not mutually exclusive, the AFL-CIO information booth, the "Christians for Keeping Christ in Christmas" advocates with a pin-striped booth like a tent at an oasis somewhere. More colors: Over there are the wood-fired sauna folks who have taken up the green cry and pronounced, "Fire-wood, fuel for the 21st century!" with a hastily tacked up green banner proclaiming "Trees – the ultimate Greenpower."

The main color is green, as expected, and the green color comes by and large on people's skin. There are some greenclothes-greenskin-green-hat-greenjewelry. But many people have just come green-skinned, dressed in regular Saturday-morning clothes like invaders from space: "Just act natural now. No one will notice." Early Japanese horror movie to Andrew. "Okay, we'll just get some earthling clothes and then casually stroll over for chapatis or maybe the pita bread sandwiches. Avocado or yogurt? Good. Now, just act normal." Others are complimenting the particularly rich green a woman has achieved with her skin.

The Green Man is with Andrew, come to see if the bands have arrived. Andrew's talking to him has progressed beyond the outbursts of the meeting day, the Marx brothers movie. Beyond? Beyond hypotenuse? The Green Man is still in the hypotenuse stage – words that sound nice but aren't really connected to anything. A collection from his language as they range around the park on Saturday morning would include: persnickety, anthrax, rezone, beeswax, row house, amiable, feeble, sacrosanct, niggling, and defunct. "Beeswax," he says, to no one in particular, as if he's singing a song quietly to himself. "Beeswax. Beeswax, beeswax, beeswax. None o' your beeswax, pleeese." The Green Man sings the beeswax ditty while they cross the park to look at the stage set up.

Then he balks when they approach the stage as if he's come to the end of a tether, and Andrew sees the reason. Above them is the electricity tap box to get juice to the stage. Mid "beeswax," the Green Man halts and backpedals into a clutch of green people congregated around the drinking fountain. Thirsty work, this being green.

Some of the green people are in the first stages of melting, apparently. The green runs down temples and congregates at the corners of eyes, where it puddles briefly before being cuffed away. The Green Man stares at the green sweat and then tests his own and looks puzzled, maybe disappointed, as if his green should run too.

A lean, young, green juggler wearing only shorts hangs five red balls in the air like a huge necklace of beads. And there is green capitalism at work: a girl sells garlands of dried flowers and fragrant bay laurel and rosemary, another entrepreneur has bamboo flutes, still another sells hammered dulcimers. The park is becoming festive as the Green Man and Andrew move around the stage area, now apparently full of the crocodiles of electricity, and then off toward where Mary and Marge are discussing the arrangement of booths. Overheard is someone discussing the price of rental trumpets for his son in a high school band.

The park is whizzing and bubbling with green people as well as more standard colors. The Green Man skitters here, there, there, sometimes grabbing Andrew's arm to pull him along, but mostly just disappearing from Andrew's side and popping up at a new site of interest. He's quiet but animated, and then he utters one of his tuneful words as if the word could account for some of what's happening. "Amiable," he says, tasting the word, and he abruptly stops walking to say it as if the effort to utter drew all his attention and energy. Surrounded by green people now, Andrew gets the feeling the green race is catching on. Something in the greenness itself is attractive.

The dolphin people are talking to the spa people. A collusion is possible: spas for dolphins in the woods.

The juggler has become legion suddenly. The air is full of unnatural objects: Indian clubs, knives, torches, feather boas.

"Rezone," the Green Man explains.

Some of the green people around them have achieved failed hues, the colors of a green person's nightmare, unwell greens and statue patinas and corrosion. Always a hazard in the development of a new race.

They cross the park the short way, and now the Green Man leads through a gathering crowd as if he's sniffed out an island in this sea. Other green people are ignoring him – no handshakes or lionizing like on Salmon Street. He is moving with a self-absorption and purpose now. Andrew is reminded of the deliberate bounds he took to assault the Horchow Company and he thinks, oh oh oh. Here we go again.

Andrew follows him to where the crowd thins out and the rose garden begins with orderly rectangles of roses in bloom. He scurries now rather than walking down the patterned lanes, with his nose unquestionably lying on the wind. He tacks again across the wind and shakes his head like a dog with a burr caught behind an ear.

Mary and Andrew have discussed keeping track of the Green Man on Green Day. Andrew is a force for reason and prudence because Mary would lock up their Green Man somewhere rather than lose him in this crowd that might do anything from shake his hand to firebomb him. Andrew proposes always keeping one of them with him during the festivities. Andrew is on duty.

The Green Man stops at the end of a row of particularly tall roses and from behind him Andrew hears his song of "Persnickety, ickety, ickety, ic-ket-tey." And then he waves Andrew off with the back of his hand, pushing the air between them, pushing him away. Andrew stops and backs up, and the Green Man continues, slower now, backhanding Andrew away, who comes forward to say something to him, and he hurries up his pushing off. Andrew goes to the end of the row and steps around the roses to find Ben's feet where he's sitting on a concrete bench. Suddenly his feet are gone, so Andrew pops around the roses playing hide and seek, and there he is sitting with his legs crossed on the bench waving off again with one hand, pointing at Andrew with the index finger of the other. Andrew goes around the roses once more looking for another opening in the foliage to keep an eye on him. By the next opening, the bench is empty. He's gone.

One of the groups had brought in fresh sawdust in wheelbarrows and made a long apricot heap into which were salted small, colorful plastic toys. Children were lined up by age group, with the youngest getting the first three-minute shot at the toys. A strident coach's whistle announced the end of the hunting time. For some reason, this activity fascinated Alstot Simpson, orchardist, as if he had come across a tribal custom he knew was important but had no idea what it meant. He stood with arms crossed on his chest, his hands wrapped around his biceps. He rocked back on his heels with the excitement of the youngest children as they crawled around in the sawdust encouraged by their mothers, and the youngest boy sat contentedly putting handful after handful of sawdust on his head and had no interest plastic toys. He had found it already while the others were still looking.

The next oldest group revealed strategies – blocking defense, scooping offense. The block was executed by a seven-year-old who spread himself over a section of the pile so no one else could enter his territory, and whatever happened to be there was his to mine. Another kid found that scooping as much sawdust as he could into a pile in front of him seemed to increase the toy-to-sawdust ratio, and so he scooped and dredged and filtered and separated from his own little mountain. One of the youngest girls in the new group gave her toys away as she found them, freeing her hands for better finding. She ended up with one, just as the whistle blew.

Alysandra, aware that fairs of all sorts were the place to get new ideas, walked with her hands behind her among the plant stalls, the pottery arranged on hastily concocted boards and brick shelves. Her pin-and-ribbon tributes to the Green Man were everywhere. She could tell her own originals from the immense variety of overstated versions, which ranged from what looked like blousy military medals to green ceramic ribbon approximations hastily fired in an unnatural yellow-green. Hard to predict glazes, she said to herself. There was even a choker of red velvet with a drop pendant of some kind of green stone that served the ceremonial purpose. She knew she would be able to sell those if no one else in town had them. But the girl was gone into the crowd. She thought she might like to go have a look at the baby camel. Oh, those big eyes and long lashes. Do camels bite? The Green Man is supposed to be here somewhere but so far she hadn't seen him.

Mrs. Little had been preparing her luggage to visit a friend in California. She was an efficient packer and prided herself on taking only what she would need. She felt rather than saw the parade of people drawn toward the center of town and the park. She found herself drawn outside first to watch the idle perambulating toward downtown but found she couldn't resist going with them as if some pied piper piped too high to register on human ears but just right for the human limbic system to pick up and guide the body. When she got to the park she forgot about her packing, and the flower stalls drew her in. Alstromeria so big in pots this time of year. So cheap.

"Aren't they beautiful?" Alysandra was back from looking unsuccessfully for the camel, and she remembered Mrs. Little as an irregular at her store.

Mrs. Little recognized her interlocutor immediately. "And they are the most generous of flowers, I find. They kill themselves with giving blooms." She held up one finger. "I've even taken to lopping off,…" and she looked around conspiratorially as if the flower police might be listening, "… some of the new buds so they don't give themselves to exhaustion. That and staking heartily for support. Wonderful things to live so generously." She had surprised herself with her own enthusiasm. Alysandra seemed to manage the testimonial in stride and nodded her consent, approval, at the harsh measures one had to take sometimes with the overgenerous flowers of the world. Mrs. Little returned to conspiracy mode. "There are other flowers that will do the same thing, but none will break their hearts to please like alstromeria." She laughed, partially to show she was not crazy, but she could see that Alysandra had joined the fun.

"I remember reading," said Alysandra, "that flowers, flowering plants anyway, made human beings possible somehow. I forget exactly why." She looked out over the park, at the possible human beings milling around, and nodded. "Yes, I'm sure that was it. None of this without flowers. I'm Alysandra Gorham. I have a small shop."

After sharing so many observations, suddenly they both felt they should reintroduce themselves, though they had spoken many times in the speak of commerce. And still the town assembled itself in the park, drawing in strangers and even cats walking by that wanted legs to rub up against.

Across the park and beyond the bamboo patch, Conroy Burbank tried to gather interest in his plan to harness the image of the Green Man to East Leven as Chicago had found Mrs. O'Leary's cow, New York the apple, Houston the steer, and San Francisco the cable car. He had concocted a petition of sorts, which he was circulating looking for signatures. But somehow, though most people thought it was a good idea, in the abstract, they were reluctant to sign up right now; they were reluctant to even read the document Conroy had fastened to a clipboard. It was really more of a resolution with some hearbys and a few whereins and one hereafter. A number of people tried to read it halfheartedly and came away empty. A few asked Conroy to tell them what it said, and he paraphrased what he thought was a reasonable proposal. But the milling of the crowd created a kind of buzzing that made it hard to concentrate, and normally very astute minds seemed to capitulate to a lower level of endeavor as a result. Conroy felt as if he were presenting people with a complex legal document asking if they were willing to give up all their rights to some green potentate, some generic Wizard of Oz in the emerald park. He shook his head. There was a drug in the air.

A mist – fine dose of something or other, of cliché and sanity and singularity – hung over the park and everyone breathed it in. For some the transformation from where they were before to where they were now was notable, and they remarked about how they got here, what they thought they were doing, and what they ended up doing. But for most, the park felt completely natural, as if they had meant to come and spend the day doing nothing in particular but celebrating some ill-defined holiday. Someone decided it would be a good place to sell her son's trumpet that he hadn't used in two years. Recipes were exchanged. Falafels were eaten.

Marge came with Al Miller (using Jake for park appearances). Marge had adjusted her usual river-person look – baggy gray sweater, tennis shoes, print skirt, white socks – to better reflect the eclectic festivities. She had on her rose sweater with the embroidered vine down one side and the rose buds on the other, a full skirt that picked up the sweater's rose color, and she traded the tennis shoes for casual flats that looked something like boat shoes, producing a land/nautical collision theme. She moved around the park as if she'd been waiting for this day to come. Jake moved silently by her side, sort of an outrigger to Marge's canoe. They were vaguely seeking the Green Man and Andrew, but in no hurry. Marge was giving her impressions of the festivities without requiring any real comment from Jake.

"I wonder where all these people keep themselves. I haven't seen this many people I don't know in a long time. I thought I knew most everybody in town at least by face. But those people, those guys over there, I couldn't tell you where they're from. The Indians I'd guess from up near Saint Paul. But that crowd looks like some kind of tamed-down motorcycle gang. Damn! And for crissakes, what's the guy with the water purifiers? Where did he come from? Could you drink river water run through one of those things?" None of which required an answer, and Jake knew it. He nodded to satisfied customers who greeted them as they strolled. He remembered each one by the outboard: classic 5½ Evinrude, 8-horse Scott Attwater, Mercury, Mercury, Mercury – all racing motors blown or dumped in the drink off hydroplanes – a long-shaft Johnson 15 for a sailboat. Marge was inspired again. "So what do you think Horchow will do? Nothing. I know nothing is what they'll do now. You don't see any of the Horchow people here do you? Of course not. But plenty of the people here work for Horchow, you bet. What? A thousand or so. Lots of money. Lots of paychecks. Lots of crap in my river. Lots of pains in the ass in the long run, you bet." Marge's running commentary became like a sound track, some sour and some sweet. "Now there's a couple of doofusses. But they look like nice doofusses. Everybody's got the goofy grin on today.

Hey Jake, it's goofy grin day and nobody told us. Just look around. Can you believe it?" Jake looked around as asked. More goofy grins than usual? More doofiness than usual? He reckoned maybe not, but kept his own council on the subject.

As they walked around the park, Jake began to muse to himself on the phenomenon encountered here. By training he first considered it a quasi-religious experience, people gathering in the name of some abstraction in order to find common ground through ritual and ceremony. All the classic definitions come to roost. But somehow he found this an unsatisfactory accounting of reality. The holy was there somewhere, but the profane flavored it so thoroughly that the compromise was very quickly complete. What was this then? He tried out the profane, some ur-gathering impulse that could be accounted for only by the fact that it felt good and kept on feeling good when even more people arrived. There would be a limit, he supposed, on the feeling good as the park filled up. What did they call it? Carrying capacity. After which there would be just too damn many people. Like the time in Costa Rica during carnival, when the street had become so packed with celebrants doing nothing but milling and drinking in tighter and tighter packs until no one could move, as if they had packed themselves into cans of narrower and narrower streets and then began to panic. He could feel the heat and pressure and not being able to raise his arms or fend anyone off and the tightening until his shoulders pried his feet off the ground and he was touching only sporadically the ground and … He shuddered and shook his head to get rid of the memory of the crushing, the panicked expressions all around him, the horror of losing all control. He thought of his repair shop, the space between the door and the bench, his consulting zone. He thought of the big double doors letting out onto the river, the moving of the river away, always away. He took deep breaths and more deep breaths.

Jake had stopped to deal with the crowd occurring in his head. Marge walked blithely on ahead still talking to him as if he were there at her side. Farnsworth had come to stand at the edge of the park and spotted his fellow mechanophile. They had had some conversations about the internal combustion engine in general, fuel injection in particular, more particularly the electronic managing of the firing sequences and fuel amounts. All that mechanical minutiae seemed to Farnsworth much easier to talk about than whatever it was he was pondering here at the edge of the park, and he figured Jake for a natural ally. He startled Jake, who had gone personally interior and was breathing measured breaths to deal with the crowd.

"Jesus, Farnsworth, you startled the shit out of me." Jake composed himself but was also glad to talk away the crush of folk. Marge continued ahead talking to the air and gesturing to point out the sites to her own personal duende.

"So ..." Farnsworth tried, and indicated with an open hand the affairs of Green Day, "what exactly do you think all this is about?" Exactly, was the key to his inquiry. Some names of some things please. A taxonomy of all this business would help. His open hand, palm up, begged to be filled with the sense in this landscape of apparent dawdling and lollygagging. For Jake the crowd was – in various moments of control and loss of control – thickening like a gravy on the stove or breaking apart as if dismissed by some hieratic gesture. For Farnsworth the crowd was chaos waiting for order in the firmament, the great naming. He waited to pronounce its name.

They began to talk but about two very different things, both of which were the crowd that continued to grow. Jake knew there was no going back to the pouting, idiosyncratic outboard-repair guy – the isolation, the alienation, the stoic aloneness. He knew by a kind of displacement, the same way he had known to move from one career to another; there was an epiphany of loss – loss of interest, loss of reasonableness, loss of integrity – in what he found himself doing. He knew from having done it over and over that there was solace and reason and coherence on the other side of the decision. And excitement. New things to learn, a new pattern, new elegance. He drew a deep breath and ventured into the crowd as if plunging underwater. The moving kept him clear. As long as he could move, even a little, he could try to catch up with Marge, who forged on ahead, through a people jam, out into the clear, into another jam, like quartering waves in a speed boat.

The Green Man quickly became irrelevant to the proceedings. In fact nobody could find him. Andrew kept looking as if something depended on his finding the great green one. But his search slowed to a leisurely gawk in and out of the rose bushes, across the bamboo patch. Mary, frantic at first to find him gone missing, thought finally that like a cat, Ben Brown could ultimately take care of himself better than anyone else could do it for him.

The Horchow apologist stood with his hands on his hips looking across the park. His boss had sent him to find out if the gathering was somehow generated by enemies, potential enemies, industrial rivals, ecoterrorsists, scofflaws, malcontents, or even discontents. He moved from group to group on the edge, trying to hear one of the above or even snatches that might suggest any manifest subversion of Horchow's economic interests. He shook hands with the dentist city council member. He greeted cordially faces he knew from the factory. He walked among them but was somehow outside the activities, although no one seemed to know exactly what activities were going on or what was to come. Speakers? Union organizers? EPA? No one knew. "I heard the Indians were going to do something later." And that seemed the most potent piece of information he could gather.

He had thought that this was all Green Man-related, but now doubts crept in. The poster-sized pictures of him, the whole parade apparatus, seemed to be missing from this gathering. More and more conversations seemed to revolve around things like seed exchange, canning tips, band instrument rental, baseball practice pickup and delivery. There was no sense to it, no pattern. He thought, if a man were given to paranoia, he might suspect that each conversation was hurled into the broad vernacular just as he arrived on its periphery. If a man were given to paranoia. He wasn't, and continued to gather the chatter of the mundane as if it were real information. Maybe it's like dividing out pi, he thought. What you find is that the mind of God is there in the random clatter of numbers, and here it is again in the random clatter of a hundred conversations about nothing in particular, exactly what we suspect must fill up God's mind like the cosmic clutter of molecules banging around. Jesus, maybe the job was getting to him. He believed in capitalism, the market economy, the opportunity to make money, even lots of money. His job was to say true things in a way that helped Horchow succeed at what it was trying to do – make money. And better, lots of money as a hedge against bad times and as a bonus to attract more capital from more stockholders. It was fundamentally a very simple proposition. What it lacked to give it the status of religion was a central mystery that could be referred to during periods of logic failure. Then there was the Green Man. He could have been that central mystery, under a different set of circumstances. The electric mystery, the chosen one to lead humankind into the future. The part man, part electricity, marked by his greenness to … He found himself laughing at the rhetoric of his old comic-book days, lying out under the red maple tree in the backyard as a kid, space traveling, bad-guy crunching. Something in the Green Man business made him remember those days. Too bad the green guy got associated with the whole ecology movement. It could have gone either way. What a spokesperson he could have been. Never mind "Better living through chemistry"; he could have brought back that old GE plum, "Progress is our most important product."

The Horchow guy sighed. The crowd milled and packed up, then released like a live thing making its way all over the park, an amoeba.

Andrew listens for the persnickety song, but nothing. He jogs around the roses and jumps up to try to see between the rows, and then he sights a green person, but it turns out to be just any green person having wandered over into the roses, not the green person he was supposed to be in charge of. The rose garden is big enough to make this hide-and-seek frustrating. Fifteen minutes Andrew is about his seeking but finds no legitimate green person – all imposters.

Andrew tries calling. Nothing. He tries earnest, wide-seeking circles of reconnaissance – frenzied, worried, parental, filling his mind with what might have happened to him as a way to spur on more and faster looking. Everything occurs to Andrew at once. He's been abducted by industrial fiends and their lackeys; he's wandered off in his new idiocy, though he shouldn't be hard to find as a missing person once all the green dye wears off the park folk; he's melted in a pool of green, and J.C. Penney work clothes mark the spot where he's returned to earth; some children have taken him for a pet; Marge has him or Mary has him. That's it! Andrew is off to check the other keepers.

Some Indians have already created quite a stir in the park. They have drums out, tapping softly as if warming up. Andrew makes his way around the crowd and finds Mary, but she hasn't seen him either. Immediately though, she looks worried enough so that Andrew knows that he only has to worry half as much now. She's off with half his burden in a whirl around the park, looking for the Green Man among the green people.

Mary, Marge, Jake, and Andrew spread out like ripples on this green pond; the four of them ought to be able to cover enough ground to find their missing totem.

CRAZY LEO WAS OUT IN JENKINS'S FIELD MUTTERING BENEDICtions over the grass; like a magician, he was working his hands to shape the magic and make the cosmos give up its marvels. He was perfect and crazy.

Watching him, Ben realized he had never really needed to go to Spain or Borneo or anywhere looking for whatever he looked for. He learned about the WPA project that generated a ghost, Crazy Leo, the town that came and went on the river pilings. He learned about the murders, about Horchow Chemical.

It was a day some days after the trial, and Ben Brown was feeling exceedingly green, one of his greenest since the early days. He had those self-absorbed green-blues based on asking himself interminably "Why me?" "Why green?" "Why not dead like everybody else who had presumed with that load of electricity?" Big useless questions as always with that particular state of mind. Crazy Leo was ebbing and flowing in Jenkins's field there in front of him when he looked up.

Leo was working like a hunting dog back and forth in a hermetic daze, and Ben walked right out in the field without Leo seeing him. Ben felt he needed the wonderful babble, the sight of his hatchet, some information on hubcaps to prod him out of his funk. Ben walked closer and still Leo didn't see him. Ben could hear his rising and falling incantations perfectly. And still he didn't see.

"Hupmobile. I had a Hupmobile hubcap once. Auntie, auntie, I'll stay in. No in and out. In and out. Flies get in. Hello captain. Hello hubcaps. Hello. Hello. Hello. The worms play pee-knuckle. Pee-knuckle on your snout."

He spun back to cover new ground just before he would have seen Ben. He shambled away, but still Ben could hear him clearly.

"Mr. Harold's in bloody snow. Gotta go. A Buick hubcap's in here. Hello Buick. Hello Mr. Harold. Glad to see you too. Tigers turn to butter. I had a Terreplane hubcap once. I don't know where it is now. Maybe I lost it in here. It's in the deep blue sea."

There were some sort of chuckles between snow and hubcaps and the deep blue sea, and snorts or parts of words. But snow and blood and, at the time, the mysterious Harold kept Ben's attention. Leo turned again as if he had reached the edge of his range.

"Mr. Harold in the deep blue sea. I didn't see, Mr. Harold. See Mr. Harold. I'll be in Auntie. It's too cold. No flies in wintertime."

He paused to tug up something shiny from under the grass but dropped it when he saw it was long and thin instead of a coveted disk.

"Bang you're dead. Bang. I couldn't find any hubcaps in there. Deep snow was all cold. I couldn't hear the hubcaps. Mr. Harold says keep looking Leo. Leo was looking all the time. Bang. I won't bang the door anymore. Walk home in the snow, so cold, nobody home, that's for sure. What's happening, Leo? Mr. Harold. A Model T hubcap could be in there."

Ben had no idea what he was hearing until he looked up newspaper accounts of the murders. There was near the end of one account:

"Harold Lansson, CEO of the newly formed Horchow Chemical, lamented the loss of one of his best friends. Lansson and the victim worked together in Hale Company's engineering department for eight years before Lansson left to work for Horchow Chemical. Lansson said, 'Charlie was a good friend and colleague. He'll be missed.'"

Another account: "A Federal State Bank loan officer and an engineer for Hale Company were murdered late Thursday evening. Apparently there were no witnesses and the fresh snowfall covered all traces of foot and automobile traffic making the investigation more difficult, according to Lt. Rendell, head of the investigative team."

Crazy Leo again: "I had a Model T hubcap but I left it somewhere. I got a bag now for hubcaps. Mr. Harold's got blood ..."

And then he saw Ben and stopped singing his tale. He quickly fumbled for his hatchet and then frantically searched for something to demonstrate it on. He found a thin stick and flailed away at it as if it were a tree. The stick flew into splinters. Crazy Leo paused and stroked his hatchet and then put it away on his belt. His interview with the universe was over.

Harold Lansson died of leukemia almost five years later, leukemia that, more years later, was connected to industrial solvents in the groundwater on his estate outside of East Leven. So the victims, Charles Elder and Melissa Crandal, the engineer and the loan officer – the "snow lovers" in contemporary accounts – were not lovers at all. They were conspirators or blackmailers or citizen heroes. They knew the price of Horchow's initial success, its complex government finances that depended on safe operation and civic value. They wanted in and Harold cut them out. Or they were going to blow the whistle on Horchow's dumping practices to the government finders. Or maybe they were lovers and conspirators and heroes. Ultimately, it didn't matter.

Crazy Leo on the witness stand. Crazy Leo wandering around Jenkins's field in full mutter, the Green Man – the younger Green Man. One slick murder plot. The parallels to the biographical character assassination of the Green Man are full of imitation. Anne Doucette conspires in this – her tale and Pinky's bug-eating life, her sweet broken neck that became part of all their dreams.

IT IS GREEN DAY AND ANDREW IS LOOKING FOR THE GREEN namesake. Every fifteen minutes or so, one of the four of them bumps into another searcher. Whatever is happening in the park seems to be quite successful if you measure by laughing and pure volume of words said and listened to. The Indians seem to provide a place and an excuse for more talking and nodding. Words are the stuff of the day, it seems.

Andrew asks himself: Where would you be if you were the lost sock, baseball glove, Ping-Pong paddles, keys? And the answer comes to him engraved on the image of the Green Man fishing in a sewer for a Frisbee. He's with the children.

The children, behind a low, white picket fence to keep the little ones in, have a face-painting party going and in the center sits the Green Man and Crazy Leo, both now assumed wholly into a society. The small hands have gathered to help paint their faces, and the color of choice turns out to be an attractive orange, yet another color people don't generate on their own. On the Green Man the kids have left green stripes showing through, but orange, pumpkin orange, is raising the noisiest of good times. The Green Man sits with his legs crossed and his eyes closed in what looks to be ecstasy, while the kids laugh and paint him in two-toned glee as if they're disguising him to hide him from Anne Doucette's watery ghost. The kids have their own painted faces in red swirls and concentric circles of purple and blue, even a few in the thematic greens of the day. Andrew stays outside the fence and lets the revelries go on inside. Mary finds him eventually, pauses and wordlessly signals that she'll stay and watch if he'll go call off the search.

The sun is overhead, the trees with the largest umbrellas casting the biggest shadows, with clusters of people out of the bright light jabbering to one another like so many roosted birds holding the colony together by sheer chirping volume.

Andrew finds himself an outsider still outside the fence of this event. Movie gestures occur to him: pull my hat down over my eyes and stroll off into the fog; wave good-bye from the ship's deck amid paper streamers; smile cautiously at first, then more and more broadly, until I light up, then taper off into wistful knowing. The day cooks on, and the shadows cock spring-loaded. Whoever the enemies Jake has postulated, they don't show on Green Day.

They don't show until evening.

Then, when the marvelous yakking has diminished to a rustle, when they are headed for Mary's in the city version of the coastal caravan – Jake has joined in with a '66 Valiant – when the orange version of the Green Man sits between Mary and Andrew on Holly's front seat, then they come.

They come on the radio. A station editorial wonders if this isn't a neo-hippy, back-to-the-earth movement that happened today in an East Leven park. What kind of antigrowth, antidevelopment, antiprogress is growing out of the case of this poor, unfortunate, green-skinned man whose industrial accident left him apparently unable to care for himself? Who is using him, manipulating him, to turn people against any project that wants to change the city? Just who is behind this so-called Green Day and what was the purpose of the gathering?

The Green Man, pumpkinheaded and garish, stares out the window.

High school boys hanging out the windows of a tiny, old Honda wave to get their attention then flip them off.

Someone driving a fierce Blazer 4×4 with windows like reflecting sunglasses suddenly weaves in front of them, and then as if to assure them the weaving is no accident of inattention, it goes off into another lane seemingly ready to turn off with its turn signal blaring and then careens back in front of them just missing their front bumper. Then the Blazer is gone in a blaze.

Farther on. An old Mack dump truck with the bulldog hood ornament crosses the median stripe and comes directly and steadily at them, air horn wide open like a throat, as if they were in the wrong lane and he were trying to shoo them away. At the last second the Mack bulldog dodges back into his lane spraying them with fine gravel, froth from the bulldog's mouth.

They clatter on toward Mary's, but the coincidence factor is building toward intolerable.

A sharp crack and Holly's back window is broken in a starburst. The rearview mirrors tell Andrew nothing, no odd movement, no assassin hanging out a car window with fists full of rocks. He drives on toward Mary's figuring there's not much else to do, that they are hung out here on the highway and the bridge over the river.

At Mary's there are placards driven into the front lawn, placards the size of political signs, except prominent among these is the immense word ASSHOLE. The *Reader's Digest* version of the coastal biographies, Andrew figures. All of language seems to be collapsing into compact versions as it comes near the Green Man. There is a rising sense of panic

Andrew shares with Mary in a look. Jake pulls his car around Holly like circling wagons.

Andrew is out and at the window saying, "Did you see what hit the back window?"

Jake saw nothing. But he saw that the driver of the dump truck didn't look like a dump truck driver – mirrored sunglasses in the evening, leather jacket in this heat, driving gloves.

More information, more evidence, no conclusions. The Green Man isn't talking. Certainly he'd have a theory. Just on the off chance, Andrew takes his arm and asks, "Well?" He sighs flat out, pats Andrew's hand as if that's why he has taken his arm. His arm muscles are completely at ease beneath his green sleeves. Even his single words of the park have gone now. It's not exactly a smile he has. Be right back, his face seems to say.

Wagons circled in the street; they wait because Jake and Marge think Mary's house might be the next point of attack. The when and where of attack seem more important to Marge than the who. She leads Jake off toward the house with Mary's key, Marge's plan clearly the same as always – barge on in and ask who the hell's there. The wind picks up and sighs across the pine duff and asshole signs.

The Green Man is out of the car, stretching and wandering off to inspect the signs. Andrew goes with him throwing a glance to Mary that means: come help me if our mutual friend skitters off into the bushes here.

The signs are standard-issue political campaign, cardboard stapled and attached by stickers to a wood stake then tapped into the turf. Nice printing too. Offset, probably, two color. Besides ASSHOLE, there are other condensed forms of the biography of the western shore: *Keep WWII in B&W. Jobs/Not green Jerks, Mind your own/damn business,* and *Keep your green mitts/Off my Paycheck.* Andrew collects the signs one by one while the Green Man tweaks each one as if grounding it or tasting it with his finger. Then he gives the whole pile a thorough snuffing, reading them like a dog, and then, still like a dog, looks at Andrew satisfied with what information he's gathered but doesn't say a word as if Andrew is supposed to know what he has found by the look in his eye. Andrew half expects him to pee on the signs to mark them.

Marge and Jake are back from the house and declare it safe, so they take the party inside. The Green Man is docile and lets himself be led up the stairs into the vegetarian rooms.

Andrew leads the kitchen table speculations, thinks he has this all figured out – what he calls the single-center paranoid flight of fancy: Horchow is still pissed off and has franchised its corporate anger to paid agents, who have the jobs of pecking away at the Green Man and company in as many different ways as they can think of. Mary makes the case for pluralism, the same case Jake began a while ago, the case of multiple pissed-offs working essentially independently. This is the essence according to Jake.

"So there are a lot of people who have figured out what all this publicity means eventually. And some of them are mighty scared that our green friend will cost them personally. Which oxen are to be gored." Andrew reaches over and lays his hand on the Green Man's arm. All of them have begun doing this lately since he fell silent; they touch him to feel for his answers in some way. Mary, standing behind him, absently pets the back of his hair.

Jake continues, "And cost is maybe the main factor here. These people are afraid for their jobs, afraid that we'll somehow drag Horchow kicking and protesting through the courts where the media will love the green guy and sensationalize the stories."

Andrew thinks the jobs stuff is a ruse and volunteers that it's not prudent to trust the signs at face value. Marge, who has been pacing and listening, and has a habit of seeming to cut through what she considers crap, holds up her hands as for a touchdown. "Okay. Okay. It maybe doesn't matter if there's a lot of people after us or only a few. Maybe it's all the same difference. Maybe we have to do the same thing in any case," she says cryptically.

Mary still pets him fondly, her child/lover. She picks up the word *do* and suggests that they take him back to his place by the river with its burned-out house and the scar where the island broke loose. She says maybe being there, things will dawn on him and he may respond to us. "Dawn on," she says as if these words hold some kind of process for unlocking what is locked, finding the lost. She's hoped these words out, but it gives them all something to do while they look out the windows for more attacks. Marge adds that they should call the newspapers and TV and gather them tomorrow in the late afternoon and tell them about the attacks, about what has happened to the Green Man and how eloquent his silence might become eventually. Andrew volunteers, "We'll fill in possible scenarios behind the attacks and suggest the papers look into who's attacking and why." "Good," agrees Jake. "Let's throw the whole thing open to the information networks to see what information comes out." "Seems a hell of lot better than calling the sheriff," adds Marge, and they settle on a plan by acclaim.

The Green Man will sleep at Andrew's house tonight, a place not implicated yet. Andrew will be his caretaker. He calls his parents and they say he's certainly welcome.

The mystery of the bio-raiders at the coast, the sheaves of papers in service of devil-information, the Green Man seems satisfied with everything the way it is, or at least his silence is a kind of consent. The plan to colorize all World War II footage to make war real doesn't seem so weird after the last few days. But what Andrew finds a happier coincidence altogether is that his own sense of history has reawakened at the very moment the Green Man's has disappeared.

It has suddenly occurred to Andrew that his father's hands appear in all the old family photos, as if hands were some kind of bookmark in his genetic stuff. His grandfather's nearly square palms with long heavy fingers made for doing and undoing also appear like white birds in the family photos, white birds against the black suit. His hands are oddly crossed, coffin style, on his chest to hold something in or keep something out as he poses with his brothers against a weathered barn. One sister in white has her hands behind her.

His father's hands are the same, lifted from the photo and screwed onto a larger frame where they fit better and seem less likely to fly off at any moment. The hands come down, undiluted two generations to him. His longness, however, takes the same hands and gives them back the birdlike skitter they had perched there on his grandfather's smaller body. Fly off, says one, fly away, says the other: roost somewhere higher and safer than here.

Besides the hands, he looks for the sagittal crest that makes his head so long. Besides the hands, he looks for the woeful countenance he has come to. The hands, and then he looks for some other relative on either side who is marked for green adventure. Theory: Sometimes it is like the island breaking loose. And then other times there is only an insistent thumping, and when you go to answer some door, there is a green man with a quizzical look on his face as if he'd just answered the door too. So Andrew looks over his relatives for signs that he would end up in conference with a vegetarian, an unfrocked Presbyterian, an escapee from the river in *The Wind in the Willows*.

He takes the pictures to his backyard where he can hear and see the river. The green is electric this spring. But the remaining buds have burst in the heat, though the evenings stay cool, and what he is about on his search in family albums seems less intense, less strident out here. The jays have taken over the yard just to do it. The juncos are in the birches out of the way. Starlings have invaded the garage eves. One hummingbird seems to move around the yard, oblivious to all other critters, at a higher speed, like the Green Man hammering at his 12-volt electrical system way back then.

He puts the photos down and looks at his hands. Is this what I've come here for? The naming of things? Has the Green Man's silence now left him only the naming of things?

He sits with the family albums like some elderly uncle puffing a pipe on a porch. He feels this whirl of the green life in the air against these buds and flowers. The rhododendrons splash open on the dark green as if they've been flung there. The early pinks are almost gone, the reds are now strong with lights from the inside, the purple is just opening royally across the yard against the reds, and he sits blooming with the photographs in his lap.

He has been to the west as far as a reasonable person can go. He drank the water. He smelled the wind. The Green Man is asleep in his house like a two-year-old. He went tired and happy to sleep. Big day today. Big day tomorrow.

The albums spread out like an invitation to go on living in an array from black and white through washed-out early colors to a true-tint now as if the world gets realer as you come toward the present. The hands he finds have stitched all this photography together, all this urge to continue.

The green person has left East Leven with nothing but silence and this particularly warm spring, both of which heft of sadness and excess and something brought on by something else. Too many secrets already and now Andrew overloaded by this permanently secret green guy. Persnickety, rezone, beeswax: the last of his sounds, apparently.

"No, no, he's fine," Andrew hears himself saying to the reporters the next evening. "Really. He's fine." Fine is a relative term, of course, but Andrew is pretty sure he's fine. There's just no way of knowing for sure. He may as well be fine. He may as well be dandy. Andrew has chosen wisely in "fine."

He sits just down there, not a hundred yards from where Andrew is standing, almost hidden by the willows. Andrew can see the green of his shirt from days of practice separating his color scheme from nature's, can read him out of the surroundings while the others can't possibly see him there at the river's edge, can say for sure he's there because he hasn't moved in two hours, and Andrew knows what's happened. The key word is quiet. He's gone quiet.

The Green Man has become completely silent. He doesn't seem tortured by the silence. There's no sign of an effort to break out of it, no sadness. The expression on his face is pleasant and his forehead is without a wrinkle – smooth as a river rock and green with a healthy chlorophyll glow. It is the light or he's actually gotten greener. Must be the light, thinks Andrew, because he was always an amazing green. Oh, he's green, the greenest "green being," he used to say laughing. Only he'd say, "Green bean, I am the great green bean. Blue Lake, Kentucky Wonder," more green beans. But this is beginning to sound as if he's gone, and he's not. He's still here. And he's fine, Andrew guesses.

The Green Man sits by the river looking off at the light on the water – maybe. Looking at the other shore, maybe. Maybe seeing something dancing in the air out there that Andrew doesn't see. The reporters will not take Andrew's word about his condition; they need to ask him themselves. As if he doesn't hear, he sits quietly. One reporter pulls him by the arm and nearly knocks him off the rock he's perched on.

The Green Man has become the green lump though his face carries that disquieting pleasantness as if someone might be interrupting something. Andrew puts a stop to handling the Green Man to make him respond. The reporters want medical tests, feel the public needs to know what the real poop is here, where this green guy has gone. And will he come back? One reporter is angry acting like Mary, Jake, and Andrew have shut off the Green Man and now they won't tell them where the switch is to turn him back on. A conspiracy, he alleges, to remove the Green Man from one arena, news, to another, martyrdom. He is public property, the reporter contends, because he is green, public property like Venus and Mars, like ocean waves.

The Green Man still sits watching the last of the light. The reporters are gone, unhappy. Mary, Marge, and Jake – the caretakers – are up here on the bank with Andrew watching the swallows thick over the water gobbling the hatch with thrilling aerobatics. The swallows' tiny sharp cheeps seem to be holding up the sunset, and the light hangs on and on while they all sit quietly. Still the light lingers like it will never leave; it holds out the night, and they peer down to the Green Man, now the man with no more color than any of them in this interminable twilight. And still the last of the thin light holds and holds, faint over the water.

Titles available from Hawthorne Books

AT YOUR LOCAL BOOKSELLER OR FROM OUR WEBSITE : *hawthornebooks.com*

Saving Stanley: The Brickman Stories

BY SCOTT NADELSON

Oregon Book Award Winner 2004

Scott Nadelson's interrelated short stories are graceful, vivid narratives that bring into sudden focus the spirit and the stubborn resilience of the Brickmans, a Jewish family of four living in suburban New Jersey. The central character, Daniel Brickman, forges obstinately through his own plots and desires as he struggles to balance his sense of identity with his longing to gain acceptance from his family and peers. This fierce collection provides an unblinking examination of family life and the human instinct for attachment.

SCOTT NADELSON PLAYFULLY INTRODUCES *us to a fascinating family of characters with sharp and entertaining psychological observations in gracefully beautiful language, reminiscent of young Updike. I wish I could write such sentences. There is a lot of eros and humor here – a perfectly enjoyable book.*
—JOSIP NOVAKOVICH
author of *April Fool's Day: A Novel*

So Late, So Soon

BY D'ARCY FALLON

This memoir offers an irreverent, fly-on-the-wall view of the Lighthouse Ranch, the Christian commune D'Arcy Fallon called home for three years in the mid-1970s. At eighteen years old, when life's questions overwhelmed her and reconciling her family past with her future seemed impossible, she accidentally came upon the Ranch during a hitchhike gone awry. Perched on a windswept bluff in Loleta, a dozen miles from anywhere in Northern California, this community of lost and found twenty-somethings lured her in with promises of abounding love, spiritual serenity, and a hardy, pioneer existence. What she didn't count on was the fog.

I FOUND FALLON'S STORY *fascinating, as will anyone who has ever wondered about the role women play in fundamental religious sects. What would draw an otherwise independent woman to a life of menial labor and subservience? Fallon's answer is this story, both an inside look at 70s commune life and a funny, irreverent, poignant coming of age.*
—JUDY BLUNT
author of *Breaking Clean*

HAWTHORNE BOOKS & LITERARY ARTS :: *Portland, Oregon*

God Clobbers Us All

BY POE BALLANTINE

Best American Short Story Award Winner 1998

Set against the dilapidated halls of a San Diego rest home in the 1970s, *God Clobbers Us All* is the shimmering, hysterical, and melancholy story of eighteen-year-old surfer-boy orderly Edgar Donahoe's struggles with friendship, death, and an ill-advised affair with the wife of a maladjusted war veteran. All of Edgar's problems become mundane, however, when he and his lesbian Blackfoot nurse's aide best friend, Pat Fillmore, become responsible for the disappearance of their fellow worker after an LSD party gone awry. *God Clobbers Us All* is guaranteed to satisfy longtime Ballantine fans as well as convert those lucky enough to be discovering his work for the first time.

A SURFER DUDE TRANSFORMS *into someone captivatingly fragile, and Ballantine's novel becomes something tender, vulnerable, even sweet without that icky, cloying literary aftertaste. This vulnerability separates Ballantine's work from his chosen peers. Calmer than Bukowski, less portentous than Kerouac, more hopeful than West, Poe Ballantine may not be sitting at the table of his mentors, but perhaps he deserves his own after all.* —SETH TAYLOR
San Diego Union-Tribune

Dastgah: Diary of a Headtrip

BY MARK MORDUE

Australian journalist Mark Mordue invites you on a journey that ranges from a Rolling Stones concert in Istanbul to talking with mullahs and junkies in Tehran, from a cricket match in Calcutta to an S&M bar in New York, and to many points in between, exploring countries most Americans never see as well as issues of world citizenship in the 21st century. Written in the tradition of literary journalism, *Dastgah* will take you to all kinds of places, across the world ... and inside yourself.

I just took a trip around the world in one go, first zigzagging my way through this incredible book, and finally, almost feverishly, making sure I hadn't missed out on a chapter along the way. I'm not sure what I'd call it now: A road movie of the mind, a diary, a love story, a new version of the subterranean homesick and wanderlust blues – anyway, it's a great ride. Paul Bowles and Kerouac are in the back, and Mark Mordue has taken over the wheel of that pickup truck from Bruce Chatwin, who's dozing in the passenger seat. —WIM WENDERS
Director of *Paris, Texas*; *Wings of Desire*;
and *The Buena Vista Social Club*

 HAWTHORNE BOOKS & LITERARY ARTS :: *Portland, Oregon*

The Greening of Ben Brown

BY MICHAEL STRELOW

Michael Strelow weaves the story of a town and its mysteries in his debut novel. Ben Brown becomes a citizen of East Leven, Oregon, after he recovers from an electrocution that has not left him dead but has turned him green. He befriends 22 year-old Andrew James and together they unearth a chemical spill cover-up that forces the town to confront its demons and its citizens to choose sides. Strelow's lyrical prose and his talent for storytelling come together in this poetic and important first work that looks at how a town and the natural environment are inextricably linked. *The Greening of Ben Brown* will find itself in good company on the shelves between *Winesburg, Ohio* and *To Kill a Mockingbird*; readers of both will have a new story to cherish.

MICHAEL STRELOW HAS GIVEN NORTHWEST READERS *an amazing fable for our time and place featuring Ben Brown, a utility lineman who transforms into the Green Man following an industrial accident. Eco-Hero and prophet, the Green Man heads a cast of wonderful and zany characters who fixate over sundry items from filberts to hubcaps. A timely raid on a company producing heavy metals galvanizes Strelow's mythical East Leven as much as the Boston Tea Party rallied Boston. Fascinating, humorous and wise,* The Greening of Ben Brown *deserves its place on bookshelves along with other Northwest classics.*

—CRAIG LESLEY
Author of *Storm Riders*

Core: A Romance

BY KASSTEN ALONSO

This intense and compact novel crackles with obsession, betrayal, and madness. As the narrator becomes fixated on his best friend's girlfriend, his precarious hold on sanity rapidly deteriorates into delusion and violence. This story can be read as the classic myth of Hades and Persephone (Core) rewritten for a twenty-first century audience as well as a dark tale of unrequited love and loneliness.

Alonso skillfully uses language to imitate memory and psychosis, putting the reader squarely inside the narrator's head; deliberate misuse of standard punctuation blurs the distinction between the narrator's internal and external worlds. Alienation and Faulknerian grotesquerie permeate this landscape, where desire is borne in the bloom of a daffodil and sanity lies toppled like an applecart in the mud.

JUMP THROUGH THIS GOTHIC STAINED GLASS WINDOW *and you are in for some serious investigation of darkness and all of its deadly sins. But take heart, brave traveler, the adventure will prove thrilling. For you are in the beautiful hands of Kassten Alonso.*

—TOM SPANBAUER
Author of *In the City of Shy Hunters*

www.hawthornebooks.com

Things I Like About America

BY POE BALLANTINE

Best American Short Story Award Winner 1998

These risky, personal essays are populated with odd jobs, eccentric characters, boarding houses, buses, and beer. Ballantine takes us along on his Greyhound journey through small-town America, exploring what it means to be human. Written with piercing intimacy and self-effacing humor, Ballantine's writings provide enter-tainment, social commentary, and completely compelling slices of life.

IN HIS SEARCH *for the real America, Poe Ballantine reminds me of the legendary musk deer, who wanders from valley to valley and hilltop to hilltop searching for the source of the intoxicating musk fragrance that actually comes from him. Along the way, he writes some of the best prose I've ever read.* —SY SAFRANSKY
Editor, *The Sun*

September 11:
West Coast Writers Approach Ground Zero

EDITED BY JEFF MEYERS

The myriad repercussions and varied and often contradictory responses to the acts of terrorism perpetuated on September 11, 2001 have inspired thirty-four West Coast writers to come together in their attempts to make meaning from chaos. By virtue of history and geography, the West Coast has developed a community different from that of the East, but ultimately shared experiences bridge the distinctions in provocative and heartening ways. Jeff Meyers anthologizes the voices of American writers as history unfolds and the country braces, mourns, and rebuilds.

CONTRIBUTORS INCLUDE: *Diana Abu-Jaber, T. C. Boyle, Michael Byers, Tom Clark, Joshua Clover, Peter Coyote, John Daniel, Harlan Ellison, Lawrence Ferlinghetti, Amy Gerstler, Lawrence Grobel, Ehud Havazelet, Ken Kesey, Maxine Hong Kingston, Stacey Levine, Tom Spanbauer, Primus St. John, Sallie Tisdale, Alice Walker, and many others.*

 HAWTHORNE BOOKS & LITERARY ARTS :: Portland, Oregon